PRAISE FOR CRAIG PARSHALL

The Empowered

"Craig Parshall is a rare breed: someone who is, mysteriously, both a great lawyer AND a great writer."

STEVEN WALDMAN, founder, Beliefnet; former national editor, *US News and World Report*

"*The Empowered*, with visible demons and angels, is a read that could make you examine your own beliefs. Is the God of the Old and New Testament, who sent angels to fight an evil underworld of demonic beings, the same today as in the days of old? Does God have warrior angels fighting for us? Does he fight the evil of pornography and child trafficking through us? This book reminded me that God uses his people to fight his battles against evil. He is the same today, yesterday, and forever. Spiritual warfare? Yes, I believe."

CONGRESSWOMAN LINDA SMITH, founder and president, Shared Hope International

"Craig Parshall's new Trevor Black series is simply riveting. In *The Empowered* we have a great cast of characters, a fascinating plot, and a bombshell or two along the way. I am especially impressed by the informed theology that underlies the Trevor Black books. Parshall knows his stuff; there is no cheesy Hollywood nonsense. The novel illustrates in graphic and frightening ways the danger of evil and the peril that is around us. Highly recommended."

CRAIG EVANS, professor of Christian origins, Houston Baptist University

The Occupied

"In the manner of Stephen King and Dean Koontz, Parshall pens a horrifying story of the unseen evils inherent in our society."

"*The Occupied* is a spiritual thriller that resurrects the lone-wolf hero and gives him a mission from God. This book is the answer for those seeking Christian alternatives to popular crime thrillers. A dash of the supernatural ups the ante, making for a grim and grisly string of murders in this first installment of the Trevor Black novels."

"*The Occupied* is a well-paced supernatural mystery that builds layers into the mystery as it also strips them away. Parshall writes with just the right amount of suspense, allowing readers to sleep at night but making *The Occupied* the first thing they pick up in the morning."

"A gripping tale that exemplifies Ephesians 6:12: Our struggle is not against flesh and blood but against spiritual forces of evil in the heavenly realms."

"One of the greatest challenges for a writer is making the invisible world real. Craig Parshall has done exactly that. . . . If you're fascinated by the supernatural and how it exists in a moral universe, then this is the book for you."

"Craig Parshall has combined gritty naturalism with believable supernaturalism to produce a real page-turner."

"In *The Occupied*, Craig Parshall takes us into the supernatural world for a thrilling ride that also educates us about the unseen realm. In the end we discover that it is crucial that we know who occupies us."

KERBY ANDERSON, president, Probe Ministries; host, *Point of View* radio talk show

Other novels by Craig Parshall

"An enjoyable romp for legal thriller aficionados."

PUBLISHERS WEEKLY ON TRIAL BY ORDEAL

"I simply couldn't put *Custody of the State* down! I can hardly wait for the next in the Chambers of Justice series. I'm addicted!"

DIANE S. PASSNO, author and senior vice president, Focus on the Family

"Fine Ironman-meets-the-Rapture style. . . . Quick pacing and a heart-pounding resolution lead to a dynamic scene of the afterlife and a cliff-hanger for the next book."

PUBLISHERS WEEKLY ON BRINK OF CHAOS, cowritten with Tim LaHaye

THE EMPOWERED

THE
EMPOWERED

CRAIG
PARSHALL

TYNDALE HOUSE PUBLISHERS, INC.
CAROL STREAM, ILLINOIS

Visit Tyndale online at www.tyndale.com.

Visit Craig Parshall's website at www.craigparshallauthor.com.

TYNDALE and Tyndale's quill logo are registered trademarks of Tyndale House Publishers, Inc.

The Empowered

Designed by Dean H. Renninger

Edited by Caleb Sjogren

Published in association with the literary agency of AGI Vigliano Literary, 405 Park Avenue, Suite 1700, New York, NY 10022.

For information about special discounts for bulk purchases, please contact Tyndale House Publishers at csresponse@tyndale.com, or call 1-800-323-9400.

Library of Congress Cataloging-in-Publication Data
Names: Parshall, Craig, date- author.
Title: The empowered / Craig Parshall.
Description: Carol Stream, Illinois : Tyndale House Publishers, Inc., [2017]
Identifiers: LCCN 2017028135| ISBN 9781496411372 (sc)
Subjects: | GSAFD: Suspense fiction. | Christian fiction.
Classification: LCC PS3616.A77 E47 2017 | DDC 813/.6—dc23 LC record available at
    https://lccn.loc.gov/2017028135

Printed in the United States of America

23 22 21 20 19 18 17
7   6   5   4   3   2   1

To every lawyer, FBI agent, or local law enforcement officer who has ever protected a vulnerable victim from terror or harm.

PROLOGUE

I was frantic. I had burst through the ring of police and ignored their shouts for me to halt. But at that moment nothing mattered except the person who was at the top of the towering structure and my getting there before it was too late.

Then the race up the stairs, hundreds of them, my breath coming in explosive gasps as I spit out a desperate prayer—*"Dear God, I have to reach her in time."* I knew what I would likely find if I failed: only the void she would leave behind after beginning her bone-shattering fall toward earth.

I was scrambling, taking steps two at a time, missing and tripping, as I tried to tear the image out of my head of what could happen—her descent from that terrifying height, spiraling downward with one long, wordless scream. Simultaneously, my mind was on fire thinking how this must be delighting the demoniac who had brought all of this to pass. The evil one I had pursued relentlessly, maybe even recklessly. The entrance to the top level was in front of me. I braced myself for the worst.

But as I neared the last concrete step, just before the summit, where I hoped to stop this tragedy, my gut was seized by another possibility, nearly as horrible. That I was responsible. That my resolve to pursue the Jason Forester case and to unravel the evil forces behind that lawyer's death might have been the cause of everything.

I felt my heart banging in my chest. The feeling of suffocation. Drowning. Panic setting in.

Then I jolted out of my sleep.

In my restless slumber, the sheets of my bed had been wound over my face. I yanked them off. After rubbing the sleep from my eyes, I looked at the clock—3 a.m. The little window over my bed had been left open, and I could hear the roar of the ocean tide that was crashing against the beach a hundred feet from my cottage. I took a few deep breaths, still groggy, and said it out loud.

"It was a dream."

But then a second later, the numbing realization as the memories smashed their way in.

No, not just a dream. It really happened. All of it.

1

Even at the beginning, when I first learned about the death of Washington lawyer Jason Forester from my friend Dick Valentine, I had that peculiar sense of mine that a supernatural force was behind it. Dick was a New York police detective. We still kept up our unique partnership even though it had been years since I left New York City.

On that particular day, I had just launched out in my fishing boat to the deep blue sea when the call came in from Dick. He shared a lawyer joke. I pushed back with a cop joke of my own. We laughed. Then Dick got down to business. He said he had a strange case involving the death of a government lawyer he wanted to share with me. Once upon a time I had been a criminal defense attorney, so naturally I was all ears.

Dick told me everything he knew about the Jason Forester matter. He explained that on the day of his death, Forester, an assistant United States attorney for the District of Columbia, had been focused on a particular investigation he had been working for months. The target was a criminal enterprise as horrible as it was secretive. He had vowed to track it down and personally drag the bad guys to justice by the collar.

"Then, at one minute after six that evening, while most of the staff was packing up," Dick said, "a secretary was trotting out of the building for the day but stopped and rapped on the door of Jason Forester's office. She tossed a FedEx envelope on his desk. 'This just arrived for you,' she said. It was probably the last conversation anyone had with Forester before he died. At least that we know of.

"So, as far as we can tell, Forester was sitting there in his Washington, DC, office when he opened the envelope. It must have been only minutes later when his heart slammed to a halt. Fifteen minutes after that, the office cleaning crew wanders in and finds the corpse of Jason Forester. He was seated at his desk."

From what Dick's source told him, Forester had a look of wild horror on his face, like something you might expect on a Halloween mask.

"Except for a couple of pens and a blank legal pad, the FedEx envelope was the only thing on his desk. Jason Forester was still hanging on to the letter."

Dick took a moment, then added, "It took two big paramedics to pry his fingers loose."

I didn't wait for the punch line. I interrupted Dick and asked what they knew about the FedEx delivery.

"It was sent from some printing, mail, and express delivery shop in New Orleans. The sender's name and address on the package were fakes."

"Any security cameras in the store?"

"Nah. And as luck would have it, the staff couldn't recall much about the person who dropped it off, except that the guy paid cash for second-day delivery."

"Any investigation?"

"Sure," Dick said. "You'll never guess who headed it up. Vance Zaduck, Forester's boss. He's the head honcho as the US attorney for the District of Columbia. But the FBI lab didn't find anything on the letter or inside the envelope. You know, no anthrax. No toxins. So Zaduck reports there had been no foul play."

"What'd the letter say?"

"Death threat. Not unheard of in Forester's line of work. So Zaduck decided it was a hoax. Just happened to arrive at Forester's office with coincidental timing. Now, on the face of it, an unsuspecting mind could concede that Vance Zaduck had a point, because it turns out Forester had a medical history of cardiac arrhythmia. Autopsy confirmed it. So Zaduck concludes that Jason Forester died of 'natural causes.' Then kicks it up to the attorney general's office for the formal wrap-up. The word I'm getting is that the AG is simply going to rubber-stamp Zaduck's findings."

I knew there had to be more to the story, otherwise Dick wouldn't have bothered to bring me into it, and I told him that.

Dick said, "Yeah. There's a backstory all right. An anonymous tipster called me and gave me all of this intel. That's how I found out. Told me everything I just told you. With one more detail."

"What's that?"

"The tipster, someone I suspect to be reliable, told me that Forester's demise was 'death by voodoo.' That's a quote."

Dick let that sink in, then asked, "What do you think?"

"Me?" I replied. "I'd file it under 'possible death by supernatural causes. Further investigation needed.' But that's just me."

"Thought so," Dick said.

He didn't push the matter. Not then.

A couple of days later, though, Dick called me again. About the same subject. Jason Forester, AUSA. The dead federal prosecutor.

When I picked up his call, Dick asked me, right out of the gate, "So, just wondering, is Trevor Black still chasing demons?"

Dick didn't have to ask. He already knew the answer. Back when I was still collecting mail at my expensive penthouse in Manhattan, Dick took pity on my plight as an attorney in a mess of trouble and hired me as a consultant to his Manhattan police precinct.

Mind you, he hadn't employed me to deal with the usual fare. Instead, I worked on a crime spree that had all the gruesome hallmarks of the supernatural. At first, Dick's partners at the precinct treated me as a joke on two legs. But they stopped laughing when we caught the demon. I use the word *demon* in its literal sense. And now Dick Valentine does too.

Dick asked me if I remembered the details he had told me the last time we talked.

I hadn't forgotten, of course. How could I? Forester, the victim of voodoo.

"Well," he said, "any thoughts?"

I asked him a few questions. Like whether he had taped the conversation with the anonymous tipster or recognized the caller's voice.

"Nope," Dick said. "It came to my cell, not to my precinct desk. And the informer was using one of those voice distorters. Couldn't even tell whether it was a man or a woman."

Then I posed the obvious question. "Why 'death by voodoo'? I must be missing something."

"The person wouldn't elaborate on the voodoo part, except to say—and I quote—'connect the dots.' That's exactly what I was told."

"Where do I fit into this?"

"Well, it's about a dead lawyer, and you have a legal background. Or at least you used to, you know, before they yanked your license to practice law."

"Thanks for the memories."

Dick rolled on. "Also, Forester's death is spooky, and we both know that's your home turf. And then there's the fact that you and Forester's superior, US Attorney Vance Zaduck, have a history together."

Dick was right, of course. My dealings with Zaduck went all the way back to law school, where we were not only classmates, we were opponents in the year-end moot court case (which I won). After getting our law degrees, we faced off again in a bitter criminal case. I still remembered, with a touch of nausea, that messed-up case with Zaduck where Carter Collins—my client, a promising young boxer—ended up going to prison, although Zaduck had to cover up some key evidence in order to win it.

"Any other reasons for sharing this with me?" I asked.

"Yeah," Dick said. "I knew Jason Forester. He was a good prosecutor. Tough. Honest. Part of a joint organized-crime task force set up between Washington and New York, which is how I met him. He prosecuted some mob bosses at first, followed by a stint going after terrorists. Switched to child porn investigations against creeps who kidnap kids and use them in perverted videos. Forester was a legal hero in my book. Then came his unfortunate black magic demise. And whenever I hear about a case that makes my skin crawl, well, I naturally think of you."

I took a moment. "Not sure. Was that a compliment?"

Dick chuckled. Then he got serious and added, "Trevor, if something from *the other side* was involved in Jason Forester's death . . . you know, unseen forces, violent and nasty—your specialty—we both know that a routine Department of Justice investigation won't be able to get to the bottom of it. Not in a million years."

I needed to connect some dots of my own. "How do you know your unnamed caller was really an insider?"

"The caller rattled off the data on Jason Forester's federal PIV smart card, along with his Social Security number, his date of birth, and the date he began work at the US attorney's office. Everything checked out."

"So why you?"

"Somehow the phone tipster knew I had a law enforcement connection with Forester, and the caller needed to tell someone 'outside the Beltway.' I asked why that was. The informant said there was a criminal investigation Forester was running, and it might have something to do with his death. That the caller didn't know, quote, 'who can be trusted on my side of the Potomac.'"

Dick Valentine ended the call by asking if I would look into the Jason Forester incident. He wondered if I could help the US attorney's office to "see the light," convincing them that this incident required a deeper look-see. I told him I'd think about it.

I knew that if I said yes to Dick, it would mean another matchup against Vance Zaduck. That could send me down a very embarrassing, very public waterslide. I had read recently in the *National Law Journal* that Zaduck was receiving serious consideration for a judicial appointment to the United States Court of Appeals for the DC Circuit. That made him a rising star in the legal universe. The DC Court of Appeals is a prestigious bench. In fact, judges from that bench are frequently culled as possible nominees to the United States Supreme Court. No question about it: in recent years, Zaduck seemed to have the amazing knack of catching the wind at his back.

I, on the other hand, was a washed-up, ex–New York City criminal defense lawyer, disbarred for refusing to undergo psychiatric examination as a condition of saving my law license. Between me and Vance, guess who wins the credibility contest.

In the big picture, though, "credibility," as attorneys use that term, has only limited utility, mostly in things like lawsuits, media debates, and Washington politics. When you're doing combat with the powers of hell, "credibility" doesn't help you much.

2

I was grappling with Dick Valentine's request. It wasn't about the money, so I didn't bother to ask who was going to pay me for my trouble if I decided to investigate the death of AUSA Jason Forester. On the other hand, since losing my law practice, I had acquired a new appreciation for three square meals a day. After my disbarment and my relocation to an island off the North Carolina coast, I had been barely scraping by, writing true-crime articles for magazines on topics that came naturally to me because of my prior criminal defense practice, mostly grisly homicides and off-the-wall lawsuits. My last one was a piece on street kids being forced into human trafficking rings.

That was my day job. But my calling—my real mission—was something different. I knew my burdensome gift of detecting the invisible world was no accident. I decided that Divine Providence was the driving force behind my special talent. My response to Dick would have to take that into account, even if the rest of the planet took me for a guy whose mind had run away and joined Cirque du Soleil.

At the same time, you can understand why the legal establishment in the New York Bar Association treated me like a psychiatric case. But then, I knew things that other lawyers couldn't fathom.

So there I was, stewing over all of that one hot day in August, sitting at my desk in the tiny corner room of my cottage, only a little larger than a walk-in closet but with a window and a good view of the Atlantic. Ordinarily I would have jumped right into the Forester case, particularly when it was Dick Valentine doing the asking. But not because I had any attraction to the subject. On a visceral level, the combination of Forester's strange, terrible death coupled with obtuse, supernatural angles turned my stomach. I knew too much about that world. At the same time, though, it stirred me deep inside. Something had to be done about it. If not me, then who? It was the kind of case that had become my niche.

Yet there was a wrinkle. I wasn't alone in my island home at the time, and I had to consider what that might mean. My daughter, Heather, had made her first visit, having just arrived at my home the day before.

That morning I had risen early to do some work and to ruminate on the Forester case, but I heard sounds like someone was stirring in the guest room. Maybe it was Heather. For most fathers that would be no big deal. But I wasn't like other dads.

For twenty-two years I had been led to believe that Heather had never been born.

Heather was the product of a college one-night stand with my youthful crush Marilyn Parlow, who insisted, seven weeks later, that her mind was made up and she would abort. In point of fact, she didn't, but for all those years, the thought of an intentional and premature end to Marilyn's pregnancy had been a backpack loaded with rocks for me. I lugged that burden around everywhere I went.

But the truth won out, thanks to Ashley Linderman, a police detective friend from my hometown. Ashley dug around until she unearthed the details about Heather's birth and subsequent adoption. Even though the news came more than twenty years late, miracles do happen. As for those years that the locusts had eaten, they can still be restored. I believe that.

In my little working room I listened for more sounds that Heather might be awake. Hearing nothing except for the noisy surf from the Atlantic just off my front yard of sand and sea grass, I mentally returned to the Jason Forester matter and his "death by voodoo" that had been hanging over me. I grabbed my iPad off my desk and started doing an Internet search on the occult subject. As usual, I quickly began a free fall, down the research rabbit hole. I was interrupted by the sound of Heather, who had quietly slipped in behind me and started clearing her throat loudly.

"Okay, so you tell me this is supposed to be our time together," she said. "To get to know each other. And you say to me, 'I dare you to drop your iPhone into a drawer.' To forget about it. Which I actually did, by the way. So who's the hypocrite now?"

With a little embarrassment I hit the power button on my iPad, dropped it on the desk, and studied my daughter, now standing in front of me. I thought to myself, *For twenty-two years I kept wondering about it. And now I know. Thank you, God, she's here.*

Heather turned her gaze toward the picture window that fronts the ocean. She was looking out to the blue-green sea, just beyond the dunes and the sea grass.

I was planning on extending an olive branch, but she was wearing a yellow T-shirt at the time, and it just happened to expose her neck. Which triggered something, and I stupidly blurted it out loud: "You know, tons of people, when they get older, regret getting tattoos like that." But I was smiling when I said it. Honest.

She whirled around. "This is not going well."

Then the voice of Ashley Linderman, the mediator. "I'm here to have fun. Why don't you two mix it up some other time?" Ashley, a skinny brunette, was wearing shorts and a faded denim shirt with the sleeves rolled up. Cute. The only thing marring her flawless face was a thin scar on one side, the vestige of her heroism in the line of police duty.

I wasn't surprised that Ashley had joined Heather on the visit to my seaside cottage. Even before Ashley helped me locate my daughter, the two of us had become close, working a murder case together in Wisconsin; she was the investigating detective, and I, the friend of the victim in pursuit of justice, was convinced that behind the killing, there was something hellish going on. Ashley seemed attracted to me, and the feeling was mutual. Still, there was that divide between us. The chasm.

During her island visit, I needed to have a difficult discussion with her about our future.

After my comment about her tattoo, Heather blew off Ashley's attempt to cool things down. She gave me an irritated shake of her head and announced that she was going for a stroll along the beach, adding, with the plural verbiage of royalty, "And *we* are walking alone." Then she stomped outside by herself.

That hurt. No question about it. Male egos pretend to be made of titanium steel, but at the core they're Jell-O.

As for Heather, she was a fully grown young woman with a mind of her own. When her opinions clashed with mine, I was faced with the disturbing reality that I didn't have the right, or even the practical ability, to control her. Instead, I was just a trustee of sorts for my daughter, and a new one at that, fumbling at this job of trying to be a parent to an adult child. Maybe my motivations had been honorable, but I was struggling.

With Heather gone and just us left in the house, Ashley gave me some advice. "I don't think you can play the *Father Knows Best* thing with her until the two of you cover some other ground first. Just my opinion. But on this, I'm right." Then she asked, "How did this start?"

"I was doing some research on my iPad. She called me a hypocrite."

Ashley stared me down.

I shrugged. "She might have a point."

"Research on what?"

"The killing of an assistant US attorney, Jason Forester."

"What federal jurisdiction?"

"District of Columbia."

"What's your interest in this?" Ashley asked.

"They mentioned voodoo as the cause of death."

The tone of her voice turned subtly cynical. "Oh, so you're branching out? Now it's voodoo?"

"I don't think it's a stretch."

She shook her head. I knew what that meant. But she plunked herself down in the wicker chair next to me, so dialogue was still open. By this point in our relationship, I was pretty sure Ashley had resigned herself to the fact that I had a strange vocation—not my day job writing news articles for crime magazines, but my other pursuit. We had continued to disagree about my other line of work. It had gone beyond just the philosophical and was getting intensely personal.

"Okay," I said, "let's forget it."

But she wouldn't and followed up with another question. "Have you already agreed to dive into this voodoo thing?"

"Not yet."

Ashley was jiggling her foot where she sat. She took a long look out the window toward the ocean, and then, after a while, she stood. After eyeing my iPad, she snatched it up and tapped the screen to read where I had left off in my research.

She announced, "I'm going for a walk. I'll catch up to Heather if I can." She handed my iPad back to me and said, "Meanwhile, just for giggles, tell me what you find out about voodoo death."

3

The next day I used every bit of my charm to get Heather and Ashley to join me for the Sunday morning service at Port-of-Peace Church. The small congregation operated out of a little weather-beaten clapboard chapel on the island, not far from an ancient cemetery where the inscriptions on the gravestones had been rubbed into indecipherability by time, tide, and hurricanes. The chapel had seats for about sixty people, which was good, because the regular attendees had numbered forty before I started showing up and made it forty-one. It had a part-time minister by the name of Banks Trumbly, who preached on Sundays and in his spare time would make visitation to the sick or the infirm. His day job was running a commercial fishing boat.

Banks Trumbly was a good man and had a no-nonsense approach to the Bible. What he lacked in theological finesse, Banks made up for with enthusiasm.

During the service, Banks preached on a touchy subject: Satan and his worldly dominion. It was touchy only because I had not spoken to Heather about my special "gifting." I had talked openly about God, the Bible, and my faith encounter with Christ. But Satan and his army of demons? No, I had left that one alone for the time being.

As I drove the three of us back to my cabin after the church service, Heather let loose. "Your pastor sounds like a Neanderthal," she blurted out. "He seriously believes there is a hierarchy of demons working under an actual devil! Like some kind of government bureau from hell."

I responded. "Yes. Not a bad description." Then I added, "Ask yourself this: Do you believe in demons or not? Seems like a perfectly legitimate question for someone studying anthropology."

She shrugged.

I pressed it. "You've said a few positive things about Jesus since you came to the island. So consider the many times in the Gospels where Jesus encountered demons that had possessed people. And each time, Jesus vanquished them. Every one. And in the process, he never hedged on the reality of the supernatural realm."

She pushed back. "Okay, Trevor, let's correct something. What I like about Jesus is what Deepak Chopra and the other mystics call 'Christ consciousness.' But you and that pastor of yours, and anyone else who goes on a Bible rampage like your pastor did, you're all victims of the anthropomorphic fallacy."

"You have to either take all of Jesus or none of him," I said. "You can't pick and choose. And you and Deepak Chopra and his mystical compatriots who want to cram Jesus into a nice, tidy box, you need to understand something: Jesus won't be crammed."

Ashley kept stone silent in the back of my Land Rover. I could guess what was going through her mind.

That night we had a quiet dinner at the cottage. Afterward Heather said she was tired and announced that she would be going to bed early. I gave her half a hug, still being cautious, and quietly whispered that I loved her. No response. Just a quick smile.

Ashley followed her to the bedroom, but not before I told Ashley that I would like some time together the next morning, just the two of us, to talk.

"I'd like to talk to you too," she said, "about things." She reached out, patted me on the cheek, and then slipped into the bedroom.

Left to myself, I swung the screen door open, cringing at the sound of the rusty groan and vowing to oil it in the morning. I strolled barefoot onto the stretch of sand and sea grass that was my front yard and kept going until I was just a few feet from the rolling tide that was edging up the beach line. The moon was full, and the ocean was calm. I was thinking back to the phone call from Detective Dick Valentine and the reasons he gave me for why I should check into the Forester death—and why I was the right man to do it.

But down deep, I was losing an appetite for the Forester case, even though I suspected that something darkly supernatural was afoot.

I wanted to focus on Heather, trying to kindle something out of the ashes of our being apart for more than two decades. I wanted to see some kind of peace sign, any kind, from her. None yet, but I was hopeful. So far she had settled into calling me just "Trevor." I suppose "Dad" was still a long way off. Maybe never.

I took a deep breath, inhaling the scent of churning salt water and the faint fish smell from seashells and tiny ocean life that would wash up with the night tide. But nothing else. Nothing foreboding in the air.

Then, as I turned to go back inside, something caught my eye. Something on the surface of the ocean, about a hundred yards from the beach. I looked closer and recognized the figure of a man, and he was definitely standing, not sinking. And something more. He was not illuminated by the moonlight. It was as if he were a black hole in space, swallowing up the light. Defying the laws of physics by standing on the sea, as if supported by solid steel. The sight of it gave me a sudden shiver, like insects scampering over me. I squinted and looked closer, trying to make out his features.

I blinked, and the figure vanished.

At another time in my life, I would have worked hard to dismiss it. But that was then. Now, in this life to which I have been called, I tucked that image away for safekeeping. My heart racing, I wiped sweaty palms on my shorts. It was time to remind myself that God still governed the affairs of the universe. Including those of men and of angels. And even demons.

I had the distinct impression that the figure out there on the ocean was issuing me a warning. Maybe a threat. About what, I didn't know.

But there was something else. Something that was missing. Unlike all the times in the past, I hadn't received my usual sensate alert, hit with the repulsive scent of burning refuse and death that had always signaled when one of the underworld monsters was near. That night it didn't happen. The absence of a sensory warning was a shocker. My head was flooded with questions. About my special "gift"—detecting the supernatural realm—and my previous early warning system. I had relied on it. Maybe too much. Was I losing control?

4

Early the next morning I was wakened by the smell of brewing coffee. Ashley was already up, so I jumped into a pair of shorts and a T-shirt and ambled into my little kitchen to join her. I was ready to ease into casual conversation with her until I could segue into our relationship. The serious stuff.

But I didn't have to. Ashley opened up the discussion as I sat next to her.

"So I've been thinking," she began. "About the compatibility thing."

I listened.

"Not just," she went on, "about our different geographies. Me up there in chilly Wisconsin, and you down here in the South, living the life of a beach bum on Gilligan's Island."

I laughed.

"It's more than that," she said. "Don't you think?"

I agreed. This was friendly direct examination, not aggressive cross-examination. So I asked a lawyerly question. "Tell me, what do you think is the biggest point of incompatibility?"

"Dirty lawyer's trick," she said with a fake complaint in her voice and a smirk. "Are you really going to make me spill it first?"

"Okay, fine," I said. "From the beginning of our time together in Wisconsin, you knew where I was coming from. You knew about my unusual work. And you knew that I consider myself on a mission from God. Now, you're in law enforcement. You deal with the aftermath of evil. Me? Whatever I am, I deal with the genesis of evil, the kind that comes from another dimension."

"Kooky, that's for sure," she said. "Your *so-called* ability to detect demons. Based on . . . let's see, what was it? . . . Oh yeah, catching their smell. You realize, don't you, there are psychological explanations for that."

It sounded pretty crazy the way she put it. "Yes," I said. "The scent, that's the way it started. At least at first. But maybe it's changing."

"You mean, now it's different? You don't have to smell them to see them?" More sarcasm in her voice.

I was thinking back to the incident the night before, on the beach. Seeing one of the monsters, but that time, minus the burning scent of rot and death.

"Look," I said, "the technical details of my ability, that's not important. What is important is about us. Maybe in one way, what you and I do in terms of stopping evildoers, we're not that different. But I've had a soul shake-up. A complete spiritual realignment. And in that, we are different."

"Different is . . . ," she began, then let her voice trail off.

"Different is fine for a vacation," I filled in, "but not for a lifetime."

She blew on her cup of coffee to cool it down. "Nice closing argument."

"Not a fun case to argue," I said. "But then, I didn't pick this case. It picked me."

Ashley changed the subject and asked me about Heather. I was frank about the problems we were having. But I told her that I would never give up on my daughter.

Ashley took a sip of coffee. "She'll come around." She stood and stepped over to me, cup in hand, and planted a kiss on my forehead. As she stepped away, she said, exhaling, "Aw, crap. I don't mind breakups with the bad boys. But it's tough when it's a good guy."

An hour later, Ashley announced that she had booked an earlier flight out of Norfolk, just across the border in Virginia, departing late afternoon, and that she would have to leave shortly.

When she was behind the wheel of her rental car, window down, I leaned in to face her. I was trying to come up with something snappy or profound or tender to say. But it didn't come. I was wordless.

"Hey, don't sweat it," Ashley said, breaking the silence. "It's painted all over your face. This isn't your fault. You don't owe me a thing. And by the way, you've given me a lot."

She turned on the ignition and added, "Besides, I'm sure

this isn't the last time we'll be talking. You'll be calling me up with some outrageous favor I'm supposed to do for you. Some police intelligence you need. So you can break another case. So you can call another nasty murder the work of the devil. And who knows? Maybe it will be."

I asked, "Will you answer when I make that call?"

"We'll see," she said. Seconds later, I saw her taillights heading away from me, down the sandy road.

When Ashley left, Heather didn't bother to ask me why. She hit me with her own theory. "I know what happened," she said. "It's all that 'I'm crazy for Christ' stuff you're into and Ashley's not. All that 'The devil made the homicidal maniac do it' stuff. And that is really too bad, Trevor. I liked Ashley a lot."

I listened but didn't go into debating mode.

For the rest of the morning I took Heather out for a boat ride, cruising around Ocracoke Island. I gave her some of the local lore about the island's most famous figure, Edward Teach, aka Blackbeard, the eighteenth-century pirate, who scuttled ships and looted and murdered around those waters until he was finally hunted down by the English navy and killed not far from my place on the island.

She seemed interested. We kept the conversation light and breezy and off the personal topics, eating sandwiches out of my cooler as I motored my forty-footer. Heather was still keeping things at arm's length. I had concluded it was going to be a marathon rather than a fifty-yard dash between us.

But my mind turned to other matters when we got back to the cottage and I found a voice message waiting on my cell phone. The call was from a young man named Kevin Sanders.

He said he was a law clerk calling for his boss, a New Orleans lawyer by the name of Morgan Canterelle.

But when I returned the call, I was greeted by a message on the other end. While the voice sounded like the Kevin Sanders I'd just listened to, the message on his answering service began with a surprisingly freaky intro: "Hello, and welcome to Marie Laveau's House of Voodoo."

5

I was midway into leaving a message of my own when Kevin Sanders picked up.

"Sorry, Mr. Black," he said. "I was just closing up."

"I'm not sure I've got this straight. I was under the impression I was calling the law clerk of an attorney."

"Oh yeah," he laughed. "So sorry. Yes, I'm the law clerk. Actually, I had to call you from this place, my job here at the museum, because the battery on my cell phone died. But yes, I do work for Attorney Canterelle when I'm not working part-time over here."

"Are you studying law?"

He said he was and that he was a third-year law student at Tulane, all the while working two jobs. I had to give him credit for that. "A lot of us law students are working two jobs," Kevin added. "It beats cleaning the toilets someplace like Six Flags."

Kevin quickly got down to business, saying Morgan Canterelle wanted to speak to me, that it was a matter of urgency, and he wanted to know when could that happen. I gave him a time later that day.

I asked, "Who is this Marie Laveau you're working for at the museum?"

He thought that was funny. "No, I don't work for her. She died way back in 1881. Never heard of her?" I said I hadn't. "She was a really famous New Orleans voodoo priestess."

Considering the facts surrounding AUSA Forester's death, he had my attention.

A few hours later, I was on the phone with Morgan Canterelle, who spoke in a deep baritone and slowly, in a born-and-bred-in-Louisiana manner. "I'm an admirer of y'all, Mr. Black. Which is the very reason I reached out."

"Admirer in what way?"

"Y'all's reputation as a criminal defense attorney pre-cedes," he said. "Y'all's cases would occasionally be the talk of the criminal law section of the ABA. By the way, I'm on the convention committee of the American Bar Association."

I said all that was interesting to know but wondered silently where this was going.

"Which is why I'm calling. We would like y'all to be a presenter at our upcoming convention. Right here in New Orleans. How 'bout that?"

"You know that I no longer practice law."

"Naturally, Mr. Black," he intoned, "I know that y'all do not presently practice law. I am fully apprised of y'all's disbarment."

"Then why have me speak to a bunch of lawyers and judges?"

"An address from an ex-criminal de-fense lawyer from New York who investigates demons? That is something I would pay Broadway-ticket prices to hear."

I waited for the gag line. That this whole phone call was a prank. But it didn't come. So I said, "I'm reluctant, Mr. Canterelle. It sounds like a TV reality show, with me playing the part of the goblin-chasing, disbarred ex-lawyer."

He shot back, "Lawyers need entertainment too." Then an added thought. "And by the way, isn't that what y'all are—a goblin-chasing, disbarred ex-lawyer?"

I couldn't argue with that. Next, the New Orleans attorney sweetened the deal. "And we pay a very handsome honorarium."

Despite my new career writing magazine articles about bizarre cases, I still had been dipping into my retirement fund. An extra cash injection sounded nice. I told him I would think about it. But I added, "When is the convention again?"

"Next week. The speaking slot would be four days from now."

The dawn was breaking. "Oh, in other words, one of your other speakers bailed on you at the last minute. . . ."

"Not at all," he boomed. "It took until now for me to convince the rest of the convention committee that *y'all's* the right man for the slot."

"A hard sell?"

"A little. But then, Mr. Black, I am a very convincing man."

Canterelle must have sensed my foot was still dragging, because he elaborated. "Look here, about that 'convincing' part, I got ahold of a speech y'all made once to the New York Bar Association dealing with the law on exculpatory evidence. I gave it to the members of our committee and told them, 'Hey, this boy Trevor Black, he's a fine speaker.' And we all know about that magazine writing now, which makes y'all a round peg in a round hole because the plenary session is being sponsored by the American Institute of Legal Authors. See how that all fits together?"

I asked when he needed an answer. He said, "Midmorning tomorrow."

After my call with the New Orleans lawyer, I checked the ABA convention website. The attorney general for the United States, George Shazzar, would be addressing the audience immediately after the slot where Canterelle wanted me to speak.

Shazzar had just rubber-stamped the decision of US Attorney Vance Zaduck to close the matter on the Forester death. A troublesome sign, I thought, particularly because the *ABA Journal* had also quoted "unnamed sources" at the US attorney's office in DC who were complaining that the matter needed a more thorough investigation. I had a bad feeling about Shazzar and was growing more convinced that this incident needed a second look. The ABA convention could give me the chance to hit the whole issue with a huge, very public LED light.

But there was also the matter of Heather. She was scheduled to stay on with me at the cottage until well into the next week. That would conflict with my flying down to New Orleans for the ABA convention. I didn't want to jeopardize our time together.

While it was still daylight, Heather and I took a walk from

my cottage, along the sandy road past the lighthouse, and then down to the harbor that was usually filled with sailboats, fishing charters, and a few crabbing vessels at anchor. There was a fish market there. She wanted to make dinner for us, so I gave her carte blanche to choose anything she wanted and told her I'd pick up the tab.

Heather decided on sea bass, red potatoes, and corn on the cob, which sounded great to me. On the stroll back, as I carried the grocery bag, we didn't talk much. I wanted to avoid the topic of my speaking at the ABA. I would save that for dinner.

After picking our plates clean at a good meal, I broke the news, talking about my dilemma regarding the ABA invitation. To my surprise she went ballistic with enthusiasm. "You've got to accept the offer, Trevor. Absolutely."

I asked, "But wouldn't you rather stay here at the cottage?"

"Uh, absolutely not. No way," she said. "I want to go to New Orleans with you. See you in action. What a trip, hearing you address all those lawyers and judges. Besides, I had actually given some thought to visiting New Orleans myself. The timing's perfect."

On a chessboard, I would have been checkmated. But in a good way.

Of course, as I meditated on her reaction, there was another explanation. Perhaps my long-lost daughter wanted to judge for herself what the legal community really thought of me. To see whether her biological father really had stepped off the deep end.

But I couldn't ignore one final factor, something completely off the chessboard. Maybe this trip to New Orleans was providential. The FedEx letter—the last thing AUSA Jason Forester looked at before he shuffled off this mortal coil, as the Bard would say—had been shipped out of a little express delivery shop. And of all the places in the world, that shop was located in New Orleans.

Yes, I would fly down to the ABA, and Heather with me. That much was certain. But before that, I decided to pursue one possible avenue on the Forester death. I e-mailed a note to a high-ranking official in the Justice Department whose name I knew, asking for a meeting on the subject. It was an ultra-long shot. The odds were slim that I would ever hear back from Paul Pullmen, assistant attorney general for the Criminal Division. Instead, I was betting that the call would come from an underling, if at all: *So sorry, Mr. Black, but a meeting with Mr. Pullmen is simply not feasible.*

6

Heather and I flew into New Orleans just as the sun was going down. Through the window we could see the Mississippi River bathed in crimson. An hour later we were driving past the venue where I would be speaking the following day, the million-square-foot Ernest N. Morial Convention Center, with the glittering symbol of the French fleur-de-lis on the facade. I saw crowds of lawyer types streaming out of the place as we passed. Little did they know the fireworks I would soon be springing on the ABA.

As we stood in line in the lobby of the Hyatt to check in, Heather gave me a nudge. "So, when'll you tell me about your speech tomorrow?"

I just smiled.

"Come on, this isn't a state secret. I'm your daughter. Give me a hint. What's the topic?"

I tried my best to dodge her questions artfully.

"Wow, Trevor," she said with a smirk. "Anybody tell you that you're emotionally closed?"

I ignored that one and booked us separate, adjoining rooms, and we parted in the hall to drop our bags.

Morgan Canterelle had promised that he would be in touch with me when I arrived in the city, but the desk had no message, and there was no voice mail from him on my cell phone, so I called his office. The receptionist transferred me to Kevin Sanders, who answered in a chipper voice and asked how my flight was.

"Good, thanks, but I was wondering if your boss might want to connect with me before my speech tomorrow."

"I tell you what, Mr. Black, Mr. Canterelle isn't in the office right now, but I will be sure and tell him you called."

Figuring that the lawyer's invitation to meet with me personally in New Orleans had merely been a courtesy, I thanked his clerk and forgot about it.

Heather and I took the elevator down for a quick dinner. As we ate, she was surprisingly chatty and had given up trying to pry into my upcoming ABA address. We drifted into a conversation about her master's thesis. She described it as "Dealing with cultural and religious syncretism. Modern-day belief systems that have their roots in older practices and then get melded together."

Then she quickly asked if I had ever been to New Orleans before.

I told her, "Long time ago. Last time was when I argued a criminal case before the Fifth Circuit, in the US Court of Appeals. Before that, I attended the ABA. And before that, a criminal case I handled in the local courthouse here in New Orleans. All of that was before Katrina hit, of course. That changed everything."

She looked pensive. "What's the legal term?"

"For what?"

"For hurricanes. Storms. Those kinds of natural disasters. One of my professors used it once."

"I think you mean *force majeure*," I said.

"Right, that's it. What does it mean?"

"An unanticipated, extraordinary, devastating natural occurrence. 'Act of God' is what the old phrase used to be."

"So, God brings destruction?"

"There's a difference between allowing it and causing it. Nature, humanity—the whole earth is out of whack. Enter chaos. Whatever his reasons, God lets the world take its course sometimes."

"And the devil? Do you believe he brings hurricanes?"

"He can. If God allows it."

"So you think God has, like, this ultimate veto power over everything?"

"That's a good way of looking at it."

"Does he let the devil get away with murder? Like your voodoo case?"

I stopped eating. "I take it Ashley told you about it?"

"Just a few things. Sounds creepy."

"Yes, very."

"I suppose you're not going to tell me why a New York policeman wants you to investigate a creepy murder of a government attorney in Washington?"

"Not yet. I'm still at the front end of that case. Wait till things get a bit clearer. Then I'll tell you more."

"You didn't answer my question."

"Which one?"

"About whether you believe that God allows the devil to get away with murder."

I took my time answering. Then, "It sounds like you're blaming God for not stopping bad things from happening."

It was her turn to take her time. Finally she said, "No, not every bad thing. Just some things."

"Like?"

"Like Marilyn dying before I got a chance to even meet her. The only thing I know about my biological mother now is the one letter she wrote to me."

"I'm sorry it happened that way."

"She really said some nasty things about you in the letter." Heather looked me in the eye when she said that.

"I'm sure some of them were true," I said. "I made mistakes."

"Like you demanding that she abort me?"

In a flash, everything seemed to change between us. One minute, a good dinner conversation that actually seemed to be opening up the relationship. Then, a minute later, I was teetering on a precipice. *Please, God,* I thought, *help me through this.* How could I tell my daughter that her mother—whom she never had a chance to meet and who had put her up for adoption and who lied to the adoption officials by telling them she didn't know who the father was—had also lied in that letter to Heather, spinning a story that I was demanding she abort the pregnancy?

Heather was still waiting for a response. She cocked her head. "Well?"

I wanted a relationship with my daughter. Desperately. So much distance between us. The whole thing seemed daunting. Even so, I wasn't about to bridge the gap by slandering her dead mother—even if she had lied about me in that letter. It was Marilyn who mentioned the abortion, not me. At the same time, though, I had played the part of the complicit coward. I had been willing to allow it. I had to live with that.

"The truth is," I finally said, "I should have fought for you when I learned that Marilyn was pregnant. And I didn't. And that was the terrible failure on my part."

Heather stared at her water glass and then picked it up like she was going to drink from it but finally set it down. She rose to her feet instead. After thanking me for dinner, she said she was going to her room, abruptly ending our dinner conversation.

As I looked at the vacant chair across the table from me, I tried to put the whole thing in perspective. Fumbling for some practical, concrete signposts. But after failing at that, I managed to construct only one lackluster word of wisdom for myself.

No one had told me that the parenting journey would be this rough or that the rules of the road seemed to be written in Sanskrit.

7

The next day, the plenary session was held in one of the big ballrooms of the convention center, an arena full of cushy seating in a semi-darkened hall. There were two jumbotrons on the stage, one at each corner.

I sat on a stage that was bathed in lights, in a velvet chair positioned just behind the lectern. The high, darkened ceiling twinkled with tiny white lights and reminded me of the night sky over Ocracoke Island—twinkling chips of refracted light in a vast canopy of black. My single emotion: I would rather have been back on my island.

But I thought about my mentor Rev. John Cannon, now a resident of a Wisconsin nursing home. He was a man who stirred up controversy himself. I thought he would have approved the remarks I was about to impart, and then, just as quickly, would have told me to buck up. I said a silent prayer and readied myself for the flailing.

When the session started, an ABA rep came to the microphone to give a few announcements about the convention schedule for the rest of the day. At that point the cavernous hall was about half-full, which was still impressive because the place seated over a thousand people. Suddenly more lawyers started to stream in. Maybe because the attorney general would be addressing them next, right after my speech. Or perhaps there was another explanation. Maybe they came to see the freak show.

I knew why I had come. Attention needed to be focused on the Jason Forester death. But it was going to be a delicate high-wire act. I still had only a cursory backstory on the incident. Yet I felt it was enough for me to suspect something foul was going on. My invitation to speak in New Orleans was not happpenstance. I was a man on a mission. Time to kick-start a further probe into Jason Forester's demise.

As I sat there on the stage, I felt like a country peasant in front of the Star Chamber, straight out of Tudor England. I scanned the audience and thought about my message. And how I would start my speech with some jokes about lawyers. The one that asks: What's the difference between a dead armadillo run over on a Texas highway by an 18-wheeler, and a dead lawyer run over on a Texas highway? Answer: There are skid marks in front of the armadillo.

In the shadows of the hall, the faces in the first few rows were visible. There was Heather, right in the front, staring up at me, mouth slightly open, as if witnessing her father in the death chamber as he was about to receive a lethal injection.

I glanced down Heather's row, noticing a female lawyer next to her. And a long line of male attorneys.

But one face jumped out. I squinted hard to make sure. Even with the passage of all those years, I was certain it was him. Vance Zaduck, United States attorney for the District of Columbia. His face was fuller, and he looked to have put on some weight. His hairline had receded over the years in an almost-perfect half circle. But yes, it was Vance all right.

My mind started to race. I knew at that moment how, if I really wanted to, I could improvise. Make some clever modifications to my speech. After all, Vance was Forester's boss. There was the hook.

Vance Zaduck had pitched a noncommittal recommendation to the attorney general that concluded Forester's death was by natural causes. Of course the attorney general had the authority to push it further and didn't, which was the true miscarriage if my instincts were right about Forester's death. So why was I fixating on Vance? I knew why, of course. And I knew that if I wanted to, I could use Vance Zaduck's status as the ranking lawyer in that office where Forester had died as the justifiable link to talk about a few of the things that I knew personally about Zaduck.

I could begin with the reality that prosecutors like Jason Forester have tough jobs and do a great service to society. Yet, at the same time, prosecutors have a truly staggering measure of power to ruin innocent people's lives under the banner of "prosecutorial discretion." Then I could relate, as an example, how ten years ago Vance Zaduck had charged a client of mine with attempted murder, back when he was an assistant DA in Manhattan, before he got the wink and the nod to become the US attorney in Washington.

I could describe my client, Carter Collins, a young middleweight boxer who grew up in the Hell's Kitchen section of Manhattan, back when the area was still roughneck and before it became gentrified with luxury condos and high-rent properties.

And how, though Carter had a misdemeanor criminal record of minor offenses, he worked hard, trained well, and created a promising boxing career for himself. He also had an attractive girlfriend who attracted a stalker. Fearing for his girlfriend, Carter took matters into his own hands, and that's where the trouble started. He tracked down the stalker, waiting for him to exit a tavern with his friend at closing time. Words were exchanged, Carter said the guy pulled a knife, and so Carter, who had an arm like a cannon, landed a quick, catastrophic right, causing brain damage to the stalker. We raised the argument of self-defense at trial, but the jury didn't buy it, primarily because the man's bar friend testified that he *never* saw his friend, the "victim," brandish a knife at all.

And then a year later I discovered that Vance Zaduck had known all along that there was an independent witness, a passerby who had actually seen the guy pull a knife on my client during the short-lived fight. What the law calls exculpatory evidence, because it tends to underscore the innocence of my client, the defendant. Something the law also requires a prosecutor to disclose to the defense. But when I raised the nondisclosure to the court, the trial judge refused to reverse the verdict, justifying it with the harmless error rule, the bane of many a defense attorney. Carter spent almost ten years in prison.

Yet, before even filing my motion for a new trial, I had a sit-down with Vance in his office, thinking that he might voluntarily agree to a new trial, seeing that I had caught him red-handed committing prosecutorial misconduct by hiding evidence from me. Thinking that Vance Zaduck might even regret what had happened to my client.

Instead of that, though, Vance went off about his being "vested with power by the state to enforce the law."

At the time, I told him in my pitch, "Vance, you also have prosecutorial discretion to do the right thing. To correct an injustice that you created yourself. Maybe Carter should never have confronted the victim in the first place, but if you drop the case, or at least agree to a new trial, Carter could have the chance to become the man he ought to be."

Vance chortled in my face and he recited a quote, along with its source: "'A man as he ought to be: that sounds . . . as insipid as: "a tree as it ought to be."' Friedrich Nietzsche."

Then Vance added, "I chose to exercise my prosecutorial authority by sending your client to prison for as long as I can. That's how I use my power."

I shot back with a quote of my own: "'If you want to test a man's character, give him power.' Abraham Lincoln."

Vance was not amused. He abruptly called our conversation to a halt.

Yes, I could have launched into all of that in my speech to the ABA, and I was tempted to.

But I didn't.

Instead I looked out at the sea of shadowy faces in the crowded convention ballroom. The armadillo joke garnered some chuckles from the audience, but then I moved on to some facts about a brave, honorable federal prosecutor.

"Let me start today with the *best* of our legal profession. Epitomized by an assistant US attorney named Jason Forester. After spending years putting away mobsters and terrorists, Forester moved against the scourge of human trafficking of the vilest form: abduction of children for sexual exploitation and even worse. Now this is a scary trend. California reported thirteen hundred human trafficking cases in a single year alone. Nationally, one in six youth runaways are swept into it. But AUSA Forester won't be chasing down that hideous network anymore. If my suspicions are right, he didn't just die from cardiac arrest. Someone, or something, wanted him stopped.

"Which brings me to a *flaw* in our legal profession."

That's when I began to address the modern shotgun marriage between the law and the world of the scientific and empirical, while divorcing itself from all things spiritual and moral. I took the audience through a quick refresher of early American law and its first cousin, the English common law, to prove how far we had wandered.

Eventually I got down to my main point, reciting a few of the facts about how Jason Forester died. I could sense some stirring in the audience, so I sped things up.

"The American public," I said, "has a right to know whether Jason Forester, a courageous federal prosecutor with a record of facing down mobsters and bloodthirsty terrorists, just might have faced an invisible enemy so horrific and malevolent that he was, literally, frightened to death."

That is when the herd really started getting restless. I could hear hundreds of them out there in the audience, shifting in their seats.

"The real question," I declared, "is whether US Attorney Vance Zaduck's decision to close that matter should be reversed by the attorney general for the United States."

A few people got up from their seats and walked out as I plowed forward.

"Do we think ourselves so sophisticated today, and are we so rationalistically arrogant, that we are unwilling to consider that there really is a devil—not a metaphor, but a being who is irrevocably evil? That belief is not unheard of, even in the most respected legal circles."

By then, scattered murmuring throughout the hall.

I tried to ignore it. "The late, great Supreme Court Justice Antonin Scalia once remarked to a reporter that he held such a belief in a real devil himself. Have you—have we—arrogated ourselves to a position of demigods? Unwilling to be taught about where evil comes from and about the God in heaven who is the only one with the power to really vanquish it?"

Voices began to rise up—only a few at first, but they were out there in the dark, complaining, protesting my message.

I kept going. "Our top law oracles have all been schooled in the world of legal pragmatism, and I get that. They comprise the majority opinion in our profession. But I've had a personal and rather painful tutorial in the school of supernatural evil. I encourage you to consider the opinion of this dissenting ex-lawyer when it comes to the demonic world and the invidious danger it represents. Including, but not limited to, the untimely death that was meted out to Assistant US Attorney Jason Forester."

That is when the audience erupted. Boos. Jeering. Catcalls. Things were quickly cascading out of control.

When two burly men in dark suits hustled onto the stage toward me, I suspected at first that they were private convention-center security. Until they got closer. Plain white shirts. Lifeless dark ties. Thick necks. Earbuds. The stone-faced look of official command.

No, not convention security.

One of them grabbed my arm. "Mr. Black, FBI. Please come with us."

When we were offstage in the wings, I asked a question that I didn't seriously expect to be answered, at least at that point. "Why am I in federal custody?"

Imagine my surprise when one of the agents actually responded to my question. And imagine my utter shock at the answer he gave me. "Mr. Black, there's a dead man in your hotel room."

8

I was backstage with an FBI agent at each elbow. That's where I encountered the attorney general for the United States, George Shazzar, surrounded by more tough-looking men with earbuds. Probably Secret Service. Much whispering to the attorney general about something I couldn't hear. Shazzar glared at me with a look of disgust.

I tried to approach Shazzar, planning to suggest to him that he do the right thing, take another look into the Jason Forester death.

"Attorney General Shazzar, can I urge . . . ?" I started out, launching into my short monologue.

But my FBI escorts closed it down, yanking me in the opposite direction and yelling for me to "get away from the attorney general."

I heard Shazzar say something about "a rotten apple at the bottom of every barrel" before he was politely but quickly whisked away.

Just as quickly I was escorted out of the convention center by a gaggle of FBI agents, though not as courteously as they'd handled the AG.

Next, placed between two special agents in the backseat of a bureau vehicle, I was driven across town, past the Army Reserve building and over to the FBI headquarters on Leon C. Simon Boulevard. The agent who drove us stayed with the car, while the other two walked me up to the red-and-tan brick building. Beyond the white arched entrance I encountered a security screening, where agents patted me down, confiscated my watch and cell phone to be kept "until later," and returned my wallet only after taking it into another room—likely to photograph the contents. An interesting procedural question from a search and seizure standpoint, but ultimately irrelevant as things turned out. The agents escorted me up in an elevator before depositing me in a nondescript beige room that was empty except for a table, two black plastic chairs with metal frames, and a TV set at the other end, probably for video evidence viewing. They told me to sit down, while they left the room and I heard the electronic click as the door was locked from the outside.

I glanced over at the large mirror on the wall that must have housed the one-way glass.

Minutes went by. And more minutes. Maybe close to an hour, but I couldn't tell.

I knew, as I sat in the beige room with the one-way glass, what to expect. The routine procedure. This was the observation stage. They were watching on the other side of the mirrored glass. Was I fidgeting? Any furtive movements? Signs of emotional stress?

After a while, I heard a heavy click as the door unlocked and two different agents entered, one young, one older. The younger remained standing. The older introduced himself as Special Agent Roger Fainlock, sat down across from me, and asked me if I needed anything.

"No."

"Water? Coffee?"

"No thanks."

They then lit into me with questions.

"Who booked your room at the hotel?"

"I did."

They followed up with some questions about my credit card, which I pulled out from my wallet. I handed Agent Fainlock my American Express, along with my driver's license, then dug into my pocket and retrieved the little folder from the hotel with my plastic room key inserted inside, and I tossed that onto the table in front of him too.

All of that to show that I was who I was, and how I had booked the room, and that yes, I had the key to the room. Which, to the naive observer, might seem to imply guilt, given the fact that a dead man had been found in my hotel room. But I knew the FBI must already have all that information anyway and my volunteering it, unprompted, ought to count for something. A small token in favor of my innocence perhaps.

Then questions about my travel route to New Orleans, which led to my telling them that there was an e-mailed boarding pass from United Airlines on my iPhone if they wanted to check it out. The agent pulled my iPhone from his pocket, and I typed in my passcode, accessed my e-mail, and showed him the boarding pass.

He didn't ask me for my cell back, so I slipped it into my coat pocket. Things were looking up.

Until he shot a question about my "traveling companion" and whether we had flown together.

"First," I shot back, "she's not my 'traveling companion.' She's my daughter. Second, yes, she traveled with her father so she could sit in the audience and watch me deliver my message to the American Bar Association. Witnessed by, oh, I'd say maybe a thousand lawyers and judges at the convention center. All of which you already know, of course, considering that your FBI agents were there and must have caught my speech, because the millisecond it was over, they grabbed me and whisked me off the stage."

That's when there was a quick eye contact back and forth between the agents, followed, finally, by an interrogation into the heart of the matter. Namely, what exactly did I know about Paul Pullmen, assistant attorney general for the Criminal Division at the Department of Justice in Washington?

"I never met Mr. Pullmen personally," I explained. "I handled a white-collar crime case in New York City once that was being reviewed by the DOJ in Washington, and I saw Pullmen's name on correspondence as the supervising attorney overseeing the case. So from that I knew about Mr. Pullmen's position at DOJ."

"Did you ever talk to him back then?"

"No. Only through his deputy, another lawyer I happened

to know at DOJ, a guy named Gil Spencer. Once upon a time Gil and I both worked in the New York City public defender's office for a short period. Anyway, having some knowledge of DOJ personnel, I speculated that Mr. Pullmen would be the logical person for me to try to contact in the Forester matter."

"Oh?"

"Yes. The death in Washington, DC, of Assistant US Attorney Jason Forester."

Agent Fainlock eyed me closely on that one, which came as no surprise. That immediately led to a waterfall of questions from him, all having to do with why I would have any interest in the Forester matter in the first place.

"A friend of mine is in law enforcement," I explained. "A police detective. He had some inside information about the death of Attorney Forester, and he shared it with me. And that piqued my interest. Plus the fact that there might be an occult connection, which is an area of special interest to me."

The agent's eyes widened slightly. "And the detective's name is?"

"It wouldn't be fair for me to share his identity without his permission. . . ."

The agent leaned forward an inch but no more. Yet an important inch. His face hardened and his eyes narrowed. "You used to be a lawyer, Mr. Black," he said, his voice rising a notch. "So you know we can hold you in custody."

"Perhaps, but not for very long," I bulleted back. "Unless you have a warrant or probable cause. And we both know you don't have either. There's no reasonable suspicion to connect me to this terrible crime, because as for Mr. Pullmen—and

I assume he's the victim and that is why you brought up his name—at the moment he was being killed by the real murderer, I was giving a speech in front of an army of witnesses that included FBI agents from this office."

The agent leaned back in his chair, his eyes never leaving mine. "Remember this: the place where a high-ranking Department of Justice lawyer was murdered was your hotel room. Not someone else's, but yours."

"Oh?" I replied. "Your forensic investigators have determined that? That he wasn't murdered somewhere else and then moved to my room and staged in a way to deliberately implicate me?"

Maybe that sounded a little paranoid, but it was a possible scenario.

"Mr. Black, I don't have to tell you what our forensics unit has determined. . . ."

"And, Special Agent Fainlock, I don't have to tell you the name of my detective friend without his consent."

A long pause. The FBI agent across from me had the age—maybe early fifties—and the calm demeanor of an experienced investigator in the Criminal Investigative Division of the New Orleans bureau. So I gauged that he had probably reached the GS-15 level, pulling six figures, and wasn't about to make a rookie mistake, say or do something reckless, especially with the video camera rolling on the other side of the one-way mirror. That was my guess.

But it was time for somebody to blink. Hopefully him. The bad thing was, he wasn't blinking. I wondered whether I had underestimated the trouble I was facing. Good heavens, did they really think I had anything to do with this?

The senior agent pulled out a remote control for the TV. "Mr. Black, I want you to see something." Then he added, "By the way, do you have a strong stomach?"

The special agent didn't wait for my answer. Instead, he clicked on the TV at the other end of the interrogation room and a video began running. Just images, no audio. I braced myself. It quickly became clear what I was watching: the FBI forensic guys documenting the crime scene. Meaning my hotel room.

As the camera slowly swept into the entrance, it caught the familiar opening to the bathroom on the left. I recognized my suitcase on the luggage rack on the right. But then an object that I did not recognize. A paper coffee cup, the kind with the plastic travel top that has a slit opening to drink from. Something you get at a coffee shop. However, I didn't put that there. Someone else must have.

The video camera moved forward a few steps and then to the left, toward my bed. Something became visible: a pair of feet extending over the end of the bed. One shoe on, one shoe off.

They had to belong to the victim, Paul Pullmen. Movement of the camera farther into the room, taking in the full view of my bed. When I saw it, I couldn't inhale. Or exhale. Or make sense of it. Not at first.

The camera was fixed on the scene. One second, two seconds. After maybe ten seconds staring at this grisly footage, I was finally able to figure out the carnage.

Pullmen was stretched out on the bed, one arm dangling off the side, his suit coat and white shirt soaked with blood. Blood everywhere.

Then I was able to see the truly horrifying aspect of the crime. His head had been slashed from his body and had been set to the side of the bed, facing upward to the ceiling. A large machete, with blood along its blade, had been carefully placed lengthwise just below the head.

The police camera zoomed in on Pullmen's right arm. More blood. Of course there was. Because his right hand had been severed at the wrist and was nowhere to be seen.

9

The agent paused the video and waited at least a minute before he asked a question. And when he did, he pointed to the television screen, which had the frozen image of the murder victim stretched over my hotel bed.

"Do you know him?"

I said, "It looks like Paul Pullmen."

"Did you do this to Paul Pullmen?"

"Of course not."

"Do you know who did?"

"No. But I'd like to find out."

"Why?"

"Just look at that video," I shot back. "The monster who did that needs to be stopped. Call it my duty as a good citizen if you like."

"What would *you* call it?"

"If I explained it to you, what really might be behind this, I don't think you'd understand."

He glanced at his watch. Then he sat for a while without saying anything, until there was a knock on the door of the interrogation room. The younger agent opened the door a crack and spoke in a whisper to someone outside, then walked over to the agent sitting across from me and whispered something in his ear.

Agent Fainlock's face relaxed as he began to stand. The two agents slipped out, and in my peripheral vision I noticed a man strolling into the room.

An instant later, I was looking into the face of my old nemesis, Vance Zaduck.

Zaduck reached out, we shook hands, and he sat down. "It's been a long time, Trevor."

"Yes, it has," I answered.

"How is that beautiful wife of yours? Courtney, that was her name, wasn't it?"

I took a moment, noticing the difference between the grammatical tenses in his two sentences.

"Yes," I replied. "Her name *was* Courtney. She died a few years ago. Shortly before I stopped practicing law."

"I'm sorry to hear that."

I studied Zaduck. Was he really in the dark about her death?

I said, "I guess you wouldn't have known. It happened after you left New York and took over as the United States attorney in DC."

"Yes, must have. But that's bad news about Courtney."

"How is your wife?" I responded. "I'm sorry I don't remember her name. . . ."

"Virginia. We separated." Then he added, "We're divorced."

"So, still single?" I asked, though I don't know why.

"Yes. You know how it is. Demands of lawyering in Washington. Sometimes it interferes with your personal life."

I nodded while I studied his face. Up close, I could see the dark, baggy circles under his eyes. Age and the trials of life take their toll. I asked, "You're here for the ABA?"

"Right."

"I know you caught my speech. I saw you in the front."

"Yes, I was there."

But this wasn't about exchanging pleasantries. In the next moment, the probing began.

Zaduck asked, "I was wondering, what's your interest in Jason Forester's death?"

"I would think that anytime an assistant US attorney is killed, it would be a big deal."

"You make it sound like an intentional killing. We looked into it. He died of complications of a preexisting heart condition. Nothing more. It was a sad loss. But that was it. So I wonder, Trevor, was there something else behind this? And why did you hit on it in your speech today?"

"I'm assuming you were behind the one-way glass a little while ago. You heard what I said about my friend in law enforcement getting a tip from a federal insider who said that voodoo was involved in his death."

"Yes," he answered. Then, after a moment, he repeated that

word again, "Voodoo," and shook his head like I had been talking about abductions by outer-space aliens.

I nodded. "Yes, voodoo."

There was a momentary smile, but it vanished instantly. "So it's really true? Trevor Black, demon hunter?"

"You heard about that?"

"Yes. And I do agree: there are demons out there."

I was taken aback. I waited for more.

"People have personal demons. Mental illness. Broken lives. Maybe being brutalized in the past. Drug addiction. Then they commit horrible crimes. But the thing is, I live in the real world, Trevor. You were a superbly talented lawyer once. What happened to you, your professional decline, was very sad."

He told me that he had to catch a flight back to DC and so he needed to jump right to the point. "Speaking of terrible crimes. Do you have any idea why the assistant attorney general for our Criminal Division would have been murdered in your hotel room?"

"No, I don't. I only know that I wrote to Mr. Pullmen in an e-mail about wanting to discuss the Jason Forester death. He didn't reply."

"The way he was murdered," Vance Zaduck said, "was horrific. As you can see."

He was waiting for me to respond. On the other side of the glass, the interrogation video camera was catching it all, I was sure. But I had nothing to hide. I had some thoughts, and they needed to be said.

I answered, "In other words, you mean to say that his head and his hand were both cut off like a ritual sacrifice?"

Zaduck's chin tightened and his lips pursed before he spoke. "You really think that's what this is about?"

"I know nothing about this homicide except what I saw on that video and what you've just told me. But two federal attorneys are dead and both under circumstances that implicate occult practices. Seems obvious, doesn't it?"

Vance Zaduck glanced at his watch, then rose quickly. "I have to go. Here's the good news. I have already talked to the FBI here in New Orleans, and to the local US attorney and the Louisiana authorities too. Trevor, just so you know, I've vouched for you. You're welcome, by the way. Sorry about the interrogation, but I'm sure you can see why. The bottom line is that you're free to go. But you obviously know that they may be in contact with you again, about the Pullmen homicide. And the Department of Justice may want to talk to you as well."

He gave me a warm handshake. "Take care of yourself, Trevor. I'm sorry we had to meet this way. And it's sad about Courtney."

Compared to the nasty tone of our last conversation together, years before, and how it had ended with his nihilistic quote from Nietzsche and his brusquely showing me the door, Vance seemed different now. Perhaps the years had softened him.

It felt good to leave the building and hit the street.

I suddenly remembered that my daughter had been left at the convention center. I hailed a cab and made it back to the ABA conclave. It was filled with milling crowds of lawyers, and the place was abuzz with gossip about Pullmen's death. But Heather was nowhere to be found. I headed to the Hyatt.

When I checked with the front desk at the hotel, I learned,

not surprisingly, that her room had also been cordoned off because of the murder investigation. They assigned a new suite of rooms for Heather and me.

"Have you seen her?" I asked the hotel clerk at the front desk.

He said he had, and he handed me a note that Heather had left for me. When I read its brief contents, I turned back to the clerk and asked if she had been alone when she gave him the note, or was there someone else with her? He couldn't recall.

All I had was that little piece of notepaper, and I kept reading and rereading the message Heather had left. In her recognizable handwriting, she had written only three bewildering and troubling sentences—

I met a woman during your session at the ABA. Traveling to Bayou Bon Coeur to do some research. I'll be in touch.

10

This was a new kind of pain for me. I had experienced life as a parent for less than a year and, even then, only as the father of an adult daughter. But Heather's unexplained disappearance, coinciding with a murder having taken place in my hotel room, rocked my world. Of course there were logical explanations for the note. I started to spin several rational scenarios to ease my mind. But none were sufficiently convincing. Heather's cryptic note didn't give me much to go on, not nearly enough to justify the nice, tidy, safe hypotheticals I tried to conjure up.

I immediately checked out Google Maps, but that didn't help. A church in Paris; a city in Idaho. But nothing in the bayous of Louisiana.

Despite my repeated attempts to call Heather on her cell,

she wasn't answering. My mind was engaged in a cruel tennis match. Alternating shots across the net.

On one hand, maybe she had simply decided to do some research for her master's thesis. *Bonk.*

But if that was true, why such a short, cryptic note, and why wasn't she picking up when I called? *Bonk.*

Of course, Heather did have an eccentric and very independent side. *Bonk.*

But how did I know for sure that she wasn't in danger? *Bonk.* Match.

My troubled mind was fixating on the many things I didn't yet know, and that filled me with dread. Had someone lured her into a bad situation? I was the one who had brought her to New Orleans. This was happening on my watch.

In my new hotel room, I uttered a hasty, clumsily constructed prayer and then opened up the state map I bought at the sundries shop in the hotel and scanned the bayous surrounding New Orleans, looking for something called Bayou Bon Coeur. Nothing.

I wanted to contact the local police and file a missing person's report, but given my recent brush with the FBI, and the news about the Pullmen murder and the connection to my hotel room, I had to be realistic about how that might play out. Worse still, it had been only a few scant hours that Heather had been unaccounted for. In addition, she was an adult, and there was absolutely no evidence of foul play. I knew too much about the process and how, down at the station, I would be summarily dismissed as an overcontrolling parent.

So I would have to wait. Staying up late. Pacing. Calling

her cell, which rang but went to voice mail each time. Sending her text messages. Sending a few e-mails. No response. Finally around 3 a.m. I fell asleep.

I awoke with a start at five o'clock in the morning. I dropped to my knees and petitioned God to give me some indication of what was going on with my daughter.

I plunged onto the bed with my cell and went through the ritual of dialing Heather's cell again, and again getting no answer except her voice mail. But I listened to it studiously. At least it was good to hear her voice. I prayed and continued praying in bed, too tired to slip under the covers, until I began to drift into sleep.

I had forgotten to set an alarm or ask for a wake-up, so it was almost midmorning on Sunday when I was awakened by a persistent tapping on my door. I headed to the door and opened it a crack. The housekeeper asked if I wanted my room cleaned. "Not today," I replied. I wouldn't take any chances with strangers coming into my room.

Then panic set in. No call from Heather had come through.

A bad way to start the day. I should have planned a day of prayer and fasting. Instead I started with cold-sweat anxiety and defeat.

I knew that New Orleans must have plenty of fine houses of worship, but I didn't know of any personally. I would conduct church in my hotel room before heading off to find Heather. It was time to set things on a better course.

I knelt at the edge of the bed. Asking for insight about finding Heather. For the power of the resurrected Jesus to fight my battles for me—after all, the combat I was engaged in wasn't just a matter of flesh and blood. It was a struggle against a dark, invisible empire.

Scripture reading for the day: I took a bypass out of Deuteronomy, which I had been studying, and went to Luke 4:5-13 instead. The devil's temptation of Jesus in the hot, dry, unforgiving desert, showing Jesus all the kingdoms of the world, and offering him dominion over all of them if he would simply worship him. But Jesus answered: "You shall worship the Lord your God and serve Him only." Then the devil unsuccessfully tempted Jesus by trying to entice him to jump off the pinnacle of the Temple in Jerusalem to prove his divinity. Jesus shut him down again, citing the Scripture about not putting God to the test.

Lesson? Even when he fails, the devil doesn't give up. For the story goes on: "When the devil had finished every temptation, he left Him *until an opportune time.*"

The dark lord and his agents don't surrender; they just regroup. Until the opportune time. Offering power as the incitement. But delivering slavery.

Morning was waning and I had run out of patience. I drove my rental down to the police station and filed a formal missing person's report. I begged them not to follow the usual routine. I told them, "I have a bad feeling about this." The interviewing officer had me sit in the chair next to his desk while he disappeared into the office of the police captain. I saw the two talking for a long while before the officer strolled back to me.

"You're the one from the ABA lawyers' meeting? Taken in for questioning by the FBI? Dead government lawyer found in your hotel room?"

I nodded.

"We'll follow up on this in *due course*." I dreaded those last two words. Then he added, "And, Mr. Black, don't leave the area without letting us know first." He handed me his card with his direct line on it.

My car was parked two blocks away. When I had trudged there, I would have ducked into my rental, except I saw something. A little jazz café, right there at the spot where I had parked, called the Blue Key. The front window was littered with small posters of music groups, and one of them struck a personal chord with me, so I strolled in. Having no answers about Heather was vexing me severely. I wanted a momentary diversion.

The place was dimly lit with a dozen tables scattered around. At one end was a bar with stools and a backlit glass case with bottles full of colored booze. At the other end, a black man was at the keyboard of a baby grand piano. I recognized the tune he was playing, an obsolete jazz number—"Some of These Days"—that said, "Some of these days you'll miss me, honey."

He must have heard me come in but didn't turn at first, just kept playing. When I took a few steps closer, he spoke without looking over. "We're closed today."

"Sorry," I said.

"It says it on the sign."

"I must have missed it."

More elegant playing of a tune dating from the end of the ragtime era. I was enjoying it. Then the music stopped, and he turned to face me.

"Can I help you?"

"That one's from the 1920s, right?"

"Sophie Tucker made it famous in 1926. You into that old stuff? You look too young for that."

"Forty-five isn't young."

"Just wait till you're lookin' from where I'm lookin'. It'll look a lot younger then."

Even in the shadows I could see his hair, cut short, was iron gray. He was wearing thick glasses. He tilted his head. "You didn't tell me what you doin' here."

"I noticed one of the posters in the window about a jazz guitarist. Jersey Dan Hoover. He played here?"

"Oh yeah. You a fan of his?"

"Yes. Good friends, too. In high school we played in a blues band together. He took off like a rocket after that. We've stayed in touch."

"Don't say." He grabbed a glass off a coaster on the piano and jiggled the ice. "I got bar privileges here. Wanna drink?"

"Thanks, but I'll pass. I was just walking by and saw the poster and had to find out about my buddy."

"You don't sound local. From outta town?"

"Raised in Wisconsin, lived in New York City for a time. Now I've got a place on an island off North Carolina."

He hit a few chords from "Bridge over Troubled Water," chuckling to himself, and then said, "No man's an island."

I responded. "So true."

"Down here in N.O. there's all kinds of people. And people got their people. Got your musicians, like me, who hang together. There's a lot of us. Then there's the Holy Ghosters who spend their lives at church. Like my momma. And you got your imports from the outside comin' here to make money—a lot before Katrina—shipping lines, oil companies, fisheries. Our football and basketball franchises, of course, and all those sports junkies that follow 'em."

"I heard you lost an arena football team," I said.

"Yeah. The New Orleans VooDoo. Them and a couple other teams around the country."

"Just wondering . . . Are there many of those still around? Voodoo followers, I mean. Not the football kind, but the real believers."

"More'n you'd think."

That was something worth pondering. I reached out my hand. "Trevor Black."

"Louis Thompson Jr. Jazz pianist." Then he added, "And human being."

I was glad to hear that. He couldn't possibly have understood why.

"That's comforting to know," I said.

He raised an eyebrow. "What's your interest in voodoo?"

"Something personal. Involving my daughter."

"Sounds serious."

"You have no idea." Taking a chance, I said, "I'm guessing you're pretty knowledgeable about things."

"Not according to my two ex-wives."

"Well, about voodoo, for instance."

"What ya want to know?"

"Ever hear of a place called Bayou Bon Coeur?"

Louis's face changed. It scrunched up and his eyes half closed. "Heard about it a few times. Always sounded to me like a bad place. Why?"

"My daughter may be there."

"Sorry for you. And her."

"I need to get there. To find her."

"Oh, I can't help you there." He leaned back, grabbed his glass again, looked into its empty contents, and gazed longingly over to the bar. When he put his glass back on the piano, he said, "But I know somebody who might be able to help."

He reached into the pocket of his sport coat and pulled out a pen, then yanked out a piece of paper from the other pocket and wrote on it.

"This here's a man who's a PI. I heard he's had some dealings with that very location." He handed me the note. "Oh, and another good thing. He comes well-armed."

11

With Louis Thompson Jr.'s note in hand, I pulled out my city map of New Orleans, looking for a place on Magazine Street. When I found it, I tapped the address into my GPS and started driving. It was a part of the city where, if you keep going and you head farther out, you start entering the edge of East New Orleans. I had heard tales about East N.O. How it's a place that sports way too many problems, especially homicides.

On the way I had a brain flash of sorts. When I was speaking at the ABA, Heather was in the front row. I recalled a female lawyer sitting next to her. Heather's note said that she met a woman who apparently told her about Bayou Bon Coeur. If I found out who that lawyer was, I could track down Heather. I called Morgan Canterelle's office and got his voice mail. I left a message: Seeing as he was on the convention committee, did he have some way of finding out the identity of a female lawyer sitting in the front row of the ABA session, right next to my daughter?

After passing some restaurants, food stores, and a strip club, I finally pulled over to the curb on Magazine Street and parked. I checked out the area, noticing a few men on a street corner a block away. The building I needed was half a block away. It housed a tavern and a palm reader on the street level, but my destination was on the second floor: the office of a private investigator by the name of Alfred "Turk" Kavagian.

It was late afternoon, so I thought I might still catch Kavagian. I walked up the narrow staircase.

The second floor was a time-warp kind of place, with worn wooden floors that creaked when you walked. The door to Kavagian's office had one of those old-fashioned glazed glass panels with his name in black letters. I jiggled the doorknob. It was locked, but I could see through the hazy glass that there was a light on. I heard heavy footsteps coming up to the door on the other side. Then a man's voice asking me to step over to where there was an eye-viewer. "I want to see you," the voice said. I saw the cover to the peephole on the other side flip open, and then an eyeball appeared. "Who are you?"

"My name's Trevor Black. I used to be a criminal defense attorney. Now I'm an investigator."

"What do you want?"

"Louis Thompson Jr. sent me. The jazz pianist."

"Why didn't you say so?" the man said.

The door opened.

Kavagian was a man in his midforties, about my age, with long hair down to his shoulders and the muscular shape of a bodybuilder. He invited me in and pointed to a wooden chair across from his desk that was piled high with newspaper clippings, magazines, and manila files.

I knew a lot of PIs in my day, and judging from his office decor, I expected him to offer me a drink—maybe straight Jack Daniel's in a dirty glass. But instead he asked me if I would like a "veggie juicer."

I declined, noticing a juicing machine on his credenza next to a bowl of fruit.

"What's up?" he asked.

"This is a personal matter. I'd be glad to pay you."

"And I'm always glad to be paid."

"It's about a place called Bayou Bon Coeur."

He took his time. Then, "You don't say."

"You know it?"

"In a manner of speaking," he said.

"Meaning?"

"Meaning there was a missing person case I had once. I was hired by an unfortunate family who was looking for their young daughter who had disappeared. The police weren't exactly burning a path to find her, so the parents got me involved through a lawyer. Make a long story short, I located some vile porno videos online that we were pretty sure had featured the daughter. And pretty sure it wasn't voluntary. Probably drugged. The guy assaulting her was dressed in a costume like some kind of voodoo devil. Anyway, I expected the worst, personally, though I didn't tell the parents. Not at first. Until I got a lead that she might have been taken to that bayou you mentioned. A place you can't exactly find on a travel atlas."

"Bayou Bon Coeur?"

"That's the one."

"Did you find her?"

"Sort of."

I waited.

"They found her body. It had been there for a while. The swamps tend to devour victims pretty fast. And whatever is left isn't pretty."

There was no happiness in my meeting with Turk Kavagian. Or in hearing his terrible story. My insides felt like they were in the jaws of a vise at the thought that Heather might be out there in that bayou. But the clock was ticking. I needed more information.

"Is this the only contact you had with that place?"

"I'd heard rumors—bad magic going on out there, that sort of thing; ceremonies and whatnot. But you know, you sort of keep an open mind until you get some hard evidence."

"That young girl who was killed. Did they ever find the perps?"

"Nope. Never did. Sickening, isn't it. Thinking they could still be out there. The cops were thinking that it was part of a larger criminal ring. Some kind of cult group."

"Voodoo?" I asked.

Turk Kavagian took a long, hard look at me. "You're not from Louisiana, are you?"

"My criminal defense work was in New York City. Now I write articles on crime subjects and do investigations."

He shot back, "In other words, you got disbarred?"

I smirked. Turk evidently knew something about the ways of the world. "As a matter of fact, I was. But that's a long story."

"The reason I asked about you not being local," he said, "is that people have all these assumptions about life down here. About New Orleans culture. Myself—I grew up in Denver and came here to play football on a scholarship to Grambling. But the very first year I tore up both my knees. Good-bye, football. I wasn't much for academics, so I bailed out my second year and teamed up with a private eye here by the name of Otis Orrman, who showed me the ropes. A good man. Died a few years ago."

"Natural causes?"

"Lead poisoning," he said and waited for my response. Then he explained, "He was serving a summons on a guy in East N.O. in a domestic abuse case. The guy shot him dead on the doorstep."

Turk wound his way back to the trail we were on—about voodoo. "See, people have this idea that every other person down here is either a witch doctor or else knows someone who is."

"Not me," I pointed out. "I don't think that."

"Good."

"But I also know," I said, "that there is a shadow world. A dark empire of evil that is mostly unseen. But the doors that lead there—they're open for business. I think voodoo is one of them."

Turk gave a weary smile. "Then I guess we have something in common."

"I'm here because my daughter wrote a note saying she was going to Bayou Bon Coeur. She's a researcher. I'm worried."

"I would be too," he said. "That criminal group I talked about, the one they thought was behind the killing of the girl in the bayou? The word around New Orleans was that it was the work of a special kind of voodoo cult. Not exactly your backwoods swamp-rat type. Or the third-world variety. This one was different."

"How so?"

"High-tech. Some kind of Internet thing. Child abduction. Trafficking. Girls getting used and abused and after a while, some of them get erased." He shook his head. "Sorry to hit you with all that, seeing as your daughter might be there."

"Do you know how to get to the bayou?"

"Not personally. I've got somebody I can call. A swamp man. Knows the bayous. He could probably take you there. For a price. Give me some time and I'll connect with him."

"Time is what I don't have."

"Tell you what, I'll put a rush on it. No charge for my time. Just gimme your card. Maybe you can help me someday."

I wrote down my cell number on one of my old "private investigator" cards from New York that I never ended up using, then told him to ignore the outdated NYC address and dropped it on his desk. I grabbed one of his for myself.

As I turned to leave, sickened over the possible fate of my daughter, I had to ask him one more time.

"About that voodoo cult you mentioned. Does it have a name?"

He shook his head. "Nope. Not that I ever knew. All I heard was just a saying that folks have about it."

"What's that?"

"That they're into sex, spells, and human sacrifice."

As I exited his office, I heard the sound of Turk's juice blender whirring. I thought back to what I had just learned, and as I did, I felt the sensation of weightlessness down in my gut.

12

Down on the street, Heather was even more on my mind after my chat with Turk Kavagian. I hunted for my rental car, but I couldn't find it. Thinking I must have gone the wrong way, I turned around and headed in the other direction along the sidewalk. After several blocks I had that sinking realization. I knew I had parked legally. Yet my car was nowhere to be found. Only one answer. It must have been stolen.

Figuring that I'd report the car theft when I was back in my hotel room, I was about to call a cab. And I would have done that, except a black Lincoln limo came cruising by and slowed down. I raised my hand, thinking maybe I could grab the limo instead. But in my unusual line of work, I had to be cautious. I checked out the license plate on the rear of the limo.

It read For Hire. I strolled over to the tinted glass window on the driver's side, which was rolled up.

"Can I see your chauffeur's license?" I said loud enough to be heard.

The window hummed down a few inches. A hand thrust out the window holding a Louisiana chauffeur's driver's license for a few seconds, as I hastily scanned the little laminated certificate. The hand disappeared and I crawled in the back, grateful for the favor this guy was offering.

It was one of those limos with a glass panel separating the passenger from the driver. I could see the driver was wearing a dark suit and a chauffeur's cap. I couldn't believe they still wore those, and to make matters worse, the cap didn't fit him very well.

I touched the intercom button and gave him the address to my hotel. I didn't care about the fare; I needed to get back and make a series of calls. My daughter was still missing, my rental had just been jacked, and Canterelle had still not responded to the message I left him.

The driver nodded. As we headed away from Magazine Street, I heard the electronic click of the doors. For a while I was buried in my thoughts, about how I needed to focus all my energies on Turk Kavagian's offer to get a swamp guide to take me to the bayou where Heather might be waiting. I had been trying her cell every few hours but still getting voice mail. Frantic thoughts of catastrophe had to be suppressed, but it wasn't easy.

Eventually I clued into my surroundings. Through the tinted windows I noticed the street sign. Clouet Street. And I looked ahead and noticed the Mississippi River looming. We were in the warehouse district. Big storage buildings, vacant lots, and few houses.

I pressed the intercom. "Hey, this isn't the way to the hotel. What's the deal?"

The driver didn't respond.

"Can you hear me?" I said.

The driver turned his head, revealing his profile, and I felt an electric shiver—an indelible sense that I'd encountered this presence before. I could picture the figure I'd seen from the beach, hovering over the water, defying the laws of nature. Except, at that moment, he was in the front seat, driving that limo.

I banged on the glass. "Talk to me. Where are we going?"

The limo took a sharp turn onto Chartres, and I heard something behind me in the trunk of the limo. A heavy rolling thud. We were running parallel to the river and the limo was picking up speed. It must have been going fifty miles an hour and accelerating.

More banging on the glass, this time with both of my fists. Finally the driver spoke. And when he did, he turned to face me. His face was like it had been carved in granite and his eyes were lifeless. Yes, it *was* him.

"Trevor Black. We meet again. But not for long . . ." He burst into a cackle like some kind of jungle animal.

The driver was the same monster that I had seen out there on top of the surf, off Ocracoke Island. He hadn't given up. Of course not. He had just regrouped. And once again, no advance warning; I never caught the scent.

The limo took a wheel-squealing turn onto an industrial

entrance to a broad concrete wharf, and there was another rolling thud in the trunk. We were heading straight at the river. No gates and no fences to stop us. Next stop, the Mississippi.

As we sped forward, the driver opened his door and stepped out calmly as if the car were in park. Even though we were going at least sixty, he never missed a step, never fell; he just casually walked away from the speeding limo, defying the rules of physics.

I grabbed the door and jammed my shoulder against it while trying to lift the handle, but it wouldn't open. I banged on the window. Break the glass, I thought. With what? The limo was maybe thirty feet from the edge of the wharf. I frantically disengaged my seat belt buckle and thrust my hands under the driver's seat, looking for anything to smash the window. We were almost at the edge of the wharf. My hand touched the handle of something under the seat. I yanked it out. A hammer. What was it doing there? And the business end was dripping with blood.

The car toppled over the edge of the wharf as I tried to swing the hammer against the car window but missed.

Whomp. The limo hit the water with a jolt, front end down, throwing me forward with the back end of the limo easing upward.

I was smashing the window with the hammer. It began to break apart. But the limo was sinking quickly into the river, the driver's compartment filling with water and the doors locked. The passenger seat would be filling next. More wild smashing of the glass. I dropped the bloody hammer and pushed the busted glass out with my hands as the river water was now up to my door.

I squeezed through the window, finally out, just as the limo fully submerged. I was underwater, having to hold my breath as the limo slipped to the bottom of the river while I did panic strokes upward through the opaque water, my lungs burning, trying to make it to the top and to the air that I needed. Pushing, pushing.

Breaking through the surface of the water and gasping for air, I saw the wharf about twenty feet away. My clothes were like lead, weighing me down, as I stroked with Olympian effort toward the wharf. But when I got there, the concrete dock was too high for me to pull myself up.

Exhausted, and mustering all that I could, I swam around the edge of the wharf until I spotted a rough beachhead and painfully stroked toward it. When my feet hit the soft silt river bottom, I pulled myself forward, waist-deep in river water, then knee-deep, finally dragging myself out of the water and dropping onto the solid dirt of the river's edge, face-first.

When I made it to the nearest sidewalk, I was trying to get my bearings straight. I tried to turn my cell phone on, but it didn't light up. So much for waterproof cells.

I needed to get to a hotel or a restaurant so I could pick up another cab and return to the relative safety of my hotel, but I was feeling disoriented and a bit lost. In the interim I had heard a few sirens, and it sounded as if they were heading down to the river's edge, in the vicinity of where the demon driver steered his limo into the Mississippi, with me in it.

All the while, I kept thinking about that bloody hammer and about the thudding sound of something heavy rolling back and forth in the trunk of the limo every time we took a turn.

13

River water squished out of my shoes with each step. I noticed a storefront that had a For Rent sign on it. The window of the empty store was covered with paper, but there were posters on the side going into the alley. They were pictures of a few younger women and several girls of varying ages, from children to middle schoolers perhaps, with their birth dates and when they had disappeared. My heart sank. I studied one of them: Peggy Tanner. Disappeared eight months ago. Blonde hair, green eyes. Twelve years old.

I remembered Turk's comment about the dead girl they found at Bayou Bon Coeur. *Please, God,* I prayed silently, *keep Heather from showing up on one of those posters. Keep her safe. And help me find her.* Then, as I kept walking and feeling more desperate, I added, *Anything, Lord. Give me anything.*

It was getting dark as I walked down Bourbon Street, feeling helpless and hungry and, of course, still soaked. The lights were on at Bud's Diner, so I stepped in. The place was crowded. All I wanted was to get some directions to the nearest cabstand.

A guy I took to be Bud was behind the cash register, cracking jokes with a customer who was paying his bill.

A waitress with a plastic menu scurried up to me and said, "Hi, honey, I've got a table for one and it's got your name on it."

I shifted in my stance, my shoes squish-squashing and creating a small pond of water on the floor. I thanked her but said I was only looking for a cab to get me back to my hotel. As she eyeballed my soaked clothes, she asked which hotel, and when I told her, she said it was only a few blocks away and gave me directions. I thanked her and pulled out a soggy five-dollar bill and handed it to her as a tip for her help.

I stepped out to the vestibule of the diner, and just for laughs I pushed the power button on my cell phone again. Incredibly, it lit up. I couldn't believe it. I immediately tried to call Heather, but it went straight to voice mail.

I tried Heather's number one more time, hoping by some miracle that Heather would pick up, and I noticed two uniformed New Orleans cops approaching the cash register to pay for their meal. As I heard the disheartening sound once again of Heather's voice mail, the police officers started up some friendly banter with Bud. He responded by saying something to them about their "fishing a limo out of the drink tonight."

I clicked off my cell phone and listened closer.

One of the officers shook his head. "C'mon, Bud, does everybody in this city have a police scanner?"

Bud chuckled. "Best radio show in town. So who was the dead guy in the trunk of that car in the river?"

"Come on, knock it off," the officer said.

His partner added, "Hey, Sarge, maybe we ought to take Bud with us to the coroner's so he can sit in on the autopsy too."

Then the waitress I had talked to swept up to the register, right in front of Bud and in front of the two cops, and she waved my wet five-dollar bill in the air and said, "Who pays a tip with soaking-wet money anyway?"

Bud replied, "Somebody involved in money laundering," and they all laughed.

Except for me. I wasn't laughing. I quickly stepped outside to the sidewalk.

The picture was clear. The corpse rolling around in the trunk of the limo must have been the real chauffeur. And my spooky chauffeur was probably his replacement—as well as his slayer.

Meanwhile, I was the person who exited the limo and crawled out of the Mississippi.

I was fast-stepping away from the diner, hoping to get out of sight before the two patrol officers left the restaurant and spotted me.

The list of my entanglements in suspicious events had expanded: insulting the legal profession in the presence of the attorney general; being hauled off stage by FBI agents; having a hotel room where a high-ranking government lawyer would end up being decapitated; and lastly, catching a ride in a limo that had a homicide victim in the trunk.

It didn't take a forensic detective from *NCIS: New Orleans* to build the chain of evidence: a car submerged in the river, containing a dead body in the trunk; the possible murder weapon in the limo, with my prints on it; and then I show up a few blocks away, wearing waterlogged clothes and handing out soaking-wet money.

That was bad enough. But there was something even worse than my being innocently implicated in yet another murder: Heather was still missing and unaccounted for.

14

I was Olympic-walking down Bourbon Street in big strides, past the strip clubs, bars, and souvenir shops, making my way into the section gated off for pedestrian foot traffic. It was lit up with neon iridescence like the Vegas strip and swarming with nightlife. I needed to become invisible. I turned to survey the diner, a few blocks back. By then, the squad car had wheeled out of the diner and onto Bourbon and was heading my way at a high rate of speed. I threaded through the mob of revelers.

In the street was a batch of musicians armed with trumpets, saxes, and a tuba, belting out jazz tunes. They were coming my way, followed by a crowd.

The band halted in front of me, switching to a rendition

of "Sweet Georgia Brown" while a mob of gawkers engulfed the street.

It was a great break. I could disappear into the middle of the impromptu audience and then out the other side, picking up my pace. But when I whipped around to check for the squad, it had already parked back at the vehicle blockade, and both officers were out of the patrol car, one looking in my direction and the other one on his radio.

I broke into a trot, off Bourbon and down a side street where the crowds were thinning and cars were parked in front of apartment row houses. A ruby-red hardtop Corvette was cruising by, but it suddenly slammed on its brakes after it passed me. Then started to back up. I had a bad feeling about that, so I jogged into another alley that was lined with an apartment building on one side and some kind of warehouse on the other, figuring I had lost the Vette.

Another flyer of that middle school girl, Peggy Tanner, had been posted there. But looking down the shadowy alley, I immediately wondered whether I had made a wrong turn. Whether I was going from bad to worse.

In a few seconds, I had my answer. Two men stepped out from a doorway, into the middle of the alley, and blocked my path. I looked at one and then the other and realized they were twins. Weird.

Then something even weirder. A tall, well-dressed man appeared behind them. I recognized him right off, and my stomach dropped.

It was my chauffeur from the underworld. And no sensory warning. My old knack of catching their stench from hell—a cross between rotting death and burning refuse—had failed me again. And this time there were two of them, plus they brought their coach. Lucky me.

Shakespeare was right. Troubles don't come by spies. They come in battalions.

The tall guy who had driven me in the limo bent forward and said something to the twins.

I tried to find a quick exit to the right or left of me, but there was none. I noticed all the overflowing garbage cans lined up on both sides of the alley. It must have been garbage pickup day. A moment later, I'd be playing the part of the garbage.

The first of the twins didn't lay a hand on me. He didn't need to. So immense was his power that he tossed me into the air with just a gesture and sent me clattering into the row of garbage cans.

Then his twin brother took over, lifting me up with a flick of his wrist and whacking me against the wall of the warehouse. Things were beginning to get fuzzy in my head.

The first twin again sent me airborne, back into the garbage cans.

They took turns playing with me like I was their stepsister's rag doll. Sending me flying. The moment I hit something and was sprawled out, the other one launched me back through the air. I expected any second for the raw, down-to-the-bare-nerve kind of pain to overcome me. To render me unconscious. I had to act.

I called out. Yelling against them in the name of Christ and in the power of his blood. But their attack didn't stop.

I found myself lying on top of a full plastic trash bag, with my head reeling and my insides short of air. Everything hurt. I called out the name of God again.

The tall guy, the hellish chauffeur and master teacher, took a few steps toward me. His voice was different. Almost soothing. Dripping, like oil. "Your God isn't here. But we are. Go back home to your island . . ."

"Or what?" I managed to mutter.

"Or the person you love will be tortured in a very ugly and very wonderful way. The animals of the swamp will enjoy what is left."

So they knew about Heather. Of course. Why wouldn't they?

I remembered the words of Jesus. Only by prayer and fasting are some demons vanquished, something I had vaguely considered but failed to follow up on. Now I was no match. Even worse, they were tracking Heather. Maybe even had her.

I was hurting too much to wonder what would come next. But it would come from an unexpected source. Someone who looked more like a muscle-bound surfer than a PI.

Turk Kavagian was in the alley behind me, unholstering his .357 Magnum. He called out to the three figures. Then he squeezed the trigger and fired a round in the air. The trio sprinted off, vanishing so quickly that I expected a sonic boom. One thing about demons: bullets can't stop them, but the same isn't true for the bodies they inhabit.

Turk helped me off the pile of garbage and apologized. "Once I realized that you were new to this part of town, I should have warned you. Should have made sure you had a ride."

"I did have a ride but lost it . . . then got another ride. It's a long story."

Despite his friendly nod, Turk still looked like he had no idea what I was talking about. "You know," he said, "that was me in the red Corvette. I happened to be driving by, just by chance . . ."

Now it made sense. "Thank goodness you did, Turk. But no, it wasn't by chance."

Then I asked if he had seen my assailants.

"Not really. They disappeared in the shadows."

As he motored me to my hotel, we passed right by Marie Laveau's House of Voodoo, where Kevin, Canterelle's law clerk, worked part-time. That gave me something to think about.

When Turk dropped me off at the hotel, he said he had already put in a call to try to get me to Bayou Bon Coeur— his bayou master, an alligator hunter and swamp expert by the name of Delbert Baldou. But hadn't heard back from him. He said he'd be in touch.

I offered him some soggy twenty-dollar bills, but he refused once again. "Nah. Forget it. Sorry our fine city's treated you rough. New Orleans is a pretty good place to live, you know."

I told him I was sure he was right.

Hobbling in pain through the lobby of my hotel and bent over like a cripple, I collected my thoughts. First, how I must have reeked of raw garbage after my dance with the dark side. Second, I was glad that Louis Thompson Jr. the piano man had been right about Turk. He came well-armed.

15

When I had settled back at my hotel room, I changed out of my clothes, which were stinking of garbage and river water. Then I jumped in the shower. I had already changed into a dry outfit when the landline in the room started ringing. On the other end was the deep baritone of Attorney Morgan Canterelle.

"Y'all come on down, Mr. Black. I am here in the lobby. We need to talk. I am the fellow in the light-tan suit, black tie. And hard to miss."

He was correct on both counts, particularly the second part. Canterelle was about my height but roundly corpulent, maybe three hundred pounds. He stretched out a puffy hand, and I shook it.

"Had dinner yet?" he asked. "It's never too late for a good

meal." I told him I hadn't, and he motioned for me to follow him to his car, which he said was outside in valet parking. I told him that I was involved in some very pressing personal business and wasn't sure this was the best time to catch a meal together.

"That awful business, the murder of Assistant Attorney General Paul Pullmen? Everybody at the ABA was talking about it. And I also know y'all been cleared. No surprise to me."

"No," I said. "Not that. You're right; the Pullmen killing is awful. But I've got another pressing issue. It's about my daughter."

"Don't mean to pry, but I did get the voice mail message about identifying some female attorney who was sitting next to y'all's daughter at the ABA. It sounded slightly ominous. Might I be of assistance in that?"

"The fact is, she was here with me in New Orleans. But she seems to have gone missing."

Canterelle was still standing in the lobby, pointing to the revolving door that led to the outside when he said, in a much louder Louisiana drawl that seemed to resonate up from his immense girth, "I do not know *any problem* that can't be solved over a good Cajun meal. No, sir. Now y'all come with me and we'll figure this out. By the way, the ABA certainly got its money's worth with that speech yesterday. Indeed they did."

He flagged down the parking valet to fetch his car, then asked me, "Now then, any idea where y'all's daughter might be?"

Not knowing whether Turk Kavagian's swamp contact would ever materialize, I told Morgan Canterelle the name of the bayou on Heather's note and asked if by some miracle he might know anything about it.

He smiled, acting as if he had been expecting my request all along. "I must confess, Mr. Black, I do not know the particulars about that bayou." Then he added, "But I just happen to know someone who might."

Minutes later we were cruising into the French Quarter of New Orleans in Morgan Canterelle's antique: a perfectly restored 1970 Imperial, the fat-tire model that was the size of a small aircraft, with a gleaming front grille that had the look of a grinning teenager's braces.

Canterelle pulled up in front of a place called Arnaud's. He hoisted his sizable girth out of the driver's seat, pulled out his wallet, and placed a twenty and his car keys into the hand of the valet. Then told me to follow him inside, to what he called his "regular table."

Arnaud's was full of fine crystal, starched white tablecloths, and well-dressed clientele served by a bartender in a dinner jacket.

The maître d' showed us upstairs to a table on the balcony that had a commanding view of the French Quarter. As we were seated, the staff fluttered around Morgan Canterelle like bees in a flower patch.

I'm a food lover and ordinarily would have feasted on their Louisiana fare, but my worry over Heather had sunk my appetite. I ordered only a bowl of lobster bisque, while Canterelle chose a huge plate of alligator sausage, adding a crabmeat salad on the side. "So's I can lie to myself about eatin' healthy," he said.

I wasted no time asking how I could get to Bayou Bon Coeur. He looked up from his starter salad and reminded me that he was not the one who knew the way there. "What I stated, sir," he said, "was that I knew somebody who was acquainted with the particulars of that place."

"Then tell me who to talk to, because I need to get there."

"It's not that easy," he complained. "In fact, it's downright complicated. But then, y'all having been a trial lawyer, y'all know what complicated looks like. There's the practice of law, and then there's the in-between parts. Those hidden spaces between the hard 'n' fast black-letter rules of the law. The cracks where the human drama comes in."

I'd had enough of Canterelle's Cajun philosophizing. "If you can't help me find my daughter, I'm afraid I'm going to have to say good-bye. I've got things to do."

As I started to rise, the huge lawyer waved me into my seat. "Such as the sit-down with the missing persons squad at the New Orleans Police Department? Yes, I have connections, Mr. Black. And to be precise, I *didn't* say I would not help. On the contrary, I will. But I must ask something from y'all in return. Quid pro quo. I'm sure y'all understand the term."

"What do you want?"

"A particular set of skills, sir. A talent for getting to the bottom of evil deeds. The ones that flow from the shadows."

"You need to be specific."

"I represent a family who suffered a horrendous loss. Their baby girl, taken from them. Little red-haired beauty. First abducted, then, a year later, found murdered out in the swamps. The police have no tangible leads, and the case has grown cold. Just like the others."

It sounded like the case that Turk Kavagian had described.

"The others?" I asked.

Morgan Canterelle wiped his mouth with a linen napkin. "There are others, Mr. Black. I represent yet another grieving family as well, whose little girl is still missing. And yet another client with a tangential, indirect connection to all this misery, but that is another story altogether. Here's the point of it. I have a good relationship with the New Orleans Police Department. I was a local prosecutor once upon a time. But they are turning up nothing but dead ends. Hence these families hiring me."

"Are all these cases connected?"

"I fear so. Which is why I brought y'all down here to New Orleans in the first place. Not just to entertain, but—might I also say—to *awaken* the complacent legal community, which y'all did, by the way. My heavens, y'all surely did. But no, sir, not just that. To enlist y'all's help. I will pay whatever the fees. Money is no object. Justice, Mr. Black, that's what we are after. Y'all said it yourself in the speech at the ABA, that the law looks only at the objective world of the empirical and the physical. But we know better. I know all about y'all's strange, remarkable abilities. And why they capriciously took Trevor Black's law license away. I need a man like Trevor Black helping me on this case."

With that, Canterelle slipped a thick envelope out of his suit pocket and handed it to me. "There's a healthy sum of cash in there for an advance toward y'all's fees and expenses, plus the meager information that we have been able to collect about the disappearance and tragic death of Lucinda—that's the fourteen-year-old girl involved. Also, background about the case I'm handling for the other family. The disappearance of a twelve-year-old blonde girl named Peggy Tanner. Still missing."

I opened the envelope. There were copies of a few police reports. I paged through and in a quick glance noticed a mention of the Six Flags theme park. There was also a missing person poster with Peggy's picture on it. The same one I had seen on the street a few hours before. And instantly I was hit with a flood tide of desperation about Heather.

"What about my daughter?" I demanded.

"I will be in touch with my contact straightaway. To get y'all to Bayou Bon Coeur."

"No disrespect, Mr. Canterelle," I said, "but how do I know I can trust you? What do I really know about you? How do I know which side you're really on?"

Morgan Canterelle set his fork down and leaned away from the table. "I am going to give y'all a very valuable piece of advice, Mr. Black. Here it is. There is a darkness spreading here. Vile. Unspeakable. Like the pagan days of old. The sacrifice of young, innocent females. Now if y'all pursue for me these demons or whoever they are, then I will help in return. And godspeed, sir, in that endeavor. I need y'all to help us put an end to this unspeakable scourge. But the evil we speak of will not be found in the person of Morgan Canterelle, Esquire. I guarantee that."

Just then the lawyer's cell phone rang, and he picked up the call. Canterelle did most of the listening and very little talking. Finally he said good-bye, clicked it off, and turned to me.

"Right now," he said, "we have a meetin', y'all and I, with an important source of information. Let's go."

Wherever we were going, I knew it had to be important, because as he rose to his feet, Morgan Canterelle had left a respectable portion of his alligator sausage with smoked onion and apple relish there on his plate.

16

During the drive to our destination, Attorney Canterelle gave me the short course on a woman by the name of Belle Sabatier, who had agreed to meet with us. He said she was the daughter of Minerva Sabatier, a woman who was on her way to becoming a modern "voodoo legend" in New Orleans folklore—that is, before "her untimely death."

That information hit me hard. Like I had just been smacked in the face with a catfish. In response, I hit Morgan Canterelle with a torrent of questions, most of which he slyly avoided answering except for a few basics: that Belle was an "artist type," she had been living for years up in Philadelphia, and she was Minerva's sole heir. "When her mother passed away," he explained, "she relocated here in order to settle the estate."

"What are we hoping to get from this meeting?" I demanded.

"As a former courtroom champ-ion yo-self," he shot back, "I am sure y'all know what a *fishing expedition* is."

He pulled his car up in front of a historic-looking three-story mansion that had a curved porch on each floor, wrapped with railings made of delicate wrought-iron latticework. "Welcome to the Sabatier mansion," he said, turning off the ignition.

As we walked up the brick path to the front door, he qualified that by adding, "In point of fact, the house technically belongs to the estate of Minerva Sabatier. But Belle, her daughter, is temporarily living here while she settles estate matters."

We were shown inside by a butler who was decked out in a dinner jacket, and then taken through graceful arched entranceways, past a library with floor-to-ceiling bookshelves accessed by reading ladders. There were plenty of dark velvet drapes gathered by gold rope and tassels adorning the windows that reached to the top of the twelve-foot ceilings. It was like walking through a slightly creepy time warp.

The butler brought us to a smaller room where there was a fireplace and an ornate black marble surround, and above it, over the mantel, a big portrait. The subject of the painting was a beautiful woman, perhaps in her late fifties, with a light-cocoa complexion and dark, piercing eyes. Her ebony hair was streaked in a few places with silver. Her dress was unusual, a black robe with stars and constellations and a few painted skulls on it, with a hood that draped over her shoulders.

"The late Minerva Sabatier," Canterelle murmured quietly with a kind of musical inflection, nodding to the painting as if there was something significant about her name. We were told by the butler to take our seats on the sofa adjacent to the fireplace.

Ten minutes later Belle Sabatier, a smartly dressed woman in her thirties, strolled in wearing a long black dress accented with flowers. My late wife, Courtney, had been a fashionista in her own right, and I had learned both by osmosis and by our checkbook to recognize the expensive brands. This one looked like Magda Butrym. Price tag probably north of fifteen hundred bucks. Apparently Belle was no longer the starving artist. Minerva's estate must have been generous to her.

Belle shook hands with both of us and then sat down on the tufted chair across from us.

Her resemblance to her mother's portrait was remarkable. Same cocoa-colored skin, dark eyes, and striking good looks. The only difference was age.

Canterelle thanked her for meeting us, then turned to me and explained that he had given Belle "some background data on who Trevor Black is."

I would have preferred to have described my curriculum vitae to Belle myself, but I let that slide.

"I understand," Belle said to me, "that you dabble in the world of dark arts."

"Not really. My job is to hunt down the powers of demonic darkness."

Belle stiffened in her chair. "So you've come here hoping to uncover things? Things in the dark?"

"Not me. God's the one who does that." Then I gave her a quote: "'It is He who reveals the profound and hidden things;

He knows what is in the darkness, and the light dwells with Him.'"

Canterelle said, "Mr. Black here is a man versed in the Good Book."

"Second chapter of Daniel," I added.

She took a moment to respond after that, letting her eyes sweep the room. Finally she said, "Mr. Black, Mr. Canterelle here says that you are assisting him in some very tragic cases. Young girls kidnapped. I am not sure how much help I can be. But if you have any questions, I can try to answer them."

Considering Canterelle was the one who wanted this meeting in the first place, I was confused—why was she directing her comments to me? I had just one crucial matter on my mind, and it was about Heather, but before I could ask it, Canterelle jumped in.

Canterelle turned to me. "The families I represent need answers about the fate of their loved ones. And they demand that those responsible be brought to justice." He nodded in Belle's direction. "Now Mr. Trevor Black here won't be timid, I am sure, in asking any questions he has."

No response from Belle. Just a smile. Things were getting stranger. Why were we having this meeting? In my prior life as a trial lawyer, I recalled a few instances like that, where the conversation seemed cloaked and obtuse. They usually involved lawyers who didn't want to disclose exactly who they represented. Or what side they were on.

Before hitting Belle with information about the mysterious bayou where I hoped to locate Heather, I decided to smoke her out a bit.

"I've heard about your mother's well-known connection to the voodoo community. You being her daughter, perhaps you can shed light on some things."

"Things," she asked, "such as what, exactly?"

"Let's start with whether you know of any involvement of voodoo in the terrible crimes we're talking about. Or any connection between voodoo followers down here and the death of a federal attorney up in Washington by the name of Jason Forester? Or the murder of Mr. Paul Pullmen, a lawyer from the Department of Justice, killed right here in New Orleans? Both dead under circumstances that implicate voodoo."

"Are you accusing my mother in some way?" she blew back, clearly offended. "Or me?"

Canterelle leaned forward, trying to smooth the waters. "Now, Miss Sabatier, none of this is to suggest, in any way, any besmirching of the memory of your late mother."

Belle shifted in her chair. "Mr. Black, I'm not sure how much you actually know about the ancient practices," she said. "But I would warn you to exercise caution before you slander the good name of my mother."

I pushed the discussion further. "Then why don't you tell us what you know about voodoo? Educate us."

"I am not a practitioner," she said. "I never have been."

"But your mother obviously was," I said.

"Voodoo is *not* a hereditary disease, Mr. Black. Daughters don't catch it from their mothers."

"Maybe not, but it's a big deal in these parts," I said. "I've heard politicians and judges coming up for election have paid good money to voodoo priests and priestesses to influence the result. Like Marie Laveau, for instance, the voodoo *mambo* who has a museum named after her. Even more relevant, voodoo includes blood sacrifice. And pertinent to my mission, it embraces spirit possession."

"You're talking ancient history," Belle replied, forcing a smile. "Marie Laveau died in 1881. Nowadays, modern voodoo is more concerned with living a happy life. Influencing attitudes in a positive way through communication with helpful spirits."

"*Helpful* spirits?" I said. "That's funny. The occult spirits I've tangoed with have always been so dangerously *unhelpful*."

"Perhaps," she said, "because you have offended the *bokors*—black magic practitioners. Maybe you should find a different pastime."

I saw the paradox. "There's something strange here, Miss Sabatier. For someone who is 'not a practitioner' and never has been, you seem to know a lot about the subject."

Belle's eyes flashed, and she pursed her lips.

Canterelle tried to cool her down. "Now, Miss Sabatier, my friend Mr. Black comes on a little strong. He does not understand the courtesies we extend to each other here in New Orleans. Let me just ask you to contact me if you have any information that can help us."

I still had questions of my own, and I was going to get them answered.

"How exactly did your mother die?"

She went wide-eyed. "That's an odd question."

"Odd or not, I'd like to know."

She glanced at Canterelle before answering. "If you have

to know, the death certificate said she went into anaphylactic shock. A severe reaction from a food allergy."

Then my million-dollar question. "Have you ever heard of Bayou Bon Coeur?"

"I have," she said, cocking her head. She studied me for a moment. "It has always been considered a place of mystery and shadows."

"Explain that."

She shifted in her chair. "I'm referring to the Cajun meaning of the words *bon coeur*."

"And that is what?"

"In the voodoo culture, Mr. Black, it means 'those who can cast spells.'"

More reasons to be uneasy about Heather.

My last question was the most important one. "Do you know where that bayou is located?"

She took a moment. Then, "No, Mr. Black. I'm afraid I do not." Rising, she excused herself and told us the butler would show us out.

17

As Canterelle drove me back to my hotel, I asked him the reason for our soiree with Belle Sabatier.

"A personal introduction," he said. "Unlike New York City, where y'all practiced law at freeway speeds, down here we are more pedestrian. We still practice the *art of the personal*. As my expert consultant, y'all needed to meet Belle. Now I agree, there is the foul smell of black magic rising from my cases. And perhaps in the slaying of that DOJ lawyer in your hotel room . . ."

"And the death of AUSA Jason Forester in Washington, DC."

"Of course. So, patience, Mr. Black. Patience. It is a sublime virtue."

"I agreed to work with you on your cases. But there's still the matter of my daughter, Heather, who may be out on that forsaken bayou somewhere. On that, I'm all out of patience."

"Y'all will be getting a call tomorrow on that matter of obtaining a trusted swamp guide who knows about that particular bayou. By close of business. It is a small, curious circle of us here in New Orleans who traverse what might be called the *unsavory underbelly* of Louisiana. Meanwhile, I am trusting y'all to get to the bottom of this horrid rash of child endangerments."

Before we separated, I urged Canterelle to remember my voice mail request: that I wanted him to track down the ID of the woman lawyer seated next to Heather at the ABA. He assured me he was working on that too.

In my hotel room that evening, I put in another call to Heather's cell and, maddeningly, once again listened to her familiar voice mail.

I dropped to my knees and pleaded with the God of heaven. I needed wisdom to figure out this tangled web, and power over the demonic powers that were surrounding me. I also had to consider the matter of endurance, because my gauge was nearing empty. But there was one shred of hope, and I was hanging on it. Even though I hadn't heard from Turk Kavagian's guy, Canterelle sounded rock-solid that within twenty-four hours I would be in touch with someone who could navigate me through the Louisiana swamps.

Then I thought about Vance Zaduck. Maybe he was different now. On the surface, at least, we should have a common interest: stopping this plague against the daughters of New Orleans. If he helped me with Canterelle's cases, in return, I could offer whatever help I was able to give him in solving the deaths of Forester and Pullmen. Best of all, Canterelle would get me to the bayou and to my daughter. The circle seemed logical enough: all of us scratching each other's backs.

But I was a realist. Before getting too close with my former nemesis, I'd better do my due diligence. I put in a call to Dick Valentine, thinking I would get his voice mail. Instead, he picked up.

I asked why he was taking a call from me rather than having a date night with his wife.

"Girls' night out," he said. "So I'm stuck home, clicking through eight hundred channels on satellite TV and learning more than I ever wanted to about cleaning products and solutions to male romance problems."

I told him I needed some very quick intel about Vance Zaduck, US attorney for the District of Columbia. He asked how extensive.

"Anything and everything. Before asking for his help and getting too close, I want to know if I'm opening myself up to a left hook."

Dick paused. "No problem. *I know a guy.*"

He sounded like William Shatner doing a TV ad about hotel bookings, so I managed a half chuckle.

But he said, "Hey, Trevor, this time I'm serious. A personal friend who does security clearances for DOJ and US attorneys. I can call him."

They don't make many friends like that. I dumped thanks on Dick Valentine to the point of embarrassment, until we finally said good night.

The next morning I woke up with a jolt, two hours before

my wake-up call. I dropped to my knees again. More praying. More pleading.

Then I picked up the Bible that had been given to me by Elijah White, a former client and now a close friend. I was plowing my way through the Old Testament book of Deuteronomy. Some of it was tough sledding.

As I fixed myself a cup of coffee in the one-cup coffeemaker in my hotel room, I had a thought. About that paper coffee cup. The one that showed up in the crime scene video of my hotel room when I watched it at the FBI headquarters. The coffee cup that didn't belong there because I didn't have any coffee in the room that morning when I was getting ready for the ABA convention. It must have been put there by someone else.

I needed to revisit that.

Then a call on my cell. From Dick Valentine. It was before ten in the morning, and he was already prepared to brief me on Vance Zaduck.

I mustered a bumbling joke. "With the blinding speed of your results, Dick, you must not be doing any actual police work."

"Where you are in New Orleans, in some sections I'd be busier than I am up here in New York."

Considering he was in homicide, that wasn't comforting.

Dick said he had a chat with his federal contact and that this was very sensitive stuff and he wouldn't be doing it for anybody but me. He said he was in a rush, so he gave me his intel in rapid fire.

According to Vance Zaduck's security references, as a prosecutor and as a man, Zaduck was known for "keeping things close to the vest. Very careful. But very smart."

Dick added, "Vance Zaduck has developed an extensive knowledge of cybercrime and Internet technology. He was married for a few years but is now divorced." That last part, of course, checked out with what Zaduck told me himself.

I asked how Zaduck assigned cases to the AUSAs under him, like Forester.

"Zaduck assigned certain kinds of cases," he explained, "like cases involving minors—endangerment, pornography, abduction, and child exploitation—to Jason Forester for day-to-day handling. Apparently had a lot of trust in him. Then Zaduck had those files supervised directly by the upper levels of the Department of Justice. By an assistant attorney general at DOJ."

"Let me guess. The assistant AG was Paul Pullmen."

"You got it," Dick said. "The same guy who I heard met his very terrible, very messy end in your hotel room."

"True," I said. "But Zaduck just happened to be down here in New Orleans, and he helped to clear me."

"I heard that too, so congratulations, I guess. Though I'm not sure that's the right word to use, considering how it ended for that poor Pullmen fellow. What was he doing in your room anyway?"

"I didn't invite him. My guess is somebody else did, posing as me. Then they waited for him to arrive."

I thanked Dick for everything, but before I clicked off, I had one more request. "If you get a chance, I would love to find out more about those child abduction and pornography prosecutions that Jason Forester was working when he died."

18

After hanging up with Dick Valentine, I was faced with a dilemma. Should I risk getting close to Vance Zaduck? Even though I had been released from custody after the FBI interrogation, what prosecutor in his right mind wouldn't still harbor deep suspicions about me after a man had been murdered in my hotel room?

But the risk was worth taking. Something infernal was going on. Maybe I could help to stop it. At the same time, with Heather still out there somewhere, a fact constantly echoing in my head, I was prone to freeze into useless anxiety. I had to fight it almost every minute.

I punched in the number for Zaduck's DC office, figuring he might be back from New Orleans by then, and I was right.

His secretary said Zaduck had a stack of calls to return. I pushed harder, saying it was time critical and that Zaduck would know what I was calling about.

I was on hold for close to ten minutes. Then Vance Zaduck answered. I talked quickly, explaining that this was a matter of urgency and concerned a family member, although I couldn't give details. But it would be very helpful if he could tell me *anything* he might know about these seemingly unrelated crimes: First, a string of young female abductions in the greater New Orleans area. Second, the Paul Pullmen death. I belabored the obvious: that I knew how an investigation into the vicious killing of an assistant attorney general was ultrasensitive, and that I understood the restraints he was under, particularly in discussing it with a disbarred criminal defense lawyer who was operating way outside the tight circle of the DOJ and FBI.

I said, "Vance, I'm in this for the public good. If I uncover leads, particularly on the Pullmen case, I will be happy to send them your way."

"This family member of yours," Zaduck asked, "is there any way she could be implicated in the Pullmen death?"

"How'd you know that my family member was a *she*?"

"Remember, I was behind the mirror during your interrogation in New Orleans, Trevor."

"Right. But no, my daughter couldn't possibly be involved. At the time of Pullmen's death, Heather was in the front row at the ABA while I was giving my speech."

A pause on Vance's end. Then a surprise.

"Trevor," he said, "many years ago, I quoted Nietzsche to you. In the DA's office in New York. Discussing the case against that client of yours, the boxer. Well, in retrospect, my quote was unfortunate. Nihilism is a dead end. We need to aspire to higher things in this world. I'd say, maybe even a need to aspire to the spiritual."

Here was a different Vance Zaduck, it seemed.

Vance proceeded to tell me that he had to be careful because a grand jury might soon be impaneled. No surprise there, but unusual for someone on the prosecution side to hand me that bit of helpful news.

"Understood," I said.

But Vance said he could give me the name of a New Orleans man who might be able to lead me in the right direction. "I withheld some evidence from you and your client years ago," he said, "and that was a mistake. Maybe it's time to make amends."

Nice to hear that from Zaduck, considering our history together. Vance Zaduck gave me the name and address of Lawrence Rudabow, a local housing official.

"That's intriguing," I said. "Not sure how a housing official could help."

Zaduck said, "You would be surprised at the clandestine information that a guy like that is privy to. Entering homes. Particularly in the bad sections. Personal information. Easy entrance into public buildings. Basement-level access to hotels, apartment complexes. Amusement areas. That sort of thing." He concluded with, "This fellow has more fingers in more slime in New Orleans than anyone I know."

A metaphor with an unpleasant image to be sure, but I saw where he was going with it.

Then he added, "Oh, and by the way, the local N.O. office of the FBI is already aware of the meeting that you and Canterelle had with Belle Sabatier. Thought you ought to know."

Apparently everyone in New Orleans knew everything, except for me.

After hanging up with Zaduck, I called my Wisconsin detective friend, Ashley Linderman. It was a stretch, but I wanted to see if she had any inside sources in the New Orleans Police Department.

She gave me a wry reply. "I told you that you'd be begging me for a favor before too long." She asked how Heather was doing.

I told her the details about Heather and how she had gone missing.

Ashley apologized for being cavalier. "I'm sorry. I have absolutely no connections down there. Trevor, you have any leads at all on Heather?"

"Just the name of a bayou. And it's not the kind of place you find on a map."

I knew it sounded dreadful.

Silence. Then, from Ashley, "I'll do anything I can. Call me whenever, Trevor, okay?" She ended by saying she was so sorry that she couldn't help me.

With my new rental car—this time a brawny Mustang, though sadly without a stick shift—I traveled crosstown, parked, and signed in at the lobby of the Housing Authority of New Orleans, or HANO. Lawrence Rudabow was listed on the board as assistant enforcement officer and special services for HANO.

I trotted up to the next floor, where I bumped into a tall black man in a suit who introduced himself as the chief enforcement officer. When I mentioned Mr. Rudabow and said that we were to have a meeting, he pointed down a hall to the last door on the left and told me to knock and go ahead in, which I did.

Rudabow, a husky guy with a buzz cut and an open shirt, was sitting at a cheap desk. His laptop was open. On seeing me, he closed it immediately. "Who are you?"

I told him my name and who had sent me.

"Oh, Zaduck sent you? Okay. Yeah. Didn't think you'd be here that quick."

"I'm sorry. Is this a good time?"

"Good as any," he said. "What's this about again?"

"About a rash of young girls being abducted. One dead. Others missing."

"And you are . . . ?"

"An investigator. Working with Attorney Morgan Canterelle."

"Yeah, I know him. The heavy guy. Drives a big old antique car."

"Can you share anything about those child endangerment cases?"

He scrunched up his face. "You know this office is strictly local housing enforcement in New Orleans, first of all. Not criminal."

"Of course, but Vance Zaduck . . ."

"Look. Zaduck knows that I know stuff. 'Cuz I'm enforcement here in N.O. and such. I'm a liaison with local police on housing complaints. Violations. Criminal activities."

"Your job is just about housing violations?" I asked.

He gave me a studied look. "I also get called into some zoning inspections. And public buildings inspections."

"So, whether housing or zoning or public buildings, I imagine your inspections make you valuable to law enforcement."

"Right. 'Cuz when I have lawful authority to enter some rattrap, and I just happen to see stuff, you know, bad things 'in plain sight' as the law says, well, then the gig's up. So to speak."

"Sure. Now, about the disappearance of young girls . . ."

"Nothing definite, you understand."

"Right. Got it. But did you ever see anything? Hear anything?"

He scratched his belly for a second. "There's this low-life apartment I entered once. Real squalor. Cockroaches. They had voodoo paraphernalia all over the place. Which in this city is not uncommon, of course. While I was doing my inspection, I overheard the occupants. They had heard something on the news and that got them talking."

"Talking about what?"

"Missing girls. There was this one name that came up."

Now he had my attention. "What name?"

"The name of somebody they thought was involved."

"Someone who was mentioned on TV?"

"Naw, not that. A name that, you know, they privately thought was involved. It was all sort of hush-hush, but I heard them."

"What was the name?"

"That lady. The *mambo*. Voodoo chick. What's-her-name . . ."

I waited as he looked like he was searching for it.

"Mini something . . . or Minerva, I think it was. Creole last name. Started with an *S*."

"Minerva Sabatier?"

"Yeah, that's it," Rudabow said. "This was just after she died. And they were saying it was like bad karma or whatever, the way she went. As 'payback' for the bad things she did. To the young girls, they were saying."

Having just questioned Belle Sabatier about her dead mother and heard her plea of innocence on behalf of Minerva, I felt like I had been kicked in the stomach by a horse.

I shot back, "I need to talk to those people. The ones who mentioned her name. I need names. Addresses."

Lawrence Rudabow shook his head and smirked. He pointed to a long row of gray metal file cabinets that lined his office. "That's just part of the inspections we've done. A ton of them. I really can't remember names and addresses. I passed it on to the cops, though. I remember them telling me that those guys who said that, they were a bunch of junkies. Always high on dope. Unreliable in court and so forth."

Stymied on that key question, I headed in a new direction. I asked him how he first became acquainted with Vance Zaduck.

Rudabow stared away, running his tongue over his teeth. "I really can't remember."

"Anything else you can tell me about the disappearance of young females in New Orleans?"

"Nope."

A final question. A kind of wrap-up, in case I couldn't get another audience with this fellow.

"Just so I understand the scope of your authority, the kinds of places that you have special access to . . . houses, apartments . . ." I let my voice trail off.

Lawrence Rudabow nodded but wasn't volunteering

anything more, so I had to go the cross-exam route. "Businesses like restaurants?"

He nodded yes again.

"And hotels here in New Orleans?"

The nodding stopped.

Then, my real target . . . "And other public places? Like theme parks, amusement areas?"

He sniffed. "Like I said, all kinds of places."

I thanked him for his time and hustled out to my car, thinking on the way how Rudabow struck me as a man who had seen the inside of a lot of dark closets and had special access to an unlimited number of places.

Then there was Minerva Sabatier, who, according to Rudabow, clearly had a sinister voodoo reputation among the local gentry. And it also struck me how the information from the city inspector collided head-on with the story that Belle Sabatier was spinning about her mother. Both could not be true. Maybe neither. It was time to sort that out.

More importantly, time to pursue my swamp guide. Where was he?

19

I called Canterelle's office and got his secretary, who transferred me to Kevin Sanders. The clerk said Canterelle was in court but was expected back shortly. I told him that he had promised to find me a swamp guide who would take me into the bayous. But it was already early afternoon, and I still hadn't heard. Kevin said he would put "the pink slip with your message on top of the pile" on his boss's desk. Next, I called Turk Kavagian, got his voice mail, and left a similar message.

Then back to the hotel. I knew I was engaged in a rarefied form of spiritual warfare. Maybe one that was way, way above my pay grade. And the sense of frustration—even oppression— was crushing down on me.

So I put a call into my spiritual mentor, Rev. John Cannon. It was time for a halftime "chalk talk" from Coach Cannon. Ever since coming to New Orleans, and even before that—when I first saw that demonic figure walking on water at Ocracoke Island—I felt that I was in the wrong league.

When I called the Lutheran retirement home in Wisconsin where he lived, I was routed to the nursing staff. I asked about doing a FaceTime video chat with Cannon. I was glad to hear they had the technology. They said for me to call back in fifteen minutes, which I did.

It was almost a year since I had last visited with John Cannon in Wisconsin. Back then, he was fairly ambulatory, getting around on his walker. This time he hummed into the room in an electric wheelchair. With a generous grin, Cannon spent the first few minutes bragging about his new ride. It had been purchased through the charity of some of his former church members, he said. I studied his face. More drooping. Paler than before. But he didn't complain.

Cannon asked me about myself. I told him I needed some advice.

"About what?" he asked. "Demonic conflict?"

"Yes. You squared off with demons in the Amazon rain forest. I don't know anyone who knows more about dealing with the dark side."

"Be specific, Trevor," he said. "Pray specific. Think specific. Study the Scriptures specific. So what's your question . . . specifically?"

"Okay," I said. "I had this ability—detecting demons, I mean. . . ."

"Yes, I remember. I'm still with it, you know."

I laughed.

"Memory still pretty intact," he added. "I recall that you could smell them coming, the demons. That burning scent. Smelled like the old garbage landfill here in Manitou. Even before you saw them."

"Right. You do remember."

Now he was the one laughing. The joke was on me.

"Lately," I said, "I've been approached by demonic forces that . . . Well, I can't sense them coming . . . no advance warning. I feel lost."

"No, no, you're not lost. You've been found, remember? Saved, sealed, sanctified, renewed . . ."

"Okay. Poor choice of words. So what happened to my ability—"

"It's not about your ability. No, it's not about you or that 'gift' you have. It's about *them*. I'd say you're encountering a higher rank of demons. These must be the captains. The majors. Not the lowly foot soldiers anymore. Not the thugs and henchmen that were coming at you with their filthy stench. No, they're bringing the upper echelon against you, Trevor. Upper management. Take it as a compliment."

"What do I do?"

"Rely on the Spirit, that's what. Make room for faith in all this, Trevor. This isn't like improving your golf game, you know. 'Walk in the Spirit,' the apostle Paul tells us. He had to learn that. You do too."

Then, after a pause, Cannon said, "What's your mission statement again?"

"I want to stop demons from doing harm."

"That's fine. What else?"

"I'm not sure. . . ."

"You ought to be sure. These hellish creatures assault innocent people. Some willingly cooperate with the devil, of course. But I'm not talking about them. Only thing you can do with those is to fight back with the spiritual weapons Paul talks about in Ephesians. No, what I'm talking about are those who are truly *victims* of the enemy. What are you doing about them, Trevor?"

"You mean exorcism?"

"I never liked that word. I preferred 'deliverance.' Or 'rescue' or 'release.' The point is you need to be ready for that."

"I'm not sure that's in my wheelhouse."

"Stop talking like a stockbroker or a lawyer. You want to help people or not?"

"Of course."

"Then be ready."

"How will I know?"

"You'll know when the Spirit of God lets you know. Be ready. Be alert. Walk by faith, not by sight. But that doesn't mean walk with your eyes closed, either. That's a good way to break your nose."

Before we ended, I told him that my daughter had disappeared during our trip in New Orleans, and it was weighing heavy on me.

I heard him sigh at the other end. Not like he was tired or bored, but like he was now shouldering my distress. "I'll pray for her," he said. "And I will pray for you, son. Every day. You can take that to the bank."

Just minutes after ending my FaceTime chat with Cannon,

my cell started ringing. I took the call. There was a powerful Cajun accent on the other end.

"Mista Trevor Black, y'all look'n' for a guide into the bayou?"

"Are you Delbert Baldou?"

"Sho' am."

"I need you to take me to Bayou Bon Coeur today."

"Gonna be sundown in a few hours. Y'all sho' 'bout that?"

"I'm sure."

"Den best get yo'self to da dock at da place Ah'm 'bout to tell y'all."

He described where his swamp boat was moored, and I wrote it down. I thanked him exuberantly for calling me and for taking me into the bayous, and then I jumped into my rental and headed to the location. Things were looking up. Way up.

In less than twenty minutes I was dockside in Little Woods, at a marina littered with expensive yachts and fishing boats. My swamp guide, Delbert Baldou, was a skinny white man with scraggly, unwashed hair, who sported a stained military-style shirt rolled up at the sleeves that revealed tattoos on both arms. He looked hugely out of place against the backdrop of the yachting marina.

While Baldou's speech was as slow and as easy as a trumpeter swan on the water, he was lightning quick about money. He quoted his fee for a day's effort in locating Bayou Bon Coeur. "Results not guaranteed," he said. That last word was spoken in three distinct syllables, Cajun style: *guar-un-teed*.

I instantly agreed to the price and looked around for his boat. He pointed to the twenty-foot flatboat on a trailer hooked to his pickup truck. "Gotta drive to da landing first. Let's go."

20

It was late afternoon. I gauged that sunset was coming in about three hours, four tops, so while we drove, I asked Baldou if he could get me to Bayou Bon Coeur this late in the day without getting lost. His answer was not comforting.

"Y' done say y'all wan-ted to get dere today. No matter what. So we goin', no matter what. Eh?"

I nodded yes, having no choice, knowing the bayou was my only clue to where Heather might be and hoping that both Turk and Canterelle were right about the swamp skills of the man. He would have to make his way through uncharted waters as daylight was waning.

I made polite conversation at first, mentioning the pretty marina at Little Woods and talking about my own fishing boat back at Ocracoke Island in North Carolina.

"Shoulda seen dat marina after Katrina," he said. "Big money boats all smashed like matchsticks, yes, dey was. Powerful bad."

He took Interstate 510 south, turned off toward Lake Borgne, then made his way to a series of roads that ceased to bear highway markers. From asphalt to gravel and finally to dirt paths.

We took a turn into a grove of trees, bouncing along a rough path until we broke into a clearing, and I spotted a tilted pier jutting out onto the dark water.

Baldou backed his truck up to the water's edge and then down, until the trailer was half-submerged. I held the bowline while he lowered the boat in the rest of the way; then he took a rope from a post on the pier and looped it around one of the boat's cleats until the boat had been snugged up.

After that he hustled up to his truck, pulled out a bottle of Sawyer picaridin insect repellent, and lathered it over his arms, neck, and face. Then he tossed it over to me. "Best lay it on right thick," he said. "Dey bugs dey eat y'all alive dis time o' day."

Last, he strapped on a Colt .45 and yanked out a 12-gauge shotgun and a box of slugs. He caught me looking.

"Gators," he explained.

Great, I thought, *looking forward to it.*

Then he added, "Now dis flatboat, she close to da water. Helps me pull in gators and big fish and my traps and such. But once a gator jumped halfway in dis boat too." He laughed.

Things were getting more interesting by the second.

Baldou cranked up his Mercury forty-horsepower outboard as I unlashed us from the pier. He kicked it out of neutral, and we motored off.

"So y'all want to see Bayou Bon Coeur?"

"That's right."

"Well, y'all goin' to see it now. . . ."

"You know it well?"

"I know *some tings*. . . ."

"Like what kinds of things?"

"I sho' 'nuff know how to get dere and back."

"Good to know. What else?"

"Some tings happen out dere, dat's fo' sho'. Low-down evil."

I asked, "Like what?"

"Y'all heard 'bout Marie La-veau?"

I nodded.

"Back dere, where we come from, at Lake Pont-chartrain, Marie La-veau, fa-mous voodoo priestess herself, she done cast her spells right back dere along dat lake, y'all can bet on it. Nasty business."

I said, "Tell me about Bayou Bon Coeur."

"What I heard from long past is dat Marie, she done make herself a brick-and-mortar man-sion in da swamp more dan a hundred fifty year ago. Not along Lake Pont-chartrain. No, not dere. But at Bayou Bon Coeur. Paid a whole lotta money to haul da brick into da swamp. 'Cuz she saw da War of *Northern Aggression* comin'. So she wanted a hiding place, to cast her *evil spells* wit her voodoo followers. But didn't live to see it done to da end. 'Cuz when dem Northern ships came stormin' down hereabouts and New Orleans was grabbed, she done give up on it. And her voodoo man-sion was wreck and ruin. And dat's da truth. Only a few know 'bout it, *'cept* for da voodoo folk, 'course. Dey still go dere to dance wit da devil. It's *bad evil* dey practice dere."

I was stuck on that last comment. If Delbert Baldou was repulsed by the black magic practice, why did he know so much about this voodoo capital in the middle of a Louisiana swamp, and why agree to take me there? Maybe it was just about the money.

But more troubling questions surfaced, ones I kept to myself so I could keep an eye on the swamp path that Baldou was taking. Questions like why some female lawyer at the ABA would have known about Bayou Bon Coeur, and how Heather could have gotten there.

We were following a narrow series of waterways that snaked between islands of cypress trees and hanging moss. As we motored across the dark mirrored waters and as the sun was getting low, the bugs came out—mostly mosquitoes—first in drones and then in buzzing clouds. We passed through them, and even though I had my old Mets cap pulled down tight, I could feel them in my hair, in my ears, and up my nose. Happily, the Sawyer lotion kept them from biting into my flesh.

I was looking for signs of wildlife, but there were only a few herons and some big fish jumping, nothing more. After two hours we entered an opening filled with the stumps of cypress trees sticking up out of the water like wooden grave markers.

Baldou slowed us down. I figured it was so he could navigate through the deadly field of tree stumps without ripping out the bottom of his boat. Just to make conversation, I offered that observation.

"Dat's true 'nuff," he said, agreeing. But then he added, "'Cuz dem gators love dis here stumpy pond, dey do. Y' get outta da boat, dey hear dat dinner bell ringin'. And y'all be dat dinner."

He cut the outboard down, slower and slower, weaving around the stumps. It was dusk and the sky was dark gray except for the moon coming out from behind some clouds.

The bottom sounded like it was scraping on something, and Baldou swore loudly, saying he'd have to trim the engine up a bit. But it didn't sound like it was coming up. I knew it would be a wretched place for us to get grounded on a mud bank or a log. Suddenly the boat stopped altogether as the engine began to rev quickly. We were hung up for sure.

Baldou yelled out, "Grab hold of dat motor. Y'all got to yank it clear!"

He cut the outboard down even more as I stepped to the stern of the flatboat. I laid hold of the engine and tried to pull it off the stumps, but it wouldn't budge. The motor was now coughing and chugging. I expected it to cut off completely any second.

I suggested to Baldou that he put it in neutral, but he argued with me and said we had to keep it in forward to pull us free.

Then silence. No more humming of the engine. It had flooded. We were dead in the water. My only hope was that he could restart the outboard.

Leaning back over the motor, I yanked at it again, but still it wouldn't budge. Baldou took his big spotlight out, switched it on, and cast the beam into the inky water. "Tink she's hung up on weeds and a log."

Baldou gave out an unhappy order. He said he would reach down and untangle the weeds on his side of the outboard motor while I, on the other side of the outboard, was to plunge down into the water, lay hold of the skeg of the motor underneath the propeller, and yank it free.

He was hanging over the stern, both arms in the water, as he grappled with the weeds and the log underneath the motor.

I was waiting for him to give me the high sign to ease into the water and to start lifting the engine up. But something caught my attention, swirling along the surface. "Baldou," I shouted. "Out there, twenty feet out."

He pulled himself back into the boat. "Where?"

"There." I pointed. "From our stern."

He reached for his .45 just as the alligator, all ten feet of him, scampered up onto a log only a few feet from our motor, then slipped back into the water.

"Get back!" Baldou shouted as he pulled his Colt out and held it straight up.

The gator kept coming. It was swirling and diving, and then with a powerful thrust of its tail it sprang toward my side of the boat. With a single leap, it was out of the water and snapping toward me, its jaws fully within the interior of the boat as I rolled to the other side.

Baldou cursed loudly, holding his Colt up to the sky while we watched the gator disappear into the dark water. My guide had only one last thing to say about alligators that evening, as he shook his head in disbelief.

"Dem gators, dey most always don't do dat."

21

If they made an Olympic event out of a dunk into a swamp to free an outboard motor from a log and then a leap back onto a flatboat in less than ten seconds, I would have won a medal. Probably gold.

Delbert Baldou restarted the outboard. It was a happy sound. He picked his way through the bog of cypress stumps as I sat at the bow with his big spotlight and pointed the beam into the gathering darkness.

Once we were out of the stumps, Baldou headed us toward a field of three-foot weeds and cattails that looked impenetrable. He cut the engine off and stood in the flatboat like a gondolier in Venice with a long oar in his hand and began to row us through the marsh.

For the next half hour he scuttled us through the grassy swamp as we listened to the flopping of fish in the water and bugs buzzing. In the beam of my flashlight I could see the swirling waters where more alligators were prowling.

And then, surprisingly, everything changed. We broke into a clearing where I could see, up ahead, an island of solid ground with a line of pine trees. Behind that, brick walls of some ancient structure that had no roof, nearly swallowed by vines and Spanish moss. There was a large flickering light within the walls and the smell of smoke.

As we pulled up to shore, we heard voices nearby, a lot of them, and some singing.

I jumped out of the flatboat and waded knee-deep through the water until I was on land. A figure was approaching us. A young woman with a backpack. Her skin glistened in the heat of the swamp, and her hair was a mess. Heather was standing before me, smiling a tense, tight smile.

I was bursting with two contradictory emotions: an outpouring of prayer and thanksgiving that I had found my daughter, and at the same time, the anger of a parent who felt ill-treated by an adult offspring.

Heather must have known what she had put me through. Or was it the foolishness of youth that she hadn't calculated or even given a thought to the full sum of that?

I strode up to her, barely able to put my thoughts into words. She beat me to it. "Trevor," she said, "you found me."

"Where have you been? What are you doing here?"

"My master's thesis," she replied. "I think I've finally landed on the subject. Isn't that great? Voodoo culture and its persistence in the twenty-first century." She turned to my guide. "Hi, Delbert. Glad you brought him here."

I was dumbfounded. "You know him?"

"Of course," she said. "He brought me here. And the others, too, I guess."

I whirled around to Baldou. "Why didn't you tell me this?"

"Y'all don't ask, so I don't say. I keep my nose outta dis."

There was the scent of meat cooking. Baldou unbuckled his holster and wrapped the Colt .45 in the leathers, then asked Heather, "Dey got cookin' goin' over dere?"

She nodded.

Baldou said, "I'll take da food. But then I bid y'all good night. I want no part o' dat evil, no, sir." Then he disappeared into the ruins of the old mansion.

When he was gone, I took a step closer to Heather. "Why didn't you call me?"

"No service," she said and shrugged.

I grabbed my own cell and checked it. It read, *No service.*

Heather said, "Look, Trevor, I'm sorry you were so worried. I mean, really, you look totally bummed about this. For that, I feel bad, naturally."

"Yes. I was worried. Worried sick."

Heather rolled her eyes.

I took a deep breath, simmering down. "I just thank God you're here. And you're in one piece."

"Of course I am. Why wouldn't I be?"

To me it seemed obvious, but not to her. "There are real evils out there," I said, picturing the adolescent face of Peggy Tanner on that missing person poster. And thinking about the grief of

Canterelle's other clients, the family living with the murder of their daughter.

"Bad things can happen," I said. "People go missing. Especially in a place like this."

Heather looked off as if trying to decide whether to endure the conversation, then turned back to face me. "Sure. But not always. Besides, like, only a few months ago, you didn't even know that I existed. Meanwhile, all of those years before we met, I had been taking care of myself. Going to school. Getting a scholarship all on my own. If we are going to have any kind of family relationship, then you have to realize that I'm not your *little girl*."

I echoed the word she used. "Relationship?"

"Yeah."

"Okay. I understand. I hear you," I said. "But there's one thing about relationships."

"Yes?"

"Caring enough about the other person that you can put yourself in that person's shoes."

She looked down at my feet and studied them for a few seconds. She grinned and said, "I think I'll pass on that. Your shoes are soaking wet. By the way, so are your pants."

She got me with that one. I burst into laughter and she did too. We studied each other, having arrived at a friendly stalemate. I reached out and gently patted her shoulder. Heather smiled the kind of smile that told me she thought for a second about reciprocating, maybe even with a hug, but then decided not to. Not yet.

We walked together into the ruins of the redbrick mansion, where a small group was seated on tree stumps within the space that must have been an interior courtyard at one time. A fire was blazing, and a pig was being roasted on a homemade spit. Most of the women were wearing white scarves wrapped around their heads.

I asked Heather about the matching headwear. She said, "They're all dressed like the voodoo priestess Marie Laveau. You know, the famous New Orleans *mambo*." Then she added, "I couldn't have picked a better time."

"For what?"

"A voodoo ceremony tonight. That's why these people are here."

It was time for fact-finding. "How did you find out about this place, again?"

"Deidre. A lawyer who was sitting next to me at the ABA speech you gave. By the way, I've got to hand it to you. You've got some backbone saying what you did back there at the legal conference. . . ."

"Thanks. It meant a lot, seeing you in the front row." But my radar was up. "Who is this lawyer you mentioned?"

"Don't know much about her. I told her about my interest in New Orleans culture and possibly investigating voodoo for my anthropology thesis, and she got me in touch with Delbert Baldou."

"Is she a lawyer down here?"

"Not sure. But she seemed to know a lot about New Orleans and about this bayou."

"This Deidre, is she a practitioner herself?"

She thought on that for a moment. "Maybe not, because she didn't come out here to the gathering."

"What's her last name?"

Heather wrinkled her brow. "Funny. I don't remember her telling me."

Behind us, the group had formed a circle around the fire, which was sending up a billowing shower of sparks.

I studied the people gathered around the bonfire, partially lit by the flames. One face jumped out from the rest. An attractive Creole woman in a flowing white dress. And when she recognized me, she stood quickly and strode over to me.

When she was close, I sensed a vulnerability beneath her peaceful expression, but Belle Sabatier's eyes never left mine.

22

A single thought flooded my mind. Betrayal.

I gave Belle a withering look. "I thought you didn't know anything about this place?"

"I didn't," she said calmly. "You must realize that my mother was an admirer of Marie Laveau, and she had this strange idea she was a kind of spiritual heir of Marie's. The heir to the title Mambo of New Orleans—priestess of voodoo. I had heard her talk a few times about the mansion ruins at the bayou. She thought it was a special peristyle."

"Say again?"

"A kind of voodoo temple. But I never heard details. So, that same night after you left, I came across a diary where my mother had described Marie's bayou mansion, including a map. Right down to the longitude and latitude."

"Why didn't you call me and tell me?"

"I had to be sure. I contacted a swamp guide. Only a few know the way to this bayou."

Heather chimed in. "Google Maps doesn't even have a satellite photo showing this place. People have checked."

Belle said, "I had every intention to call you if I made it here. Especially if I found your daughter." She raised her cell and pointed it at me. "But no service."

Salt in the wounds. But it made sense.

There was pathos in Belle's voice, and for a moment, I felt parts of me being drawn in. Pulled. Metal shavings moving to a magnet.

Belle invited us to walk, and all three of us strolled toward the edge of the island. "Trevor," she said, "you need to know something. After our conversation at my house, I thought about something you said from the Bible. About *hidden* things. It sparked a memory. I hadn't been back to our mansion for years until Mother died. Things were not good between us. But after your comment, I remembered it."

"Remembered what?"

"A secret place. A little hiding place I used to play in when I was a girl. Underneath a stairway and covered by a bookcase. Once, when Mother wasn't looking, I saw how she would go in and out. She would remove a book on the top shelf to push a button behind it and swing the bookcase out, revealing an entrance. From then on, I started playing in there myself. I saw books and pictures and boxes there that were filled with strange objects—talismans and amulets that she kept. But when she found out, she scolded me terribly. Told me she would 'tan my hide' if I ever went in there again. So I never did. Not until last night."

"And then?"

"I knew that my mother used to keep diaries on her nightstand in her bedroom. After she passed, I went through the house. Strangely, I didn't find any of them. Until I rediscovered that secret place last night. In the one diary I found, the dates of her entries started only a few days before she died. Where the other diaries went, I have no idea."

"Who could have taken them?" I asked.

She shook her head.

"Who else was in the house with her?"

"She had a housekeeper, but she was a very trusted friend. The only other person was the man who was with her the day she died. The man who cooked her meals and did some odd jobs."

"Besides the location of this bayou, what else did she write?"

Belle hesitated. She parted her lips like she was about to share something but stopped.

"Belle, please," I said. "I am hunting down very bad people doing some very bad things. I don't know whether or not they're all connected. Your mother's diary might help."

Another pause, then, "Mother and I had parted ways long before I started art school up in Philadelphia. Regardless . . . I can't think she was involved. Not the way you might think. Not the way it looks on the page . . ."

"What are you saying?"

Belle was shaking her head in disbelief. "It's not the way it seems, when you read it. There has to be another explanation."

Before I could respond, we heard the sound of drums coming from the interior courtyard of the crumbling mansion.

Heather had a conflicted expression on her face. She looked over to the ruins strangled in overgrowth, where the bonfire was lighting up the night sky. "I . . . I have to go. I can't afford to miss this. My research . . ."

The father in me leaped out. "Heather, I care more about your soul than your research. Don't go. This is dangerous stuff."

She shook her head.

I pressed in. "It's not about some ridiculous voodoo ceremony. There's more at play here underneath all of that— a supernatural enemy with an aim to maneuver you, entice you, until you're a slave. He's just looking for an open door, that's all. Any door will do. Heather, please don't step into it."

Before I could explain any more, Heather exploded. "I'm not doing this with you right now. Especially in front of this nice woman," she said, nodding to Belle. "I'm not going into your medieval junk, Trevor. Satan and his minions. Heaven and hell. Your comic book theology."

Heather turned and strode toward the lights from the bonfire that were flickering up the cypress trees encircling the ruins, where the drums were beating louder.

Belle looked away from me, like a child who had just reluctantly chosen sides against me in a schoolyard argument. "There's something I have to do," Belle said and then quickly followed after Heather.

23

It was late, and I was alone. I was resigned to the fact that I was stuck at Bayou Bon Coeur till morning. I planned to have Delbert Baldou ferry me back to New Orleans at daybreak along with any others who wanted to join us.

Wanting no part of the concert of voodoo spell-casting taking place by the bonfire, I sauntered down to the water where Baldou's flatboat was tied up. I had delivered my warning to Heather. What else could I do?

I sat down on a grassy spot and listened to the swamp that was alive with the sounds of night animals in the brush and creatures on the water. While the sky was pitch black, the bonfire blaze inside the mansion courtyard cast a light all the way to my place at the water's edge. The moon had come out full, and it painted a yellow beam of light across the water.

My mission had been to locate Heather and make sure she was safe. That part was finished. But I was uneasy about all that was still undone. Between Heather and me. And why I had come to New Orleans in the first place. The death of Jason Forester. And now Paul Pullmen. And the abductions of young girls. Canterelle was right about that; it resembled Old Testament atrocities. Practically Canaanite.

On the visceral level, it all felt connected. But in my head, it dead-ended.

Back at the mansion ruins the drums were unceasing, followed by chanting and singing. Louder and louder. Someone was hitting a tambourine. The din was rising.

Then, a bolt out of the blue. What was I doing down by the water anyway, when my daughter was back there, just two hundred feet away, in the middle of an occult hoedown? My reasons for avoiding the ceremony suddenly rang ridiculously hollow.

I was on my feet and heading to the wall of the crumbling brick mansion. The front door was missing, and the opening gave me a good surveillance position into the courtyard. I could see Heather seated on the other side of the bonfire but outside the inner ring of participants.

Several of the white-turbaned women were swirling around the flames to the beat of the drums. One of them was swinging a machete in one hand while holding a bottle of liquor in the other. In between swaying and swooning, she thrust her head back, taking big gulps. First she sprayed it from her mouth at a big Latin cross that looked like it had been borrowed from a graveyard, then turned to the fire and spit liquor into the flames, causing it to momentarily flare up, to the delight of the caterwauling dancers.

Two of the gyrating women were swinging headless chickens over their heads, obviously having sacrificed them to the voodoo gods. I was no expert, but I had done enough research to understand the point of this cacophony: to summon the "spirit gods" from the other side.

One of the prancing women in white stood out from the rest. Her dance was more graceful, and she was holding a huge pink chalice containing some liquid that she was delicately sprinkling here and there with her fingers. The point was to invite a supernatural presence into her body. I kept watching. Suddenly she jammed to a halt, dropped the chalice, and began screaming and writhing, swinging her arms but still rhythmically in sync with the beating of the conga drums. Now all focus was on her. The other dancers gathered around her as she straightened up and began to physically assume another persona, this time a sashaying celebrity, with one hand raised high to the crowd, waving and provocatively swinging her hips as she walked. Whoever or whatever she had become, the revelers must have recognized it, because they began to shout, *"Ezili Freda! Ezili Freda!"* An onlooker rushed up to her with a satin cape and wrapped her in it while the others danced around her with white candles.

But it didn't last. Another abrupt change. The woman's cocky strut was over as her shoulders slumped and she put her hands over her face. Her shoulders began to shake, and her sobs came in loud waves of hysterical weeping. The other dancers encircled her, reaching out as if wanting to comfort her but afraid to touch her.

The drums stopped. I glanced to the far side of the bon-fire, where Heather was seated. She had grabbed her knees and tucked them up close to her, the light flickering over her. There was an expression of sad astonishment on her face.

I had seen enough. Heather was safe, but only physically. The ceremony was finished. I returned to my place at the shore and sat down, feeling oppressed by the heat and by the cultic rituals that were going on and my daughter's interest in them. Doors had been flung open to a demonic enemy. Only by the grace of God had a supernatural army not marched through the portal. Then again, maybe it had.

The sound of footsteps. Someone was coming up behind me.

Belle Sabatier was clutching two bottled waters, and when she sat down on the grass next to me, I noticed she was holding something else that she quickly slipped into her pocket.

When she offered me a bottle, I asked, "Is this a peace offering?"

"Maybe."

The bottle was chilled, and I put it to my forehead. In the sweaty heat of the bayou, it felt good.

I asked her, "Why weren't you in the middle of that fracas back in the mansion? I would have thought you'd be reveling right in the thick of it. Voodoo queen of the ball."

She tilted her head and leaned in closer. "I thought lawyers look for evidence. Where's your evidence for that idea?"

"I'm not a lawyer anymore, remember?"

"Of course. Mr. Canterelle filled me in. Your belief in the supernatural got you tossed outside the city gates."

"So," I asked again, nodding toward the bonfire, "why weren't you dancing with the others? I didn't even see you."

She uncapped her bottle and took a healthy swig, then held it against her neck to cool herself. She kept it there for a few seconds.

Looking out to the waters of the bayou, she began to explain. "All I ever wanted to do was to run my little art studio back in Philadelphia. After I left New Orleans, I studied at the University of the Arts in the city. When I got out, I painted. My medium was watercolor, memories of the houses that I remembered in the French Quarter growing up. I rented a little shop and sold some of my work and that of other local artists on consignment. That's who I really am, Trevor. Not part of my mother's voodoo congregation. Just a struggling artist."

"Okay," I said, cutting it short. "And what about your mother? What was in that diary of hers?"

She put down her water bottle and pulled a small leather-bound book from her pocket. There were symbols etched into the leather.

"My mother's diary," she said, handing it to me. "See for yourself. The last entry was the day before her death."

I opened it. Just as she had described, the first page had a meticulously drawn map of the waterways leading to Bayou Bon Coeur with a large X and, underneath it, the words *Ruins of the Mansion of Marie Laveau.*

Then, only two handwritten entries.

The first one said:

I am so vexed in my spirit. Am I the Mambo of New Orleans or not? Will cleanse myself from the blood with a special spell.

Then the last one. I had to read it twice, just to make sure. And when I was sure of the words that were written, I was stunned.

Something must be done about all those young girls. I am QUEEN. And my power shall not be trifled with.

I closed the diary and looked into Belle Sabatier's eyes. "What 'young girls' was your mother writing about?"

In Belle's eyes there were tears glistening, welling up. She tried to reply but couldn't talk, making just a garbled sound. Then she snatched the diary from my hand, rose to her feet, and hurried toward the bonfire. I thought I could hear the muffled sound of weeping as she swept away.

I tried to untangle the meaning behind the entries in Minerva Sabatier's diary—that part about "all those young girls." And having to be cleansed from the blood. What else could it mean, other than that she was part of the vile abductions that had been taking place? More dread. For all the world it seemed to corroborate the rumors that Rudabow had told me about Minerva Sabatier.

Belle seemed contrite. Even appalled by her mother's notes. But then, looks can be deceiving. I had learned, in my hunt for monsters, they sometimes come pleasantly disguised. The innocent facade can be fatal. Was Belle just one more?

I looked out at the moonlit water on the bayou.

Immediately I was aware of a menacing presence, nearly palpable.

Maybe I had lost that one peculiar sensory ability to detect the dark forces in advance, but it seemed to have been replaced by something else. A sense that was now more refined. Just like Rev. Cannon had said. An inner spiritual certainty that, at least when I was attuned to it, was even more powerful and accurate. A discernment telling me to be alert.

Just then, I had the overpowering notion that one of them was out there.

I checked my surroundings. Then I saw him, this time out on the mirrored surface of the water. In the moonlight. The dark figure. And I knew it was him. The one I had first seen from the beach on my island, standing on the ocean. My hellish chauffeur. The mentor for the demon twins I met in the alley. He had not given up on me. Of course not. He just waited for a more *opportune time*.

Now he had come back, and he was on the surface of the water in the bayou. Not sinking. But this time his arm was raised and he was beckoning me.

I was trembling and suddenly weak, hardly able to stand. I couldn't run or fight back. Against everything that was in me, I felt myself being drawn to take a few steps toward the edge of the land, toward the dark waters where the menacing figure was waiting and summoning me to himself. His power was increasing, and mine decreasing.

"Lord Jesus," I whispered, "your strength, not mine."

The sound of laughter echoed over the waters, mocking me. Toying with me. It was coming from my enemy out there on the surface. Then, an instant later, he was gone.

24

It was well after midnight when the flickering lights from the bonfire began to ebb and people started hunkering down for sleep on Bayou Bon Coeur. I wanted to collect Heather and get out of there immediately, but that wasn't going to happen.

Delbert Baldou asked me if I had a place to sleep. I told him no, but that I was waiting for my daughter, and after that I would have to figure it out.

He grinned. "I got da answer for y'all and Heather." He pointed to his swamp boat. He explained that in the footlocker on board, he had a homemade tent setup that would cover the boat and create a sleeping space. We could use the life jackets for pillows.

Sleeping bags and mosquito nets were being mustered by

the voodoo crowd within the walls of the roofless mansion ruins. Compared to that, Baldou's boat looked like a night at the Plaza. I accepted his invitation, though I privately wondered why the special treatment.

I hung out at the shoreline pondering the appearance of that ghoul on the water and my helplessness, thinking about the horrible toll visited on those children and their families, considering what Belle had told me, and wondering why she had come clean like that about her mother and her diary. Perhaps there was more to Belle than I thought. And more to Minerva, as well.

When Heather showed up, she gave me a polite hello and I told her about Delbert Baldou's offer. She was happy to join the two of us on the flatboat. In less than half an hour Delbert was snoring loudly. Heather couldn't hold back a giggle.

In the shadows I rolled over so she could hear me, and I whispered, "Give me your impressions."

"About what?"

"What you saw. The voodoo ceremony."

"Educational," she said. A few seconds later, she added, "Informative." More time went by before she ended with "And very strange and kind of unsettling . . ."

"Me too," I said.

"You watched?"

"Keeping you under surveillance. But yes, I saw it." I let a few seconds go by, then asked, "You're the anthropologist. Tell me—what was going on with that woman at the end? Strutting around like she was a Hollywood starlet, then crumpling into tears."

"They said it was the female spirit god, Ezili Freda, taking her over."

"Meaning what?"

"They say Ezili Freda is very powerful. Brings love and success. But also feared, because her jealousy and vengeance are all-consuming."

"Why the tears?"

"They told me that Ezili Freda always ends her visits in weeping. Because the world is too much to endure."

"True," I said. "It can be. The dark side always makes enticing promises that are never kept. What's left is sorrow. Broken hearts. Enslaved souls. I've lost friends to it."

For a while Heather said nothing. But in her total silence I knew she was still awake.

After a few moments she said in a whisper, "I suppose, now you've found me and your ABA speech is done, you'll want us to head back to Ocracoke."

That's when I told her about Morgan Canterelle hiring me as a consultant. I mentioned a little about his cases but tried to be discreet.

I finished with "So this rash of abductions, those young girls, I've been hired to track them down. And find the monsters who are doing it."

"How many? Where?"

"Several in this area. Close."

I thought about the cold case dating back a decade and a half—involving the horrible death of fourteen-year-old Lucinda, whose body had been found right there on Bayou Bon Coeur. But I spared Heather from that one.

"So," I said quietly, "I'll pay for your airfare tomorrow. Fly you back to Florida or wherever you want to go."

But Heather protested so loudly that Baldou began to stir and I thought he might wake up.

"No way, Trevor," she said. "I'm staying here with you. I'll be your research assistant or something. Where else am I going to get this kind of experience?"

Experience? I thought to myself. Heather still knew nothing about the real dangers of the demonic empire. And how those battles aren't forensic or scientific but spiritual.

I told her we would discuss it in the morning, but in my heart I didn't want Heather anywhere near the forces I'd be confronting.

Her last words before we both slipped off into sleep were "Just so you know, Trevor, I'm staying here in New Orleans. I'm working on those cases with you." I tossed her a skeptical look. A moment later she added, "Anyway, it's about human trafficking. In anthropology, you know . . . it'd be field experience."

When morning broke, Delbert agreed to ferry the both of us through the swamps and back to the landing at the Little Woods marina before returning for some of the other visitors. The other swamp man was on his way, he said, to help transport the remaining voodoo followers, including Belle Sabatier.

On the way back, there was little talking. Watching a few cranes winging over the water. Spotting splashes that made me think alligators were close. As soon as we reached cell phone service, I would have to call our hotel and, once again, extend our stay, and the same went for the car rental. Since being retained by Morgan Canterelle, I had an envelope full of cash, so that would help.

After Delbert Baldou docked the boat at the edge of the water and loaded us into his pickup truck, he suddenly became talkative, as if on cue.

"I seen y'all talkin' to Miss Belle. The Sa-ba-tier daughter."

I nodded.

"Y'all know dat her momma, Minerva, the voodoo gal, she done got poisoned."

It caught me off guard. Then I said, "No, it was an allergic reaction. Food allergy. Maybe allergic to peanuts or something."

"Dat's what dey wanted y'all to tink, sho'," Baldou said. "But I know better. She done got soup for dinner. When she dead, the FBI done a test. Found peanut oil fo' sho' in her body. But dat don't kill her. Got poisoned by black-magic beans."

Heather was in the backseat of the truck, and she leaned forward, hanging over the console at that point.

"Where'd you hear that?" I asked.

Baldou shrugged. "Got all kinds o' in-fo'mation round here."

"You get this from Attorney Canterelle? Or a private investigator named Turk Kavagian?"

Baldou shook his head. "Not from any lawyer. And not from a pri-vate eye."

When we pulled up to the marina where my rental was waiting for us, Baldou parked, quickly got out, and opened the door so we could exit. He waved to us as he jumped back behind the wheel of his truck and shouted out the window, "Y'all have a good day now."

On our ride back to the hotel, Heather commented on my

new rental—a Mustang. I told her about my stolen rental and getting a replacement.

She said, "Things are getting weirder."

"You mean the stolen car?"

"Not just that. What Delbert said. *Poisoned*," she said, repeating the word. "Black-magic beans and all that."

"Yeah, that was news to me too," I said. I grabbed my cell, called the hotel and extended our room stay, and dialed Morgan Canterelle, who was in his office. I put him on speaker. "Morgan, what do you know about Minerva Sabatier being poisoned?"

Silence on the other end. Then, "Well, sir, I do know that she died from the rich soup concoction she ate that evening. Some kind of peanut soup. Her personal chef didn't know about her allergy. Nor anyone else, I gather."

"You didn't answer my question."

Another silence. After a few seconds Canterelle said, "There was an investigation. And it found something else in her system besides the peanut oil from the soup."

"Like?"

"Some kind of toxic plant. A bean, found somewhere in Africa. I do not recall the name of it. But it is highly poisonous."

"What did her private chef have to say about this?"

"Not a word. He vanished."

I asked, "How do you know all this?"

"Can't tell y'all. Attorney-client confidentiality, my friend."

"Who's your client in that matter?"

"That also is con-fi-dential."

I pushed back. "I can't help you if you tie my hands."

"If I think it's essential to advise y'all," Canterelle said, "I'll obtain the appropriate client waiver."

I had to get Canterelle on record on at least one point. "Then answer this," I said. "Did you ever tell Delbert Baldou any of this business about the poisoning?"

An instant denial. "No, sir. I surely did not," he said.

I was drawing a blank on what this new revelation meant. As Heather said, things were getting weirder.

After hanging up, I noticed that Heather had just done a Google search on my iPad, and she was grinning. "Okay. About those 'black-magic beans' that Delbert Baldou mentioned. The botanical name is *Physostigma venenosum*. Common name: the Calabar bean," she said. "Just as Canterelle said, derivation is from West Africa. Sometimes used in—get this—*voodoo ceremonies*. In sufficient strength, it causes paralysis and even death."

Heather capped it off with *"Booyah."* If she had a microphone, she would have dropped it.

"Hey," I shot back, "this is not a game. This is deadly serious."

The wry grin on her face told me she wasn't buying the risk. Not yet.

"I happened to notice that in your phone call to the hotel, you extended *both* of our room stays."

Yeah, she had caught that.

"I'm taking this one day at a time," I said. "But the minute I think there's any personal danger to you, I will order you straight out of New Orleans. Is that clear?"

She grinned again. "Understood, *Czar* Trevor."

25

Our hotel was coming into sight when my cell phone lit up with a *No ID* call. At that moment, I had the visceral sense, the hair-raising-on-my-forearm kind of sense, that it would be important. I pulled into the hotel parking lot, found a spot, and took the call. When I picked it up, I put it on speakerphone so Heather could hear it too. If my daughter was going to work this case with me, I needed to loop her in.

The voice at the other end jolted me back against the head-rest. It was a deep, metallic, basso profundo voice—the kind you would expect in a dark opera starring monster robots or Darth Vader.

I recognized the ultra-low digital tonality. The caller was using an electronic voice distorter. Like the person who had called Dick Valentine at the beginning of this creepy case.

"Trevor Black?" the caller asked.

"Yes," I responded.

"Good. You've got me on speaker. Now you both can listen."

Lucky guess? I wondered . . . but no, nobody's that lucky. The caller knew that Heather was with me. I waited for more.

"Two federal prosecutors are dead. Children are disappearing. Lives destroyed. Get moving on this."

Time to bring the caller out of the shadows. "Give me a reason why I should?"

"Get serious. This is your thing. You live to expose this kind of terror. Voodoo. Exploitation of young, defenseless girls. Murder. That's why I pulled you in."

"Where do I go from here?"

"Think Batman and Gotham City. Except the Jester is not out in the streets. He's on the inside, running things."

"How inside?" I asked.

"Touchy question. You find it out. You're on the outside looking in, so that's good. But time's wasting. Just be careful who you trust."

Sudden silence. The call went dead.

Heather was agape and staring at my cell.

I asked, "Are you sure you're ready for this kind of 'field experience'?"

My daughter nodded but looked shaken and had to take a second before asserting, "I'm ready." Then she added with a bit more certainty, "Yes, I'm ready for this. But please," she said, pointing to my cell, "tell me what just happened."

"Okay, now we know some things. First, the caller with the voice distorter knows you're with me. And knew something about me and also wanted me on this case. And must be the same person who originally called Dick Valentine after AUSA Jason Forester's death. Believes voodoo is behind this and that it involves child exploitation. The kind of abduction crimes that Morgan Canterelle is handling for some grieving families."

Then I tossed her a cleanup question. It was meant to be professional courtesy to my new partner. "Did I miss anything?"

"Only one."

"Which is?"

"Batman," she said. "Did you catch it?"

"Which part?"

"The part about the Jester. I saw every Batman movie. That's not what the character is called. He's called *Joker*, not *Jester*."

I chewed on that. My partner was impressive.

"Interesting. The fact that the caller said that, it may have been a Freudian slip."

Heather smirked. "So you believe in Freud?"

I gave that a think. "There's a Sigmund Freud quote I remember. He said that no one who confronts 'demons that inhabit the human breast, and seeks to wrestle with them, can expect to come through the struggle unscathed.' I agree."

Heather raised an eyebrow. "Sure, but I bet he meant *demons* metaphorically."

"Which is where Freud and I part company. Anyway, the bit about the Jester could be important. Do a word search using *Jester* plus *New Orleans* and see what you come up with."

She noticed that I was climbing out of the car. "Where are you going?"

"To the hotel desk. Be right back."

I fast-walked into the hotel lobby and talked to a desk clerk to confirm the extension of our stay. Yes, she said, our rooms were extended, per my telephone call. "Good," I said. "Now, please change our rooms to a different floor."

With Heather joining me, extra precautions had to be taken. I had to keep our whereabouts unpredictable. The clerk churned out two new keys, one for each of us. I asked for doubles. She complied. Heather would have a key to both her room and mine, and so would I.

By the time I climbed back into the car and explained the new room situation and handed Heather the keys, she explained what she had found.

"Okay, there's a connection between *Jester* and *New Orleans*. The Jester was a roller-coaster ride in Six Flags amusement park here in New Orleans. It's still standing, but the whole place was totally wrecked by the floodwaters of Hurricane Katrina and was closed down." She added, "So maybe your Freudian slip idea is on the mark. And by the way, there's a Gotham City section of the theme park."

A memory flashed. My first telephone conversation with Morgan Canterelle's law clerk, Kevin Sanders. Something he said. A random comment.

I started the car and wheeled it out of the parking lot.

Heather asked, "Where now?"

"The voodoo museum."

I called Kevin on the ride over, making sure he was working there that day. He was. He said there was another staffer on duty and tourist traffic was slow, so, yes, he could chat with me.

I gunned it over to Bourbon Street, and Heather and I strode into the lobby.

Kevin greeted me and then turned to Heather, whom I introduced. He shook her hand and stood there staring at her. I suddenly realized that Heather was not just my daughter. She was also a woman, looking every bit as attractive as her mother, Marilyn, ever did. I had to refocus Kevin's attention.

I said, "Tell me about Six Flags. You mentioned something about people who worked there. Do you still have contact with any of them?"

"Yeah. I think so." He thought on it for a moment. "Sure. One of my classmates has an older brother. He used to work there."

"Does he know a lot about the park?"

Kevin gave a covert smile and lowered his voice. "The place is closed down. Kids go in there because it's so spooky-looking. But the cops have been cracking down. More patrols. Even so, Bert—that's the older brother of Tom, my classmate—he's like this amateur filmmaker type. I heard he's still slipping into the park to do this horror movie of his."

"Call him," I said.

"Now?"

"Yes. Right now. Tell him I want to find out when his brother Bert is going into the park next, and anything else he knows about Six Flags."

Kevin shrugged. "Okay. I'll try." He took a few steps away and started making some calls.

That gave Heather and me a chance to glance around the museum. The place was covered with cultic statuettes, "magic potions," herbs, and talismans for sale, along with the typical tourist trinkets like T-shirts and coffee cups sporting a variety of images of skulls and magic symbols. I spotted "spell kits" on the wall, to cast curses against former spouses—like one called "hex your ex." Heather thought it was strangely amusing. I, on the other hand, had a very different take.

Once upon a time I would have snickered along with her at the seeming old-world, flat-earth stupidity of it all. But not now.

Ever since the spiritual turnabout in my life—and my own battle with the underworld—things were different. I knew that behind the veil, there was a swirling sinkhole populated with forces that were energized by a horrible mission and a ruthless master. The danger of voodoo lay in its portal of entry, even if unintentional, not in any innate power that its ceremonies and potions possessed. Either way, the consequences could be just as devastating.

Kevin trudged back to us, cell phone in his hand. "Okay, Mr. Black, I called my classmate Tom. Bert shares an apartment with him, and he works at a little local film distribution company. What he actually wants to do is either go the indie film route, you know, like the kind of movies they preview at Sundance, or else go to Hollywood someday—"

"Kevin," I blurted. "Sorry to cut you off, but time's of the essence. About Six Flags. What can you tell me?"

"Okay, well, Bert told Tom, who just told me on the phone, that he still has to finish shooting his little homemade horror movie at Six Flags, but he knows the schedule of the police patrols so he doesn't get caught. Anyway, some of the girls he's using in his movie kind of got scared about going there. . . ."

"Why is that?"

"Because of the rumors."

"Explain that."

"It's about this guy who shows up, hanging around the abandoned Six Flags ruins, wearing a hat and sunglasses. Tries to get girls to come with him. Tells them he's with a legit movie company and that they're holding auditions."

I said, "I'd like to talk with this Bert fellow. Immediately, if possible."

"That may not be possible, Mr. Black."

"Why is that?"

"Because he's on his way to Six Flags right now to finish shooting his film."

26

When we left the voodoo museum, I could tell Kevin Sanders was troubled. I had asked that he put me in touch with Morgan Canterelle and said it was urgent and that it had to do with the abandoned Six Flags site.

"You aren't going to get my friends in trouble, are you?" he asked. I promised I would do my best to make sure that didn't happen. Then I asked him everything he knew about the entrance that Bert and his amateur film crew would use to get into the park. I had Heather take careful notes as he laid it out for me.

I was driving toward the Six Flags site when Canterelle's call came in. I put it on speakerphone.

"First thing," I said, "about that abduction of Peggy Tanner. I notice that the police report you supplied me on her case has some information about Six Flags."

"Yes, sir," he said. "Correct."

"Let me guess. Did Peggy sneak into the abandoned Six Flags theme park before she went missing?"

Silence on the other end. "My oh my, y'all are resourceful. I am certainly getting my money's worth."

"And the other girl who was tragically killed and found on Bayou Bon Coeur, same thing with her?"

"Yes, sir, same thing. Both of them happened at the Six Flags park. The other girl who died and was found in the bayou—she disappeared in the theme park when it was open for business."

"Before Katrina hit?"

"Exactly. Now, to their credit, the police have stepped up security considerably to keep out trespassers, as I believe my law clerk told y'all. All this information is *off the record*, understand. . . ."

"Understood. But now I need something else from you, Morgan. You said you were friendly with the police. I need to get into Six Flags immediately. Myself. Without obstruction and without getting cited for trespassing. In fact, I'm on my way over there with my daughter, Heather. Can you tell the patrol officers who I am and that I am working with you? If I find any thrill seekers in that abandoned site, I will get them out of there myself. But I don't want them arrested or cited. Deal?"

Canterelle had to think about that. Then, with a sardonic chuckle, he said, "Y'all are a man with a lot of demands. But yes, I will make that call." After a pause he went on. "Do you have a concealed carry permit? I have one myself. Y'all best be armed. . . ."

"No, I'm not carrying a weapon," I said. "At least nothing physical."

Heather chuckled and shook her head.

I pulled the car off of Michoud Boulevard and eventually into the mammoth Six Flags parking area—a vast concrete wasteland of tall weeds sprouting from cracks. Beyond that, I could see the ruined theme park landscape that had been wrecked by the unstoppable power of the floodwaters from Hurricane Katrina.

I told Heather, "I need to find Gotham City Hall in the park. The area where Kevin said Bert and his film crew would be shooting."

She pulled up a map of the site on my iPad. "Okay," Heather said, "you can find it in the Super Heroes Adventures section." A smile spread over her face. "So does that make us superheroes as we enter that area?"

"You mean, as *I* enter that area, not as *we* enter."

"You're shutting me out of this?"

"Absolutely. According to what Kevin Sanders just told us, some character trolls these ruins looking for females. You're staying in the car. Sorry."

My cell phone lit up. It was Morgan Canterelle, reporting back that he had talked directly to the police chief and that we had a deal. We should expect a patrol to show up in the next ten minutes.

In the interim, Heather wanted some answers.

"Tell me again, what do you expect to find here?"

"I'm not sure. Maybe nothing. But I'm talking to Bert directly.

About this guy in the sunglasses and hat who approaches girls who show up here."

"Because . . ."

"Because our anonymous caller used Batman nomenclature, and there's a Gotham City area at this park. Plus, the caller may have either subliminally or deliberately inserted the Jester reference because of the female abductions that have taken place here, and there's a roller coaster called the Jester. And we're here because we need to stop this savagery somehow. And yes, it's a stretch, but this is the best I can come up with right now."

Heather looked doubtful. "Okay, but maybe this guy that Bert is talking about is just some lone nutcase wandering around the park. . . ."

"You know the old saying about criminals returning to the scene of the crime?"

"Yes, actually thinking about that."

"Well, it's not true. Not in most crimes. But there are two types of crime where it is true. One's arson. Not applicable here."

"And the other?"

"Crimes of serial violence. Kidnapping. Rape. Murder. I'm thinking that if Mr. Creepy is part of these abductions, he may be showing up again. Just a hunch."

She did some head bobbing. Then, "So why the business about voodoo? The caller has mentioned it twice. Once to your friend, the detective. And again in the call just now to you. But I don't see the connection."

"Paul Pullmen was overseeing Jason Forester's work, cracking down on child abductions and child pornography. First Forester dies by some voodoo curse, according to an insider.

Then Pullmen is killed in an orgy of blood that practically shouts cultic ceremony. No signs of a struggle. A coffee cup was found in my room that didn't belong there. If he was poisoned first, then it matches the death of Minerva Sabatier, the voodoo queen who was done in by a toxic plant used in voodoo practices. And Minerva's diary was talking about girls and about blood and some kind of atonement. I think we're just inches away from pulling all the threads together."

"Even if you're right that it's all connected, you haven't given the 'why' behind any of that."

"Sometimes that's the very last piece."

I had an assignment for Heather while I tromped through the theme park. "Why not look up the use of the poisonous Calabar bean in voodoo ceremonies? In your search, see if you can tie it into the disgusting core of these cases—child abduction and human sacrifice."

She smirked. "You're not giving up on the voodoo angle. . . ."

"No. I saw with my own eyes on that FBI video what was done to Paul Pullmen."

A police cruiser made its way toward our car, with a two-man team in the front seat. I got out and approached the squad on the driver's side.

After showing my driver's license, I thanked them for allowing me access to the park.

The officer behind the wheel spoke up. "Look, I'm just following orders from the captain. You enter this park at your own peril," he said. "And it's understood you'll advise any frequenters to exit the park." I nodded. He handed me a card with his cell number on it. "You'll report any suspicious circumstances immediately." I agreed to that too.

He ended with "I'm guessing you must have some pull, Mr. Black."

"No. I just know somebody who does."

With that, I started trekking across the busted concrete parking lot, toward the wreckage of Six Flags.

27

The Six Flags theme park was ringed with a new chain-link fence to keep the public out. Kevin told me about the spot where the fence had been cut. Not far from the Super Heroes area.

As I walked along the chain-link boundary, I could already see up ahead the twisted metal and rusting signs. The flood tides of Katrina had inundated this place and laid it waste. When the powerful waters receded, the theme park that was left behind looked as if it had been hit by some cosmic blast. Not decimated entirely, but ravaged, leaving only its skeleton behind.

I trotted along the six-foot-high fence until I found a part that buckled slightly. When I looked closer, I could see that the chain link had been cut from top to bottom and closed up with some thin-gauge wire. I plucked the wire open and bent the metal mesh back so I could slip through.

At one time there must have been a manicured grove of trees where I was walking, but the trees had been uprooted by the floodwaters and strewn across the wasteland.

I tried to get my bearings. Not easy when you are surrounded by four-foot weeds and rusting outbuildings. I ended up doing a tour of the devastated grounds. At one point I could see in the distance the sign for the Jester and the outline of the mangled roller coaster that had been tilted by the force of Katrina's waters. A giant clown's head lay sideways on the ground, its eyes blankly staring ahead.

Eventually I spotted an entrance to my destination—an archway that read DC Super Heroes Adventures.

Scanning the area, I noticed some tall scaffolding that had at one time been a supporting structure. I studied it closer. It had been the theme park facade of an art deco cityscape building, now in shambles. That was all that was left of the Gotham City Hall. At one time a fun house for children and families, now a sagging false-front building with peeling paint.

But there was no Bert or anyone else. Until I started calling out my name and yelling that I had been sent by a law student by the name of Kevin Sanders.

Then, the sound of feet shuffling through the wreckage. A tall young man in jeans and a T-shirt, maybe in his late twenties, stepped out from behind the fake scenery. Followed by another male about the same age, shouldering an expensive-looking steady-cam. A few seconds later, they were followed by two girls, maybe eighteen or nineteen.

I showed him my ID and explained that I was an investigator

looking into strange occurrences and abductions, some of which happened in the abandoned park.

One of the girls elbowed Bert and yelled, "See. I told you so. I told you this place is creepy."

I asked him if he saw anything unusual the night Peggy Tanner went missing.

"Nah, nothing at all," Bert said. "We're just shooting a film, that's all."

"You see anyone else here?"

He shook his head.

"I'm here on behalf of the local police. I need to advise you of something."

All four of them flashed a panicked look. For a moment, I could relate. I was back in my own crazy youth thinking about all my stupid risk-taking and brushes with cops and near misses with the law.

I said, "So here's the deal. I promised the police that I would get you people out of the park. Count yourselves lucky. They've agreed not to prosecute you for criminal trespass. But you have to leave right now."

A disappointed expression on Bert's face as he puffed his cheeks out, then exhaled loudly.

"Sorry about that," I added. "Hollywood will have to wait."

Just then, one of the girls went wild-eyed. "Uh . . . uh," she stammered. She slowly raised her arm, pointing to something out there, beyond.

I whirled around. About fifty yards away, there was a stocky male who quickly turned away from us. But before he did,

I caught the fact he was wearing sunglasses. And a little, short-brimmed bebop hat.

I yelled to the group. "Get out of the park now!" Then I took off after the man in the hat, who had disappeared behind a dilapidated ice cream booth, heading toward a field of chest-high weeds.

Wheeling around, I saw Bert urging his partner with the camera to start filming my chase.

"Shut it down and get out!" I yelled again and sprinted toward the collapsed ice cream booth.

As I ran, I plucked out my cell and punched in the number for the patrol officer in the parking lot. "I've got a possible perp on the run in here, wearing a hat, sunglasses—"

He bulleted back. "Where are you?"

"Leaving Gotham City, heading past an ice cream vending kiosk."

He ordered, "Do not engage that individual."

Ignoring that, I clicked off my cell and burst into a full sprint. But at the ice cream shack, I lost sight of the man in the hat. I stopped for a moment because I was winded. Time to get back into shape, I thought as I bent over to catch my breath.

It would be my last thought. Next, a heavy blow to the back of my head, shooting stars, the world beginning to tilt, and the sensation of falling forward.

28

When I opened my eyes, I was lying on the ground facedown, and I heard a voice. I rolled over, swooning with nausea and with a swirling pain in my skull.

Bert was standing over me, next to his amateur film assistant, who was still clutching his shoulder-mounted camera.

My scrambled brain was able to frame a single question. "Did you catch his face on film?"

The camera guy shook his head. "Nah, just his back."

I stumbled to my feet. I could see two patrol officers running to my location with their hands on their sidearms. When they arrived, I struggled my way through a rundown of the incident and the few details I could tell them about the potential predator.

One of the officers said, "Sir, you should go to the emergency room to get checked out for your concussion. We'll call an EMT unit."

"Don't bother," I said. "I'll have my daughter do the driving."

The officers gave a stern warning to Bert and his crew, but true to the deal I had struck through Morgan Canterelle, they let the group go without charges.

I finally made my way out through the cut chain-link fence to the cracked cement parking lot that was choked with weeds.

As I approached the rental car, Heather must have noticed something odd about me because she jumped out of the passenger seat and trotted up to me.

"Okay, what happened? Something happened to you. . . ."

"An incident," I said. "I'm okay."

She stared into my eyes. "Trevor, you're looking goofy. I'm driving."

When I settled into the passenger seat, she turned on the ignition, then tossed me my iPad. "You've got to read this. This is sickening. A game changer."

For me, it wasn't a game changer at all. But I had danced with the dark side for several years and Heather hadn't, so by then nothing surprised me except the constant realization that the God of all compassion continued to look out for me in the process.

On the iPad, she had come across a series of articles dating back to June of 2014, including one in *International Business Times* and another in *Business Insider*. They were spawned as a result of a report from the United Nations Committee on the

Rights of the Child warning about voodoo ceremonies involving children and sexual abuse.

She found a link to an earlier online article in the *National Geographic News* dated February 10, 2005, recounting the horrific death of a child brought into England by voodoo followers and apparently killed as a human sacrifice.

But it was the manner of death that jumped out and accounted for Heather's reaction. An autopsy showed signs of poisoning by the toxic Calabar bean.

"This needs to be stopped!" Heather yelled as she began to wheel our rental car across the parking lot. "But first, let me tell you something, Trevor: you don't look good. Tell me what happened."

I gave her the Twitter-length version of my being knocked out, but I stressed that the loss of consciousness maybe lasted only for a few seconds.

"Well, I've got to get you to the ER. You need a doctor to check you out."

"I'm fine. We don't have time for that. I have someplace else in mind."

I gave her the address for Belle Sabatier's mansion in the French Quarter.

When we arrived, I marched up to the front door, turned the old brass handle on the doorframe several times, and heard the tinny *ring-a-ling* as I did.

No butler came to the door. Instead it was Belle herself, looking unsteady. She wiped her swollen red eyes, and with that same hand gave a sloppy wave for us to follow her inside. In the other hand she held a wineglass that had clearly been

drained and probably more than once. We were led to the familiar sitting room with the fireplace and the portrait of Minerva
Sabatier hanging over the mantel.

Heather began apologetically. "We're so sorry to disturb you.
I hope we didn't catch you at a bad time—"

I interrupted. "Belle," I said, "time for straight talk."

"Of course, Mr. Black. Straight as an arrow . . ."

She took the last swig of red wine, then set the empty glass
on the little table next to her. That's when I noticed a worn
Bible on the tabletop. It was open to a page where an old-
fashioned embroidered bookmark was draped.

Belle struggled through tears to say something, pointing
to the open page of the Bible. "After finding Mother's diary,
I needed to know . . . to know what she meant about the young
girls. And what it had to do with her power as the New Orleans
mambo. So I tore this mansion apart, looking for answers. Until
I found this." As she said that, she put her finger on the page
of the Bible.

I checked the passage she was pointing to. It was the New
Testament. The Gospel of Luke, chapter 17.

It would be better for him if a millstone were hung
around his neck and he were thrown into the sea, than
that he would cause one of these little ones to stumble.

Next to that verse was a long, handwritten note down the
entire margin of the page. It had obviously been written there
by Minerva.

O God, forgive me! They just wanted names of my followers. "To help expand my influence," they said. But then they recruited them. I didn't know about the girls. Have I aided this terrible slavery? The rumors are that Sulphur is the path to Hell, leading to the sea. I must stop this.

"What does this mean?" I asked.

"You're smart," Belle said. "Figure it out. Her diary showed she was concerned. About some girls. You thought it was a confession, didn't you? Well, here's your confession," she said, jabbing a finger at the Bible. "It's all coming back now. I heard a comment from one of her voodoo friends when I came back for Mother's funeral. That someone had been asking for her help in 'networking' all of her voodoo followers together. Some kind of Internet thing. And how Mother and her voodoo power were going to 'go global.' That was the carrot they used. Her pride. But all they really wanted was to enlist some of her followers. Looking for the worst of the worst."

I asked, "Why? For what purpose?" But as soon as the words came out of my mouth, I knew the answer.

"The girls . . . ," she began to say but then broke down in a sob.

Heather left her seat, put her arms around Belle, and tossed a look back to me. It seemed to be saying, *Now what do we do?*

I leaned toward Belle. "You know what I think? Your mother was an unwitting pawn in that horrific scheme. She opened the door. And hell walked in."

Belle couldn't talk. All she could do, as she tried to stifle the sobs, was to nod yes to my question.

"Why didn't you tell me?" I asked. "About your mother being poisoned?"

After a few heavy sighs, Belle let go of Heather and said, "Didn't know who to trust. Besides, Mr. Canterelle was handling that. Investigating her death."

"So you're one of his clients too?" I asked. She told me she was. Belle had to be that client whose case Canterelle said was *indirectly* related to his other cases: the murder of Lucinda, who was found at Bayou Bon Coeur, and the still-open case of Peggy Tanner. But still related to all that because she was poisoned by someone involved in the wider network. Someone responsible for the crimes.

"Do you think your mother was killed because when she learned the truth, she was guilt-ridden and was going to expose the criminal network?"

"With all my heart," Belle said. "Mother was raised Catholic. But left it when she decided to devote herself to voodoo. I always thought, though, that she had some unfinished business with God."

I glanced at the page of the Bible that had been opened to the words of Jesus in Luke. "It looks like it," I said.

Then I added, "Belle, I want to find out who—or what— was behind her death. And behind the occult network orchestrating these females being abducted, and even worse."

29

Heather drove us back to our hotel. We grabbed a table in the downstairs restaurant and began to debrief each other on the events of the day.

She kept asking how I was feeling after my knock on the head. I got a kick out of her concern.

Back at the mansion, before we left, I had asked Belle whether she knew what her mother meant by the reference in her Bible to "Sulphur," as well as the cryptic note about "the path to Hell, leading to the sea." But she hadn't the faintest.

"Sulphur," I said out loud to Heather as we ate. "It could be a euphemism for evil. The subtext relating to the burning fires of hell."

That stopped Heather, fork in hand, right in the middle of her Cobb salad.

"So," I continued, "was that what Minerva Sabatier meant?"

Heather saw where I was going and shook her head. "I wouldn't expect a voodoo priestess to think in terms of hell like that. Too orthodox."

"But not for a lapsed Catholic."

Then I remembered how the note about sulphur in the margins of Minerva's Bible actually read.

I said, "Minerva capitalized *sulphur*. Maybe it's not a theological reference. Maybe it's geography. A place name."

A second later Heather was frantically typing a search on my iPad.

"Talk to me," I said.

She raised a finger. She was onto something.

I asked, "What?"

"Okay, this is it. You said geography. So I checked place names with the word *sulphur* in them."

"And you found what?"

"Something about an hour from here."

"Give me more."

She smiled. "A place called Port Sulphur."

"A port?"

She nodded. "On the Mississippi."

I waved to the waiter to bring me the check.

"That's our destination tomorrow," I said. Then I repeated that part of Minerva Sabatier's note: "'Sulphur is the path to Hell, leading to the sea.'"

On that happy note, I suggested we both head to bed.

My original plan was to set out early the next morning. But I decided against it. We didn't know where to look, so it wouldn't do any good arriving before shops and offices had even opened up. Instead, I opted to use the early hours for something else. My reading routine first thing each day had me slogging through the book of Deuteronomy with its complex Israelite history and intricate Judaic law.

I was nearing the end of that Old Testament book, and I was looking forward to finally finishing it and moving on to the book of Joshua, full of stories of battle and conquest, the thrill of victory and the agony of defeat.

My wake-up call came just after dawn. I splashed water on my face and opened my Bible to the place I had left off the day before, marked with a leather bookmark: chapter 29 of Deuteronomy.

But as I read the account about the covenant between God and the sons of Israel at Moab, and the warnings of God, my mind refocused on the journey Heather and I would be taking that day. To a place that was a tiny dot on the map in southern Louisiana. I didn't know why we were going there. Not exactly. Except for the hint that Minerva Sabatier had dropped in the margin of her Bible . . . It was all I had to go on. A hunch? I yearned for more. Where was God's leading in this?

I returned to Deuteronomy. About two-thirds of the way through the chapter, I stumbled onto God's judgment on wickedness and on the flagrant rejection of his moral law. Stern stuff. To those people, the consequences would be horrifying. And then I read the features of that divine curse:

All its land is brimstone and salt, a burning waste,
unsown and unproductive, and no grass grows in it.

Brimstone. The King James word for sulphur.

I had to read that one again. A wasteland of sulphur and salt.

I didn't believe in coincidences. Not anymore. Having come to understand that the Lord of the universe is a sovereign architect, I expected his hand always to be instrumental. Even when I couldn't see it. The timing of my Bible reading and our destination for that day could not have been an accident. His hand. Using his Word. For his mission. Yeah. That made sense.

By the time I had finished the end of the chapter and knelt at the edge of my hotel bed, the words of my prayer had already been placed in my mouth. They were taken from the last verse of that part of Deuteronomy, an Old Testament book that had surprised me with its relevance:

> The secret things belong to the Lord our God, but the
> things revealed belong to us and to our sons forever,
> that we may observe all the words of this law.

I had to keep my eyes and ears open for what was about to be revealed.

30

The drive to Port Sulphur was slightly over an hour, as we traveled Highway 23 through the low delta land that followed the Mississippi. When we entered the little burg, we found a humble scattering of houses, some churches, a school, and several industrial buildings along the river that serviced the shipping industry. Forty-five miles to the south, the Mississippi wound its way to Port Eads, where the mouth of the river opened to the Gulf of Mexico.

Heather asked the obvious. "What now?"

We had just passed a municipal building off Levee Road.

"I might pop into the Plaquemines Parish Sheriff's Office. Pay them a visit."

"A cold call?"

"Right."

Heather looked dubious. "This should be interesting."

I sent a quick text to Morgan Canterelle in accord with the agreement I had with him that I would report on my investigation progress.

Things were quiet at the sheriff's department. I bumped into a deputy leaving for patrol. He told me that the sheriff, Clay Haywood, along with most of the command staff, were at a law enforcement conference at the other end of the state, way up in Shreveport. The detectives were out in the field.

I played the Morgan Canterelle card. "I'm here investigating a case for a New Orleans attorney."

"Well, Deputy Ben St. Martin is still here. He's in the Marine Division. Water search and rescue."

That didn't sound hopeful. But my options were limited. I asked if Deputy St. Martin could see me, along with my "assistant." We were taken to his office.

Ben St. Martin was a square-shouldered man in his thirties with his hair buzzed, military style. I gave him my card and told him that I was working a case for Attorney Canterelle about a missing girl. I handed him Peggy Tanner's poster.

I had unknowingly yanked the string at the end of his lightbulb, because there was a flash of recognition on the deputy's face. "I know about this," he said. "A rash of missing girls. Apparently Mr. Canterelle—and you, too, I guess—think law enforcement isn't doing its job."

"Not really. We're after the same thing you are. It's about finding a young girl named Peggy Tanner. And many more like her. And finding out why another young girl named Lucinda was killed and left in a bayou."

He looked dubious. "Really?" Then he added, "I know law enforcement in New Orleans. They're totally dedicated to finding that girl. Just like we are. You know how many cold cases our detectives are dogging? Plenty. And they never give up."

"I don't doubt that," I said, then decided it was time for the wide-angle lens. "I think this Peggy Tanner case is just the tip of the iceberg. We're trying to locate the criminal enterprise behind this. Child abduction and pornography. Homicides. Awful stuff. With a heavy dose of voodoo mixed in."

"What does Port Sulphur have to do with this?"

I noticed a small plaque on his desk with a section from the book of Proverbs:

Trust in the Lord with all your heart, and lean not on your own understanding; in all your ways acknowledge Him, and He shall direct your paths.

I figured I could get down in the weeds with him.

"Big picture, I'm not in Port Sulphur just for an assignment. For me it's a mission. God is in the center of it. I'm tracking down these evildoers because it's the right thing to do. Not a job. A calling. Just a guess, but I'm assuming that doesn't sound totally crazy to you."

He smiled and thought on that for a moment. Then he said, "Child abduction?"

I nodded.

Deputy St. Martin glanced at Heather. "And what's your interest in this, miss?"

I answered for her. "She's my research assistant. An anthropologist."

"Almost," Heather said, slightly qualifying my dad brag. "Currently working on my thesis."

The deputy said, "Anthropologist. You mean the experts that analyze human remains? Bones?"

She said, "That's forensic anthropology. I'm into other things."

Our meeting didn't look productive, so I was about to cut it short. "I appreciate your meeting with us, but I don't want to take up any more of your time. You may not be able to help us. . . ."

Deputy Ben St. Martin leaned forward and lowered his voice. "I wouldn't be too sure about that."

He picked up the phone and put in a call, right in front of us, explaining about me, what I was investigating, and asking whether the person on the other end was willing to talk to me.

The deputy went silent, listening, and after a few more minutes he gave a warm good-bye, hung up, and turned to me. "This is a complicated situation. Pastor Ventrie isn't sure he can talk. He'll consider it."

"Does he know something?"

"I can't comment. Except to say he's the head pastor of Levee Road Community Church here in town. If he gives the green light, I'll give you a call and put the two of you together."

I wanted to probe further, but before I could, Heather jumped in. "Is this pastor trying to protect someone?"

Deputy St. Martin straightened. "Can't comment."

Heather got pushy. "Oh, so you're trying to protect this pastor. . . ."

He turned to me, forcing a grin. "Mr. Black, your assistant's pretty aggressive."

"Well," I said sheepishly, "she's my daughter."

By then I had a theory on what was going on. I threw Heather a stern look to stop giving the deputy the third degree. I thanked him for taking the time. I snatched one of his cards. "Let's stay in touch."

As we drove away from the sheriff's office, I cautioned Heather. "We can't stomp into a place like that and treat law enforcement like they owe us something."

"Aren't they public servants?"

"That doesn't mean just *our* public servants. They serve everybody." But she wasn't buying it.

So I kept going. "Have you given it much thought, their jobs? Monotonous rounds to keep the townies safe, day after day. Traffic stops. Angry citizens. Impatient judges. Protecting everyone but pleasing almost no one. Until one day they respond to a domestic dispute, and an angry spouse fires a loaded weapon at them at close range. Just because they wear the uniform. All the while, getting paid a pretty meager salary. Did you notice those little houses and trailer homes on the way down here? I'm betting one of those belongs to Deputy St. Martin."

"Wow," she shot back, "I didn't realize you were so gung ho on cops."

"Not always. Remember, I used to be a criminal defense

lawyer. Then I started dueling with evil, face-to-face, started to see the world through God's eyes. Things change. So did I."

I remembered seeing a sign for a Subway sandwich shop when we first entered Port Sulphur. I asked about catching something to eat, and Heather said she was up for it.

I doubled back and headed out of town, back to where the billboard had pointed the way. The route took us on a lonely road through low fields of grass, scrub brush, and red clay dirt. It went on longer than I expected and without signs or other traffic. I thought we'd better get our bearings. But the GPS on my phone couldn't get a fix on our position. Then that fleeting sense as we drove that maybe we should turn around. Head back into Port Sulphur.

31

I shook off the paranoid apprehension. There was only one car at the sandwich shop, and it was parked around back, which meant it likely belonged to the young fellow wearing the paper Subway cap who was standing at the counter, reading a magazine until customers showed up.

After we ordered and collected our humble eats, I suggested to Heather that we dine in the car. I had my reasons for privacy.

I asked for my iPad from Heather, clicked it on while I ate, then booted up my LexisNexis search engine for legal research and handed it back to her. "There's a reason the local pastor might be hesitant to talk."

"You mean, like protecting his flock?"

"Might have something to do with it, but I have another thought."

"I'd be interested to hear it."

"You've been a good research partner on this case. How about doing another online search?"

She chomped down on her sub and laid the iPad in her lap. "Looking for what?" she said with a mouth still full.

"I suggest you find some cases with the following search terms: 'Louisiana, clergy privilege, disclose.'"

She tapped it in and scrolled down some online articles, then stopped at one and started reading. As she read, she summarized it. "This is fairly current. April 2016. A teenage girl confessed to a priest about sexual abuse that occurred to her. . . . The priest didn't report it because of the 'seal' of confidentiality in the confessional. . . . A judge ruled the priest didn't have to report it despite being a 'mandated reporter.' . . . Appeal to the Louisiana Supreme Court . . . Doesn't look like that court has ruled on it yet. . . ."

"That confirms my suspicion."

"How? A pastor isn't a priest."

"He doesn't have to be. The clergy privilege of confidentiality prevents an official of a religious body from being forced to disclose what was said by a lay member in a private spiritual setting, especially where it might involve a confession of some serious wrong."

"So in our case, a wrong done by a church member?"

"Perhaps. Some admission made to the pastor that Deputy St. Martin talked to on the phone. Maybe some terrible thing that could relate to child abductions. Or the vile things done to those victims. Things available for viewing on secret porn sites. The pastor in this town could be trying to figure out where he stands under the law right now. Whether he can talk to us or not."

"It still sounds fishy."

"Welcome to the dark swamp of the law. I used to swim in it regularly."

The sun was getting low as I pulled away from the Subway sandwich shop in our rented Ford Mustang. I clicked on my headlights as we headed down the road.

Then, in my rearview mirror, I saw a vehicle approaching, and it was coming fast. A jacked-up, heavy-duty pickup truck. A single driver in the front. As it roared closer, I could see him, a skinhead with a full beard and a nasty expression.

I picked up speed, but the truck was bearing down on me. I could hear some headbanger rock at maximum volume pouring out of the truck's radio. The truck switched its lights on high beam. I accelerated. But I couldn't shake him. The big pickup was a foot from my rear bumper. I could sense the fear in Heather, as her eyes kept darting up to see the lights in our rearview mirror.

There was a dirt pullover coming up on the right-hand side of the road, and I slowed and eased off the road to let him pass.

But when the pickup roared past, it swerved over onto the pullover in front of me, then slammed in reverse toward my front bumper.

I jammed my foot on the accelerator, wheeling to the left, and skidded back onto the paved road. I floored the Mustang. I grabbed my cell to call 911, but we hit a bump and it disappeared in that dreaded space between my seat and the console. I told Heather to use her cell instead.

"I lost it."

"What?"

"Back at the bayou," she said. "That's why I've been using your iPad. . . ."

It was time for emergency measures. I was already calculating how long it would take, if we were run off the road, for me to pop the trunk and grab the tire iron.

I could hear the roar of the pickup even before I noticed the high beams racing up behind me. I had my foot to the floor, going over ninety as we took the turns on the country road. No streetlights. I prayed no cars would pull out from a hidden farm driveway, and no stray deer either. And that I could reach the little river hamlet of Port Sulphur before something wretched happened.

I strained my brain to remember how long the ride was from Port Sulphur to the Subway. Twenty minutes? Thirty? I had to make it back to civilization.

We were squealing tires through the turns. I knew the high-riding pickup had more power on the straightaways, but we had more agility. I was counting on that.

I was nearing a hundred and the pickup was gaining. Heather was whimpering next to me. I told her we would get back to Port Sulphur and drive straight to the sheriff's department.

A billboard for a shipping supply store in Port Sulphur went flashing by. We were getting close. But the truck was getting closer.

I saw an intersecting side road coming up on the left with a deep ditch on each side. I took my foot off the accelerator.

"What are you doing?" Heather screamed.

"Bluffing."

The muscular pickup roared past me on the left and swerved, trying to force me off the road. I slammed on the brakes, then feinted to the left as if taking the side road. The pickup swung in front of me to block me at the intersection but went too far and tipped into the ditch.

I swung the Mustang to the right, barely missing the pickup, and gunned it straight ahead. Heather started hooting and hollering in a victory chant.

"Too early to celebrate," I yelled. "That big rig is made for off-roading. He'll be back on the pavement in minutes."

A few minutes later I saw the high beams of the pickup far behind us. It was picking up speed.

But by then we were entering Port Sulphur. The pickup began to slow and then did a quick U-turn and disappeared in the opposite direction.

32

We skidded to a stop at the sheriff's department and I tromped in, Heather close behind me. Deputy Ben St. Martin had left for the day, so I talked to the deputy at the desk. I filed a complaint of road rage against the other driver and identified the big pickup as a Chevy Silverado.

When I finished filling out the mundane data, the deputy asked me an obvious question. "Did you give that driver any reason to come after you?"

I told him no.

"You sure? Didn't cut him off? Didn't go too slow, way below the speed limit? Make an obscene gesture? Try to provoke him?"

I started to explode. "I don't know what passes for entertainment down here, but that maniac came after us for no reason.

It was all I could do to keep him from killing us. It was unprovoked, attempted vehicular homicide. My daughter here was in the front seat with me. Ask her."

But he didn't. Instead he calmly spoke as he finished the report on his keyboard. "Complainant says he did nothing to provoke the driver."

I signed my statement and left.

"Hey," Heather said with a sly grin on her face. "'We can't stomp into a place like that and treat law enforcement like they owe us something.'"

I stopped in my tracks and my mouth eventually spread into a grin. Couldn't argue with that.

I suggested we check in to a motel chain that we had passed. On the way over I told her I was sorry about the aggressive driving scare.

She offered an explanation. "Maybe he was on drugs."

"I wondered that. But his driving was too intentional. Too precise. We were being targeted."

"Why? And please, no demon stuff."

"Okay, here's a question: Who knew we were here?"

Heather didn't have to think long. "You texted Attorney Canterelle. You told him you were down here."

"Nah. I may have trust issues with Canterelle, but that's a stretch."

"Deputy St. Martin knew we were here," Heather said. "And so did that pastor he talked with on the phone."

The list was getting longer.

We checked into the motel, and I made sure we had adjoining

rooms. Heather hung out in my room for a while, watching TV on my bed. I knew down deep that she was frightened.

Then my cell lit up. It was Dick Valentine.

"Dick, why aren't you snuggling with your lovely wife, rather than calling me?"

"She's at a ladies'-night-out thing again. Women wearing red hats. I don't get it, but she's into it."

"So you're stuck with me?"

"Yeah, fun city. Briefing a guy who's all hot on devils and such."

After the chuckles, he launched in. "Got a little more on the Jason Forester case. When he died, he was homing in on an international child abduction and porn ring. Really sophisticated. Well-financed. Very high-tech. Part of the 'dark net.' The dirty basement of the Internet that's heavily encrypted and accessed by twisted types with expensive passcodes. Back-alley stuff. Except it's all digital."

"Where's the command center of this disgusting website?"

"The server is overseas. But there's a control administrator somewhere in the continental United States. Also, there's a Russian name attached to this group of creeps. You'll need a pen to write this down."

I told Dick I was ready.

"*Kuritsa Foks Videoryad,*" he said, following up with the spelling.

I took a moment to absorb that. "Any hint of voodoo in this?"

"Depends on how you define voodoo."

I needed more. "Dick, I know you've got homicides to crack

up there in NYC. And you do me a lot of favors. Don't ever think I take this for granted. . . ."

"Yeah, blah, blah. Listen, how many times do I have to tell you, it's the least I could do for you after you broke that rogue cop case for me up here."

"Okay, then here it is: it would be grand if you could get me more on this international criminal bunch. And that control center in America, that'd be a home run."

"Anything I can, I'll do. Shouldn't be a problem, seeing as there is always a New York City tie-in on those criminal enterprises. In my contacts log, I'll mark these as calls with one of my confidential informants. Which I guess you are."

I laughed. "But, Dick, you're the one informing me . . ."

"So you're saying the informant would be me? Dunno. I'm getting on in years. I get mixed up."

By the time the jokes were over and I was off the phone, Heather was asleep on my bed and snoring. I clicked off the TV and pulled the covers over her. I jotted down a note for her that I was sleeping in her room and put it on the nightstand next to her. I took a moment to give her a fatherly look. Neck tattoo and all.

Thank you, God, for my daughter.

As I lay in bed in the other room, fading into sleep, I wondered whether it was fair for me to have pulled Heather into danger. I was willing to assume the risks. But she had no idea what she was venturing into.

At what point should I pull the plug, get her safely away from me and light-years away from the hideous organization that I was messing with?

33

I awoke the next morning to the ring of my cell. I had left it on and plugged into the wall for charging. The voice on the other end was a man's, but it wasn't familiar. A slight drawl.

"Mr. Trevor Black, this is Pastor Wilhem Ventrie of the Levee Road Community Church in Port Sulphur."

I told him I was grateful for the call.

"We need to talk. But not over the phone. Have you had breakfast yet?"

I was still waking up. Food wasn't on my list. "No . . ."

"Good. Meet me at Captain Jack's Oyster Bar."

"Yeah, I think I saw it off of Levee Road yesterday."

"That's the one. I'm buyin'. My treat."

I was glad to oblige, though I couldn't see how oysters at 8 a.m. would be anybody's treat.

I slipped into the other room where Heather was sleeping soundly and dropped a second note on the nightstand, telling her where I was and why.

Pastor Ventrie was a man in his sixties, heavyset, with a ruddy face. He was already sitting in a booth by the window of the café when I arrived. He asked me to recount again what brought me to Port Sulphur, and I gave him a paper-thin account—investigating on behalf of a New Orleans attorney the death of Lucinda and the disappearance of young Peggy—and showed him the same poster I had displayed to Deputy Ben St. Martin. "I suspect it all might be part of a wider criminal enterprise involving young girls."

He looked at the poster and shook his head. "No, she's not familiar. Don't know about this one."

"This one?"

"Yes. This particular one."

"There are others?"

The waitress hustled up to us, and the pastor ordered oyster quiche. I went for the tamer stuff: scrambled eggs and crab cakes.

He leaned forward and asked in a low voice if I was a "saved man."

"God changed me radically when I had my faith encounter with Christ, if that's what you're asking."

He nodded. "Ben . . . Deputy St. Martin, he thought as much. He's a member of our church. Well, then you know about the battle with demonic forces, as the Word of God says, not against flesh and blood, but with the principalities and powers of the unseen world . . ."

"More than you can imagine." I nudged closer to the issue. "Can you give me specifics, why you wanted to meet with me?"

He glanced around the café, which was already more than half-full. He was about to tell me something, but our plates showed up and he stopped. Pastor Ventrie prayed a blessing over the food, expressing gratitude for the grace of God and the sacrifice of Christ on the cross, and for "Trevor Black, that he may fight the good fight for the faith, not only opposing the deeds of darkness, but even exposing them . . ."

When he finished, I thanked him for praying for me and for the Scripture that he had mentioned. "Paul's letter to the Ephesians. Powerful and true," I said.

He nodded. Then he drilled down deep. "I have a member of my church. He's been in turmoil ever since he turned his heart over to the Lord Jesus Christ. Wrestling with something. I know a little about it. But I've got to figure things out."

"Legal things? In my prior life I was a lawyer."

"Yes, legal. I did talk to a member of our board of elders who's an attorney. I won't be able to share things unless that church member gives me permission to tell his story. I want to do the right thing, but these legal matters are like quicksand."

"I'm guessing you're probably caught between being a mandated reporter of sexual abuse on the one hand and honoring the privacy of a church member who has confided in you spiritually."

"That's it exactly, Mr. Black."

"I don't want to put any pressure on you, Pastor, but time is of the essence. There are young girls out there at risk. Every day that goes by, more of them are abducted and turned into human traffic for a ruthless business. Some disappear forever. I'm sure Port Sulphur is a fine place to live. But evil doesn't know boundaries. Of course, who am I to preach to a preacher about that?"

He smiled.

"Who knows," I said, "maybe you've been called to help us stop this."

A nerve had been hit. I could see it in his eyes. "Port Sulphur is a good little place. Honest, God-fearin' people. Tough times, though, economy-wise. But lately there's been . . . not quite sure how to put this . . ."

"I'm all ears."

"A spirit of demonic oppression is comin' over a few of the people. Floatin' in like a poison cloud. Involvement in vile sensual appetites for children . . . *children*, mind you. On the Internet. Horrible things. I've preached against it. Summoned the powers of Christ against it. Prayed and fasted over it. It breaks my heart."

Then he added something that screaked like a siren. "What's worse," he said, "is that I am hearing tales of voodoo worship being involved in all of this. Rumors of spells being cast and such. To give these child predators special powers of protection. My land, Mr. Black, this is Armageddon taking place."

I wondered how much I could share with him. I opened the door a crack. "Last night I was harassed by a man in a big pickup truck as I left the Subway sandwich shop outside of town. He was driving a Chevy Silverado. It could have turned deadly. I don't think it was an accident. Who, besides you and Officer St. Martin, knows I'm here or why I'm here?"

Pastor Ventrie's eyes widened, mouth pulled tight. "Only

that church member of mine. Just him. I didn't even tell our attorney about you. Maybe I should have . . ."

"I have a favor to ask."

"Yes, if I can."

"Don't tell that church member of yours about our meeting today. Or anyone else. Not yet."

"I can honor that. You know, I felt led to meet with you this way. In person. Just the two of us, privately. I didn't even feel right about us talking over the phone. This church member of mine that I've been talkin' about, he thinks somethin' funny is going on with his phone."

Note to file: that registered with me. Meantime, I needed to hustle back to the motel and check on Heather.

34

Heather was awake when I got back and was sitting by the motel room window sipping coffee from a Styrofoam cup. "So," she said with a pout, "do you need me on this case?"

"More than you know. But you were deep asleep, practically unconscious. Besides, I thought my first meeting with Pastor Ventrie ought to be solo. I didn't want him to feel double-teamed."

Satisfied she wasn't being cut out, Heather perked up. "Find out anything useful?"

"Predictably, the pastor sought legal advice. He can't talk unless that church member of his gives him the go-ahead. It sounds like the member thinks his telephone line might be tapped."

"Could it be?"

"Not legally. Unless there's a warrant."

"Good grief, do you think this church member's involved with child abduction?"

"Don't know. If he is, right there is a basis for the warrant. But maybe there is no warrant, and someone just thinks he knows too much."

"Why don't the cops bring him in for questioning?"

"Deputy St. Martin could be playing this cagey. He's a member of the pastor's church."

"Sure . . . or maybe he's covering this up, just like I suggested. An interchurch conspiracy."

"Then why would the pastor invite me to breakfast and discuss it with me? And why would Deputy Ben St. Martin make that call to the pastor right in front of me? I'm seeing transparency, not conspiracy."

She didn't look convinced.

I said, "I'm not pressuring you to believe the way I do. But there's no need to be so suspicious. Not every person who uses 'Jesus' as a proper noun rather than a swearword is a crackpot."

"I'm not a raving secularist."

"Of course not. But you do cast a jaundiced eye at all of us Bible-thumpin', devil-fightin' members of God's army of crazed zealots . . ."

I got a smile from her.

I said, "I think these are good people down here. Trying to do the right thing. They may be facing an enemy of overwhelming force."

"You want to elaborate on that?"

"Not now, but soon."

I suggested that we cruise around Port Sulphur. We had a little time to kill while waiting to hear whether anything would come from my meeting with Pastor Ventrie.

We drove down Levee Road, past the little clapboard church that was Pastor Ventrie's. I slowed to take a long look at the greenish-brown water of the Mississippi on the other side of the road. And as I did, I had a thought. Something had to be checked out, but I needed a place to park. The small parking lot of the church was as good as any.

I had Heather pull the travel map out of the glove box; then I asked her, "Show me where the river ends, due south from here."

A minute later, with her finger on the spot, she said, "Port Eads. Like we said before."

"It makes sense."

"Meaning . . ."

"Funny. Always wanted to compete in the famous billfishing tournament there, down where it pours into the Gulf of Mexico."

"You're thinking about fishing? In the middle of this case?"

"Not really. I'm after bigger fish."

Out of the corner of my eye, I noticed a man strolling toward us from the church. It was Pastor Ventrie. He bent down at the driver's-side window, waved to me, and then eyed Heather. I rolled down the window, said hello, and explained that I was using his parking lot to study our travel map.

By the look on his face, he had a crisis on his mind. "This must be providential, you being here. I was on my way to your motel. My church member . . . He was here this morning, waiting for me. This is so hard for him . . . but urgent, too. It just weighs heavy on the heart, Mr. Black. This whole thing." He glanced at Heather.

I introduced my daughter and explained she was my "investigative assistant."

The pastor launched into it. "His name is Henry Bosant. He's a boatman and ship's mechanic. Worked the river from here up to New Orleans. He was known as pretty much of a roughneck around town. He served time in jail. But praise God, he has come to Christ. His heart's burdened; the Spirit's been whisperin' to him. Now, he wants to talk."

He plucked a piece of paper out of his pocket and quickly sketched a map, giving us directions north up Highway 23 to a location where Henry said he would be waiting for me.

"It's off 23, along Diamond Road, and then straight toward the banks of the Mississippi until you see a sign for an old cemetery."

"We're meeting in a graveyard?" Heather blurted out.

"Not really," he said. "But it used to be. Back in the 1940s there was a major flooding of the river, and when the water subsided, they decided to dig up all the graves and move them farther inland. Folks call it Dead Point."

I asked, "Why are we meeting there?"

"An expression of remorse on his part, I truly believe."

I thanked him. He pledged to "pray us all the way to Dead Point." His last words were "Be careful. Be safe. These are dangerous times. So you be of good courage, Mr. Black." Then addressing Heather, he said, "And you too, young miss."

It was a short drive from Port Sulphur north along the river and just past Fosters Canal, where we turned off 23 and onto Diamond Road and cruised slowly with the Mississippi on our right, bursting into view from time to time through the overgrowth. We drove until we spotted a dirt road cutting through a tangle of scrub brush. We could see, fifty feet away, there was a sign made of gray, warped metal that arched over the dirt road. At close view the lettering on the sign was legible, but only as a ghostly trace.

River Bend Cemetery.

There was a rusted gate made of metal tubes, like a farmer's gate, and it could have blocked us from entering. But not that day. The gate had been swung open.

After we bumped along the root-infested dirt path in our Mustang, the scrub brush disappeared and the river lay before us. A white utility truck was already parked there at the banks of the river. A man was leaning against the truck, smoking a cigarette.

I parked and turned to Heather. "Stay in the car. Let me do the talking. If I give you the signal, you can join us. But not before I signal you. Understood?"

She agreed, and I trotted up to Henry Bosant, a short man in his fifties with a tan, creased face and fingernails darkened with grease.

As we shook hands, I said, "I understand you have something to tell me."

Henry took one more drag, then tossed the cigarette down and crushed it. "Gotta kick that ol' habit now," he said. "My body's the temple of the Holy Spirit. Goin' to quit. But not today. Too much on my mind . . ."

I invited him to tell his story any way he wanted.

He didn't have a problem telling it. To me, even though I was neither a policeman nor a priest, it felt as if I was hearing his confession. And it became clear, almost immediately, why he had picked that particular spot to tell it.

"You know, Mr. Black, why they call this place Dead Point?"

I explained the little history I knew about it.

"Well," he continued, "this was the very spot where I knew it for sure. How I knew my soul was stone-cold dead inside. And all them others? Well, they was dead too. They just didn't know it."

35

Henry Bosant had two qualities that made him the right man for the wrong kind of job. He was a man with a criminal record, and he was a boatman who had a knowledge of the river.

Henry told me that it had started simply enough, with a call from a small shipping outfit he had never heard of. Something with a Russian-sounding name. Their boats would depart from the New Orleans area, pass by Port Sulphur, and eventually reach the end of the Mississippi where it met the Gulf. When the boats reached Port Sulphur, they wanted him to act as a "tender," motoring food, supplies, and fuel to their boat while it was in the middle of the river, about once a month. Always at night and in the dark. The money was pretty darn good. Two thousand a pop, plus supplies. It didn't make a lot of sense, Bosant said. He asked why they didn't simply dock at one of the ports along the way so he could shuttle supplies to them there much easier. Their explanation, Bosant said, was "to save time." Of course, there was another explanation, one that came too late.

"The first time," he said, "it went off real smooth. I'd anchored my tender boat just off Dead Point, right here, and waited for a signal."

Then his voice dropped. "But the second time, that was about all I could take, 'cuz of what happen'd. I motored out to their ship, hung on to the net ladder, while them sailors, they'd scamper down the ladder and fetch the food and the big containers of fuel for their onboard generator. And then I hear it. Sounded like a young girl screamin'. I looked up and I saw her."

"Who did you see?"

"Young'un. About ten or eleven. Hangin' over the railing. Like she was gonna jump. But she was acting all strange. Like she was doped up. Drugs maybe."

"What happened?"

"One of them sailors slapped her good, and then I hear a couple of other young girls screamin'. All of a sudden, it got quiet."

The picture Henry Bosant was painting was so troubling and so evil that I understood his desire to rid himself of the guilt. The vilest kind of human trafficking.

Bosant said he tried to get out of his monthly rendezvous after that, making excuses why he couldn't continue the deal. But his contact told him that wouldn't be allowed. Bad things would happen, he was told, if he failed to cooperate. Then, in a twisted turn of events, his contact said he needed Bosant to access an Internet site. He was given a code and a password which would be good for only one day, and then it would be changed, but he was to sign in and "take the required online lesson." He was warned that if he failed to log in to the site, they would know it.

Henry Bosant did what he was told. "I hadn't been able to sleep a single night since then," he said. "Not till I got right with Jesus."

It was, he told me, a private Internet site with a Russian name, made up of three words, but he couldn't recall the specifics, though he thought the word *video* was in there somewhere.

Once he downloaded the file, he was to click the Play arrow. That was when, sitting alone, he watched in horror as on the screen a young girl was repeatedly raped and beaten by men wearing masks. "I don't know how she could be alive after all of that," he said in a low moaning voice. "Dear God, please forgive me for tendering supplies to their boats. Taking their money . . ."

It was clear, the video "lesson" the Russian shippers wanted him to learn. That if they were willing to inflict that kind of hellish brutality on an innocent girl, how much more they would be willing to do to him if he turned on them. Even more diabolical, once he downloaded and watched the video, he would be guilty of a crime himself and therefore afraid to go to the authorities. Double indemnity to keep him quiet.

In Bosant's eyes, red and watery as he told the story, I saw a man in grief who was still learning that the price paid for his redemption came without loopholes. But one thing he would have clearly understood: the depth of evil that had conspired to ravage the human race. Henry Bosant knew it well because he had been rescued out of it.

I patted Henry on the shoulder. "Grace and forgiveness," I said, "swim down deeper than the hell you were swimming in. They rescue drowning people like you. And like me."

I expected it to end there. His epiphany of confession. Finally saying the words to a stranger. Expressing his repentance and remorse, and that would be the end of it.

But I was wrong.

"There's more," he said. "Another ship is comin'. Two nights from tonight. It'll be filled with young girls again."

"Past Port Sulphur? Through Port Eads?" I asked. "And into the Gulf?"

He said that's exactly what would happen.

There it was, the passageway for kidnapped kids: taken from the greater New Orleans area, down the Mississippi, past Port Sulphur, and out to international waters.

Then off to how many other countries? How many dirty dungeons? How many more videos, tortures, and deaths?

I asked, "They still expect you to arrive with supplies?"

"Sure they do. But I ain't comin'. Only, I've been worryin' about my landline phone makin' odd sounds. Maybe it's bugged."

I couldn't give him legal advice. That privilege had been stripped from me years before. But I could ask him a question. "Have you considered talking to the authorities?"

"Yes. But I know they could prosecute me. Then I think to myself—Henry, you're saved by the blood of the Savior. What can they really do to you?"

I had no desire to see Henry behind bars. Besides, burning inside me like a furnace was something else: the passion to stop these evildoers in their tracks. They might even be the same beasts who had snatched Peggy Tanner. And so many others.

I looked back at the Mustang and saw Heather with her arms crossed on the dashboard, waiting with an exasperated expression. I was glad she hadn't heard all the details. Yes, she was a woman, not a little girl, and I would have to tell her in my own way. But the thought of that—describing to her the true depth of evil out there in the world—it'd be like sharing a curse.

In fact, it was a curse. Welcome to the world. Still, a curse that could be lifted, the stain removed forever. As far as the east is from the west. I knew how deep my redemption was. Now it was time to find out how deep my faith was.

I had an idea. I told Henry Bosant that I wanted to talk to Deputy Ben St. Martin, that I trusted him, and that I wouldn't use Henry's name but would alert the deputy to the facts as Bosant had shared them with me. We needed to interdict the next ship that would be waiting out there on the Mississippi, expecting another tender boat delivery from Henry Bosant.

36

On the ride back to Port Sulphur I explained to Heather the gist of what Henry Bosant had told me, but not all of it. Not the hideous abuse of the young girls.

Heather wouldn't let it rest. "First you had me sit in the car like a child. Apparently I'm good enough to do research on your iPad, but you don't think I'm old enough to hear everything that guy told you, whoever he is."

"Henry Bosant. That's his name."

"Whatever. You need another voice in your head besides your own."

"Because . . ."

"You said it yourself: this guy's got a criminal record. His credibility is questionable. How do you know he's telling the truth? And if he is, maybe that's even worse. Maybe he's actually deep into this repulsive video porn site, and he's just using you."

"Or maybe," I said, "his life was transformed. Like mine was. Experiencing the personal revolution that takes place, from the inside out, when you do honest business with Jesus. I'm convinced that Henry Bosant went through that. Otherwise, what's his motive for exposing himself? The law calls that a declaration against interest, by the way. It ranks high on the credibility scale."

Upon reaching Port Sulphur, I drove straight to the sheriff's department. I had called ahead and told Deputy St. Martin that we were coming in and had some information that required immediate attention. He sounded distracted and didn't respond except to say, "I will be waiting for you. See you soon."

When we arrived, I invited Heather to join me, but she refused at first. "I suppose this is just your makeup to me for being an absolutely controlling jerk lately?"

I struggled not to smile. "Fine, let's say that's it."

She stared me down.

I added, "Just remember, this is the officer who thought you were being overly aggressive. Despite that, I want you next to me. That should tell you something. About how much I trust you. But there's a flip side too. My job to *protect* you."

That broke the ice. She said, "Did you ever think that, you know, maybe you've got things turned around?"

I asked what she meant.

"Look at the facts. Your obsession with demons that you think are after you—that got you disbarred. You gave a speech to the ABA that almost caused a riot. And an assistant attorney general was murdered in your hotel room. Maybe I'm the one who ought to be protecting you."

I gave her a big, fatherly grin.

She swung open the passenger door and said, "Let's get this party started."

We trotted into the lobby. A female dispatch officer was at the desk and said, "They're waiting for you, Mr. Black."

I hadn't asked for a group meeting. That should have been my first hint that things were about to get very strange.

The dispatcher led us to a room and opened the door. Heather was right behind me.

Inside, Deputy Ben St. Martin was standing against the far wall, harboring a disturbed look. A middle-aged man in uniform with an all-business expression stepped up to me, identified himself as Sheriff Clay Haywood, and asked if I was Trevor Black.

I gave him the expected response and asked what this was about. Then I noticed the two audience members for this tragicomedy of errors, also standing against the wall. One was Special Agent Fainlock, the FBI agent who had interrogated me about Assistant AG Paul Pullmen being executed in my hotel room. The other was one of the New Orleans police officers who had eaten at Bud's, the diner I entered trailing puddles of water from my shoes after my limo plunge into the Mississippi.

The FBI agent, his arms crossed, asked me, "Find any demons in Louisiana, Mr. Black? I know you've been looking."

Unfortunately I took the bait and swallowed the hook as well as the sinker. "They're everywhere," I said. "You just have to know where to look."

I was ready to launch into the news about the upcoming rendezvous with the Russian ship at Dead Point and the complicity of the crew in child abduction, horrendous abuse, and violation of federal obscenity laws. But I never had the chance.

"I'm afraid, Mr. Black," the sheriff announced, "that we have no alternative but to take you into protective custody under Louisiana Revised Statutes section 28, paragraph 53."

"I practiced law in New York," I shot back. "Not Louisiana. So, humor me . . ."

"It's the statute," Deputy St. Martin blurted out with a pained expression, "that permits a peace officer to place you in temporary involuntary mental commitment for purposes of psychiatric evaluation."

"We are advised," the sheriff said, clearly not taking any pleasure in what he was about to say, "that there are reasonable grounds to believe you suffer from a grave mental condition requiring treatment and that you are a danger to others."

The sheriff put zip-tie cuffs on my wrists and said, "I'm sorry. You'll have to come with us."

"There's a hellish criminal enterprise that has to be stopped in the next forty-eight hours!" I yelled. In retrospect, I suppose that sounded ludicrous and just fortified their skewed assumptions about me, but I didn't care. It was the truth.

Heather cried out frantically, "Where are you guys taking him?"

"Morehaven Psychiatric Hospital," the FBI agent replied. "For observation, treatment, and medication."

"We'll see about that," I shouted back and told Heather to grab my car keys from my right side pocket, which she quickly did. I whispered, "Follow me to this hospital; I need to talk to you. And bring a pad of paper and a pen." Then I added, "Looks like you'll be protecting me after all. . . ."

They loaded me into the back of a squad car and we began the two-hour journey to Morehaven. I turned around several times, each time spotting Heather driving the Mustang, hugging the road right behind us. Somehow I always expected this. Convinced that the worlds of law and law enforcement would not long endure a disbarred ex–criminal defense lawyer who believed in real demons and then acted on that belief.

But in the quiet of that squad, my wrists uncomfortably bound, I was formulating a backup plan in my head. It was a long shot. I didn't want it to come to that. But if it did, Heather's help would be crucial. And it had to be quick.

37

I was escorted up the front sidewalk of Morehaven by the sheriff and another deputy. They walked me along the pavement to the four-story redbrick hospital that sported four tall pillars in the front, antebellum style. By the looks of its sagging porch and peeling paint, it could have been used back in the Civil War.

Before turning me over to the guys in white coats, Sheriff Haywood said with a shake of his head, "You understand this is out of my hands."

I didn't fully understand his comment at the time. But I didn't forget it.

After admitting me, they shuttled me through the large day-room, a sad place filled with milling and fidgeting souls, many of whom were talking to no one in particular. Finally I was placed in a locked room where my zip-tie cuffs were removed.

I was told that Dr. Alex Schlosser, a psychiatrist, would be interviewing me. I took some pleasure in that thought. My former criminal defense practice in New York had me in contact with a parade of some of the nation's top mental health experts. Surely I could convince him of my mental stability and my orientation to reality. But it needed to be fast, so after my release I could speed back to Port Sulphur and explain to Deputy Ben St. Martin the story about the modern-day slave ship that would be cruising down the Mississippi River. What's more, St. Martin would be the perfect guy. The river was his jurisdiction.

Minutes ticked by. Every hour of delay increased the chances that a manifest of human cargo locked in the hold of some ship and trafficked by some shadowy voodoo fraternity would slip past the Louisiana authorities and glide into the Gulf, bound for parts unknown.

When the door opened, the psychiatrist, a man about my age and dressed smartly in a suit and tie, entered with a clipboard in his hand. He was undoubtedly carrying the routine questionnaire, the psychiatric inventory. All the typical questions. Did I know what day it was? Did I know where I was? Did I know why I had been hospitalized? Followed by the clinical determination—privately, of course—whether I was oriented in terms of time and place. Was my manner appropriate to the setting? Any flights of fancy? Evidence of auditory or visual hallucinations?

I thought I was ready.

It started simply enough. Dr. Schlosser sat down across from me, crossed his legs, and took the time to straighten his pant leg before he began. I had guessed right. The standard psychiatric inventory questions. I answered each of them calmly. His face showed no emotion.

Then questions about my criminal defense practice in New York. And the decision of the legal ethics committee to revoke my law license.

"You were given a chance to save your license?"

"Yes."

"You were only required to cooperate with psychiatric examination and treatment; is that correct?"

"Yes."

"But you refused?"

"Correct."

"Why was that?"

"I wasn't suffering from a mental disease. I didn't need treatment."

"Oh?" he said calmly. "Explain that."

"The problem was twofold: First, I believed in the existence of demons. More to the point, it was my considered judgment that a client of mine, someone charged with a very disturbing homicide, was occupied by demonic forces. Therefore, I didn't believe I could effectively represent him, so I asked the judge to allow me to withdraw from the case."

"And the second thing?"

"A former client of mine got my late wife hooked on cocaine, which ultimately led to her death. So when I ran into that same man in a courthouse elevator one day, I took the opportunity to punch him in the face and break his nose. To put it all into context, at that point in my life, things were going downhill."

Dr. Schlosser seemed particularly interested in that last part, about my life unraveling.

"Do you see these demons—visually, I mean?"

"Occasionally."

"What do they look like?"

"Very hard to describe to the uninitiated."

"Uninitiated?"

"Spiritually, I mean. God gives his Spirit to those who put their trust in Christ. And spiritual abilities accompany that. This is orthodox theology, by the way. Followed by Christians for two thousand years. You can find it in the Bible. Anyhow, that's the only way I can remotely explain my particular spiritual gifting."

"Do you feel a calling to destroy—to kill—these demonic forces?"

"Not really. Just to stop them."

"But if the only way to stop them is to kill them, would you?"

"I hesitate to answer hypothetical questions. I need more facts."

"Do you believe God commands you to oppose demons?"

"Of course."

"What if God commanded you to kill someone? Would you feel compelled?"

"Your question is posed in a vacuum, which makes it difficult to answer. All I can say is that God doesn't contradict himself. He reveals himself in his Word, the Bible, which God orchestrated to record what he wanted to record. Historical events. Places. People. And yes, also miracles and theophanies . . . like those involving his Son, Jesus Christ."

"I don't believe you answered my question. . . ."

"Let me try it this way. The Bible lays out moral principles. And from those, I glean three situations where God might— I emphasize *might*—command a person to kill. First, in self-defense. Second, in good-faith defense of another. Third, in obedience to established government order in defense of itself. Which I guess goes to the issue of the theory of a just war. But that's a whole other subject. Does that answer your question?"

"For a trial lawyer, you seem to be well-versed on subjects outside of the law. Why is that?"

"When I had my faith encounter with God and trusted that Jesus Christ was and is who he said he was and that he came as a suffering servant who was a sacrifice for all the rotten things I was guilty of, that sort of lit my mind on fire. Before that, my focus had been narrow. Basically three things. To hone my legal craft. To crush my opponents. And to make a lot of money. But after faith was born in me, it was different. I wanted to understand everything, because once you understand that God is, you suddenly know that everything has meaning. Absent that, everything is meaningless. I suppose you can try to invent your own meaning and value for things. But in the end, it doesn't hold up."

Dr. Schlosser had stopped writing in his notebook. He looked me in the eye and said, "And this is what you believe? God is everything? Without God, everything is nothing. Yes?"

Hadn't I just said that? I wondered. I nodded.

Then he made his move. Pawn takes knight. "So you harbor a view of the world that necessarily requires the existence of demons and evil forces. God is good, and therefore everything else must be evil, and therefore you must fight such forces to the death. Wouldn't you agree?"

At that moment I had the sense, coming over me like a neurological shiver, that there was something foreboding about this mild-mannered psychiatrist. Among the dozens of mental health professionals I'd encountered during my years as a trial lawyer, most of them were honest, dedicated professionals, and some of them even brilliant. But just then, at Morehaven, sitting in the room with Schlosser, I was convinced of one thing. This psychiatrist was being influenced by an outside force. And his dark influencer from the underworld had a temporary visa to menace us.

38

I asked the psychiatrist a question of my own. "What do you believe, Dr. Schlosser?"

Which prompted the expected response. "I'm not here to talk about myself."

"But you should."

"Why is that?"

"Pure objectivity is impossible," I said. "Psychiatrists like you, if you're honest, try to identify your natural biases so they don't affect your clinical judgment. True?"

"Is objectivity important to you?"

Oh no, I wasn't going to let him off the hook that easy.

"Let's stop playing philosophical games," I said. "Do you think I'm dangerous and therefore should be confined in a mental hospital against my will because of my spiritual beliefs about demons?"

"Those who feel they are doing God's work can sometimes be dangerous, yes."

I deserved an answer. "Am I dangerous? Yes or no?"

"That is what I am trying to find out."

"What about doing God's work, stopping human slavery of young girls? Opposing an evil cult? Are those things dangerous?"

Dr. Schlosser's eyes widened ever so slightly. "That's a very interesting concern you have."

"It ought to be everyone's concern; don't you agree?"

"I avoid generalizations."

I dug in deeper. "Dr. Schlosser, do you believe that when an occult group is engaged in the enterprise of abducting young girls and women and placing them into sexual slavery— videotaping them by coercion or outright force and sometimes even murdering them—such conduct is an evil that should be exposed and stopped at all costs?"

"The way you put it tells me you are very concerned."

"Of course I am. I have objective evidence that it is going on, and if it weren't for this commitment proceeding, I would be out there trying to stop it. So tell me, do you think my opinions on that subject make me dangerous?"

"It's your mental status that I am trying to explore."

"Oh, so then you think it's okay for human monsters who are part of a voodoo cult to kidnap girls, drug them, and sexually abuse them on camera?"

He smirked. "You oversimplify."

"How?"

I had the intangible but irresistible feeling that I had just touched something deep inside of Dr. Schlosser.

He said, "There is something to be said about men who are able to achieve a higher level of living, beyond the conventional categories of good and evil."

"The Übermensch," I said.

"So you are familiar with Nietzsche. The ideal of the superman. The Nazis took his ideas to an extreme, you know. Distorted them. And sadly, the Third Reich became Hollywood's favorite villain. Which of course defamed Nietzsche's genius along with it."

I looked into Dr. Schlosser's eyes. A light was missing. I said, "Do you know something about these girls?"

He smiled. "No. Not really. But what if I were to tell you that I know someone who you have already met. Someone very powerful. Someone involved in this criminal business you speak of. Would you like to know who that is?"

At that precise moment, something happened. I was suddenly aware that a tall figure had entered that locked room with us. How, I didn't know, and it was only for a few seconds, yet long enough for me to recognize him. The figure was standing behind Dr. Schlosser, with his hands on the doctor's shoulders.

It was the chauffeur from hell. The sinister figure I had seen out on the ocean and in the alley in New Orleans with the savage twins and then again standing on the water at Bayou Bon Coeur calling to me.

Though not possessing this psychiatrist, the figure was there for a reason. Skewing his judgment. Moving him on the chessboard. Did Dr. Schlosser understand he was just a pawn in this game? Almost certainly not. Blind to his captivity.

Sure, Schlosser must have told himself that he was exercising his professional judgment, shaped by years of training. But all the while, starting from a purely naturalistic premise, hedged in by unyielding presuppositions. And resistant, in the most extreme die-is-cast kind of way, to any evidence to the contrary.

The demonic monster was there behind the therapist for only an instant, and then he vanished.

I whispered a prayer. But it must have been audible because Dr. Schlosser acknowledged it. He said, "You've just had another one, haven't you? One of your private visions? And you believe they are real. They must seem, to you, so very real. . . ."

No response was necessary. Or wise. I kept silent.

"Prayers can make you feel better," he said. "But they don't change reality. I am going to recommend strong antipsychotic medication. And possibly ECT. That's how we can change you, Mr. Black, in a healthy way. You do want to get better, don't you?"

I knew about ECT—electroconvulsive therapy. Electric current sent through the brain, sometimes triggering seizures. Helpful to some psychotic persons and others with certain forms of mental illness. But with side effects: possible loss of brain function and memory.

"I'm done with this, Doctor. This is a battle between light and darkness. I'm sorry you've picked the losing side."

He studied me with a calmness that was unnerving. "You're a smart man. What if I could prove certain things to you?"

I followed his lead, having no real choice. "Prove what things?"

Schlosser settled back in his seat. "That the most important beliefs in your life, the things you hold most dear, are fundamentally untrue." As he said that, he was drumming the fingers of one hand on the leather folder he had laid on the table.

"Have at it," I told the psychiatrist.

So he did. "A few minutes ago, I told you that I knew someone you were familiar with. Someone powerful."

I nodded.

"And when I said that," he continued, "you visualized him. Standing right here in this room. For only a moment. But seemingly very real, nonetheless."

My expression must have given me away. He said, "That figure must have been a very menacing one for you. Very threatening. Do you deny that?"

I couldn't. But I wasn't going to give him the pleasure of admitting it.

"So," he went on in a soothing tone, "that caused you to seek self-comfort and reassurance by praying to God."

By then, even though disturbed by the degree of Schlosser's perception, I couldn't soften. I stared him down and waited for more.

"That figure, whoever it was, seemed very real to you. Until your cerebral cortex kicked in and corrected your emotional response with logic, causing you to abandon the image you had concocted."

"My imagination? You're actually going down that route?"

He smiled. "I have just used the power of suggestion on you, Mr. Black. Stage magicians and charlatans have used it for ages.

It can be very effective. Especially when it is used on someone under a high level of stress."

"Oh, and you're saying that's me?"

"The death of a spouse. The end of your successful career. Personal and professional humiliation. Followed by a series of violent encounters that suggest to me you may be dealing with post-traumatic stress disorder. According to the Holmes and Rahe scale of stress—the SRRS—you have had some of the top stresses a human can experience."

"You told me that you'd prove I was under the influence of lies. So far, I've heard only your psychological theories."

"To be precise," he countered, "Holmes and Rahe were not psychologists. They were psychiatrists. Medical doctors specializing in the psyche like me. Psychologists, on the other hand—"

Classic put-down. Queen takes bishop.

"I know the difference," I shot back. It was time for the banter to end. "Proof, Doctor. You said you had proof."

He smiled and unzipped his thin leather case. "Up to now we've been going into some of your more abstract ideas and beliefs," he said. "God. Demons. Good. Evil. And the reason why you believe the way that you do. The things that motivate you to imagine that supernatural beings appear to you but to no one else. Have you ever wondered why that is? Why they make themselves visible only to you?"

I sat in silence.

"I know that in your criminal practice you represented clients who suffered from psychosis. Visual hallucinations. Professing to see and hear things that neither you nor anyone else could see or hear. Only them. That has a name, Mr. Black. It is called mental illness."

Dr. Schlosser was slipping some papers out of his black leather case as he spoke. "These images you see, they provoke you to joust with them. I know you are familiar with Miguel de Cervantes. You must be."

I could see where he was going. "Sure. *Don Quixote*, Man of La Mancha."

"The full title of Cervantes's work was *The Ingenious Gentleman Don Quixote of La Mancha*. Or in the original Spanish, *El ingenioso hidalgo don Quixote de la Mancha*."

More one-upsmanship.

"Fascinating," I said. "And I suppose that I would be Don Quixote, imagining windmills to be my mortal enemies, attacking me. Forcing me to fight back. But all the time, just windmills."

"You are getting close," he said. "Good for you."

By then he was holding the papers and waving them in front of me. "You believe in objectivity. Yes?"

I nodded.

"You have a daughter?"

I nodded again, slower.

"Her name is Heather?"

I wondered where he was going with this, but it didn't sound good. I didn't respond.

"Please," he said. "Humor me. You have a daughter named Heather?"

"Okay, yes, I do."

With that, he shook his head. "No, Mr. Black. In fact, you don't."

He handed me the papers. I scanned them quickly. I had been a criminal defense lawyer, not an adoption lawyer, so those kinds of papers weren't usually in my area of practice, but I recognized soon enough what they were. Family court documents from a case in Virginia. Termination of parental rights, pending the adoption of the single mother's infant girl. The papers read:

Mother: Marilyn Parlow

Marilyn, my high school crush, my sometimes girlfriend, with whom I had that ill-fated, one-night intimate encounter in college.

My eyes scanned the form.

Female Baby: Heather

I read farther down the paper.

Name of putative father . . .

I expected it to be blank. I had heard, some twenty-odd years later, from my friend Detective Ashley Linderman, that Marilyn lied and told the paternity court she didn't know who the father was, all the time hiding the birth from me, telling me she was having an abortion.

I read that column in the court papers again. Then, as a numbing sense of shock engulfed me, I had to keep reading the next six words on the court document over and over.

Name of putative father: David Fleming

The world was tilting. Gravity was giving way.

David Fleming. Captain of the high school varsity swim team at the same time that Marilyn was the captain of the girls' swim team. I had heard somewhere that he entered Virginia Military Institute after high school. Not far from where Marilyn was going to college.

I repeated a part of that in my head, this time connecting it to the heartbreaking end game. *Not far from Sweet Briar, where Marilyn was attending college at the time she became pregnant.*

Dr. Schlosser had a look on his face that was almost compassionate when he said, "Mr. Black, this is what the truth looks like. I'm sorry."

39

Stumbling through an unlit alley. All the while, being punched and kicked by the world, the flesh, and the devil.

That was my feeling at that moment. Despite my onetime encounter with Marilyn and all my assumptions about her pregnancy resulting from that, I had been shown in black and white that Marilyn had been pregnant by another man. Heather was another man's daughter.

But equally stunning, Ashley Linderman, who had access to the juvenile court records through her law enforcement work, had lied to me. She must have known. Yet she told me, after researching it for me, that Heather was my daughter. Ashley, who had become a close friend and confidante during that case in Wisconsin. Ashley, the woman with whom I had found myself falling in love, until our time together on the island when we both finally agreed to call it off. Why had she hidden the truth from me?

And then there was Marilyn. She was gone, of course. Cervical cancer. But when she had called me so many years ago as I sat in my college dorm room and told me that she was carrying my child, did she know she was lying? And if she did, why had she played such a twisted game of deception?

I needed to make a call to Ashley Linderman. I was crazy with grief and anger. I needed to hear it from her own mouth.

After that, I would have a second conversation. An even harder one. This one with Heather. But after everything we had been through, and all the years apart, then my stumbling attempts lately to earn her trust and make things right . . . what would I tell her now?

Once the interview with Dr. Schlosser was over, I was led into the dayroom with the other patients. A television was blaring on the wall, but no one was watching. I strained to keep a handle on things as I walked slowly around the perimeter of the room. Trying to focus. I had become, to the idle observer, just one more patient, as I stared at the floor sorting things out in my mind, trying to avoid all the ghosts that had been summoned to plague me. All the doubts.

I had a plan, didn't I? Yes. I remembered it. I tried to tell myself that I might be down but I wasn't out. I needed Heather's help to execute the scheme. But how could I bring her into my plan without telling her what I now knew?

I forced myself to organize. Emergency triage. First things

first. There would always be time later to get into the painful details with her about David Fleming, her real father.

I strolled up to Nurse Aldrich, the managing nurse who carried herself as stiff as the white starched uniform she was wearing. "I'd like to make a call out. Actually, two."

"I'm sorry, Mr. Black," she said. "Calls out are not permitted for you right now."

"I know my rights. This is a legal matter."

"Are you calling a lawyer?"

"Not exactly. But my calls are connected to my legal defense."

"I don't think it's possible."

"Who's the director here?"

"Dr. Manfred Touley."

"I'd like to speak to him."

"He's not here today."

"Who has the authority to give me telephone privileges?"

"Dr. Schlosser, whom you met. Unless he's already left. He sees other patients at several other hospitals."

"Can you check? This is urgent."

Nurse Aldrich disappeared into her office.

I dropped into one of the chairs in front of the television set. It was a program about genealogy. Finding your genetic and familial roots. Given the recent turn of events, I would have preferred anything but that. I looked around, foolishly, for a remote control. Of course it wasn't there. Probably controlled exclusively by Nurse Aldrich. Yes, I had seen *One Flew over the Cuckoo's Nest*. I thought I knew how things went down.

An hour later, I noticed Nurse Aldrich stroll back into the dayroom, where she resumed her position at the far end. Before too long, Dr. Schlosser joined her and they talked together briefly before Schlosser disappeared.

Nurse Aldrich motioned for me.

"Mr. Black. You are being given an exceptional privilege. You may make one phone call. Five minutes in length. You can use the hall phone. I will put the code in and then hand the phone to you. If you abuse the privilege, there will be consequences."

I called my own cell number, hoping that Heather would pick up. She did.

"Where are you?" I asked.

"I tried to see you but they wouldn't let me. I'm coming tonight during visiting hours."

"When you do, bring some pens and a legal pad. Do you have a tape recorder?"

"Wow, that's really old-school, Trevor. I have your smartphone—it has audio-recording capacity, remember?"

I asked her to do something else. To call Detective Ashley Linderman and have her call me at the hospital. "It's important that you tell her," I said as I practically choked on the words, "that I have been involuntarily committed for observation. I'm a patient here. So it may be tough for her to get through. But she's pushy. I'm counting on that."

There was a time when Ashley and I would have laughed at that last part. But not now.

Dinner for me that night was in the dining hall, where one unfortunate soul had an explosive episode and had to be restrained and taken away. I shared a table with a short, white-haired gentleman who described himself as "Saint Sebastian." He warned me that if I crossed him he would pump me full of arrows, just like they used to kill him under Emperor Diocletian. Either he was a time traveler or he was suffering from psychosis. I was betting on the latter.

I told him that I wouldn't think of crossing him, but I asked if I could pray for him. He shrugged and said, "You may, my son."

After we bowed heads and I asked God to help him achieve clarity and peace of mind as well as peace in his heart, he looked up, said, "Well done, my son," and then quickly consumed a mouthful of mashed potatoes. Returning to his previous conversation, he added, "You notice I refer to being shot with arrows. Of course, that was the technique—arrows from my crossbow—that I also used on that rotten neighbor of mine."

When Heather arrived, visitation hours gave us a little less than an hour, so I had to talk fast.

But before I could speak, Heather leaned in and asked in a low voice, "How are you?"

I quickly passed it off, ready to dive in. But she wouldn't let it go. "No, really," she said, her voice trembling a little. I could see a glistening in her eyes. "How are you really doing in this place? It has to be so hard. . . ."

"Yes. Harder than I would have imagined."

She nodded.

"What's even harder is that if I don't get released immediately, it could change everything. My credibility to law enforcement. My mission. What I said publicly at the ABA. And most important, I won't be able to convince Deputy St. Martin, and perhaps even Sheriff Haywood, about a boat full of girls, taken captive by monsters, motoring right past them."

I gave her a confident smile even though my heart was

sinking under the weight of the family court document that Dr. Schlosser had shown me. Which in turn had raised a logistical question: Who had provided that court document about Heather's adoption to Schlosser? For that matter, who was the motivating force behind this mental commitment proceeding against me? Sheriff Haywood seemed genuinely apologetic when he told me, "This is out of my hands."

Heather interrupted my stream of consciousness when she asked, "What's the plan?"

"It's called *habeas corpus*," I said.

"Meaning what?"

"Latin for 'bring forth the body.' Forcing officials to produce an imprisoned person who is being kept illegally. An old English Common Law procedure. Today that right is protected by article 1, section 9, clause 2 of the US Constitution."

She shook her head. "I didn't go to law school. Break it down for me."

"Better than that. I'll dictate it."

I grabbed my cell phone and started laying it all down. Heather would have to type it up. After I hand-drafted a declaration on the legal pad and signed and dated it, I told her, "Attach this to the end of the petition for habeas corpus."

Then I quickly used the phone to do five minutes' worth of legal research. I found what I was looking for, jotted it down on another piece of paper, and stuffed it in my pocket.

"Now the tough part," I told her. "After you type this up, you need to get it to the clerk for the US district court in New Orleans and request an emergency hearing."

She looked overwhelmed.

As I handed my cell phone back to her, I added, "And the court hearing has to be tomorrow."

Before she left, I told her, "Heather, no matter what happens—no matter what comes of any of this, or even what might come between us—just know how proud I am of you. And what an extraordinary woman you are."

Her chin trembled a bit. We heard the night nurse call out that the visiting period was over. "You have to go," I said. "God bless you."

40

In the rush of my final instructions to Heather, I gave her my old federal court PACER number and described how to electronically file my petition for habeas corpus with the court. One good thing about electronic court filing: you don't have to wait until the courthouse opens up in the morning. Heather assured me she would get it done that evening. I was glad our hotel rooms in New Orleans were still good for a while. She had a bed to sleep in.

Heather was smart, so I knew she could handle the logistics: filling out the petition on my laptop, printing out copies of the legal document in the business office in the hotel, and e-mailing it to the US District Court for the Eastern District of Louisiana, with a copy e-mailed to Morehaven. She also had to serve a copy personally on the sheriff's department and on the hospital director the next morning, and then hopefully visit with me again to give me a status report.

The night nurse gave me a little paper cup containing what she said was an antianxiety pill and ordered me to take it. I refused. I was aware of the groggy side effects with some of them.

"I have to be in court tomorrow," I said. "Need to be sharp. At my best. Tell you what, if the court hearing doesn't go on, or if it does and they send me back here, then I'll take it as ordered. Promise. Cross my heart and hope to die."

She wasn't amused. She called the male aides and told them to force-feed me the pill. In response, I warned her that after two decades as a defense lawyer I knew a few things about making life miserable for people who violated other people's rights. I told her to call the director or even Dr. Schlosser to get authorization to give me a pass on the medication.

Eventually the issue went away. I wasn't sure why. But I thanked God for it. The last thing I needed at that moment was fuzzy-headed thinking.

I was wakened early the next morning, and the staff introduced me to the usual routine. Bed check, breakfast, and a meeting with a psychiatric nurse, this time going over medical insurance, more background information, how I was feeling, my sleep patterns, my sleep the night before, medical history, social relationships, work history.

But my mind was somewhere else. I was a captive. No outgoing contact or phone calls. Where was Heather?

I was placed in a small group therapy session. I knew I had to volunteer some limited insights about myself. A modicum of cooperation, and I complied, but without specifics. After all, those poor, confused souls shouldn't have to hear my stories about demons. I was pained to see the broken minds and ruined lives that were seated in the folding chairs in that circle. I remembered what the Bible says about the whole creation groaning as a result of humanity's collective break with God. Brokenness comes in many different forms.

Lunch came and went.

Then afternoon "free time" in the dayroom under the watchful eye of Nurse Aldrich. I leafed through some *National Geographic* magazines. Looked at the clock on the wall. Praying for some sign that Heather had been able to accomplish my plan with the court.

But all the time, hearing the voice of Dr. Alex Schlosser in the back of my head. About my susceptibility to suggestion due to my stressful situation. And about God. And demons. And Friedrich Nietzsche.

There were other thoughts. Mostly about Heather and how she might walk out of my life forever once she learned the facts about her biological father.

Then dinner. Still no Heather. Then visiting hours.

That was when Heather finally came in with the small stream of other family visitors and sat down next to me on a vinyl couch.

"It's filed," she said. "Your petition for habeas corpus."

"And?"

"Well," she began, "I know you wanted a hearing today. But it wasn't possible. I'm really sorry, Trevor."

Considering the dockets in most federal district courts,

I wasn't surprised. It was a long shot. I braced myself for the rest of the story. I asked Heather where we stood, knowing that, realistically, getting a federal judge to hear my petition on any short notice would be extraordinary. Getting it heard in time for me to help stop the next ship loaded with human cargo— that would take a miracle.

"There's more," Heather said. She took a dramatic pause.

I was glued to her next comment.

"As far as your petition is concerned, US District Judge Manning Levall will hear it in his courtroom tomorrow. Five o'clock in the afternoon. The last case of the day."

I scrambled to rethink my conversation with Henry Bosant. The day before he had told me that in a matter of days another ship would soon glide past Port Sulphur. He thought maybe forty-eight hours. Twenty-four hours had already passed. But he also said the ships motored at night, under cover of darkness. That meant sometime tomorrow evening.

The long gauntlet of obstacles before us was staggering. I calculated that the hearing would need to conclude with a ruling from the bench by 6 or 6:30 p.m. Judge Levall would have to grant the petition and order me released. That release would have to be effected immediately. No complications with my discharge from the hospital. No administrative snafus. With my credibility reinstated, I would connect with Deputy St. Martin and tell him what I had learned from Henry Bosant. And he would have to buy into it and then set up an immediate blockade on the Mississippi.

High hurdles. Olympic ones. Time for backup. We needed a plan B.

"Heather, we can't put all our eggs in one basket," I said. "You need to call Deputy St. Martin. Tell him what I've told you about the juvenile slave trade on the Mississippi, happening right under their noses. But don't mention Henry Bosant's name. And tell him that he has to get out there on the river and apprehend any suspicious vessels tomorrow evening."

"Me?" she responded. "You do mean me, right? The one Deputy St. Martin thought was too 'aggressive' during the meeting? Plus, how do I tell him I'm delivering a message for you—a resident of an insane asylum . . . ?" She caught herself. "Sorry. I didn't mean that last part."

"It isn't pretty," I said, "but it's true. At least true until the court hearing tomorrow and then, depending on the outcome, maybe longer than that."

Inside, I was wrestling with other things that were true, things I knew but Heather didn't. Assumed "facts" she believed, and I had too, but that I had just learned were lies. Things about us. I was still convinced that I needed to pick the right time to tell her, and this wasn't it. Not at a psych hospital. Not like this. But I couldn't put it off too much longer. It was crushing down on me.

Heather said she would reach out to Deputy St. Martin on my behalf, calling him the minute she left Morehaven.

After she left, I ran through the probabilities. Strictly analytical. And from that perspective, the outlook was dismal. Sheriff Haywood and Deputy St. Martin had already been served with their copy of my habeas corpus petition. Which suggested they had almost certainly consulted with the Plaquemines Parish attorney's office about the case and had been told not to talk.

Besides, even if they *hadn't* been served, once they saw me taken into custody, all communication with me would end—at least while my legal challenge was pending. Result: Heather was going to be shut out no matter what.

That meant we had only one chance. I needed to win our habeas proceeding the next day. About the same odds as hitting the jackpot at Harrah's casino in New Orleans.

41

The next day, two Morehaven staffers transported me to the US district court building located on Poydras Street in New Orleans. They hustled me up the elevator to the courtroom of Judge Manning Levall.

I should have been thinking just then about the finer points of my argument for release from a mental institution. But instead, I had an overpowering thought about courthouse architecture. It had to do with my own legal history.

The building that housed the United States District Court for the Eastern District of Louisiana had an aesthetic like so many in the federal system: bland, functional, exuding a heavy sense of authority but in an unimaginative office-building kind of way.

Local court buildings, on the other hand, often have an aged mystique—case in point, the New Orleans courthouse across town. That's where I had served as cocounsel years before for a wealthy New York client who had business interests in New Orleans. We defended his extortion case in the criminal courts for the Orleans Parish and won a verdict of acquittal. The local paper covered it and printed a splashy headline. Then a victory bash at a local eatery and drinks all around. In retrospect, fleeting glory. A vapor that appears for only a moment and then vanishes.

What a contrast. Now I was being escorted into Judge Levall's sterile federal courtroom under the custody of two security guards from a mental hospital. Still, I wouldn't have traded places, wouldn't have gone back to my old life—not for a billion dollars. I was part of a divine drama. That kind of life never gets dull. Tiresome, perhaps, and often daunting. But never dull.

I was seated at counsel's table, representing myself. I had declined the offer of public defender representation. Not the wise thing to do in almost all cases. But this was not the typical case.

The hospital director, Dr. Manfred Touley, was seated at the opposing counsel's table next to a parish attorney. In the gallery chairs directly behind him sat Dr. Alex Schlosser, and next to him, Port Sulphur's finest: Sheriff Haywood and Deputy St. Martin. Behind them, there was FBI Agent Fainlock as well as a New Orleans patrol officer who had spotted me in that late-night diner, along with my soaked clothing and dripping-wet shoes.

Then the customary parade into the courtroom. First, the court reporter, followed by the judge's law clerk and the court clerk.

As we waited for the judge, I thought about my early morning Scripture reading at the hospital. I had asked for, and been given, a Bible to read. I'd picked up where I left off in my reading. I had traveled out of Deuteronomy and by then had arrived at chapter 2 of Joshua. An interesting story about Rahab, the Jericho harlot who protected the Israelite spies from the enemy.

Rahab, the town harlot. A wonderfully unlikely hero.

Finally a black-robed Manning Levall strode in from his chambers and sat down at the bench. A handsome man in his late forties, with dark hair and the stiff air of a disciplined jurist, he struck me as a judge not prone to flights of imaginative jurisprudence. Which could be bad for me, considering my unorthodox and imaginative habeas corpus petition. But he also struck me as a judge who read the law, knew it, and would follow it wherever it led, come what may. Which could also be good for me.

The clerk called the case. My opponent, Nancy Cougin, appearing as attorney for the Parish of Plaquemines and for the Morehaven Psychiatric Hospital, rose and announced herself.

I stood and informed the judge that I would be representing myself.

Judge Levall looked over the glasses perched on his nose. "I understand you were at one time a successful criminal defense counsel in New York City. So you've heard, I'm sure, the old maxim. That a lawyer who represents himself has a fool for a client."

"In most cases," I said, "that would hold true. But with due respect, not in this one, Your Honor."

"That remains to be seen," he said curtly.

Then he got down to business. I acknowledged, in response to his pointed question to me, that I would bear the burden of proving that my apprehension under the mental health laws of Louisiana had been unlawful. If I failed, I would be immediately returned to Morehaven.

"Let's make this clear. This is not a full-blown mental commitment hearing," the judge stated. "That is for the State of Louisiana to conduct, not a federal court. This is a petition for habeas corpus alleging illegal apprehension and confinement of you, Mr. Trevor Black. It is for you to prove that. And frankly, you've got a high hill to climb."

He told me to call my first witness. I turned and glanced at the large clock on the wall. It was 5:17 p.m. I needed to hurry.

Then I noticed the one friendly face in the courtroom. Heather was seated a few rows back. She gave a restrained wave when our eyes met.

I called as my first witness the New Orleans beat cop who saw me in the diner. I needed to trim down my examination. Would the court accept, I asked, the fact that the officer was a hostile witness so I could question him through cross-examination rather than direct examination?

Opposing counsel jumped to her feet and objected. "Police officers by definition are not hostile, representing as they do the interests of the State of Louisiana."

The point I had made seemed simple enough, almost painfully obvious. No need for a Supreme Court argument on the matter. Judge Levall considered it and agreed with me. So I inserted the scalpel and began to cut—cross-examination-wise, that is.

Was he the officer who signed the apprehension order against me, I asked, seeking "protective custody" on the grounds that I was a danger to myself or to others by reason of mental illness?

Yes, he was.

"On what grounds?" I asked.

"I had reasonable grounds to believe that you were appropriate for commitment and evaluation, were gravely disabled by reason of mental illness, and were acting in a way that was dangerous to yourself or to others."

"I'm glad you've memorized Louisiana Revised Statute 28:53 L (1) before coming here today," I shot back. "But I was looking for facts, not legal conclusions."

Nancy Cougin was up again, yelling that my statement was argumentative.

Judge Levall sustained the objection. I apologized and moved on.

"According to you, was I a danger to myself?"

"Not really that," he said.

"Oh, then a danger to others?"

"Yes, that's it."

"How so?"

"You were implicated in the murder of a limousine driver. His body was found in the trunk of his limo, which you had stolen and driven into the Mississippi River. I would say that constitutes a danger."

Judge Levall's eyes widened at that.

Rather than object to his wildly speculative answer, I asked, "Did you ever, at any time, see me steal a limo? Any limo?"

"No."

"See me drive any limo into the Mississippi?"

"Not exactly."

"Ever me see me lift a hand against the limo driver?"

"I wasn't there when it happened."

"Then, Officer, you made absolutely no personal observation of any facts which would make me a danger to others, right?"

Opposing counsel was up again. "Your Honor, 'personal observation' would include also the inferences drawn from the observations of other credible people. For instance, the officer is entitled to rely on the observations of an FBI agent. . . ."

"Well," I shot back, "that was a badly mangled statement of the law. But we'll get to that later. Meanwhile, Your Honor, I can't tell whether Ms. Cougin is making an objection or suggesting to the witness how he ought to answer my next line of questions."

Ms. Cougin exploded over that one, even though I had caught her in one of the oldest trial tricks known to the legal profession.

Judge Levall quietly chastised me for insinuating that Ms. Cougin was trying to improperly influence the witness's testimony. But underneath the ruling, his unenthusiastic tone made me think that, down deep, he hadn't missed the opposing counsel's high jinks.

I returned to my question. "Did you have any observations of my being a danger—?"

"FBI Special Agent Fainlock," the witness cut in, utterly fulfilling my prediction, "is a credible witness, and he led me to believe that you were implicated in the murder of an assistant attorney general who had been found in your hotel room."

I could have objected to his hearsay answer, but it would have accomplished nothing. The FBI agent was in the courtroom, and the other side would probably call him anyway and elicit the same facts directly from him.

The only thing left was to plant my flag and salute it. "But,"

I asked, "none of that information from the FBI agent was from your own *personal knowledge*, was it?"

"Of course it wasn't."

"Any other reason for taking me into custody?"

"Yes. You were in a diner where I was having supper with my patrol partner. It was the same day that the limo was retrieved from the Mississippi and the dead limo driver was found in the trunk. And I noticed that you were sopping wet. Drenched."

The judge gave the officer a wide-eyed look of disbelief.

Perhaps noticing His Honor's reaction, the officer gave a boost to his answer. "In fact, you even paid the waitress a tip with sopping-wet money. And it hadn't rained that day. The weather was clear as a bell. And the diner where you ate was walking distance from the river where we found the limo."

"So you are assuming I had been in the limo, right?"

"Not just in it. Driving it. After you killed the driver and put him in the trunk."

More creative speculation, but I ignored that and asked, "But none of that was *personally observed* by you, right?"

"No. But it seems logical."

"Okay, let's take a look at it *logically*. Were you present when the limo was dragged out of the river?"

"Sure was."

"Was the driver's-side door open or closed?"

"Uh . . . closed."

"Was it locked?"

"No, unlocked."

"How about the rear doors?"

"Well, they were locked."

"Driver's window open or closed?"

"Closed."

"How about the window in the backseat?"

"Uh, it was open."

"Open or actually *smashed out*?"

"The glass was broken, yes."

"Was there a glass separation panel between the driver's compartment and the passenger compartment that was shut?"

"Let me see . . . Yes, I guess there was."

"So let's concede for a moment that I was in that limo. Still, wouldn't you agree it's more logical to believe that I was just a backseat passenger and I was *not the driver*, and that I escaped through the busted window after the driver, who was the real killer, dumped the limo into the river?"

"I'm not sure. Maybe."

There's an old saying in trial practice. If you get a good answer from a witness, don't gild the lily by trying to improve on it. I quit while I was ahead.

Then I looked at Levall. A judge who I thought couldn't be judged by his face. Except that right then, he looked unimpressed by the case I was putting on.

Cougin decided not to question the officer. I must have inflicted some cuts, and she wasn't sure how she would patch it up. "I reserve the right to recall the officer for examination during my case," my opponent announced, but I was willing to bet Morgan Canterelle's next dinner tab at Arnaud's that she never would.

42

I rested my case. To win my freedom, I had to prove only one point—that my apprehension by a police officer under the mental health law was illegal because it wasn't based on *his personal observation*. I thought I had shown it. But I wasn't sure.

Attorney Cougin was smug when she argued for my petition to be dismissed. She seemed buoyed by Judge Levall's apparent disinterest in my examination of the New Orleans officer.

"Mr. Black is wasting the time of this federal court," the hospital's attorney argued. "What is a mental commitment case doing here? It belongs down the street, in the Orleans Parish court." Gaining steam, she not only argued that my case be kicked out; she also demanded that the judge assess attorney's fees against me as a penalty for bringing "a frivolous, ridiculous case."

Judge Levall nodded to me for a response.

I made it short and sweet. "Your Honor, habeas corpus has been held to be a perfectly legitimate approach to object to an illegal violation of the mental health commitment laws. I suggest the court read the opinion in *Jackson v. Foti*, a 1982 decision of the US Court of Appeals for the Fifth Circuit, right here in New Orleans."

The judge didn't waste time. "I'm familiar with the opinion in *Jackson*," he said. He turned to Attorney Cougin. "Your motion to dismiss is denied. It's your case now, Ms. Cougin."

I glanced up at the clock. It was ten minutes after six. When would the sun go down and darkness fall? When would that ship glide past Port Sulphur? When would it be too late for the human traffic on board to be rescued?

Cougin called Special Agent Fainlock as her first witness. He described in great detail how he had interrogated me regarding the death of Assistant Attorney General Paul Pullmen, pointing out with exuberance that the victim had been murdered in my hotel room.

She asked, "Did you consider Trevor Black to be a potential suspect in that homicide?"

"Obviously," Special Agent Fainlock replied.

"Did you consider Trevor Black to be a potential danger to the public?"

"Considering the violent way in which Paul Pullmen was murdered, I certainly did."

"Were you present when Trevor Black recently delivered a speech to the American Bar Association convention in New Orleans?"

"I was there."

"Describe for the court what happened."

"Mr. Black went off on a rampage that upset the audience."

"In what way?"

"By demanding an investigation into the death of an assistant US attorney by the name of Jason Forester, who died of natural causes but who Mr. Black thought had been the victim of some kind of voodoo curse."

"When you were with the parish sheriff just minutes before he took Trevor Black into custody for mental observation and treatment, did you have a short conversation with Mr. Black?"

"Yes."

"About what, pray tell?"

"About demons."

Attorney Cougin feigned astonishment for theatrical effect. "Pardon me, but did you just say *demons*?"

"I did," the FBI agent said. "I asked him about it because he has a reputation for chasing what he believes are demonic forces."

"And what did Mr. Black say?"

"That demons are 'everywhere.' That's the word he used. Then Mr. Black added, 'You just have to know where to look.' That is an exact quote."

As I stood for my cross-examination of the special agent, I had only one line of questioning. It was about his interrogating me at the FBI headquarters in New Orleans.

"Agent Fainlock, did you release me after questioning me about the murder of Paul Pullmen?"

"You were allowed to leave, yes."

"Do you customarily release men who have murdered other men?"

"Not usually, no. But in your case, there were other factors."

"Like what?"

"Like the fact that Mr. Vance Zaduck spoke to me. He's the United States attorney for the District of Columbia."

"What did he tell you?"

Attorney Cougin was up again, objecting on hearsay grounds.

"No, not hearsay," I replied, explaining that I was not offering it for the *truth* of what was said, but only to show that Vance Zaduck had said it.

Judge Levall allowed the question and told the FBI agent to answer it.

Agent Fainlock said, "He told me he knew you, Mr. Black, professionally. And he was in the audience at the ABA convention when you spoke."

"Any comments from Mr. Zaduck that I had run amok, acted like a crazy man during my speech to the ABA?"

"Not that I can recall."

"Did Mr. Zaduck also tell you that as a result, it would have been impossible for me to have been in my hotel room killing Assistant AG Paul Pullmen and simultaneously in the auditorium giving my speech?"

"Mr. Zaduck and I are not pathologists, Mr. Black. Coroners and pathologists are the ones who fix the time of death."

"But you'd agree with me, that it's implausible to believe I killed Mr. Pullmen in a bloody melee in the hotel room, then cleaned up in a matter of minutes and calmly trotted over to the convention in time to deliver my speech. . . ."

"Not impossible."

"But if you really believed that is what happened, would you have released me?"

Long pause.

"Probably not."

I ended my cross there, and Judge Levall announced a break. When I turned to check the time, it was then 6:45 in the evening. I also noticed that Heather had left her seat in the courtroom and was quickly approaching me.

"Trevor, on that last witness, the FBI guy, I was just wondering . . ."

"Wondering what?"

"Why didn't you try to nail him about your comment about demons being 'everywhere.' I mean, I was there, in the sheriff's department when you said it. You were perfectly calm. Said it almost offhandedly. But he made it sound like you were totally crazy."

"You're wondering why I let that go?"

"Right."

"Strategy. I'm leaving the demon stuff for the next witness." Then I asked, "Did you strike out with Deputy St. Martin?"

"They wouldn't let me talk to him."

"Thanks for trying. You're a trouper."

"All rise."

Judge Levall was striding back into the courtroom.

Ms. Cougin called Dr. Alex Schlosser to the stand as her next witness. As I had guessed.

43

A belabored introduction of Dr. Schlosser followed. His medical background and training. His professional accomplishments. His scholarly articles, and on and on. Time was running out. I rose to my feet and told the court I was willing to concede he was an expert in the field of psychiatry. We needed to get to the heart of his testimony.

Unfortunately, when we arrived at the heart of his opinion, Schlosser's opinions were devastating. He testified that I was suffering from auditory and visual hallucinations most likely brought on by an early onset of paranoid schizophrenia. "Such a condition of mental illness," he elaborated, "can often appear mixed in with rigid, fixed religious ideology—or in Mr. Black's case, a hyper-extreme form of Christianity. It gives him the psychic defense, an intellectual justification, for his delusions. In his case, the delusions take the form of so-called demonic beings that regularly appear to him and with whom he thinks he is doing battle."

"Dr. Schlosser, can a person suffering from such a condition pose a danger to other people or to himself?"

"Most certainly. And in Trevor Black's case, his dangerousness is heightened by his rationale that God has blessed his mission against demonic forces. Some of the most horrendous crimes are committed by mentally impaired people who believe that God has commanded them to act in a certain way."

Then the kicker. Cougin's coup de grâce.

In this case, my reason for representing myself, among others, had been tactical: showing the judge that I was a man who could present a cogent, intelligent defense, with well-reasoned arguments and insightful questions. Raising grave doubts that such a man could be as mentally disabled as Dr. Schlosser said he was.

But Cougin was prepared for that.

"One last question, Doctor. Could a person suffering from paranoid schizophrenia, as you describe it, in the early stages as is the case with Trevor Black . . . could he have episodes of normality? In other words, appearing intelligent and mentally oriented, even capable of conducting a legal defense of himself as he is doing today?"

"Absolutely. There can be transient periods where the person seems poised and mentally healthy and confident, and could be mistaken by nonexperts for a person who is not mentally ill. Especially when his delusions are not challenged and he feels secure in his own private world of fractured reality. Eventually, however, he unravels. And that is when he can be the most dangerous, unless properly confined and treated, of course. Which is what we plan to do for Mr. Black at Morehaven."

Cougin rested.

I took a few seconds before plowing in. In the old days it would have been a trial lawyer's tactic. Letting the courtroom fall into silence, which would put Schlosser a little on edge and would also rivet the judge's attention on what was about to come.

But that day, I needed a few seconds to pray silently. I glanced back at the clock. Ten minutes after seven. I could see, through the windows of the courtroom, the sun nearing the horizon. Barbaric inhumanity was on its way down the Mississippi and had to be stopped. I wanted to freeze the hands of that clock on the wall.

I took a relaxing breath. Then I began.

"Dr. Schlosser, I took good notes while you were testifying. You said a mentally impaired person—to be a precise, a paranoid schizophrenic, which you testified under oath that I am—that such a person can appear normal for periods of time and can even participate in complex legal proceedings, 'especially when his delusions are not challenged.' That is what you said, correct?"

"Correct."

"Have you been in this courtroom today during all the testimony in this case?"

"I have."

"Heard it all?"

"Yes."

"Then you know that Judge Levall has heard testimony, first . from a police officer, then an FBI agent, and now you, each of you attacking my mental state. So it's clear my beliefs about demons have been aggressively challenged in this courtroom, have they not?"

"Of course."

"So, according to your opinion, I should have unraveled. Now, have I unraveled before your eyes today?"

"That is for the judge to decide."

"No, it's for you to decide, because my question is put to you, the psychiatric expert. So I ask again. Despite having my beliefs assaulted in the most militant way, have I unraveled, sir?"

"Not entirely."

"My beliefs as a follower of Jesus—do they make me vulnerable to mental illness?"

"That is not what I said."

"You testified that my Christian views contributed to my delusions. That my 'rigid, fixed religious ideology,' 'a hyper-extreme form of Christianity,' as you called it, provided me with a convenient 'psychic defense,' which contributed to my psychotic beliefs about demons. You said that, didn't you? I can have the court reporter read it back if you doubt me. . . ."

"No need. I'll concede the point. It's getting late."

Indeed it was, later than anyone in that courtroom really knew.

"I'll be brief," I said. "Here's my question: Do you believe that Jesus was psychotic? Delusional?"

"I wouldn't know. I didn't have the chance to examine him." Schlosser smiled and looked around the room, probably hoping for reinforcement and some evidence that his attempt at humor hit home, but if that was his plan, he found none.

"You do know," I continued, "that the accounts in the New Testament describe Jesus meeting and talking with the devil. In your professional opinion, does that make Jesus psychotic and in need of mental confinement and treatment?"

"As I recall the story, he was in the desert. Hungry. Exhausted. Under such conditions a person can be rendered temporarily delusional."

"But there are numerous accounts in the four Gospels where Jesus encountered, talked to, was recognized by demons, and then he in fact cast them out. In *none* of those instances does it say he was suffering from malnutrition or physical exhaustion."

"I wouldn't know."

"Well, you took an oath to tell the truth by placing your hand on that Bible sitting over there on the clerk's desk. I can pick it up right now and walk you through those accounts."

"I'll take your word for it."

"Some of the most brilliant minds in history believed in the God of the Bible and the miracles of Christ. The apostle Paul. Augustine. Copernicus. Francis Bacon. Johannes Kepler. Isaac Newton. Blaise Pascal. C. S. Lewis. And they believed in the existence of the devil and demons, too. Were they all hopelessly mad?"

"They can be excused as products of their times and cultures, I imagine."

"How about you, Doctor, with your presuppositions against the supernatural world and against the reality of the spirit? Can your mistaken biases be excused as a product of your elitist scientific culture?"

Of course my question was argumentative. And of course

my opponent leaped at the chance to object. And as expected, the judge sustained it. But sometimes, come hell or high water, the question simply has to be asked.

Next I asked him, "How about the late Supreme Court Justice Antonin Scalia? A brilliant jurist, he stated publicly that he believed in both God and the devil. Was he mentally disabled, or was he just a product of his culture?"

"I'm not an expert in the law."

"Nor are you an expert in spiritual warfare, right?"

"I never said I was."

"But you have presented yourself in this court as an expert in the matters of the mind."

"That is my area of expertise."

"In that case, can you explain to the court where exactly is the dividing line between the matters of the mind and the matters of the soul?"

"I couldn't say."

"So if this court finds that my devotion to opposing evil supernatural forces is entirely a matter of the mind, then it should listen to you. Right?"

"I would hope so."

"But on the other hand, if this court finds that my devotion against supernatural evil is best explained as a matter of the soul, then your testimony would be irrelevant, correct?"

Dr. Schlosser took a while to consider that. Judge Levall finally had to intervene and ask him if he had any answer to my question.

In the end, Dr. Schlosser said simply, "I do not."

44

My opponent had rested her case. I hadn't intended to present any rebuttal evidence. After all, what could I have possibly offered?

By my estimation, there were several ways in which Judge Levall could have justified dismissing my petition and bundled me off to Morehaven with a bang of the gavel. While I felt that I had done a yeoman's job of casting doubt on my mental health incarceration, it might not have been enough. I had to go further. I had to prove the illegality of my apprehension by the government. A tricky matter.

In any case, at that point the testimony on my habeas corpus petition would usually have been closed and the case submitted to the judge for his decision. Would usually have been. But wasn't. In a universe governed by a God of surprises, always be prepared to be surprised.

After all, if God can use a town harlot named Rahab to protect the ancient Israelites from their enemies, then anything is possible.

I felt a hand on my shoulder. Upon turning around, I was looking into the corpulent face of Attorney Morgan Canterelle.

He whispered to me, "Y'all might want to offer a rebuttal witness, Mr. Black."

"Any suggestions?" I asked.

"Yours truly," he said with a big grin. "As a witness to y'all's sanity. Y'all's normality."

Of all the people capable of judging normality, Morgan Canterelle was not at the top of my list.

"Remember," he added, "I'm the one who picked y'all to address the entire American Bar Association."

"What are you doing here?" I asked.

"I shall explain later."

I wheeled around to face the judge. "Your Honor, I have a rebuttal witness. Attorney Morgan Canterelle."

"On what issue?" Attorney Cougin belted out.

I replied, "My sanity."

Opposing counsel exploded with objections like confetti from a party gun.

Judge Levall looked undecided.

"Your Honor," I said, "my opponent, by calling Dr. Schlosser, opened the door to this issue of my mental status."

Levall rocked awhile in his big judicial chair, then glanced at the clock. "I'll permit it. But please get to the point, Mr. Black."

Canterelle lumbered up to the stand. When he arrived, Judge Levall nodded to him. "Hello, Morgan," he said.

"Judge," Canterelle replied with a smile. "I missed you at the ABA."

"I was there," Judge Levall replied, "but tied up in judicial conference meetings."

Their cordiality was nice to see. But Canterelle was still a wild card with unclear motives. I was now entrusting my case, my freedom, and the welfare of young sex slaves held captive in the bottom of a ship to a lawyer who was still a mystery to me.

I was taking a risk, and I knew it. I silently asked God to protect those victims from any of my mistakes and miscalculations. Legal, strategic, or otherwise.

I began my direct examination of Canterelle. His knowledge of my legal reputation in New York, his relationship with me, his inviting me to speak at the ABA, the ABA session itself, my speech, and the reaction of the audience.

Then I asked, "Attorney Canterelle, based on all of that, have you formed an opinion, strictly as a lay witness and based on your own perceptions of me, regarding my mental state?"

"Yes, sir, I have. Mr. Black, I've got to say, y'all are the most unusual person I have ever met. Bar none. And I've met some pretty strange folk."

Out of the corner of my eye, I could see Attorney Cougin gloating.

I found myself in a box. To get out, I had to violate the number one rule of every trial lawyer: never ask a question when you haven't the faintest idea how the witness is going to answer.

But having no other alternative, I ventured down that darkened alley. "Unusual in what way?" I asked.

He cocked his head. "Well, sir, most folks believe in

something. Doing the right thing, maybe. Or stopping things that are wrong. They believe in heaven. Or in hell. Those who believe there's a God. And those who believe there's a devil. I've met some of each over the years. But Trevor Black, y'all's one of the few men I've met who's all of that, all wrapped up into one. Crazy? I say right now that Trevor Black's not crazy. Unless crazy means seeing things that cynical folks, nearsighted people just can't fathom. I don't know about demons, Your Honor. But if a person wants somebody to hunt 'em down with a crystal-clear mind and the heart of a lion, then Trevor Black's the man."

When I rested, Attorney Cougin was smoldering. Then she hit him with her cross-examination.

"Mr. Canterelle," she began, "you are a high-ranking member of the ABA. And you are a well-known New Orleans attorney. As we all know, this is the twenty-first century. Are you seriously telling this court that demons are real and they are out there doing evil?"

Canterelle grinned. "Miss, y'all really think that demons and the twenty-first century *don't* mix? This is New Orleans. Y'all ever been to Mardi Gras?"

I heard laughter. It sounded like it was coming from Heather, and also like the sheriff or Deputy St. Martin, or maybe both, were joining her.

Cougin quit while she was behind, probably fearing she could slip even further.

Another glance at the clock—7:42 p.m.

Attorney Cougin must have figured that she could make a closing argument, because she started to rise.

But Judge Levall put an end to that. "Be seated, Counsel. I am ready to rule."

The federal judge proceeded to remind all of us that the state courts are vested with the authority to decide mental commitment cases, *not* the federal courts.

"The authority of this court is extremely limited. Very narrow. Particularly in a habeas corpus proceeding. Which is the legal basis that you have chosen to pursue, Mr. Black. This was your petition. And I am constrained to rule within the four corners of that petition, according to the evidence I have heard. I cannot rule out of sympathy for you, Mr. Black, or even out of respect for the way in which you have conducted your very able effort in this courtroom. And I can't second-guess the decision of Morehaven to confine you or the opinions of the psychiatric staff who want to treat you."

To most people, that would have sounded like a death knell. Me? I was waiting for the big turnabout. It usually starts with a judge saying, "But . . ."

Judge Levall paused. Then he said, "*But* . . . this case isn't about any of that. Although as a side note, I would have found Attorney Canterelle's lay testimony fairly compelling, if sanity were the issue here. But it isn't. It's about the Louisiana state statute that gives the police the authority, on their own impetus, to take Mr. Trevor Black into custody for the purpose of a mental examination and possible treatment *only* if a certain condition is met. That condition is that the officer's determination of Mr. Black's impaired mental state and dangerous potential must be based on his 'personal observation' of Mr. Black. I do not doubt the good faith of the New Orleans police officer who took Mr.

Black into custody. But I am convinced it was *not* based on his personal observation. The habeas corpus petition is granted, and the court orders Mr. Trevor Black to be released forthwith."

I jumped to my feet. "*Forthwith*, Your Honor?"

"Yes. As in, this very instant," Judge Levall replied, then gaveled the case to a close and slipped from the courtroom and into his chambers.

The two Morehaven staffers shook my hand and asked if I needed transportation. "No need," I said excitedly. "My daughter is here to drive me." I'm sure they didn't notice the catch in my voice when I spoke the word *daughter*.

Heather was at my side and squeezed my hand. "Oh, wow, I can't believe this!"

Canterelle slapped me on the back. "Congratulations, Trevor. We did it."

But I was baffled. "Morgan, how did you know about my case?"

"Gossip spreads fast. One of Minerva Sabatier's loyal followers works here in the courthouse. She called Belle Sabatier and told her all about it. Belle ordered me to do everything I could to help you in this case. To get y'all freed."

"What do you know about that," I said. "Belle Sabatier, daughter and heir of a voodoo priestess. What a wonderfully unlikely hero."

I strode up to the court clerk before she could disappear and asked her for a copy of Judge Levall's order granting my habeas corpus petition and containing his finding that my apprehension and commitment to Morehaven had been illegal. She promised to e-mail it to me.

45

As the courtroom began to empty, I scanned the room for Sheriff Haywood and Deputy St. Martin. But they were gone.

"The two of them ran out of here like the place was on fire," Heather explained. "The very second that the judge ruled in your favor."

Something came to mind, and I whirled around to Attorney Canterelle. "About that favor you were going to do for me, finding the identity of the attorney who sat next to Heather at the ABA . . ."

"I've been working on it. But now that I see y'all found her, do y'all still need to know?"

I told him yes. My private reasons for wanting that information had changed by then. But I still needed it, and more than ever. It had to do with my phantom caller with the digitally distorted voice. I had a hunch the caller was the same lawyer sitting next to Heather during my speech, the person who knew about the voodoo ceremony planned at Bayou Bon Coeur and who led Heather to Delbert Baldou.

I pressed Canterelle again to get me the lawyer's ID, adding that her name might be Deidre.

Canterelle said, "It's complicated. I located an ID that the lawyer used to get into the session, but the name doesn't match. Now I've got a friend who's in the facial recognition software business, and he's running the video that caught the faces of the first few rows in the audience and checking it against a federal database. Y'all should have an answer shortly."

It was almost eight in the evening when we hustled out of the courthouse and into the dusk outside. As Heather handed over my cell phone, I told her we had to rush to Dead Point along the banks of the Mississippi.

On the way, I called the sheriff's department for Plaquemines Parish and said I needed to talk to Sheriff Haywood immediately. That I knew he was on his way back from federal court because I had just been with him in the courtroom. I gave my name and cell number and said that if the sheriff wasn't available, then Deputy St. Martin needed to call me back instead, but that it was urgent and I needed to hear back from someone.

Dead Point was a good hour away. I laid my cell down on the console of the Mustang and waited for a return call.

Heather said, "Back in that courtroom . . . that was so

amazing." She was smiling. "So that was what you did, all those years as a lawyer?"

"Something like that. Never represented myself before, though." Then I smiled back. "By the way, a lot of the victory belongs to you. Nice work on the petition."

I saw a wide grin from Heather.

But inside I was in turmoil. I wondered when it would be the right time. When I would tell her what Dr. Schlosser told me. What those legal papers said about her biological father. And what they failed to say about me.

And then I thought about Ashley Linderman and wondered when I might expect a call back from her.

A half hour into the drive we passed a gas station with a small sundries shop. It was getting dark, so I dashed in and bought the biggest flashlight I could find. I told Heather, "There are no lights out there at Dead Point."

For the second time in two days we took the turn off of 23 and onto Diamond Road, with the Mississippi River to our left, and then to the dirt road cutting through low scrub brush until we could see the rusting metal sign arching overhead announcing River Bend Cemetery. This time the gate was closed. Heather scampered out of the car and opened it. Then the bumpy ride over the rough terrain that had once housed the caskets and crypts of the departed, before flood tides finally forced the grave-yard caretakers to dig them up and relocate them.

We arrived at Dead Point but hadn't received a call back from either the sheriff or the deputy. I jostled the Mustang across the field and stopped close to the banks of the Mississippi, and we jumped out.

In the shrouding darkness, we would have to listen for the sound of ships approaching, knowing there was a chance we had already missed the awful one, the vessel carrying its young cargo. We had no idea what kind of boat we were waiting for. Our informant, Henry Bosant, hadn't told us. At first we heard only the lapping of waves against the shoreline and the wind in the trees, but nothing else. The moon was poking in and out of a thick blanket of clouds, and the river itself was almost invisible in the inky night, yet we knew it was there because we could hear it rushing along the banks.

Heather and I stood silent, fixed at attention. Waiting.

I put a call into the sheriff's office again, received the same message, and told the dispatcher that it was urgent and they needed to meet with me at Dead Point immediately. Then the same reply, that my call would be noted and that Sheriff Haywood and Deputy St. Martin "would be advised."

More waiting. Then a sound. In the distance, the low hum of a boat engine approaching and the swishing of a wake as a river craft cut through the water.

I held the big spotlight in my hand but hadn't turned it on.

Heather asked if we should turn on the Mustang's headlights.

"No, too wide a beam. And I don't want to alert them to the fact that a car is at the banks of the river. Flashlight's better."

As the boat was approaching, I noticed a periodic beam from the vessel's bow light flashing on and then turning off. They must have been checking their bearings on the river but didn't want to keep the light on, possibly to avoid detection.

By the sound of the engine, this was no oceangoing ship. It

was a smaller craft. I knew there was a chance that this boat had nothing to do with child sex slavery or some bloody voodoo cult.

When it sounded as if the boat was parallel to our position at Dead Point, I ran up, right to the water's edge, with Heather close behind me. The clouds parted a little and I could make out the outline of the craft in the darkness. It looked like a long fishing boat or a trawler, with a cabin area belowdecks. There were a few portholes along the starboard side, facing us. A dim light shone in the cabin, but something covered the porthole windows.

My index finger was on the slide button of my big spotlight. I pointed it straight at the outline of the boat and clicked it on. The beam cut through the hot mist rising off the river and lit up the boat.

There, within a porthole, a hand was holding open a curtain. Then a face peering out. I looked closer, keeping my beam fixed on it. It was a young girl. Her eyes were half-closed and her mouth was wide-open, face contorted in a scream, hands waving next to her face, pleading.

I heard Heather yelp next to me. "It's a girl. They've got a girl. . . ."

Then some confusion in the porthole. Something was happening. The girl's face appeared again, but only for a moment. She was struggling with someone. She was yanked to the side and I saw who had done it. For just a fleeting second a man's face was in the porthole, staring out with a fierce expression; then he pulled the curtain shut and the lights went out in the cabin.

Feeling numb and gut-punched, I clicked off my spotlight. Heather was weeping softly next to me.

I put my hand on her shoulder. "I'm sorry. There was nothing we could do." But those words seemed so pitifully inadequate and pathetic. Even cold.

Was I growing callous to the depravity that I had been fighting ever since my spiritual awakening? I prayed to God that wasn't true.

I looked at Heather. She was still staring at the dark flow of the river rolling past us. She was sniffling, trying hard to hold it back. Suddenly she burst into tears.

Heather turned to me and sobbed in my arms. I held her yet felt a catastrophic tension pulling me in two. Wanting to share with her everything that the Lord had shown me about the separation of the darkness from the light, and that even with all the horror and wretchedness of the devil—and the struggles against the world and the flesh—there was still hope because it had all been overcome by Christ the King, whose power was so cosmic that even the grave couldn't contain it.

But Heather was not my daughter to console, I told myself. Genetically, biologically, and in every way in which a father and daughter can be linked through the mystery of conception and birth—I was none of that, merely a third party. Just a friendly stranger to her now. Even an unwitting impostor. The truth of that still had to be spoken to Heather. It would lie in my mouth like poison until I said it aloud.

I finally said, "Let's get back to the car. Someone may try to track us to this spot."

As we turned from the river, a fire had been lit inside me. The carnage had to stop. The terrorizing of young girls, the cruel caravans as they were carried off to slavery—it had happened right in front of me. On my watch.

But no more. If God had called me to this, then he would empower me to stop it.

We were halfway to the rental when a pair of headlights came roaring down the path toward us and broke into the open where our Mustang was parked. I recognized the jacked-up pickup as it skidded to a stop. When the driver opened the door and the dome light was on, I knew who he was. The skinhead male with a full beard who had chased us down the highway outside of Port Sulphur.

"Get in the car," I told Heather, "and lock the doors."

"But—"

"Now!" I shouted.

The driver stomped toward me. I didn't see a weapon, but I was already getting the signal. My senses were filled with the old incendiary scent of a landfill on fire; of dead animals, garbage, and death. Which meant that the man coming at me had been taken over by one of the lower-echelon demonic thugs. I knew what would come next: I would soon see the demonic being that had taken him over, in all of its grotesque essence.

When he was about ten feet from me, things started to happen. He hunched his shoulders, and his arms flailed in all directions. Before me, his face transformed into the demonic creature within: the essence of the thing was like some kind of hairy spider with large lifeless eyes.

He screamed in a voice that was high and screechy like an untuned violin, "Why have you come to torment me?"

"Who do you work for?" I demanded. "Who's your boss?"

"You can't defeat him. The overlord is too strong. The king

of lust and pain. The destroyer of children. He rapes. Ruins. And he'll ruin you."

A sudden, inexplicable calm washed over me. I held out a hand to him. "You can be rid of this."

"Get away," he yelled. "Leave us alone, or you'll be chopped up. Fed to the alligators."

"No, I won't. You know who I serve. I serve the Son of the living God."

He shrieked so loudly that it echoed off the river and through the woods, like a creature whose leg had been caught in the jaws of a trap.

I took a few steps toward him. He backed up and stopped, then lunged at me and grabbed me by the throat, no longer the hellish insect creature but a man again, yet there was no power in his grip.

"I am going to help you," I said as I removed his hands and forced him down to his knees. Then the words, from a place within me, began to flow out. "In the name of Christ the Lord, and by the power of his blood, and by the power of his resurrection, I cast you out, you foul spirit. Get out of this man, into the outer darkness, back to the dry, desolate, godless place where you came from. Out!"

The man screamed, shivered and shook, and collapsed. He was still for a while, lying there on the ground. Then he began to move. After wiping the spittle from his mouth and beard, he looked up, his eyes darting around.

He asked, "Where am I?"

"By the river. At Dead Point," I said. "Welcome back to the land of the living."

46

I helped the man to his feet and asked him what he remembered. He recalled very little, except to say that a repulsive but unstoppable darkness had been growing inside him like a cancer, until it took him over entirely. But now, he said with a look of astonishment, "It's gone. . . . It's been lifted."

"Do you know why you are here at Dead Point?"

He shook his head no.

I asked him if he was familiar with a church in Port Sulphur, and he nodded. "Yes, sir. I've driven past it. I know it."

"Good. Go there. See the pastor first thing tomorrow. His name is Wilhem Ventrie. Tell him what happened and that I sent you. I'm Trevor Black."

When I climbed inside the Mustang, Heather was drop-jawed. "You want to tell me what all that was about?"

"Well," I asked, "what did you see out there just now?"

"You sort of wrestling with that man. And he shouted. You were on top of him on the ground and you shouted something. Then, all of a sudden, the two of you were talking together like nothing happened. Almost buddies."

She waited. Then, finally, "So . . . what was going on?"

I said simply, "Deliverance. Rescue."

Heather was quiet after that.

There was a heavy silence in the car as we drove back to the hotel in New Orleans. Heather was the first to break it. But when she did, she avoided asking about my encounter with the pickup driver.

Instead she went back, several times, in several different ways, to the girl in the window of the boat and whether there was an innocent explanation for it. I wanted there to be, but I told her I doubted it. "The chances that a freak coincidence could have happened exactly like Henry Bosant predicted, at night, forty-eight hours later, going down the Mississippi? Slim to none."

She was carrying a desperate expression. I said, "Heather, this kind of work will break your heart. But then, it ought to. Look what's at stake. On the other hand, there's hope. . . ."

"Oh yeah? I'm not seeing it."

"Hearts get broken. But I know someone who can fix them."

I saw a struggling smile. "Yeah . . . I know what you're talking about. Thanks for the mini sermon," she said.

Still, I was struggling against desperation myself. No call back from the sheriff's department. And despite the fact that Heather left a message on Detective Ashley Linderman's voice mail, asking her to call me, no call from her either.

The toughest question Heather asked was the next one, and the most obvious. "What now?"

I wasn't sure. Not at first. All I knew was that the sheriff's department at Port Sulphur needed to know what we saw. But despite what I had just said to Heather, I realized that skeptical minds could still discount it. Especially if they didn't know the backstory from Henry Bosant.

As we entered the city limits of New Orleans, I called the sheriff's office once more, this time demanding to be put through to Deputy St. Martin's voice mail.

I left a detailed message. In accord with what I had promised to Henry Bosant, I omitted any facts that might implicate him personally. But I described everything else: how a credible witness had told me about a child abduction ring operating down the Mississippi with ties to New Orleans, and that boats would periodically motor past Port Sulphur, getting supplies on the water near Dead Point from a smaller tender boat as they headed south toward Port Eads and then eventually into the open waters of the Gulf of Mexico.

I continued my voice mail message, saying, "I wanted to tell you all of that at the sheriff's department, but before I could, I was placed into custody as a lunatic, cuffed, and carted off to Morehaven."

In closing I said, "In any case, Deputy, on a tip, I went to Dead Point tonight around nine thirty and spotted a young girl who looked as if she were being held captive in the hold of a forty- to fifty-foot craft heading toward the Gulf as it passed by my position. I saw her in the porthole of the boat, and it appeared she was yelling for help. Exactly as my tipster said would happen."

I left my cell number and asked that he return the call.

Then I was hit with a last-ditch idea. I asked Heather to look up the number for the local branch of the Coast Guard and place the call for me on my cell so I could talk to them.

I was transferred to the master chief of that sector, and I told him I had evidence of illegal conduct taking place on the Mississippi around the area of Port Sulphur. A possible kidnapping ring, and that the boat was on its way to Port Eads.

Then the predictable answer. "Sir, you need to contact the local sheriff's department. They'll decide whether they need our backup for an interdiction."

I was unable to tie the female abduction cult to the possessed pickup truck driver who encountered us at Dead Point, but I had a strong suspicion that he had been one of the worker bees in the conspiracy. In Reverend Cannon's words, one of the low-level "henchmen." Whoever he had been working for, whoever the "overlord" was at the top of the pyramid—"the king of lust and pain . . . the destroyer of children"—he had successfully intimidated his followers through a pitiless exercise of power.

As we drove closer to our hotel, I knew there were still mountains to climb and so much that I still didn't know. We hadn't stopped the boat floating past us on the Mississippi. And every hour that passed, more innocent young lives would be swept down a demonic sewer, orchestrated by a level of evil I had never experienced before.

Yet despite all that, something struck me out of the blue. And when it did, I was buoyed. Lifted unexpectedly by a quiet but powerful current. My presence at Dead Point wasn't in vain after all. Why did it take me so long to realize it? The dark side owned that tough guy in the pickup truck. He was lost. Possessed. But I was there by the banks of the river just in time to meet him. I was used by the same God who raises the dead and rescues the living. And he used me to raise that man from the walking dead and breathe life back into him.

Heather must have seen that in my face, because I was smiling. She bent around from the passenger seat to take a closer look. "Hmm" was all she said, but there was a half smile on her face.

Heather and I caught a late dinner in the hotel restaurant. Conversation was sparse. The exhaustion of the day had set in for both of us. But before I paid the check, I asked Heather what turned into a long, rambling question. "What you've experienced lately . . . you know, the ABA convention and my speech, and being approached by that female mystery lawyer, and the goings-on at Bayou Bon Coeur and at Six Flags; then our meeting with Henry Bosant at Dead Point, and my being taken into custody and admitted to Morehaven, and the court hearing; what happened tonight at the river and what we saw, and then the possessed guy in the pickup . . . I was wondering . . ."

"Wondering what?" she asked.

"Well, just wondering what you've thought about all of it."

"I'm still processing it."

A safe answer. I didn't blame her.

Then she said, "Look, I don't want to get into it right now—I'm too tired—but basically, I'm glad I've been here. Seeing it all. And seeing it with you. How you fit into this crazy stuff. You're . . ." She took a moment before she ended it. When she did, she said, "You're kinda unique, you know? I wouldn't have missed it for the world."

There was so much swimming just below the surface of her words.

I said, "And it's not over yet."

I looked at the fatigue on her face and decided right then that my important conversation with her would have to wait until tomorrow morning. The talk about her real father. Over breakfast. When our minds were fresh.

47

Heather said something to me that night, right before slipping into her hotel room. "Trevor, someday we're going to talk about what really happened between you and that pickup truck guy at the river."

I nodded, and we said good night.

In my room, I pulled out my iPad and plugged in my search terms: *David Fleming Manitou Wisconsin.*

There were some references to his having attended VMI, the military college in Virginia. But then some surprises: according to the *Milwaukee Journal Sentinel*, at some point David joined the Army, served in Somalia, and ended up being killed in action in the battle of Mogadishu. A war hero, to be sure.

My head was swirling. Not only did I have to tell Heather

that I wasn't her father; I also had to break the news that her biological father had been killed in the horrific fighting in Somalia. I remembered seeing images of dead American soldiers being dragged through the streets by armed rebels. Was Heather's father one of them? This meant that both of her parents were gone.

I put in a call to Detective Ashley Linderman. Not her regular law enforcement cell, but the other one: the "supersecret" cell that she used for private contacts, informers, and clandestine operations. And for me.

Ashley's voice. "I knew you'd call me again sometime. And I am assuming Heather is okay . . ."

"Located, safe and sound," I said.

I could hear the relief in Ashley's voice when she said she gathered as much when she received the voice mail from Heather.

"Right," I said, "Heather's message to you about my being involuntarily committed."

There was a long pause. "Yeah. So, Trevor, I have to say, that was really a sick joke. Only mildly funny, by the way."

"Not a joke. More like a tragicomedy."

"Well," Ashley said, moving on in the conversation, "I've been swamped with cases here in Manitou. Including a double homicide. I planned to call you. In that weird message from Heather she sounded rushed. A little distracted . . ."

"Because I had just been taken into custody and dragged into Morehaven."

"What's Morehaven?"

"A mental institution in Louisiana."

"Uh, wait a minute . . . so you weren't joking?"

"That's what I'm trying to tell you."

"Trevor, how did this happen?"

"Too complicated to explain now. The point being that it was all a mistake and I had to challenge it in federal court, and now I've been released. But I have something personal to discuss. Very personal."

I took a second, then plowed ahead. "Specifically, about your telling me that I was Heather's biological dad. That was a big deal to me, obviously. And now I learn that what you told me wasn't true."

Another pause at the other end, this time longer. "What are you talking about?"

"A psychiatrist at Morehaven showed me the paperwork from the termination of parental rights proceeding when Marilyn gave Heather up for adoption. Don't ask me how he got his hands on it. In any case, Marilyn listed the father. She put down the name of a high school classmate of mine: David Fleming."

"Oh, that . . ."

I listened for more.

"Let me think," she said. "Okay, right. He was some kind of swimmer in high school."

"Exactly."

"Joined the Army," she said.

"Something I just found out."

Ashley said, "The same David Fleming who was killed in action . . ."

"Same one."

Then Ashley said, "Yes, he's the one."

I waited.

She continued. "In the beginning, Marilyn tried to peg him as the putative father on the paperwork because by then he had been killed. Oh, I don't know what was going through her mind. Maybe she thought the baby—you know, Heather— could collect some military benefits or something. Or maybe she was trying to protect you from the fallout. . . ."

After letting that shocker sink in, I had a question. "I thought David Fleming went to a military college in Virginia."

"The social service investigators said he left college almost immediately and enlisted," Ashley said. "It became clear that this young man would have been in active military service and completely out of contact during the time when Marilyn became pregnant. When Marilyn was confronted with those facts, she recanted, did a one-eighty, and told the adoption people that she didn't know who the father was. But I was told that after the adoption was concluded, the investigating social worker strongly suspected that the real father was an unnamed student at New York University, and that it was a onetime encounter involving Marilyn and that young man, someone she had known from high school. Of course, that fit you perfectly."

"Why didn't you tell me about David Fleming?"

"Because he wasn't the dad; it was irrelevant."

"Not to me."

"Maybe not. But when I told you that Heather had been born and then adopted, and that you were the father, and you were super excited about it, I had this thing for you and enjoyed seeing you so happy. Didn't want to rain on your parade and all that."

My mind had been blown. Again.

"So," I said, "just to be sure. Are you telling me that you know of absolutely nothing that would raise doubts about my being her biological parent?"

"That's what I'm telling you," she said.

A hurricane just miraculously evaporated. In a matter of seconds I had experienced a complete reversal of fortunes about Heather. I was her dad again.

"I bet you're relieved," she said. "You must have been really bummed about the David Fleming curveball. Truly sorry. I should have told you that."

Then her tone changed. The detective came out. "You say you got that information from a psychiatrist? That seems odd. Out of place."

"To say the least. In hindsight, the guy was eminently sketchy. But at the time he was doing a masterful job of poking holes in me and filling me with doubts."

The call ended with my telling Ashley how great it was to connect and thanking her for the fantastic news, and I promised to keep in touch.

As I lay in bed in the dark, I was buoyed again, riding a second tide. Thankful that Ashley had taken my call and dispelled the false doubts that had hounded me. I had my daughter back. *Thank you, God.*

But then another image flashed in front of me. The face of that young girl, peering out from that porthole of the boat, mouth open in a silent scream for help.

I imagined that somewhere out there a father was missing his daughter and living in quiet desperation. Continuing to glance at the phone, hoping it would ring; yanking his cell phone out when it did, praying that he would hear the news that she had been found, yet all the time knowing that such a call might never come. And through it all, the father dying a little each day. Like never before, I could relate to that.

I decided that come morning, first thing, I was going to set my mind to the task. With the time I had left, and with the faith and strength that were mine, I had to throw myself against that terror.

48

While I dressed for breakfast, the news on TV was droning in the background. Heather was to meet me in the café downstairs. I didn't want to be late. Among other things, I would be telling her what I had learned from Ashley the night before. She deserved to know everything.

Then a news report on CNN grabbed my attention, starting with the name mentioned: Attorney General George Shazzar. I turned to check it out.

Video shots showed Shazzar at the Department of Justice podium in the briefing room, giving a press conference. A reporter narrated a backgrounder: antipornography groups had criticized him for the slow pace with which the DOJ was pursuing obscenity cases. Particularly child pornography. He was being accused of "deliberate foot-dragging" when it came to the endangerment of children.

In a clip from Shazzar's presser, the attorney general stated: "The Department of Justice has a solid commitment to enforce obscenity laws. We also are fully committed to aggressively prosecuting predators who prey on children and endanger them, particularly through the channels of the Internet. I am personally reviewing our efforts to date and can guarantee that we will be as vigorous as we can to eradicate harm to the youth of America."

It had the sound of typical Washington-speak, but I tucked it away for future reference. While I waited in front of the hotel elevator on my way down to breakfast, my cell rang. Surprisingly, it was Ashley.

"Hey, it's me again," she said. "Now it's my turn to ask a favor."

"Sure. Name it."

"Back at the island, you were researching voodoo on your iPad. Specifically, 'death by voodoo.' Something about the death of a government lawyer in Washington . . ."

"Right. I'm still trying to sort that one out."

"What'd you find out—about 'death by voodoo,' I mean? You never did tell me."

I had almost forgotten that conversation.

"Two possibilities," I said. "One's the supernatural definition, or you might say 'cultural' if you're a secularist. For true believers, it's the old-school idea of mixing potions, casting curses, that sort of thing—and in the case of black magic voodoo, actually causing the death of an enemy. Then there's the second one, the medical definition. The idea that a prediction of one's demise can become so powerful and real that a coronary event occurs. The person is literally frightened to death."

"Interesting."

She had me thinking. So I had to ask, "What triggered your question? Was it my calling you last night?"

"No. Something else. Remember, before I got my detective's shield, I used to do child protection investigations as a patrol officer. I'm still on this law enforcement e-mail alert about child predators. This morning, an e-mail alert pops up in my in-box about child abductions and sex trafficking."

"What does that have to do with voodoo?"

"The alert was referencing an Internet article talking about a voodoo cult involved in child abduction and exploitation, apparently trafficking in the New Orleans area."

"A credible news article or just some Internet junk speculation?"

"The jury's out. The web domain that's being used for the article was questionable. But when I read it, I immediately thought about you being down there in New Orleans and the voodoo connection to that government attorney's death you told me about. Anyway, I thought you ought to know. Besides, you owed me an explanation on 'death by voodoo.'"

While I had her on the phone, I needed to get personal. "Listen, Ashley, I want to thank you again for talking to me last night about Heather and Marilyn. What a game changer that was for me. Really. Thanks for being a friend."

I could tell she was trying not to get emotional. Ashley quickly changed the subject and shared some tidbits about her latest cases until we both said we had to run. Then I jumped in the elevator.

Heather was already sipping her coffee when I got down to the hotel café. I told her about my conversation with Ashley that morning—about the Internet rumors on the voodoo/New Orleans link to the kind of child sex trafficking we had both been exposed to. She seemed interested.

I slowly shifted to my conversation with Ashley the night before about David Fleming and how her mother, Marilyn, had fingered David as the father at first—conveniently timed, because David had been killed in action in Somalia. Then, when faced with the fact that he couldn't have been the father, how she changed her story.

Heather was holding the coffee cup halfway to her mouth and just kept it there for the longest time, like one of those street performers posing as a statue. Finally she put it down.

She said, "Wow. You'll have to give me a minute. I don't know how to feel about what you just told me. Really mixed emotions."

"I understand, and you don't owe me an explanation. But you deserve to know everything that I know. That's why I told you."

She folded her hands on the table. When the waitress came, Heather said she wasn't hungry. I paid for her coffee and we left without ordering.

In the hotel lobby, Heather looked confused and vulnerable. "For the record, I have no idea what we're doing or where we go now or what I'm supposed to do."

She was opening up, and that was good. Then the irritating

ring of my cell. I didn't care who it was; I was ready to ignore it and let it go to voice mail.

"Aren't you going to take it?" she said.

"No, this conversation we're having, it's important."

"You left messages with the sheriff's department. What if it's them?"

I glanced at the screen. It was a 504 area code. "Don't think so. It must be from New Orleans."

"But Port Sulphur has that same area code."

Sharp girl. I took the call.

It was Deputy St. Martin. He said he was calling for Sheriff Haywood. I didn't wait but jumped in and asked if he'd heard my voice mail, and went straight into the business about the boat on the river and the girl in the window.

"Sorry, we're not authorized to comment on any of that," he said. "The only thing I can tell you is that right now Sheriff Haywood is over at the FBI headquarters in New Orleans. He told me to specifically tell you that. Are you in New Orleans?"

"Yes. How long will he be at the FBI?"

He paused. "Uh, until his meeting is over, which should be just about now."

"But about this child abduction ring . . ."

"Like I said—" the deputy began to speak slower and louder—"the sheriff is just about through with his meeting. At the FBI headquarters. In New Orleans."

Either we were having a communications disconnect, or the sheriff's department was giving me a message below radar. It had to be the latter. Which told me something, and if it meant what I thought, it was crucial. After I thanked him, I ran over to the hotel valet desk and asked for the Mustang to be brought around.

Heather and I jumped in and headed for Interstate 10 to Franklin Avenue and then up to Leon C. Simon Boulevard, thinking we could beat the crosstown traffic. But it was still slow going.

When we pulled up to the parking lot at the FBI building, it was crowded and we had to cruise through, checking each lane. Heather looked to the right, while I did the left, trying to spot a sheriff's squad from Plaquemines Parish.

Then Heather cried out, "There it is."

I swooped the Mustang around to the adjacent lane, but I saw the backup lights of the squad turn on as it began to ease out of the parking space. I slammed my rental into park and told Heather to get behind the wheel while I sprinted to the driver's side of the squad.

When I was at the window of Sheriff Haywood's squad car, I waved and yelled. Haywood was startled, slammed on the brakes, and momentarily grabbed for his sidearm. Given his line of work, I couldn't blame him.

He kept the window up for a few seconds, eyeing me like he was weighing the risk of unintended consequences that might come from our talking. Then the window lowered.

Sheriff Haywood kept his peace, staring me down.

"What did you mean?" I finally asked him.

"About what?"

"When you had taken me into custody and were about to escort me through the doors of Morehaven, you said something. You said, 'This is out of my hands.' What did that mean?"

He didn't answer.

I continued. "What did you mean by that?"

"What did you think I meant?"

More game playing. I had a hunch why. So I answered, "I think you meant that you were getting pressured from above. The question is, how far above?"

Sherriff Haywood stayed mum.

I said, "Okay. I can see this is a guessing game. Here's my guess: Was the heat coming from the state capitol in Baton Rouge?"

"I've got places to go," he said.

"Pressure from here at the FBI?"

"Like I said, things to do . . ."

"Then it must have come from outside of Louisiana."

He settled back in his seat. "I'm listening," he said.

I was getting warmer.

"Washington, DC—is that it?"

"I'm still listening," he said.

By this time I was thinking out loud. "So where in Washington? It's a bureaucratic jungle with lots of buildings and lots of marble. Blocks and blocks of federal agencies and institutions. More lawyers per square mile than anywhere on earth. And more power per inch than any other city on the planet."

Finally Haywood spoke up. "Mr. Black, why don't you think about what you just said. And then think about where I'm sheriff. You know what Port Sulphur is? It's so small, they call it a CDP. Census-designated place. I guess it's a reminder that people actually live there in Port Sulphur and it's got its own dot on the map. Population never gets above two thousand or so. So you think about that, Mr. Black, as you figure things out, and why they've happened the way they have, and then you decide where you go from here."

I nodded. I gave him a half salute, half wave as he finished backing out and drove out of the parking lot.

I trotted back to the Mustang, where Heather scampered out of the driver's seat and jumped into the passenger side. She said, "You get all the interesting conversations while I get stuck in the car."

Heather badgered me about my dialogue with the sheriff. I gave her the condensed version. That some outside federal authority might have come to bear on local law enforcement— including pressure to tie me up in a mental commitment, to get me out of the way.

I called Morgan Canterelle's office and got his law intern, Kevin, again. Because we were in a rush to get to the river the night before, I hadn't followed up on something with Canterelle. I put Kevin on speakerphone and asked him whether Morgan had uncovered the identity of someone at the ABA convention.

"You mean the lawyer sitting next to Heather?" Kevin asked.

"That's the one. Did he identify her?"

"He sure did. It just came in."

"Great. Who was she?"

"Mr. Canterelle never told me."

"Where is Morgan now?"

"In the Orleans Parish courthouse."

Of course I knew the building and where it was. After Kevin told me what courtroom Morgan was in, I roared out of the FBI parking lot. But before I could close the conversation, Kevin asked, as I was driving, "Are we on speakerphone?"

"Yes, we are."

"Mr. Black, is Heather with you?"

Heather giggled and I gave a fatherly shake of the head. "Yes, Kevin. She's right here."

"Hi, Heather," he said brightly.

She returned the greeting.

Time to close the front door and turn off the porch lights. "Kevin, you've been great, but we have to run."

49

In half an hour I was leading Heather through the shadows of the dimly lit corridors of the old state court building. It was all coming back to me, just as I had remembered it: the dark wood, the glazed glass doors, and the high arched ceilings that sported ornate plasterwork.

Outside a courtroom, Canterelle had a file tucked under his arm, and he was strenuously arguing some point with his client. Then he noticed me, excused himself, and trotted over my way.

"Trevor Black," he bellowed, "what y'all doing here?" Before I could answer, he lowered his voice and whispered, "I'd love a favor in return for what I did for y'all's case in federal court by helping me with my case here in state court. I have got a client over there who just won't accept the misdemeanor plea I have bargained for him. Y'all know how clients can be. . . ."

"Actually, Morgan," I said, "I'm here on some urgent business. I need to know who the female lawyer was who was sitting next to my daughter at the ABA session. Kevin Sanders said you found out."

"Indeed I did. Facial recognition didn't give us enough. But we found her full name on her registration application—which was classified, by the way, so it took some time to obtain permission from the feds. Her name on the registration was Louisa Deidre Baldou. Her registration said she was from Washington, DC."

The last name hit me like a bucket of ice water. "Where does she work?"

"Couldn't find that out. Privacy issues. Homeland Security reasons too, I guess."

"So she works for the federal government, then?"

"Possibly. By deduction."

The money-ball question: "The woman's last name, Baldou," I asked, "any relation to Delbert Baldou, our swamp guide?"

"Can't say for sure. Try a PI in town by the name of Turk Kavagian. He might know."

I chuckled. The web of connections in New Orleans—the degrees of separation between the people who knew people—was growing more and more intricate.

As I turned to leave, I broke courthouse decorum and shouted down to Canterelle's client in the corridor, "Hey, friend, want some friendly advice? Be glad that you've got such a good lawyer."

I tracked Turk Kavagian down having lunch at a place called Mother's, a redbrick diner that had the look of a three-story warehouse. It was jammed and noisy, so Heather and I pushed our way over to his table, where he was feasting on a catfish salad.

"When you called and wanted to see me," Turk said, "I went ahead and ordered some grub for the two of you."

Two huge po'boys were sitting on plates for us.

"Fabulous!" Heather shouted. I remembered that earlier she had passed up breakfast and I had followed suit. We thanked him and tore into the food.

Turk craned his head to check out Heather's neck tattoo. "Nice tat," he said. "What is that . . . a tree?"

"Yeah," she said without blinking. "An umbrella tree. You know, those big spreading trees in Africa. I think they're beautiful."

"Why a tree?" Turk asked.

I had a flashback to the spat between us about that tattoo. Wow, that felt like a long time ago. But now I was enjoying the conversation; Turk Kavagian had unwittingly led her into it, and she was opening up.

"When I was a kid," Heather said, "I used to watch this children's TV show called *Under the Umbrella Tree*. I guess it was that and, well, other reasons too."

It was a television show she had watched as a girl. It felt good to know that. But I wanted more. So much more I needed to know about my own daughter.

"Cool," Turk said to Heather. He turned to me. "So, Trevor, you wanted to know about Louisa Deidre Baldou? I can tell you what I know."

"Anything."

"As I remember it, Delbert had this girl he was raising as a daughter, because of some family problems. She was a niece of

Delbert's. Everybody called her Deidre, but her given name was Louisa. Deidre's father—Delbert's brother—lost a daughter, Deidre's younger sister. Her name was Lucinda." Turk took a second, looked me in the eye, and then said, "She was the one we found at Bayou Bon Coeur."

Wake-up call. I blurted out, "Abducted at the old Six Flags park . . ."

"Exactly. Well, after they found the remains of poor Lucinda, the father just fell apart. Booze and drugs and a busted heart, I suppose. They found him sitting in his easy chair one day. Died from an overdose. So, next thing, Delbert takes Deidre in and raises her."

"Delbert became a substitute father?"

"Yeah."

"What happened after that?"

"Deidre did good for herself. Really good. It sounds like she was close to being some kind of genius. Straight As. Scholarship. Ended up going to college."

"What kind of school?"

"Something in science. Or technology."

"Stanford?"

"Isn't that in California?" He thought on it for a second. "Nah, that wasn't it."

"MIT possibly?"

"Yeah, that might be it. Definitely on the Eastern Seaboard. Big-name school."

"And after that?"

"I can't help you there."

"We have information that she also became a lawyer. You know anything about that?"

Turk shrugged. "No, sorry."

"Would Delbert be willing to talk about her?"

"Don't count on it. For some reason Delbert closes up like a clam anytime you ask specifics about what she's doing now. Just says he's real proud of Deidre, given all the family tragedy. And he grins real wide whenever he says it. But won't say anything else about her."

We finished eating, and against Turk's protest, I paid for everything and said that Heather and I had to hurry on to our next destination.

Turk stuck out a strong right hand, gave me a crushing handshake good-bye, and wished us well.

When we were back in the rental, Heather led into a question. "Back at the hotel I told you something. That I didn't know what I was supposed to be doing at this point. Or where I should be going."

"I remember."

"So," she said, "now's your chance. Any suggestions?"

The best I could do was to put it into a question.

"Have you ever been to Washington, DC?"

She shook her head.

"I think the two of us should catch a flight to DC as soon as possible."

"Why there?"

I said, "That girl we saw in the porthole of the boat two nights ago? We may be her only hope."

She gave me a long look. "That sounds noble."

I said, "I'm hoping it's providential."

50

Several facts pointed to Washington, DC, as our target.

I was convinced that the federal insider who called Dick Valentine originally about the "voodoo" death of Jason Forester was the same person who called me, using a voice distorter both times. And I was betting the caller was Louisa Deidre Baldou. After all, she had a motivation to get someone—obviously me—to investigate the cruel abduction and exploitation of young girls. In my first conversation with Turk Kavagian, he mentioned that an occult-sounding voodoo network with Internet prowess was behind it, and Dick Valentine's intel pointed the same direction. All of that rang familiar.

The fact she attended the ABA told me she was a lawyer. And Morgan Canterelle's intel told me her bailiwick was the

District of Columbia. According to Turk Kavagian, she did graduate work in technology, which is a bewilderingly vast field. But if her particular niche was Internet-focused, that would also explain a lot. Dick Valentine said Jason Forester was closing in on criminal child exploitation activity on the dark net at the time of his death. Those pieces also seemed to dovetail with the data shared with me recently by Detective Ashley Linderman.

And the fire-breathing creature flapping its wings over all of this—orchestrating and reveling in it—was some demonic voodoo cabal yet to be identified.

As I talked to Heather that night about plans for our flight to DC, I shared it all with her.

She had a pointed question: "You're telling me this Deidre who talked to me at the ABA, and who you think was the anonymous caller to Dick Valentine as well as to you, was a double threat in terms of expertise: an expert in technology as well as the law?"

I told her that was my best guess.

"So the bottom line is, what . . . ? You want to talk to her?"

"Exactly. Bring her out in the open. Stop the shadow games. Find out what else she knows."

Heather shrugged. "Washington, DC, is a huge place."

"Right. Lots of lawyers and lots of technology experts."

"Where do we start?"

"I'm betting she's in the government sector."

"I don't see it," she said. "At least not that clearly . . ."

I gave her the short list of facts we knew up to then.

"Morgan Canterelle thought that she could have government employment based on all the federal barriers raised to his getting more information about her—including those from Homeland Security—despite his ABA insider status. I'm also reading between the lines with Sheriff Haywood's comments to me in that FBI parking lot. He made it sound like some official in a heavy-duty capacity was behind my apprehension and lockdown at Morehaven. Somebody outside Louisiana."

"How does that lead back to Deidre?"

"Because that's why she needed an outsider like me. *Outside* the system. Beyond the Beltway. In her call, she described our ultimate overlord bad actor—*not* as an outsider who's running wild in the streets, but as someone *inside* the power structure. Which means she has to watch her back.

"Also, Dick Valentine looked into the federal personnel data she shared with him about AUSA Jason Forester, and it all checked out. It sounds to me like she's a whistle-blower— except she's not squawking about the usual corruption fare, like cost overruns or padded federal contracts, but about a whole different deal altogether. A cancer embedded deep inside Washington. Engineering an occult campaign of hellish female abduction and perversion. Even human sacrifice."

That night, as Heather was in her hotel room booking our flight for the next day, I was slumped down in the chair next to my bed, practically tasting the bitter despair. The battle had become so elevated and the odds against us so astronomical that I felt overwhelmed. And then there was the crazy immensity of the evil we were facing. The enemy was a giant. And we were insects.

I plucked up my Bible, returning again to the book of Joshua, where I had left off. It was the part where God sent the Israelites through the Jordan River and into the Promised Land by holding back the waters, just like the Red Sea. Another miracle. Then God directed them to do something unusual. To collect stones from the river bottom and set them up as a memorial on the dry land so they wouldn't forget the victory. And wouldn't forget who had won it for them.

I was deep into it when a call came to my cell from Dick Valentine.

"Trevor, breaking news. Still sketchy, but I thought you ought to know. That international child exploitation ring we've been talking about? Our sources tell us there's a major rush now to get a large number of abducted girls out of the United States. Like, right now."

"Why the hurry?"

"Not sure. Maybe they think someone's onto them and they'll be shut down. . . ."

"What part of the country are we talking about?"

"Sorry, we don't have that. Just some chatter on the Internet that was picked up by our guys here in NYPD doing surveillance for a terror cell, and they happened to land on this instead."

While I was mulling it over, Dick said, "So frustrating. We're trying to figure out how they plan to drag these poor girls outside the country—transportation routes, that stuff. But we don't have enough hard data to make an educated guess. To do that, we'd need to know where the command decision is coming from. That's the key."

"Any closer to identifying who's calling the shots?"

"Our guys are sure there's a controlling administrator in America who's running this entire putrid business and using the dark net to do it. But we can't pierce it. Too sophisticated, digitally. We've asked the feds for special IT assistance, but no answer yet."

The image of that girl's face in the window of the boat was in front of me again. "You're talking possible transportation routes," I said. "I've got a story to tell you."

"Should I grab some popcorn?"

"Not unless you're into horror. I've got solid information that some of those girls are coming down the Mississippi River, being motored into the Gulf of Mexico, and then into international waters."

"Makes sense. Our terrorism guys tell us about the vulnerability of ports and harbors. Good deduction, Sherlock."

"I can't take the credit. I have a credible witness. He dropped it right in my lap. I checked it out and saw it with my own sorry eyes."

I could tell Dick was thinking. Then he said, "Are you still down in New Orleans? You're right near the mouth of the Mississippi. You need to talk to law enforcement down there."

"Already tried that. Their hands are tied."

"Want me to give them a call?"

"Let's hold on that. I want to keep our relationship close to the vest."

"Coast Guard?"

"Tried that too. They sent me back to the local authorities."

"What's your next move?"

"I'm flying to Washington tomorrow with my daughter."

"To do what?"

"Solve the problem."

"Washington actually *solving* a problem? That's strange logic."

I smiled at my end. "To kill a snake, you have to strike at the head."

He wished me luck and we both promised to keep in touch.

I popped into Heather's room to check on her progress.

"Done," she said. "I've got us on a direct flight leaving tomorrow morning from Louis Armstrong International Airport." Then she asked what I had been doing.

"Mostly reading the book of Joshua."

She smirked. "Old Testament."

"Yes. Glad you're familiar with it. . . ."

"Well, you know, those of us in the anthropology field have to acquaint ourselves with all the ancient *mythological* religions."

I was tempted to take the bait but let it pass.

She asked, "Anything else going on?"

I told her about my phone call with Dick Valentine. And the extreme urgency now behind our trip to Washington.

I saw in her face that she was shaken, as I already was, by the news that captured girls were about to be hurriedly exported out of the United States.

Heather's voice cut like a knife. "How can we stop this in time? Keep them from being shipped out of harbors? Or down the Mississippi to who knows where . . . ?"

I thought on it. "Here's how. By drying up the river," I said. "And then, when that happens, we take stones from the river bottom and build a memorial. So we don't forget who gave us the victory."

She gave me a funny look.

I smiled. "I'll explain later."

51

The next morning, after we returned the rental car to the airport, I sent a quick text to Ashley Linderman:

Thinking about that article you mentioned, the one from the underground Internet site—about some voodoo cult involved in child exploitation. Anything more about the web source of that article? Your true-blue friend, Trevor.

Our flight was scheduled to depart from gate B-12 at the very end of the concourse, so we knew we had to hustle. First the typical drill: received our boarding passes at a kiosk because we only had carry-ons, and then on to security. I received the "random" extra security screening. I thought nothing of it. It had happened before.

I lifted my arms and spread my legs for the full body scan,

and then was told to wait while my carry-on bag and laptop were searched. Nothing came of it. Until I was told to keep waiting exactly where I stood, with no explanation about the delay. I stood there, turning only to raise my hand to wave over to the next line, where Heather was also going through security.

The TSA woman grimaced and said, "Put your arm down, sir."

I complied, but by then I was getting wary of the nonroutine treatment. I didn't blame the woman in the blue TSA uniform, or the airlines or anyone else. But I had the sinking feeling that they might just be pawns on the wrong side of a drama more dangerous than they could have imagined. I steeled myself for the worst.

At that point, my belt, coat, shoes, laptop, keys, and cell phone were lying in front of me in two trays at the end of the conveyor belt, having already been successfully scanned through the X-ray machine. Then I heard a digital ding from my cell. I leaned toward it and noticed a text. I reached down and pushed the message icon. It was from Ashley.

Urgent. New information. Call me ASAP.

The TSA lady grabbed the cell out of my hand. "Step back, sir, behind the line immediately."

My premonition came true when two men in suits rushed up to me, one on each side, and ordered me to follow them. Again I began to comply, but I asked about my luggage. I was told it would be "taken care of." I half turned to Heather and yelled for her to follow me.

That must have been some kind of last straw for them, because I was thrown to the ground, hands behind my back, and handcuffed. While my face was being smooshed to the floor, I tried to process my dilemma. The men were definitely not TSA. FBI? Homeland Security? Yes, probably DHS.

What did they have on me? Whatever it was, it was time to extricate myself yet again from more administrative quicksand that could stop me from getting to the monsters who were preparing at that moment to convey a caravan of victims toward international waters.

I was yanked to my feet and fast-walked up to the second-level lobby of concourse C. I tried to turn around to see if Heather was behind me, but each time I was warned that if I did that again, I would be tasered.

After being pushed into a small, unadorned office by the two agents, the door was closed behind me. No pictures on the walls, just a few telephones on bare desks. It had all the naked ambience of a telemarketing station. I was seated on a plastic chair by one of the agents as the other looked on.

"What is your reason for leaving New Orleans?"

"A trip to Washington."

"Your business in Washington?"

"Meetings."

"With whom?"

"I'll know when I get there."

The other agent smirked.

The agent questioning me said, "You need to explain your travel plans, Mr. Black."

"And why is that?" I asked.

No answer to my question.

Meanwhile, in my head, a quick review: events were

breaking. Ashley had just sent me an urgent text. I had to get to Washington ASAP and couldn't afford to miss my flight.

I grabbed the discussion by the tail. "Okay, what list was I erroneously placed on? Watch list? No-fly? I believe in those lists, by the way. When they're accurate. But yours can't be."

My criminal practice had given me insight about the process. FBI gives data to the NCTC, the National Counterterrorism Center, which inputs it into the Terrorist Screening Database for the creation of watch lists used by the Terrorist Screening Center. Yeah, at that moment, I thought I was so very smart.

Until the agent spoke.

"Who says you're on a list?"

Having just been humbled down to size, I asked, "Then what's this all about?"

"Tell us about Morehaven. . . ."

Just then, daybreak in my brain. All that was lacking in this drama was a choir of soprano voices, high and airy, in the background as the sun burst through the clouds.

This was no watch list. I was being specifically targeted. Probably by the same entity that caused the New Orleans FBI and Sheriff Haywood to round me up on phony psychiatric grounds and drag me to Morehaven. To stop me or at least slow me down. And accomplishing that required not only manipulating federal and state law enforcement, but also feeding slanted information to a supernaturally skeptical psychiatrist and now sending a directive to the Department of Homeland Security.

Of course, all of that would take immense power, coupled with malicious resolve, something on the level of molten-hot road rage. The thought gave me pause.

With ironclad certainty, I had arrived at one uncomfortable realization: ever since leaving Ocracoke Island, and even before that, I had been swept into extreme spiritual combat, version 2.0.

Had I really faced up to that?

By then I didn't consider myself a novice. And maybe that was the point. This battle wasn't ultimately about flesh and blood. No mere battle of wits between "experts." Not some political power play. This was an ancient conflagration raging between heaven and hell, and I was sitting in the front row. Or actually, closer.

As I looked at the agent from DHS, I decided to lay it out.

"Morehaven was a mistake," I said. "But behind that mistake, just like behind this mistake you are making right now—and I'm sure yours is a good-faith mistake, by the way—behind all of it, there is something malevolent. Here's the truth: I'm being targeted. Someone a rung higher than you mistakenly informed you, based on orders from someone higher than them, that I was a court-committed psychiatric patient at Morehaven. Probably gave you a song and dance about my being an escapee from that institution or being a public danger or both. You currently have possession of my cell phone. Along with my laptop, my suitcase, and my belt, by the way. Now, if you bring my cell phone to me, this can be handled quickly."

Neither agent budged.

I added, "I have great appreciation for what you gentlemen do for our country. Nevertheless, there is something you need to understand: God wants me on that airplane. If you give me my cell, you'll learn everything you need to know about Morehaven. And why you have to release me immediately."

The DHS agent who had been questioning me looked at his partner and nodded. A minute later I had my cell back in my hand. I pulled up my in-box and showed him the message from Judge Levall's clerk of court—the e-mail that contained the judge's order granting my habeas corpus petition, vindicating me, and declaring that my confinement at Morehaven had been unlawful.

The agent read the e-mail and then showed it to his partner. After a few seconds, he opened the door. "Have a nice flight, Mr. Black."

52

Heather was waiting outside the office, along with my luggage, my laptop, and my belt.

"What's going on?" she shouted. "Oh, my gosh, I couldn't believe it—they took you down, I mean, right to the ground, like some kind of terrorist. . . ."

I told her we had to hustle to the gate and make sure we made the flight. I would fill her in about everything else during our flight to Washington.

By the time we arrived at gate B-12, we had a good fifteen minutes to spare before boarding started. A miracle.

I used that little window of time to respond to the text from Detective Ashley Linderman. I phoned her. She picked up.

"Ashley, Trevor here," I said. "Talk to me."

"You sound hassled."

"You have no idea."

"Okay, so here's what I found out," she said. "Another e-mail alert today. This one's got some really juicy information dealing with that Internet article, the one about the supposed voodoo child-abduction and sex-abuse cult. The domain name associated with the article is real sketchy. It's part of something called Odin. An underground Internet network full of shadowy postings and nefarious activities."

"I heard about this. It's part of the dark net."

"Right. Well, let me give you a comparison. There's this other site out there, pretty well-known, called Tor, where some of the content is legit, but other activities described on that web engine are questionable or illegal. But Odin? Trevor, it's even worse. Practically everything that goes on Odin is criminal. Really vile, awful stuff. That's where the article originated."

"So where does that leave us?"

"Here's my guess," she said. "Whoever authored that piece is not a nice person. The article, by the way, never condemned the idea of a voodoo cult that captures girls. Just talked about it. Other than undercover cops and researchers, anyone who travels down the Odin Internet road is rotten to the core. Does that help?"

"I think so, thanks."

"You still down in New Orleans?"

"Just about to board a plane with Heather, heading to Washington."

"Say hello to Heather for me. She's a special young woman. And you be safe."

The last hurdle would be boarding. I still knew that anything could happen, and I wouldn't relax until we were on board and in the air.

Thirty minutes before takeoff, boarding started. As we stood in the crowded line that snaked to the boarding desk, I suddenly felt played out. Empty. Out of nowhere, a sense of fatalism washed over me. Maybe it was the natural result of an endless series of attacks, most of them when I had least expected. The frailties of the flesh. But when it's coupled at the same time with the onslaught of the world and the devil, it can be an utter drag.

Just then the advice from Rev. John Cannon came bounding into my head, like a big dog demanding attention and pressing its wet nose into my face.

"Rely on the Spirit, that's what. Make room for faith in all this, Trevor. This isn't like improving your golf game, you know."

Time to quit complaining. Self-pity is a destroyer. A tool of the enemy.

To my delight, boarding was uneventful. Heather and I had seats together, and after stowing our carry-ons in the overhead, I plunked down into my seat with my laptop and gave her my iPad.

She immediately demanded a recap of my experience with the two men from the Department of Homeland Security. I told her everything.

Heather asked, "All it took was your showing them the e-mail about winning the Morehaven case?"

"Technically, yes."

"Technically?"

I added, "I also told them God wanted me on this flight."

She looked at me funny, studying me for a while, but didn't respond.

I wrapped it up. "And so here we are."

Heather wanted to know about the call from Ashley Linderman. I told her what Ashley said about the sinister Odin web network.

Then I let her into my head. "Something's been bugging me."

"Like?"

"Like the fact that voodoo is like a virus: it has a number of different strains."

She gave a knowing nod.

I continued. "Of course, you're the budding anthropologist, so you already knew that."

More nodding from her, this time with a sarcastic wink.

I continued. "Minerva Sabatier was into voodoo big-time. Then some outside outfit shows up and wants to team up with her. She unwittingly sticks her big toe into it and then realizes what it's really into: child abduction, human trafficking, and murder. The worst. She decides in a moment of personal conviction to pull out, maybe even expose it, as documented in the notes in her Bible. Soon thereafter, she's poisoned by her personal chef, who uses a toxic potion that is a favorite of the most nefarious kinds of voodoo cults. Something that may also have been added to a coffee cup offered to Assistant Attorney General Paul Pullmen in my hotel room to disable him before he was so terribly mutilated. After all, there weren't any signs of a struggle."

Heather said, "And your point is . . . ?"

"I need to get a handle on a voodoo cult that fits our profile—specializing in violent, sadistic behavior. Not just spell casting or dancing around fires. But sexual abuse. Bloodletting. Human sacrifice."

Her answer was simple. "I've already done some thinking about that. Let me check it out."

When we were up in the air and the restriction on devices was lifted, Heather dove into my research project, using my iPad again.

Meanwhile, on my laptop, I checked out the three-word phrase that had intrigued me ever since Dick Valentine spoke it—the name of the Internet enterprise being investigated by Jason Forester before he died. The outfit connected with sex slavery of young girls. *Kuritsa Foks Videoryad*. It must have been the same hideous site that Henry Bosant was told to access. Russian-sounding, he said.

So I went with that and fed it into an online translator. It spit out the English version: Chicken Fox Videos.

In sex abuse and prostitution cases, the word *chickens* is a twisted term of art, referring to young sexual victims of older predators. I could guess the meaning of *fox*.

I closed my laptop, suddenly aware that Heather was staring at me.

"What's up?" I asked.

"I've got something for you."

"Hit me."

"The dark net stuff and specifically the Odin site that Ashley mentioned."

"What did you find?"

Heather said, "It's about Odin. Do you know who he was?"

"A mythological god."

"A Norse god, to be exact. But that's not the important part. What's important is what Odin might have to do with that criminal Internet site."

"Teach me."

"He was one of the chief gods. There are three things about him that might be important. The first is that he was the god of outlaws. Think about that. The Odin network is all about masking criminal activity."

"I follow you."

"Second, he had a lust for power."

That grabbed me.

"Lastly, and I think you'll especially like this," Heather said, "Odin was able to enter the world of the dead. There's the supernatural angle. I know you've been looking for it."

Heather was right. From where I was sitting, that was a home run.

Then she gave her last comment, a kind of throwaway.

"One final tidbit. Just a footnote. One author said if she had to align Odin the Norse god with one philosopher in particular, it would probably be Friedrich Nietzsche."

There was that name again. I found myself staring off.

Heather squinted at me. "Did you hear what I said?"

"Yes, sorry. I was just thinking of something. Good research."

"Then there's that other thing you wanted."

"Right, on the violent side of voodoo . . ."

She said, "Well, I found something. A very scary variation of voodoo. It's called Palo Mayombe."

"Great. Maybe we're getting closer."

"I'll have to dig a little further. But that's a start." There was weariness in her voice. "Boy, I'm feeling brain-fried." She sighed and said, "Can I ask you something?"

"Sure."

"Do you ever get tired of this?"

I could see where she was heading.

"I'm talking," she said, "you know, about the battle. Against horrible people who do horrible things. Chasing monsters."

"Tired?" I said. "Yes."

As I spoke, I noticed the dull fatigue in her eyes. I gave a nod to the overhead screen above her seat. "Why don't you give yourself a rest. Catch an in-flight movie. Get your mind off this stuff for a while."

53

For the rest of the flight, I was lost in my own thoughts, trying to construct a rough game plan for our Washington expedition.

By the time our jet was approaching Reagan National Airport and the announcement came for electronic devices to be shut off, I glanced over at Heather and noticed that she had not been watching the movie. Instead she was glued to my iPad, which she had open in her lap.

Finally she turned to me with a Cheshire-cat grin and said, "I found something."

I said, "Sorry I ruined your movie by laying research projects on you."

Heather shot back, "And I'm sorry to ruin your appetite with the research I'm about to dump on you."

At that point, she proceeded to explain the tormented life of a Mexican drug lord named Adolfo Constanzo.

"He died violently in a 1989 shoot-out," she said.

"Not unusual for a drug dealer."

"This guy's not your usual cocaine kingpin. As a boy, his mother had taken him to Haiti, where he became an apprentice to a local voodoo witch doctor who was a practitioner of Palo Mayombe."

Now she had my attention.

Heather explained, "Palo Mayombe cult followers believe that the ceremonial killing of living victims is the key to empowerment. Animal sacrifices are considered useful, but human sacrifice is the real deal. The bones and body parts are used in a *nganga*, a cauldron ceremony to impart that power."

"How did this drug dealer use it?"

"Constanzo figured that the practice of Palo would make him rich and would also protect him from the police. And for a while, it must have looked like it was working. In Mexico, he became a powerful crime figure, even though he was a young guy, about my age. At first he dug up corpses in graveyards for his cult practices. Then he moved on to murder and mutilation of live victims. He ran a drug cult called the Narcosatanists, and he killed more than twenty people whom he then used in his ceremonies. One poor victim was a University of Texas student. When that happened, it hit the news in the US."

Recalling the macabre dismembering of Paul Pullmen and the machete lying next to his corpse, I asked, "Any mention of the use of a machete on his victims?"

"In fact," she said, "that was the weapon of choice in

Constanzo's warped Palo Mayombe world. Then there's this, a headline from the *New York Post* from 2000—'Human Sacrifice Rare, but It Happens'—tying it to Palo Mayombe. More recent reports too. One from the *National Geographic News* in 2005. Plus a report from the United Nations Committee on the Rights of the Child, warning about ritualistic abuse and killing of children connected with certain voodoo practices. It was picked up in June 2014 by publications like *International Business Times* and *Business Insider.* Trevor, this stuff is real. . . ."

As Heather closed the iPad, I was thinking through what she had just told me. The voodoo subcult she described was a close fit to the murder of Assistant AG Paul Pullmen. My own knee-jerk was to assume that this violent form of voodoo only flourished in third-world countries and that it didn't seem to fit with urbane Washington, DC, the global seat of power and sophisticated politics. It was hard to fathom a Palo Mayombe mastermind lurking somewhere in the federal bureaucracy. But then I knew too well that evil didn't have cultural or geographical borders.

The landing gear lowered, and the wheels of the jet hit the runway with a squeal.

By then, I had picked the starting point for my investigation. It was the only name that made sense to me at that moment. Someone who worked in DC. But it had been years, and I wondered if he would remember me.

By the time we left the terminal, I had already left a voice message for Gil Spencer, deputy assistant attorney general in the Criminal Division of the Department of Justice.

Gil and I were fresh out of law school when we were both hired as attorneys in the New York City public defender's office.

Eighteen months later, I took a job in the private sector to handle criminal cases at Tobit, Dandridge & Swartz, eventually becoming a full partner. Not too long after, Gil landed a job as a staff attorney in the DOJ and moved to Washington and then up the legal ladder at Main Justice.

I was hoping my history with Gil Spencer would open the door, though perhaps only barely. It had been a lot of years with no contact between the two of us.

But Gil was a logical choice. He had close access to key players in this tragedy. When Jason Forester died, Gil had been the assistant to Paul Pullmen and would have inside intel that I didn't have but needed. Whether he could share it with me was another matter.

Heather and I were standing on the airport's public transportation level, waiting for a car rental, when a return message from Gil Spencer came through. His voice was high-pitched and thin, and he was talking fast. "Trevor, this is Gil. Please call me back, but only on my cell."

Once he had delivered his cell number, he hung up. No good-byes, no "talk to you then," no salutations. Nothing.

When I reached him, he was practically hyperventilating.

"Trevor, I can't believe you're calling me right now. In terms of the timing, I mean. This is absolutely spooky. You have no idea."

"Why so?"

"Your name came up."

"How?"

"Meetings. Postmortems about Paul Pullmen's murder. Came up again today, in fact. It's crazy."

"In what way?"

"Can't really talk now. We need to rendezvous."

"Can we do it quickly? Time's of the essence."

"I haven't taken a lunch break." He gave a sardonic laugh. "Yeah. Like that's something new. I'll tell my secretary I'm taking a late lunch. Right now, in fact. We'll meet. But it's got to be off-site. Out in the sticks somewhere. Nowhere near Capitol Hill."

There was a momentary silence. Then he said, "Okay. I've got the place. Rock Creek Cemetery. My aunt is buried there. There's a statue on the grounds called *Rabboni*. Ask at the cemetery office; they'll tell you where it is."

I walked with Heather to the Metro station at the airport and handed her my cell phone. When I had time, I would have to pick up another for myself—one of those TracFones, something to use until Heather could replace hers.

I told Heather about my upcoming meeting with Gil Spencer at Rock Creek Cemetery. I asked her to take the rental car into the heart of the city, and we set a time and place to meet for dinner later.

I wanted her to be my proxy in the interim. "Book two rooms for two nights at the Mandarin Oriental. Then call Pastor Wilhem Ventrie in Port Sulphur. Ask him to contact Henry Bosant. The guy at the Dead Point abandoned cemetery."

"You ever notice how you have this thing for graveyards?"

"Hey, I'm not the one picking the spooky sites."

She laughed.

"So," I continued, "have the pastor ask Henry Bosant to call you. When he does, he needs to give you an update on the nasty business going on along the river. Maybe Bosant can corroborate what Dick Valentine told us about the rushed timetable."

"Why don't I just call Bosant directly?"

"Better to have the pastor pave the way."

"Send me your number as soon as you get yourself a phone. I'll call you if I find anything. And, Trevor . . ."

I eyed her as she seemed to be sifting through things in her mind.

"Just . . ." She bit her lip. "Just be careful."

54

I rode the Yellow Line Metro, getting as close as I could to Rock Creek Cemetery. I exited at the Petworth Metro station, finishing the rest of the trip on foot. When I arrived, I passed under a black wrought-iron archway that announced the three-hundred-year-old cemetery, and I went right to the office.

A map showed the location of the *Rabboni* statue, and there was a written blurb about it. I headed through the landscape of trees and rolling hills and grave markings until I found it— a life-size bronze image of a woman in a robe emerging from a stone alcove, her right hand lifting the hood from her head and her left arm outstretched to something beyond. There was pathos in her face. The meaning of it required an understanding of the story where she was an important part.

I spotted a bench in front of the statue and sat down. It wasn't long before I heard a voice.

"She looks scared. The statue, I mean."

I turned toward the voice and recognized Gil Spencer right off. But he had changed, his hair thinning, his face pale, and bags under his eyes. The toll taken on Justice Department lawyers by endless hours and working in a cauldron of professional pressure.

Gil pointed to the bronze likeness of the woman that over the last century had turned a streaked, greenish hue. "One description I read said she looks 'horrified.' But I think that's taking it too far."

I said, "It's supposed to be Mary Magdalene. A woman who had seven demons. Then she met Jesus and was healed. The Gospels tell the story." I pointed to the spot next to me on the bench. "Have a seat."

Gil looked around in all directions before sitting down. "Thanks for meeting here. I can't afford to have eyes on me."

"Look," I started out, "before we talk, in full disclosure, you need to know I've had an *unconventional* career path since we last met."

Gil cocked an eyebrow. "Always the prince of understatement. Yeah, I know what you've been doing. *Litigator Today* called you one of the top five criminal defense lawyers in New York City. Then everything went south for you. Including your license to practice law. Followed by your stint with the NYPD as their chief Ghostbuster."

I didn't react. No need to quibble over job titles.

Gil said, "Yeah, I heard it all. But to me, you were always the guy with the killer trial skills, especially during cross."

"No more," I said. "Now I'm out there on the fringe. But look at you . . . one rung away from being the top dog for the Criminal Division at DOJ. Good for you."

Things got somber when Gil changed subjects. "So on the phone, I said your name had come up. My advice: be careful who you trust. If you go skipping into DOJ with your story, you'll be digging your own grave. Better not do that. And by the way, reading the case files that Jason Forester and Paul Pullmen were working, I think you're onto something."

"Tell me more."

"I've got to be careful what I share. One thing for sure— someone inside the system is sabotaging things. Documents missing. Hard drives erased. It's getting dangerous. Jason Forester gone. And now Paul Pullmen murdered."

"About my name coming up . . ."

"Yeah. You see, he was planning on talking with you right before he died."

"Right. Paul Pullmen must have thought he was meeting with me in my hotel room in New Orleans. Instead, the killer showed up."

Gil Spencer was shaking his head. "No, no, not that. Sure, I knew my boss wanted to meet with you after he got your e-mail. But that's not who I am talking about."

"You don't mean Jason Forester?"

"You got it."

That was a shocker.

"His handwritten notes are missing from his prosecution file in the case against that Russian child porn site. But we were able to retrieve his log from the metadata on his computer. Three days before he died, Jason Forester made an entry about planning to talk with you."

I immediately wondered who could have pilfered Forester's files. "This data sabotage you described and the missing files—who would have had access?"

"Well, his supervising US attorney, of course. And also our Criminal Division over at DOJ."

"Anyone else?"

"Sure. Attorney General Shazzar."

I chewed on all of that while Gil Spencer kept talking.

"Anyway, Jason Forester was planning on talking to you about some magazine article you wrote. He wanted to know if you had picked up any useful leads when you did your research on the human trafficking of young kids. Runaways . . ."

I was trying to process that. "I never knew . . ."

Gil charged on. "Then the next thing that happens, he's found dead at his desk."

"An inside source in DC called it voodoo. You know who that might be or why the tie-in to voodoo?"

He shook his head. "No. But there was a very menacing message in the FedEx letter Forester received right before he died. Weird symbols. A skull wearing a top hat. Skeletons dancing. It also had letters from a newspaper cut out to spell these words: 'You will die in five minutes.' And according to the coroner, that's exactly what happened."

After checking the time, he said, "Gotta go. I may have eyes on me. Have to be careful."

We both stood.

I pointed to the *Rabboni* statue and explained. "By the way, that isn't fear on Mary Magdalene's face. It's amazement. And joy, too, I think."

"How do you know?"

"The story lays it out," I told him. "She runs into the resurrected Christ. She'd thought he was dead. She saw him die with her own eyes. But then she finds him alive, just after Jesus had performed the ultimate act of supernatural empowerment—rising from his own grave, *bringing forth his body*. You know, habeas corpus."

At the corner of Gil's mouth, a flicker of a smile. Then he strode off.

55

I made the long trek to the closest Metro station and on the Green Line subway to the belly of the beast in DC in order to meet up with Heather. We'd agreed on an approximate time for us to gather at 1789, an upscale restaurant in Georgetown. Because she had my cell, I felt disconnected. But according to my watch, I was on schedule.

It was shoulder-to-shoulder in the subway car and I was standing, but after the first stop several seats freed up, so I sat down. Only two pieces of intel had surfaced from my conversation with Gil that might prove useful in pinpointing the leadership of Kuritsa Foks Videoryad. One bit of information wasn't new but corroborated everything I believed. The fact that someone with influence inside the federal government in DC was behind the cruel enterprise. I came to Washington expecting it, but somehow it sounded even more disturbing coming from Gil Spencer.

Secondly, three days before he died, Jason Forester had made notes to himself on his computer about wanting to contact me about my article. He must have been following up on any leads he could find about child abduction or adolescent sex trafficking. Clearly he was zeroing in on Kuritsa Foks Videoryad. I wondered who else might have known about Forester's plan to talk to me.

The subway cars slowed to another stop. The doors slid open. That was when I noticed him, not ten feet away, reading the *Washington Post*.

"Vance?" I called out.

Vance Zaduck put down the paper, looked over, and smiled when he recognized me. The seat next to me was open, so he trotted over and joined me.

"What are you doing in Washington?"

"Business," I said.

Vance shook his head and lowered his voice as he got personal with me. "Listen, when I found out about that Morehaven episode, I called the US attorney for New Orleans and read him the riot act. They should have called me before they roped you into a custodial situation. They knew that you and I had a professional relationship, for crying out loud. I could have helped you. Prevented all of that embarrassment . . ."

"No apologies necessary," I said. "I filed a habeas corpus and was released quickly. But that was a first for me."

"What were they thinking?" he asked. "I would like to know who gave them the directive to pick you up. Do you know?"

"Not yet. But no matter. I've got other fish to fry." I looked at my watch. "You know, Vance, I'd figure you to be the work-aholic type. You heading home already? It's not five yet."

"I'm playing the good uncle," Vance said. "I'm heading out to my niece's birthday party. She's officially a teenager. Her mother—you know, my sister—she put the pressure on me."

I nodded.

Vance looked down at the floor, his jaw clenched like he was struggling. "I have a decision to make," he said.

I waited.

He hesitated. "Deciding how much I can tell you—ethically, I mean."

"What about?"

"About you."

"Me?"

"Yeah. See, I'm on the team leading an internal investiga-tion. Ever since Jason Forester died."

"Natural causes, isn't that what you determined?"

"Right now that issue is moot. The point is, he was threat-ened in a FedEx letter. And that was followed by Paul Pullmen's murder. We're looking at a possible federal insider who could be involved with both of those events. A traitor in our midst." He looked me over. "Do you find that hard to believe?"

"As time goes by," I said, "I'm surprised by less and less."

His eyes narrowed. He was giving me a closer look. "I guess you're talking about your moonlighting job, right? Chasing spooks and demons?" He gave a little snort.

"Let's just say that when it comes to rotten apples, I don't believe evil has geographical boundaries—or professional ones either," I said, looking him in the eye. "The real enemy is unseen. Malicious. Committed. Equally at home in halls of government as he is in suburbia or in the hood or in rural America."

Then I turned it around. "Vance, about what you just said—about what you can, or should, share with me. And about my name being involved in some way with the Jason Forester matter."

"Just be careful," Vance Zaduck said. "If you are approached."

"Approached by who?"

"Can't name names. But I can warn you about one thing: be very cautious of anyone from the Department of Justice who tries to speak to you about Jason Forester and Paul Pullmen. And their deaths."

"Can you be more specific?" I said, sliding over a few inches on the bench to get a better look at Vance's face as he drilled closer to the mother lode.

Vance's expression tightened. "Anyone who worked closely with Paul Pullmen at the Department of Justice. Someone who knew his comings and goings. We're close to nailing the bad actor. And he's dangerous."

"Anyone I know?"

"I'm afraid so. That's all I can say."

My skin crawled. Vance had practically pasted Gil Spencer's face on a wanted poster. And I had just come from a meeting with him.

I said only, "Thanks. Food for thought."

Zaduck smiled. "Just be cautious. I remember, during your FBI interview in New Orleans when I was on the other side of the glass, that you mentioned you've got a daughter. She was in New Orleans with you."

"Yes. Heather."

"My advice? Take care of her. And yourself. You may want to get out of the city for a while until we can clear things up."

After that, Vance closed up the conversation. He exited at the next station, giving me a quick wave good-bye.

I took the Green Line all the way to Chinatown, then hailed a cab and headed over to 1789 at the corner of Thirty-Sixth and Prospect. I was looking forward to dinner with Heather. Another glance at my watch told me I was on time.

Funny, the things that can go through your head in the backseat of a taxi. Excitement about reconnecting with Heather after being separated from her for hours. But after Vance Zaduck's warning, wanting to keep her out of harm's way. I was even entertaining the possibility of getting her out of town ahead of me, while I continued to dig.

The clock was running. It was time for me to do something bold. If I shook things up, maybe the bad actor out there would come out of the shadows.

56

I had hoped dinner could at least be a brief respite when I could talk to Heather about her life. About growing up, and her interests, friends, school, sports, and dating life. All the things I had missed for more than two decades.

Heather, on the other hand, couldn't wait to spill some sordid details that she had learned.

We were at a corner table at 1789 restaurant, and Heather was bursting with news. We ordered quickly, and then she started.

"Oh," she blurted out, "do I have something for you. That guy you met at the Mississippi River, at Dead Point, but not the guy you ended up wrestling with—you know, the pickup truck driver—but the one before that . . . the guy with the boat who was halfway guilty . . . or maybe not, maybe just a dupe."

"Right, Henry Bosant," I said. "The man I wanted you to talk to."

"Well, there's breaking news at Port Sulphur. I called Pastor Ventrie, and get this: Henry Bosant was found dead. Hanging by his neck from a tree."

That was a gut punch. Tragic news for Bosant, the new convert to Christ from a rough background, struggling with his possible complicity with a human trafficking ring.

I had to ask, "Suicide?"

"That's the strange part," she said. "The pastor talked to that officer who goes to his church, Deputy St. Martin, who investigated Bosant's death. There's some question about whether he hanged himself or whether he had a blow to the head first—blunt-force trauma—and then was hanged by the neck by someone else."

"Head trauma . . . based on what?"

"Don't know exactly. But the hanging part sounds fishy."

"Tell me more."

"In addition to Henry Bosant possibly suffering a fractured skull and being set up for a fake suicide, there was this business about his landline. His phone line was apparently tapped."

"He had suspicions about that. What else?"

"Just that an official of some kind from New Orleans was the one who discovered his body."

"What kind of official?"

"In the housing department."

That didn't make sense to me. "Why would a New Orleans housing department person be in Port Sulphur?"

"According to a news report, Bosant had been named as a

witness in a housing violation, and the housing guy went down there to take a statement from him."

"That sounds like overkill, just to process some slumlord complaint or settle a rental dispute. What's the official's name?"

"His last name was a little different."

I knew only one name at the Housing Authority of New Orleans. "Was it Lawrence Rudabow?"

"Wow, yes, that's it."

Heather peppered me with questions, so I told her about my meeting with Rudabow in New Orleans. She also wanted to know more about my meeting at the cemetery with Gil Spencer and the odd happenstance of my running into Vance Zaduck on the Metro, and whether I thought Spencer was as culpable as Zaduck was intimating, and how voodoo could be involved in any of this.

On that last question, I simply said, "Circumstantially, voodoo is staring us in the face."

"Because . . . ?"

"Your research on Palo Mayombe. Human sacrifice. Paul Pullmen was decapitated with a machete. It was left behind at the crime scene, carefully placed next to his corpse. As if arrogantly daring us to put it all together. Flaunting their ceremonial power. And Pullmen's hand was missing. They use body parts of their victims in their ceremonies."

She asked, "Then what are we doing in DC? I mean, look at the last Palo Mayombe celebrity. Adolfo Constanzo, a drug lord. Raised in voodoo-saturated Haiti and tutored by a voodoo priest. Lives and dies in the most crime-ridden part of Mexico. All that's a far cry from the nation's capital."

I nodded. "It's a conundrum."

"Where next?"

I said, "Getting a face-to-face with Louisa Deidre Baldou."

"Yeah. She seems to be in the middle of everything," Heather said. "Attending the ABA, where your address was on the death of Jason Forester and demonic involvement. Then she gets me to Bayou Bon Coeur, where voodoo is all over the place. Calls you with some coded message about Batman and Gotham City. Uses the word *Jester*, which helps lead us to the ruins of Six Flags . . ."

"Where her sister Lucinda had been kidnapped," I said. "Her remains found at Bayou Bon Coeur, a place with a dark voodoo reputation."

"Finding Louisa Deidre Baldou won't be easy." Heather thought on that some more. "Correction. Finding her will be next to impossible. She could be working anywhere. Just think how big the federal bureaucracy is."

"I've got a pretty good idea," I said.

Heather shook her head and winced. "I keep thinking back to that night at Dead Point and seeing that girl's face in the porthole of the boat."

That image hadn't left my head either.

A few seconds later she looked at me, narrowing her eyes. "All right. Time to tell me what in the world was going on between you and that pickup truck guy by the river. That guy starts to scream. It sounds otherworldly. Honestly. You wrestle him to the ground. You're shouting to him real loud, and then everything changes."

"You didn't see him change physically, did you?"

She took a second. "Of course not."

"Well, I did."

"Okay, you'll have to explain that one."

I decided it was time.

"I see things, Heather. Demons. When they inhabit people. And even when they don't. Things that others can't see."

She sat back, slack-jawed, finally saying only, "Oh, wow."

"Hard to believe, I'm sure. But there it is."

"And what you were doing with that guy by the river . . ."

"Helping him. A rescue effort. Expelling a demon."

"You do that stuff?"

"Never before. That was a first. It seemed like the right thing to do."

"You've been attacked by . . . demons, or whatever . . . attacked before?"

"Often."

"In New Orleans?"

"Several times."

"Where was I?"

"Somewhere else, thank goodness."

She gave me a look, one that I won't forget. It told me a lot about her, things that I had wanted to know but hadn't heard from her yet. Just then, I saw it in her eyes.

Then I heard it in her voice. Heather said, "I want in. All in. I want to stop this horrible stuff. All those girls . . ." Her voice was constricted, her eyes filling. "And I want to do it with you, Trevor. No more sitting in the backseat, watching like a spectator. Please, let me start now. Partners. You and me."

After I paid the check, we left the restaurant and readied to cross over to the other side of Prospect. I noticed how busy the traffic was in both directions.

Heather told me she had parked the car on the street level below, down on M Street. It was a steep drop and we were looking for a quick route to get down there. Heather said there had to be a shorter walk than the long, roundabout one she had taken to get up to the restaurant.

But while Heather talked, I was thinking about the real horror she knew nothing about: something she was willing to confront. Courageously, sure, but maybe a little recklessly. I had a great caution about it. On the other hand, she wanted to do it with me. That was the best thing of all.

Heather was talking fast about how we might locate Louisa Deidre Baldou, and as a result she didn't see the oncoming cars as she stepped off the curb and walked right into traffic. I pulled her back from the curb just as a big Escalade SUV came roaring by.

She looked stunned. After a second she said, "Wow, thanks, Trevor. Really. Thanks for the rescue."

I said, "My job. Always."

57

Heather and I stepped fast across Prospect, dodging traffic, till we made it to the other side.

For some reason, my skin was crawling. Tingling all over. I decided to look back, past the 1789 restaurant that fronted Thirty-Sixth Street. The sidewalk outside the restaurant was crowded with pedestrians. But it only took a second or two to understand why I had the sense that we were being followed.

There were two burly men in the crowd. And I recognized them right off because I was seeing double, except that one was wearing a red golf shirt and the other was wearing a yellow one. I impulsively shouted out loud to Heather.

"Demon twins."

Heather stopped and half laughed. "Uh, what are you talking about?"

"Bad news coming. They're passing by the front of 1789. We've got to run."

"To where?"

I noticed some steps that led to M Street below us. "We're going down."

"Since when do demons come in twins?"

"Since they attacked me in an alley in New Orleans."

I grabbed her by the arm and urged her straight ahead of me, down an ultra-steep stone staircase that plunged between a redbrick building on the left and a three-story limestone wall on the right. As we scampered down, I looked behind us, but no one was coming.

At the bottom, we caught our breath. I surveyed the area. I could see the traffic on M Street dead ahead between some buildings. Another look back up the staircase. Still no sign of the demon twins.

I heard Heather shout something and then a short, explosive laugh. She was pointing to a bronze plaque on the wall of the building at the foot of the perilous stairway. I asked her what it said.

She cried out, "You've got to be kidding!" She opened her arms wide and said, "These stairs are called '*The Exorcist* steps.' They were used in the movie. The part where a priest possessed by a demon throws himself down the stone stairway . . ."

She never finished, because by then I had looked up the steps one more time and the demon twins were standing at the top, grim-faced, one looking down Prospect Street and the other up Thirty-Sixth Street.

"Gotta run," I yelled and waved for her to follow me to M Street.

When we were almost to the street, I cranked my head around one more time. The twins were sprinting effortlessly down the stone stairs after us.

We turned onto M and fast-stepped along the sidewalk until we were able to hide ourselves in a crowd of students from Georgetown University.

I asked Heather where she had parked our rental. Half out of breath, she said it was a side street off the right-hand side of M Street.

"You carry a makeup compact?" I asked.

"Okay, so is that some chauvinist comment . . . ?"

No time to explain. "I need it now," I snapped.

She passed it to me and I plucked out the makeup pad, then cupped the mirror in my left hand so I could see behind us without turning around.

Heather said, "I thought they don't show up in mirrors."

I shot back, "That's vampires. That's Hollywood. This is real." Then I told her, "Don't look back, but they're heading this way, on our side of the sidewalk."

"How close?"

"About a block and a half behind us."

All of a sudden the college kids halted and bunched up in front of Clyde's restaurant while one of them strolled in to check the wait time for dinner.

We shot ahead, pulling into the middle of a large group of tourists who were gathered together chatting. They gave us curious looks and polite nods. I whispered to Heather, "We need to break free right now. Walk fast to the next cross street."

"Good. That's where I'm parked."

We almost plowed into a man and a young woman about Heather's age who were window-shopping. We excused ourselves as the couple nodded back and then entered the store.

The two of us quick-walked Olympic style until we were almost at the corner. I looked back with the mirror. "They're closing on us. Don't know if they see us right now, but we can't take chances."

We took power strides to the corner. Another look in the mirror. "Okay. They were jogging, but now they're stopped at the window of a shop, looking for us. Maybe they think we went in."

We picked up the pace.

At the corner, one last glance in the mirror. "They've started jogging again. I think they've seen us."

We sprinted down the side street until we reached the rental that she had parked at the curb. "You drive," I shouted. "I've got a plan."

She jumped behind the wheel, and I buckled into the passenger seat. I told her to do a U-turn, get back to M Street, and turn left.

Heather wheeled the car around and pulled up to the red light at M. Seconds ticked by as we sat in the stopped car. I knew that any minute the demon twins would be appearing on the sidewalk from our left. They would run right into our car. We would be sitting ducks. More seconds elapsed. Traffic was snaking slowly past us on M Street.

I shouted, "Run the red light. Pull onto M."

She gunned it and jackrabbited us in between cars coming and going in both lanes, followed by a flurry of blasting horns. But at least we were in the lane heading toward the Key Bridge.

Except that the twins on the sidewalk were now parallel with us and had us in their sights. They lowered their heads and charged like rhinos. Leaping in front of oncoming cars in the other lane to get to us.

"Pass!" I yelled.

"There's no passing lane!"

"Make one!"

She pulled out of the traffic jam and slammed her foot to the floor, speeding us into the oncoming lane of traffic.

"There's a spot." I pointed to the space in front of a seafood delivery truck that had slowed down. She accelerated past it and tucked the car neatly into the space that had opened up in front of the truck.

"Nice work," I shouted, then checked my visor mirror. Behind us, the twins were yanking some poor unsuspecting couple out of their vehicle.

Heather glanced over at the look on my face. I gave her the reason.

"The chase just got faster."

58

I told Heather to bear left and take the Key Bridge. I half turned to check on our pursuers as we followed the fast-moving traffic across the Potomac River.

"They're driving behind us, on the bridge. About five cars back. Here's my plan: we have to split up."

Heather shouted, "No!"

"It's the only way. They want me, not you. I'm hoping they'll tail me and leave you behind."

"But there are two of them," she said. "One for each of us."

She had a point.

"Give me a second," I said, booting up Google Maps on my phone. "Okay. Get me to the Rosslyn Metro, which is straight ahead, only a few blocks from here. I'll dash out. You'll have to backtrack and find the exit to I-66 heading into Washington. You'll cross another bridge, then get onto Constitution Avenue. A couple of miles down Constitution, you'll bear left on Louisiana over to Union Station. That's where we'll meet. Can you remember all that?"

"Trevor, I'm a grad student, remember? But what will I do when I get there?"

"Just keep making your way around Union Station. There's a circle drive. I'll be in the front coming out of the building. Meet me in an hour."

"Until then?"

"Lose them if they're still in the car. Hopefully they'll both come after me. If not, make it over to the DC side, across the Potomac. Once you're on Constitution Avenue, you'll see loads of squads and Metro police. Just pull over, get out of the car, and start screaming that you're being chased."

Heather asked, "What about you?"

"I'm taking the subway. The Metro rail."

We were across the bridge by then, and I told her to stomp on the gas and gun us over to the Rosslyn Metro. A quick look in my side mirror. "They're only two cars back," I shouted. "Closing in." I pointed to the Metro subway sign. "Slam on the brakes!"

We screeched to a stop, and I tossed the cell phone down on the passenger seat and bolted out of the car as Heather squealed the tires. She was out of sight by the time I hit the lobby of the Metro station, frantically grabbing for my wallet and debit card. Quickly inserting it into the ticket kiosk, yanking out the ticket, and hurrying down the steep escalator crowded with travelers,

I glanced back to see if I was being followed. Not yet, but that wasn't good. I wanted me to be the magnet for the duo, not Heather.

Silent, rushed prayers for the safety of Heather. For the vanquishing of the dark forces that were at play in this city. For the obliteration of Kuritsa Foks Videoryad, and for the rescue of all those girls who had been captured in that web of torture, terror, and perversion.

And as for the voodoo cult leader hiding somewhere in Washington who had to be the force behind it all—undoubtedly demonically empowered—I prayed for the searchlight of God to illuminate that twisted monster for me.

I stepped off the escalator, pressed through the crowd, and searched for the tunnel leading to the Silver Line of the Metro until I found it. Another glance backward to the escalator. I heard the sound of the Metro train rushing up to us, and as it pulled to the curb in a long line of conjoined cars, I heard the chimes and the canned announcement telling everyone to step back to allow passengers to exit the car. When the doors slid open, I was about to dash into the nearest car, but looked back to the escalator. The red-shirt twin was now sprinting my way.

I jumped into the Metro car. Then the double chime and the recorded voice: "Step back. Doors closing."

"Yes, good idea, close, close," I said under my breath.

I put my face to the glass as the doors slid closed and saw the twin in the red shirt squeeze into the car behind mine.

The Metro railcar sped forward with a jerk as I prayed for Heather, wherever she was. I had to commit her now to the protection of God.

I knew I had to transfer to the Red Line at Metro Center in order to get to my destination and rendezvous with Heather, and the red-shirt twin would be only steps behind me when the Metro came to a stop.

Then the realization struck me. There were multiple stops in between. At each stop, the doors would open. The demonic twin would be in my car in an instant. To avoid that, I would have to dash out at each stop and make it down to another car just before that door was closing. A game of chase-and-dodge, with my life on the line.

59

As the subway car slowed down and passed through a station without stopping, I checked the Metro Line map overhead. The Foggy Bottom stop was closed for repair, which meant I would be arriving at the one after that—Farragut West. That gave me an extra minute or two to decide my next move.

In our crowded subway car there was a huge guy standing close to me—maybe six foot five and must have weighed close to three hundred. He was trying to keep his balance as the Metro car rocked slowly to a stop.

As the chimes told us the doors were about to open, I stood and took a position—rudely, it must have seemed—directly in front of him.

The doors slid open effortlessly, and once I felt him hovering behind me, I departed the car and tried to match the big man's pace exactly, using him as a visual shield from the demon twin to my rear.

The platform was crowded, and I managed to stride several cars ahead before opening Heather's compact. In the mirror, the red-shirt twin was charging toward me. I ducked into the car as the door began to slide shut.

Then it banged open. In an instant the red-shirt twin was inside and dragging me out of the Metro railcar with one hand clasped on my shirt. As I punched wildly at his face with both fists, I began to see the inner creature that occupied him. The human face was fading into another—the image of a hairy, foul-smelling beast with yellowish animal eyes and razor teeth. Behind him, I saw the Silver Line Metro whisking away.

The monster had me by one hand on the platform. A cop was rushing up to him from behind, but the twin never turned. He didn't need to. He lifted his free arm, and with a flourish in the manner of a perverse orchestra conductor, he sent the policeman flying back without ever touching him. Passengers were stumbling as they sprinted madly away in all directions.

The monstrous twin tossed me down onto the platform. Before I could get up, he simply waved his hand, and I felt myself lifted into the air. In a single, bizarre, slow-motion moment he began to move me through the air until I was poised over the far rail. And then I heard the rushing thunder of a Metro liner coming my way. First only the sound off in the distance. Then the deep rumbling.

On the platform on the other side, two men rushed over and reached out to take hold of me. They searched the air around me, trying to figure out how I was being held up, hovering four feet over the rails.

They didn't see the other twin with the yellow golf shirt, who had just appeared on the platform behind them. He moved both of his hands as if performing a magic act and sent the two men tumbling backward along the concrete platform. I dangled in the air, unable to move, as if caught by some dark magnetic force. Heather's pursuer had joined his twin, one on each side of the rails, double-teaming me. I had two thoughts: They planned to drop me in front of a speeding Metro train. But at least Heather was safe from them.

The rumbling sensation was growing, and I heard the rushing sound of the Metro rail liner. I would be a bug on its windshield.

But I saw something else. A square-shouldered soldier in fatigues was standing within arm's length of the demon twin closest to me. The soldier held his hand over his head, palm outward, toward the twin, who was recoiling and letting loose with a hideous roar. The twin was being overpowered without ever being touched and finally was knocked head over heels by the gesture of the soldier. When he was, I dropped straight down onto the rails in a dead fall. The wind had been knocked out of me and I gasped for air, struggling to get to my feet. As I rose unsteadily, I saw the Metro liner hurtling toward me, just fifty feet away.

I scampered toward the platform but knew it was too tall for me to pull myself up. With the Metro liner now only five feet away, I shouted out a frantic prayer as I tried to reach the dugout section past the rails where I might be able to hide from the subway train.

The Metro liner was right on me, engulfing everything. Death was certain.

Then, inexplicably, I was flying through the air. But not struck. Yanked into the air and off the rails by a powerful hand that had reached down, grabbed my shirt, and brought me up to the safety of the platform as I felt the rush of wind from the Metro liner speeding past.

I crouched on my knees on the concrete platform, looking up into the face of the soldier, whose expression was so calm it seemed to be carved in stone.

"Thank you," I breathed to my rescuer.

Through the windows of the railcar, I looked at the platform on the opposite side of the tunnel, where another soldier in fatigues was standing strong and had vanquished the other demon twin as well. The identical demons sprinted out of sight.

As the chimes sounded and the Metro train pulled out of the station, I glanced back at the man next to me. But he was gone. And when I looked across the rails, so was the soldier on the opposite platform. Both had vanished into thin air.

My life had been spared. But the enraged enemy was increasing the attacks. The ferocity of the battle convinced me that I was getting closer to the truth. To the deep, dark center of it all. The place where monsters shriek. No time to lose.

60

Night had fallen on Washington, DC. I made my way along the cavernous white marble interior of Union Station, threading through the mob of train travelers and weary end-of-workday Metro passengers, and then outside to the circle drive. Only a few people seemed to notice my ripped sport coat and grease-stained white shirt. I was nursing a painful shoulder that felt like I might have reinjured an older rotator cuff issue. The one I had received from a prior run-in with the dark side.

The Capitol dome was lighting the evening sky. As I searched for Heather, I wondered at the fact that somewhere below the superficially civil and politically correct surface of Washington bureaucracy, there was a voodoo sadist lurking. His demonic lieutenants had already taken their shot at me in the Metro. But I knew things had to get even worse.

It didn't take long before I saw Heather cruising by slowly in the rental car. I flagged her down with my good arm and jumped in.

She greeted me with a half-grinning, half-shocked expression. "You're looking pretty rough. What happened?"

I explained only in vague terms about my tussle with the twins; then I asked about her.

Heather said she was tailed closely until she reached Constitution, when she pulled up right next to a Metro police squad as I had suggested, and the twin chasing her took a quick U-turn and disappeared.

It was after eleven when we arrived at the Mandarin hotel. I said I needed a shower and a clean shirt and suggested we meet for a bite downstairs. But Heather nixed the idea.

"Let's order room service instead. I'll ask for a bag of ice for your shoulder. Then we can get down to work."

I smiled. "Work, meaning . . ."

"How we find Louisa Deidre Baldou."

We were mind melding. "Good," I said. "Dinner to be delivered. Let's meet in my room. There's a small conference table. And I'll need a pot of coffee."

I knew that in less than an hour the clock would turn. Another day gone. We had to get to the head of the snake before more girls disappeared.

I changed into clean clothes, and a little before midnight Heather and I were dining and talking, mostly about the chase through the Metro and my levitation over the rails as the speeding subway train was heading straight for me.

Heather asked a lot of questions about that, not disputing it, but careful not to endorse the reality of it either. Cautious, yet faced with the increasing possibility of a supernatural world she had never suspected.

"The soldiers who rescued you . . . you really think they were something more than just military . . . ?"

"They were part of an army. Just not one that gets its orders from the Pentagon."

The beginning of a smile at the corner of her mouth.

"You think I could hunt down demons without believing in angels? Not the cultural picture you see in art galleries— androgynous figures with fluffy wings. In actuality, they are powerful beings of pure spirit. If you and I saw them in their true magnificence, standing in front of us, we'd fall to our knees. They're powerful heralds and messengers . . . and warriors, engaged in an ongoing battle with the underworld. And they just saved my life. Once again."

From Heather, no debate, no playing the devil's advocate. Simply listening.

"So," I said, "let's put together a game plan for tomorrow."

The missing person poster in New Orleans of a young girl named Peggy Tanner flashed into my head once again. Back there, a family was grieved. And their lawyer, Morgan Canterelle, was counting on me.

I took out a legal pad and a pen and started talking. "We start with what we know about Louisa Deidre Baldou. What she told us about herself, even indirectly."

We both knew the facts: She attended the ABA because she was a lawyer and, according to Turk Kavagian, was an over-achiever with an advanced degree in some technology field and was probably incentivized to put a stop to child abduction due to the death of her own sister. And she was likely in the public sector of employment, someone whose full identity was classi-fied, according to Morgan Canterelle.

"Fine," Heather said. "That's all we have. So I ask once again—imagine how many federal employees there are in the District of Columbia."

"Actually I can," I said. "I checked on it. There are more than two million employees on the federal payroll. A large percentage right here in the greater Washington area."

She shook her head. "I thought we were supposed to lay out a game plan."

"We will. As soon as we hone it down. Vector the grid."

Heather gave me a crooked smile. "Nice lingo. Now you're just trying to impress me."

"How am I doing?"

She laughed.

"Actually," I said, "I'm serious. When I had complex cases to defend, some white-collar crime with hundreds of transactions, I'd diagram the thing on a vector chart. This is much simpler. We're trying to find out the federal agency where our woman is likely employed."

"Technology and law," she said.

"Which means maybe a person in the intelligence sector or law enforcement."

She said, "Huge categories."

"We can narrow it down. Turk Kavagian thought she might have attended MIT. There are a few federal agencies that seek out lawyers with technology training. Department of Justice is one of them. That also explains her inside knowledge about the death of an assistant US attorney like Jason Forester."

Heather turned to the iPad. She started there.

After a few minutes she said, "Okay. DOJ's got something called the High Technology Investigative Unit, HTIU. Right here in DC. And they have a child exploitation division. Cybercrime. Internet child pornography. A perfect fit for her, given the tragedy of her own sister and the nature of what we are pursuing. Maybe she was even aware that Forester was intending to talk to you when he died."

She checked the staff information for HTIU but gave out a long sigh. "Sorry, no Louisa Deidre Baldou listed."

"She could be lower down the pecking order," I said. "They don't list every federal employee in every DOJ division, just the higher-ups." I told her to do a name search on sites with news articles dealing with legal cases or legal or tech conferences where she might have been mentioned or have been a speaker. But Heather came up dry.

We also checked the FBI online, which of course had its own technology and forensics unit. And yes, it also had a cybercrime division that covered child pornography. I told Heather that our target person could be in either the DOJ or the FBI, but it might be neither, because she could also be working for the CIA or the NSA or even the Department of Defense's technology sector.

Heather looked tired and exasperated. "So, in which basket

do we put all our eggs? Because we may only have enough time to pursue one."

She was right, of course. By Dick Valentine's estimate, the boats, cars, or private airplanes could already be preparing to exit the country by the next day.

That's where it stood when I decided we should close it up for the night, which was close to three in the morning.

Heather was insistent. "I'm not going to sleep until I know where we start tomorrow. My mind is already racing."

I told Heather that the Department of Justice was our best bet, and we would try to get an audience at the HTIU office somehow. After all, the DOJ is an exclusively legal office, filled with lawyers, more so than the FBI, and by every indication Louisa Deidre was a lawyer with intel that only a DOJ staffer would likely have. I also reminded Heather that we were hunting down a ghastly enterprise whose chief appeared to work domestically, inside the United States. Intelligence and military agencies, on the other hand—unlike the DOJ—don't have domestic jurisdiction, and therefore she was less likely to be employed there.

If my plan didn't work out at the DOJ, I wasn't sure how we would have the chance to head over to the FBI, our other option, and force a meeting or start another search for Louisa Deidre Baldou. We were running out of time to locate the monster in the system and interdict the flood of young female sex slaves about to leave our shores.

When Heather said good night and disappeared to her room, she still had my iPad under her arm.

Half an hour later I was already in bed and starting to doze off when I heard a frantic pounding on my hotel room door.

It was Heather, with a stunned look on her face.

When I let her in, she shoved the lit screen of my iPad in my face and shouted, "Three-quarters of a million hits on YouTube. In just the last few hours."

"What are you talking about?"

She pointed to the screen. Then I understood. Someone with a cell phone had shot a video in the Metro station. It showed my back as I hovered several feet over the rails at the Farragut West station. The video also caught, in the background, a two-second glimpse of the confrontation between the demon twin and my rescuer in Army fatigues.

I smiled and nodded. "Glad they didn't catch my face."

Heather handed me the iPad. "I don't know what to say."

I said, "It's more important to know what you believe."

61

I don't know whether I had dreamed it or whether it was one of those first thoughts that flash into your head just as you're waking up.

Whichever it was, I knew I had to call Turk Kavagian, the New Orleans PI. It was early morning, but I couldn't afford to wait.

When Turk picked up at the other end, I heard the dull roar of a crowded restaurant in the background. Turk was at Mother's eating some kind of local breakfast fare that he tried to describe to me, something with crawfish and okra. He asked what he could do for me.

"It's regarding our conversation about Delbert Baldou and that niece of his who he raised like a daughter. Louisa Deidre."

"Yeah, I remember."

"Did she use Delbert's last name, Baldou?"

At the other end, Turk thought about it for a while. "She may have. Makes sense."

"Was her biological father's last name Baldou?"

"Nah. It wasn't that."

"Really. What was it?"

"Gaudet. See, her father was only Delbert Baldou's *half brother* because they had different fathers. Louisa Deidre was a Gaudet."

"So her birth name would be Louisa Deidre Gaudet?"

"You've got it."

"Turk, once again, you've been great."

"Hey, that one was easy," he said.

"For you maybe, but not for me. Thanks again."

I rounded up Heather, who was sleepy-eyed, and handed her a big coffee laced with espresso along with a little bag that had a sugary piece of bakery inside. Then I told her we had to be on the move.

"I was thinking," she started out in between slurps of her coffee. "Didn't Vance Zaduck warn you about talking to people at the DOJ?"

"Only if someone from DOJ reached out to me first."

"Anyway," she said, "didn't that guy, Gil Spencer, also tell you to be careful . . . not to barge into the DOJ and start spilling your story?"

"Right."

"Okay. Two warnings. So tell me again: why are we heading there?"

"Because this is not about spilling *my story*. It's about Louisa Deidre Gaudet's story."

We parked the car in a garage and walked along the south facade of the Department of Justice building.

Near the entrance, I halted in front of a bronze statue that was darkened with age. The kind of little statue easily missed by passing traffic and hurried pedestrians. I nodded to it. "Nathan Hale. Hanged by the British when he was caught doing reconnaissance for General George Washington's army." I added, "He was just about your age."

She smirked. "And on that pleasant note . . ."

"But it does raise a question," I said. "About what we're willing to live for. And willing to die for."

She tightened her face. "Not sure. But I know one thing. I don't want any more young girls victimized, and maybe butchered, by some crazy voodoo cult running an Internet porn service."

"Well then," I said, "let's both of us walk into the DOJ and shake things up."

There was hesitation on her face. Her eyes were wide, her mouth drawn. She said, "Uh . . . you sure you want me with you?"

"Positive."

"Okay," she said. "Just checking."

We entered and went through the security check in the crowded lobby and handed over our IDs. At the desk the officer asked, "How can I help you?"

"We're here to see someone in your HTIU office."

"Both of you?"

"Yes, she's my research assistant."

"And you are . . . ?"

"Trevor Black. Legal investigator."

"Who exactly are you here to see?"

"Louisa Deidre Gaudet."

The official at the desk blinked slowly. No smile. "Say again?"
I repeated the name.

Then a flash of recognition on the security officer's face.
"Oh, you mean LD Gaudet?"

I was inching closer to the goal line.

"Yes," I said energetically. "That's right. LD."

"Do you have an appointment?"

"Not exactly. But she'll know what this is about."

"I'm sorry. I can't allow you inside without an appointment."

Heather gave me a side-glance. I was preparing to leap over
the high jump in front of me. "Well, you see, this is a follow-up
from my assistant's meeting with LD in New Orleans recently.
And it's an emergency. LD considers it a matter of extreme
urgency. I know that as a fact. She's the one who tasked me to
work on this project."

The officer stared at me and tapped a finger on the desk. She
pulled out a list, looked it over, then reached for the phone and
typed in a short number. I was guessing that it was LD's extension. The officer lowered her voice to murmur something and
listened to the response. Then, very audibly, she repeated my
name and listened again to the voice on the other end.

When she put the phone down, she looked me over one
more time. Then she double-checked our IDs and typed out
two paper tags with our names on them and little metal clips
on the tops.

"Make sure you keep them on your person," she said, handing our name tags to us.

In the elevator, when the doors closed, Heather whispered, "Do you have a plan?"

"It's a bit sketchy."

"Okay, but at least a script in your head for what you're going to say?"

"Not exactly. More like an impression."

Her eyes widened. "I'd love to hear it."

"Hope for the hopeless. Encouragement for someone trapped in the past. Healing for the brokenhearted."

Heather raised an eyebrow. "That sounds more like a sermon."

I didn't respond because just then the elevator stopped, the doors opened, and we walked into the busy corridor of the High Technology Investigative Unit.

62

We had been told that a tech assistant to LD Gaudet would greet us at the elevator on the HTIU floor. When the elevator door opened and we stepped out, we were passed in both directions by hustling staffers in shirtsleeves and pantsuits with their federal ID tags swinging from their necks, but none of them looked our way.

I stopped one of them and asked directions, and we were directed to LD's office, two halls down. We stopped where we saw the little white name card inside a metal frame on the wall next to the door:

LD Gaudet
Assistant Computer Forensic Specialist

Heather raised the notepad she clutched in her hand. "Do you want me to take notes?"

"Not unless I tell you. I don't want to spook her. The legal pad was mainly to give us a business look in the lobby."

I knocked on the door. No response. I put my knuckles to the door a second time, this time louder, and heard a noise inside. And then the sound of footsteps until the door swung open.

The woman with untidy brown hair who opened the door didn't greet us but walked straight back toward her simple metal desk. There were two large, ultrathin computer monitors on the desktop and two more monitors on the credenza behind the desk.

She kept her back to us, looking out the window, which had an unimpressive view of the walls and windows of an adjacent office building behind the Department of Justice.

Heather and I stood silently in the middle of the room and waited for Louisa Deidre, aka LD Gaudet, to begin speaking.

The silence went on for at least a minute, and I could sense that Heather was stressing out next to me, so I reached over and gave her little finger a squeeze. Then LD Gaudet wheeled around and started to talk.

"Well, hello, Heather. They told me that you were coming up without an appointment."

Her leadoff was all I needed to know, addressing Heather rather than me. LD Gaudet was buying time, trying to sort out her options. Wondering what her next move would be. Worrying about her future in light of her unorthodox actions. Understandable.

I waited for Heather to respond. For a split second I

wondered what would happen if Heather didn't recognize her. And whether I had made a tactical mistake in assuming the lawyer at the ABA who had been responsible for arranging Heather's trip to Bayou Bon Coeur was the same one who had been my anonymous caller.

But all that evaporated as the conversation continued.

"Hello, LD," Heather said. "Or is it Deidre?"

A quick, strained smile from LD. "For some reason my classmates in middle school always made fun of *Louisa*. So I started using my middle name instead. You know kids, how mean they can be. Never as malicious or damaging as grown-ups, though. It was *Deidre* from then on, until law school. And then I started using LD."

I joined the conversation. "Are you surprised?"

"By what?" LD replied.

"That I found you."

She eased herself down behind her desk. "Part of me was actually hoping for it."

"And the other part?"

"You were a big-shot New York lawyer once upon a time. You should know the answer to that."

"I think I do. That's why I want you to know you have nothing to fear from me."

"Oh, really? So this isn't some kind of shakedown?"

"Of course not. I'd do nothing to harm you, LD. The fact is I didn't need to get an anonymous, digitally distorted phone call from you to convince me that there was something rotten going on behind the scenes. Or, for whatever reason, that I am the one who has to find the answers."

"And have you found them?"

"That's why I'm here. To finish the puzzle. I'm into task completion."

She gave a strained smile. "We have something in common. So then, let's get down into the weeds. Why are you here, specifically?"

"I need you to tell me everything you know about someone. Probably a respectable-looking federal law enforcement official, but down deep, a monster. This person may be into a voodoo cult called Palo Mayombe and moonlighting as the mastermind of a perverse Internet child exploitation syndicate called Kuritsa Foks Videoryad."

"You've been doing your homework."

"Thank you. What can you tell me?"

"Considering that I have a top secret security clearance, am bound by federal law to keep confidential information confidential, and signed a lengthy agreement with the Department of Justice when I was hired, what do you *really* expect me to tell you?"

"Just the truth. I think you owe me that, after first seeding Detective Dick Valentine about the Jason Forester death, knowing he would pass it on to me. And then trying to motivate me to finish the job, all the while keeping yourself at arm's length."

LD straightened in her chair.

"But more than that," I said, "you owe it to somebody else. You risked your professional career here at DOJ to make sure I was incentivized to help stop this human tragedy. And then you nudged me a little in the right direction, all because this investigation is critically important to you. Professionally, of course.

But even more important, personally. Honoring the memory of your slain sister, Lucinda. So, because of all that, LD, this is important to me too."

I could see a softening in LD's face.

I said, "You need to tell me the truth because *you* are the person who deserves it: to see this scourge stopped, because it hit home in your own family. Maybe even if it's just telling your story to a wreck of a guy like me, who's lost some things too. But nothing like what you've lost. The ruination visited on your family. Sort of similar to the ruination that Katrina brought to that Six Flags theme park and to all New Orleans for that matter. One minute, life as usual. Next minute, disaster."

LD's face was struggling for composure. Her chin was wobbling. "How could you have known?" she said, her voice cracking.

"Just some facts I learned about your background. Coupled with my own life experience. My dealings with the world, the flesh, and the devil. And all the while, trying to walk a path illuminated by a God who has proven to me beyond a reasonable doubt that he can take a junkyard of a life and turn it into a garden."

In my peripheral vision, I could see that Heather was staring at me.

LD made a little sound like the muffled chirp of a bird, a half cry that was struggling to get out.

In front of me, LD Gaudet, assistant computer forensic specialist for the Department of Justice, was trying desperately to suppress a primal lament that had been welling up inside for too long and was now looking for a voice because of her bruised and tortured past. The murder of her sister. Then the collateral damage of her father, who doped and drank himself to death out of grief for his savagely slain daughter.

LD Gaudet put her hands over her face, and the weeping began.

63

LD Gaudet was crying softly as Heather and I slipped into the two chairs across from her desk. After a while, she opened a drawer and pulled out a Kleenex to wipe her eyes and her nose.

Finally she said, "I'm a mess, and not just what you're seeing here on the surface."

I nodded. I knew the feeling. "I'm not here to dig into your past, LD."

"But you have, you must have, to say what you said just now about my past."

"A private investigator I contacted in New Orleans knew about your family. About your father. And about Delbert Baldou, your uncle, who took you in when your father died. I just put the pieces together. But some pieces are still missing."

She opened her mouth, and at first nothing came out.

I didn't say a word, but I had a good idea what was coming.

LD said, "We came to New Orleans to stay for a few months over the summer with Uncle Delbert. My father had a new construction job and he would be traveling a lot. Dad took us to Six Flags down there as a treat because he was leaving the next day to head back north. I was in the girls' room when . . . when Lucinda wandered off to look at something. And disappeared. Oh, poor Lucinda, she just vanished."

As LD struggled to keep her composure, I gave her time.

After a moment, she continued. "My dad and I pushed the police to find out what was going on. There was talk among the detectives who were doing the investigation that her killing might involve some mysterious group. Abductions of girls. Human slavery. Even cult sacrifice. You can imagine my horror. . . ."

"Just barely . . ."

She kept talking. "I thought at the time, that if I ever do anything in life, it's going to be in law enforcement to make a difference. To put a stop to this kind of evil. No more lives destroyed. Like Lucinda was. Like my family was."

There were so many things I wanted to say but wondered where to start. Heather said them for me.

Heather was weeping softly, and her voice was broken when she said, "We are so, so very sorry for what happened to your family. Our hearts break for you. And please forgive us for having to bring up those painful memories."

"I'm fine," LD said. "I got counseling for a couple of months after it happened," she said. "After they found Lucinda's remains in the bayou." She paused for a short, heavy-laden moment and added, "I've moved on. I guess."

I said, "I know there's an internal affairs team investigating the identity of the insider who's running Chicken Fox Videos. And the possible connection between that criminal scheme and the deaths of Jason Forester and Paul Pullmen."

Her eyes were clear of tears by then, and she was watching me closely.

I continued. "I know all the legal ropes the DOJ has tied around you in terms of confidentiality. But I also know that those rules might not stop you from bringing in outside consultants. So treat me as your consultant. You can talk to me within the scope of that consulting relationship. Right?"

LD was still studying me.

"I'm not new to this. I had that kind of relationship with Detective Dick Valentine at the NYPD."

"Yes, I know," she said.

"Of course, that's right; you already talked to him."

She tipped her head in a slight nod. "You really do have it nailed down, don't you?"

"Not nearly enough. You mentioned 'death by voodoo' in your call to Dick, which is where this all started for me."

"That's because I knew the two of you had a relationship. I was hoping he would bring you into this."

"But the voodoo connection . . ."

"As part of the team, I saw the actual FedEx letter that Jason Forester received. Remember, I may have been born up in Connecticut, but I spent a lot of time later in New Orleans with

Uncle Delbert. I know voodoo when I see it. All the symbols. It's all right there if you can recognize it."

"And Paul Pullmen's death?"

LD said, "I think you're onto something about the manner of his death. The voodoo subcult of Palo Mayombe certainly fits."

Heather jumped in. "But of course, nobody in the federal law enforcement field is ever going to hint about being a follower. . . ."

"Right," LD said. "Which brings us to current status. Our team is getting bogged down. Maybe even blocked. As a result, we haven't located the evildoer inside the federal system. Call it desperation, but that's why I reached out to you via Dick Valentine."

"Hence the digital voice distorter, so you could keep your distance."

"We had one lying around in an evidence locker."

"There's a rush on this," I said. "I heard the bad actors are going to ship all their female captives out of the United States soon."

She was nodding. "And even more Internet chatter as of yesterday. We think it's going to happen in the next twelve to twenty-four hours."

It shouldn't have hit me that hard, actually hearing the timeline narrowed down like that. But it did. "Anything else you can give me? Anything?"

She paused. "Okay. So, you're here. You found me. Impressive. You've passed the test, *consultant*."

I grinned.

She said, "Here goes. . . . I'll share some intel with you. First, a code we've discovered."

"Digital coding?"

"Yes."

Heather jumped in. "You're talking about the dark web? The networks that are sharing these child porn videos?"

"Exactly," LD said. "I've been working with some Internet steganography experts, and we've located a code fragment that has appeared on the network protocols used by Chicken Fox Videos. It showed up three times. Used, I believe, as a type of kill order. It first appeared twenty-four hours before the death of Jason Forester. Then a day before the murder of Paul Pullmen. And after that, just before the very recent death of a Louisiana local that was contrived to look like a suicide."

Heather said, "Henry Bosant. In Port Sulphur. A hanging."

"That's the one," she said. "Meanwhile there are other code strands we think might also be kill directives. We're still trying to decipher those."

"What's the code that you've identified?" I asked.

LD snatched up a pen, wrote something down on a small piece of notepaper, and shoved it over the desk to me.

Adj111C62

I asked the obvious question. "Any idea what it stands for, or is this just an operational cipher?"

"Haven't the faintest. We located the code yesterday and our encryption guys are working on it."

I wanted to know if she had something else to share, anything that would help me tag the culprit.

"Yes. One other thing," she said. "Our foreign agents have picked up this one word in the dark net chatter. We think it's linked to Chicken Fox Videos."

"Just a single word?" I asked.

"Yes. The word was *Matamoros*."

Heather asked, "The city in Mexico?"

"That's one possibility," LD said. "It popped up each of the three times that the kill-order protocol code also appeared."

I wondered out loud if there was a deeper significance for the word.

Heather chimed in. "*Matamoros* is a Spanish word. It has something to do with a vision experienced by a Spanish king. As a result, during a war he ordered the slaughter of thousands of Moors."

LD gave an admiring nod of the head. "Father and daughter. You guys make an impressive team."

I said. "She's the smart one. Me? I'm just persistent."

"There's another possible meaning too," Heather said. "It has to do with a cult leader and drug dealer in Mexico by the name of Adolfo Constanzo. He was known as 'the Godfather of Matamoros.'"

I asked LD whether his name rang a bell, but she shook her head no.

I had one last question. "The internal affairs task force looking into all this, is Gil Spencer in DOJ part of it?"

"Yes."

"Anyone from the US attorney's office for the District of Columbia part of the group?"

"No."

"How about the attorney general himself, George Shazzar? Is he part of the team?"

"Nope," she said with an air of certainty.

64

Before we left, I assured LD Gaudet of two things. First, that we would keep our meeting and the details she had revealed about her past and everything else strictly confidential. Second, I pledged to pray for her.

After thanking LD for her courage in speaking with us, we left the DOJ building. The note with the protocol code message written on it was securely tucked in my pocket, but I hadn't the faintest what it meant.

I could think of only one next step. And it involved Gil Spencer, a member of LD's internal affairs investigative team looking into the Forester and Pullmen deaths. On the other hand, Vance Zaduck had given me a dump truck full of reasons to stay clear of him.

As a preliminary, I called Zaduck at the US attorney's office.

I had something that I needed to ask him before my next move. But I was told he was in meetings and he would have to call me back. I couldn't afford to wait for his return call before I reached out to Gil Spencer.

Heather stopped me on the sidewalk, right in front of the Nathan Hale statue. She announced, "I've got to get over to the Library of Congress. Right now. I'm only ten minutes away from the best information resource center in the world."

"Fill me in."

"*Matamoros*. I've got to research that beyond just an Internet search. There may be a deeper meaning behind that word. And I intend to find it."

I told her that I would be running down Gil Spencer. I had no idea when, or if, I would be hearing back from Vance Zaduck, but our backs were against the wall. I still didn't have a cell phone replacement, so I told Heather to hang on to mine, and I would pick up a cheap cell phone and try to track down Gil.

I felt uneasy about separating from Heather. On the other hand, I was proud of her initiative. And then there was that comment from LD about our father-daughter team. Amazing how great a simple thing like that can make you feel.

I told Heather, "Let's plan on getting back together in three hours. I'll call you."

While we waited for a cab for Heather, I put in a call to Gil Spencer, and his secretary informed me he was in court. After explaining my past history with him and our being legal colleagues, I was able to ferret out from the secretary that he was arguing to oppose a Freedom of Information Act demand that had been filed against the Department of Justice.

"So," I asked, "that means he's over at the US district court?"

"Yes. 333 Constitution Avenue NW." She gave me the courtroom number. A taxi pulled up and I wished Heather luck, gave her my cell, and shooed her into the backseat. I decided to leave my rental in the parking ramp and catch a cab myself to save time. One showed up a few minutes later.

My destination wasn't that far away, so I knew the cabbie would be ticked off about a low fare, but I told him I would drop a heavy tip on him if he could thread the needle quickly through traffic.

After eight minutes of a hair-raising ride, he slam-parked the taxi on the other side of Constitution, across from the courthouse. I paid the fare, plus twenty bucks, and danced my way across oncoming traffic, dashing past the statue of Sir William Blackstone and into the federal courthouse building.

On the sixth floor I peeked into the courtroom. The judge was rendering his opinion. I decided to wait outside in the corridor. Ten minutes later, the door swung open. Gil Spencer's opponents were smiling. A forlorn-looking Gil trudged out with his extra-wide briefcase.

I stopped him in his tracks. "Well, Gil," I said, "better luck next time."

He looked surprised to see me. "Yeah, well, you know these FOIA cases. The motion today was just a skirmish. The case itself? More like the Hundred Years' War."

"Since when are you doing Freedom of Information litigation?"

He looked down the hallway in both directions and said in a hushed voice, "Keep it down." Then he added, "I have been temporarily reassigned out of the Criminal Division. Get this:

somebody within the federal legal establishment filed an internal ethics complaint against me."

"Do you know who?"

"Not yet. But I will soon. I'm wondering if it is because of our off-the-record conversation at the cemetery." Then he asked, "So what are you doing here?"

"Bringing you a question."

"Make it quick. This doesn't look good, my talking to you like this."

"Okay, here it is: when I say the word *Matamoros*, what does that bring to mind?"

His head jerked back a bit. "You've been talking to someone on the internal affairs investigative team, haven't you."

"Sorry, I can't confirm or deny."

"That's fine," he said. "Okay. *Matamoros* . . ."

"Right. Let your mind wander . . . any recollection at all. Why it might be important. Whether you can see any connection to the case that Jason Forester was investigating and your boss, Mr. Pullmen, was supervising."

"What are you looking for, exactly?"

"Anything. Everything."

"You look a bit frantic, Trevor. That's not like you."

I managed a tight smile.

Minutes ticked by. Gil kept looking this way and that, like he was under surveillance.

"Look," he finally said. "Obviously you got that word from somebody in internal affairs. And obviously we all know it's a city in Mexico."

"Right. I'm trying to figure out whether any of Paul

Pullmen's cases, for instance, or those of the DOJ, or cases of Jason Forester have anything to do with *Matamoros*. Or for that matter, any other case you've ever heard of in your life."

Gil bobbed his head.

While he was struggling, I asked him a question out of left field, just to catch his response. "Gil, one more time. I need to know this. I can trust you, right?"

"Yes," he shot back, looking me in the eye. "And I'm pretty sure I can trust you. Otherwise this conversation wouldn't be happening."

I nodded. He kept thinking. Then he jerked his head up like someone just jabbed him. "Wow, that's odd."

"What?"

"After all these years, remembering it. The human brain's a strange thing."

"Explain."

"Oh, this goes back. Way back, all the way to the New York City public defender's office. It was just after you left to join the Tobit law firm. You remember that boxer client you had? Convicted of attempted murder or something close to that? Beat up some guy who was stalking his girlfriend."

"Carter Collins. How could I forget?"

"After he was convicted and was already serving his prison sentence, we got this letter from him, addressed to the public defender's office and saying he wanted to talk to you. I arranged a phone call to Collins at the prison and explained you were now working as criminal defense counsel in a high-priced private firm, but that we could forward any message to you. Carter Collins said that of course he couldn't afford private counsel but needed someone from the public defender's office to talk to him about something. So I paid him a visit in prison.

"The details are foggy—about our meeting, I mean. I don't recall exactly what the guy wanted, though whatever it was, it struck me as pretty strange at the time. Typical prison gossip stuff—railing against the system, that sort of thing—but my memory is that he was making some pretty outrageous claims against a government lawyer. But he wouldn't give me the name of the lawyer unless I promised that he could strike a deal with the prosecutors for a reduction of his sentence, which I was supposed to work out for him and which of course I couldn't do. The point being, the city of Matamoros came up in our conversation somehow. That much I'm sure. Anyway, your client struck me as just trying to get a free-pass-out-of-jail card, and I wasn't buying it."

"You're positive about all this?"

"That's the weird thing about it. That part just leaped out of my memory bank. So, anyway, there it is."

I knew I had to talk to Carter Collins but had no idea where to start after all these years.

When I mentioned that out loud to Gil, he shrugged real nonchalantly and said, "That's not a problem. He's been out of prison for quite a while and he's actually not far from here. I read an article in the local news section of the *Post* about his heading up a boys' boxing club for underprivileged kids. You know, some kind of self-help, motivational nonprofit group with a pretty good record. His outfit is being sponsored by two congressmen who serve together on the Judiciary Committee. And they're actually from opposite sides of the aisle if you can believe that."

65

The Olympian Boxing Club and Gym was in the Chinatown section of Washington, only two blocks from the ornate Asian arch that stretched over the roadway at H and Seventh Streets. The gym was housed in an aging redbrick building in the otherwise-upscale section, a building that could use some fresh paint, with crumbling mortar between the bricks that needed tuck-pointing.

I stopped for a moment outside the gym because I had already picked up a cheap TracFone in Chinatown a few doors down and had texted my new number to Heather. Now she was texting me back with some research.

U.S. gov't, over several yrs, has issued advisory for Americans not to travel to Matamoros, Mexico. They say that city & surrounding state of Tamaulipas is nest of "lawlessness," with rampant

murder, gangs, kidnapping, drug running. Law enforcement "non-existent." Will send U more as I get it.

Somewhere in my cerebral cortex, that word *lawlessness* meant something.

But I needed to get back to Heather on a piece that had fallen into place in my head on the cab ride over. It had to do with *Matamoros* as a code, the connection it had to Adolfo Constanzo, and its relationship to that other strange digital code they found in the Internet network protocol of Chicken Fox Videos: Adj111C62.

I was no code breaker, but there's something that happens when you spend two decades as a trial lawyer: you get adept at untangling facts. Grouping similar things into similar piles, then looking at them up, down, and from every angle.

So first, I grouped the letters together: AdjC.

I had already pegged the code maker, the chief administrator of Chicken Fox Videos, as not just evil, but something even worse. The careful, systematic kidnapping, torture, and even murder of young girls while in the business of making porn videos told me that it had all the markings of a demon-influenced operation. And if that was the case, then it seemed to me that the sin of pride, that ultimate demonic fantasy of achieving god status on the earth, might be buried in that code somewhere. Flaunting it in an exercise of grotesque hubris.

The initials of Adolfo Constanzo—AC—obviously. But also the letters *d* and *j*.

Next, I tried to unscramble the numbers in the code: 11162.

It could be an address. A location. Part of an international telephone exchange. Or a date. What if it was a date? It could be January 11, 1962. Or maybe November 1, 1962.

The exercise seemed fruitless. If the federal code breakers hadn't figured it out in the last twenty-four hours, what chance did we have? On the other hand, Heather and I had the background data on the possible voodoo connection, and real-life on-the-ground experience with the nasty supernatural forces behind Chicken Fox Videos. That ought to count for something.

I sent a lengthy text to Heather summarizing those thoughts and asked for her input. Then I shoved the phone in my pocket and walked into the gym.

At the far end of the Olympian Boxing Club and Gym were two black teens sparring in the ring. A half-dozen other young men were working out on the speed bags.

An Asian man wearing a shirt emblazoned with the gym's logo approached me. He asked if I was looking for someone.

"Yes, Carter Collins."

"Busy now," he snapped.

"I'm a good friend of his."

"So are all these guys," he said with a smile, sweeping his hand over the room.

"This is urgent," I said.

The man looked into my face for a second, then said, pointing over to the far corner of the ring, "Don't bother him now, but he's over there."

I recognized that face, hunched below the corner turnbuckle, eyeing the ring from his position just about even with the canvas. He was yelling, not loudly, but in a calm, powerful directive.

"You guys know English, don't you? When I tell you to move your feet, you gotta do exactly that. Now keep them moving!"

I stood off from the ring, waiting for an opening. The boxers were standing and jabbing, but not dancing or circling. More yelling from Carter Collins. The young boxers, dwarfed by their padded headgear and big gloves, started picking up the pace and moving their feet. Carter looked pleased.

My cell dinged. I picked it up. A text from Heather.

U nailed it! His full name was Adolfo de Jesús Constanzo. Thus—the letters AdjC. He was born on November 1, 1962. All that gives us: Adj111C62. That's got to be it. See you in an hour.

Carter Collins glanced momentarily in my direction, then back to the ring. And then back to me for a longer look. He grabbed the little hammer and rang the bell.

"Take a breather," Carter yelled to the boxers. He grabbed the ropes, pulled himself to his feet, and began walking my way. I tucked my phone away. Carter's walk was slower, his reddish sandy hair was thinner, and his lean, muscular fighter's build had put on a few pounds. But otherwise, he looked remarkably the same.

When he was closer, he gave me an easy smile and extended his powerful right hand. "Counselor," he said. "Good to see you after all these years. Big surprise. Here on legal business?"

"Not practicing law anymore," I said.

"Too bad. Man, you were fierce."

"Not fierce enough for your case, sad to say."

"That wasn't on you," Carter said. "That was on the guy who put me away. Dirty tricks. But I'm not looking back. I'm pressing forward." He pointed to a tiny office in the corner, and I followed him over there.

After Carter Collins closed the door to his office, he dropped into a swivel chair behind an old wood desk. "Something tells me you're not here to talk about the old days."

"Maybe I am," I said.

Carter raised an eyebrow. I explained what Gil Spencer had shared with me about his conversation with Carter in prison.

"Yeah, well, that was a long time ago," he said. "Let me think a minute. A lot happenin' since then. I'm a different man."

I looked over his head. On the wall behind him was a poster of Christ with a crown of thorns on his head and boxing gloves on his hands, and underneath was the title "Undisputed Champion of Redemption."

After he'd been quiet for a while, Carter said, "Matamoros. Yeah. Okay. Here's the deal. In prison there was this guy who was doing some hard time for drug running, kidnapping, and some very bad stuff. He got to be a real high roller, until he got caught. Rolex watches. Fancy cars. He was a Mexican guy. Can't remember his name. Anyway, there's this under-ground, you know, of information that runs through prison. If you know the right people. I got to know the right people. I heard that this Mexican guy was born in Matamoros, and I knew it 'cuz he was always boasting about it. Like that was something that would scare off people who might otherwise be thinking about sticking a shiv in his ribs or something."

"So that's the way Matamoros came up?"

"Yeah."

"That's it?"

"Mostly, yeah."

The feeling of defeat was palpable. A bumpy, unlit road at night, and my headlights had just hit the Dead End sign.

"Any mention of a guy named Adolfo de Jesús Constanzo?"

"No, I don't remember that."

I asked, "After all these years, why would you remember the fact that Matamoros was mentioned by another con in prison?"

"Because of the meeting I had with your public defender friend . . ."

"Gil Spencer?"

"Yeah, I guess that was his name. At the time, I was just looking for a break, some way to shorten my prison sentence. Grabbing for straws. I don't think he believed me, and honestly I don't blame him. My meeting with him never went anywhere."

"How would this thing about Matamoros have helped you out of prison?"

"'Cuz of the lawyer, you know, who wanted to cut some deal with that Mexican inmate to get him out of prison, and in return, all he had to do was open up some doors so this lawyer could go down there to Matamoros and—oh, I don't know, it all sounded crazy—but the lawyer wanted to learn about something down there. Some, like, religious cult thing—voodoo, I guess—and this Mexican guy in prison would, like, be a guide or something, or else I guess hook him up with someone who could be a guide."

"What happened?"

"You gotta understand, not very many guys in the joint knew about those rumors, just a couple of us—a small bunch of Irish guys from Boston and New York mostly, that was our gang—and that's how the word spread in prison, starting with an Irish guard from the Bronx who told one of our gang . . ."

Anyway, suddenly this inmate, the Mexican, he's not there any-more. I don't mean transferred to another facility. I mean he's outta prison. Bam. Out on the street. All because he cut that deal with the lawyer, having to do with Matamoros."

"Carter, no disrespect, but this doesn't sound right. A lawyer can't just negotiate someone out of prison like that."

"Well, there was more to it than that."

"Tell me."

"See, the inmate knew some other gangbangers. So the way it went down was that this lawyer was going to make it look like the inmate was giving a huge bit of inside information to the cops about those gangbangers. Then the lawyer would go into court and say that he was a real help to the police, and that's why he should get his sentence reduced to time served. That was going to be the talk to the court on the surface. But underneath, all that the lawyer really wanted was to get intros to that weird cult group down in Matamoros. Why, though, I couldn't tell you."

"The lawyer who arranged all this, was he a public defender?"

"No, no, no. You know the guy."

"The lawyer?"

"Yeah, you know him. Geez, you oughta remember him."

"Why?"

"He was the prosecutor who sent me to prison. The one who prosecuted the case against me at trial."

My brain went numb. An instant later I put the name out there.

"Vance Zaduck?"

"Yeah, yeah. That's him. Zaduck was the guy cutting the deal with the Mexican drug dealer. All so's he could get down there to Matamoros to meet that voodoo cult group."

The room felt like it was tilting.

I thought about how he helped cut me loose from the FBI interrogation in New Orleans. It must have all been for show. And his cooperation in lining up my interview with the New Orleans housing official, Lawrence Rudabow—Vance Zaduck's unusual local contact in New Orleans. He had to be in on it with Zaduck. Rudabow—perhaps the last person on earth who had seen Henry Bosant alive in Port Sulphur before Henry was found dead, in a setup made to look like a suicide. They must have learned that Henry had spilled his story to me and needed to shut him up. The whole picture was forming.

But that was instantly followed by a tsunami of dread. Heather had my cell, and I had left a message for Zaduck from that number. What if he connected with her?

Carter must have been oblivious to it, because he just kept talking. "But like I said, I'm looking forward, not back. Prison broke me. When I got out, a boxing friend introduced me to Jesus. After that, Jesus fixed the broken parts."

I was hit with a second wave. A sense of certainty. About what I knew to be true. I knew who was in charge of the universe, and that included Washington, DC, New Orleans, and wherever my daughter was at that moment.

I grabbed his hand, gave him a warm handshake good-bye, and told him that Jesus had fixed my broken parts too. Then I apologized for having to run. But I motioned to the poster in back of him and said, "You and I, we have something in common. We have the Champ in our corner. But we've also got the devil in the ring. That's why I have to fly out of here right now."

66

The instant I was outside, I dialed my own cell phone number to reach Heather. No answer. I texted her. No response. I called again and left a voice message. "This is urgent. Take no calls on my cell from *anyone except me*. Especially no calls from Vance Zaduck. Stay away from him. As far as you can. I'll explain later." I sent her the same message as a text.

I jumped into the street and flagged down a taxi.

When the cabbie asked me where I was going, I hadn't the faintest. Heather and I hadn't decided on that yet. I told him to start driving toward the Mandarin hotel.

Bullet prayers all the way to the hotel. I was pleading with God to keep Heather safe. Once I had her with me, I needed to get her out of town. Then I would find a way to face Vance Zaduck. And stop him somehow.

The driver must have heard me praying. "Are you in trouble?" he asked.

"No, but my daughter might be."

"I'm sorry."

"So am I."

He asked, "I help you?"

"I don't think so. . . ."

"How about I pray for you? And your daughter."

"Yes. Good idea. Pray for us both."

He asked for both of our names, and I told him. My driver turned his radio down as he maneuvered his way through Washington during five o'clock rush hour. He began, in broken English, to pray for us by name, imploring the God of heaven to bring his angels down and surround us both with "miracle power."

Seconds after the taxi driver had finished praying, my TracFone rang. I picked up, hoping that it was a miraculous answer to prayer.

But the voice on the other end wasn't Heather's. It was a man's voice. He didn't tell me who he was at first, just spoke to me in an odd way as if I had broken into a conversation that he was already having with me. It took me only a few seconds to realize who it was, and when I did, I was sickened inside.

The caller said, "So the point is, you have been a busy little bee. Buzzing around town. Talking to Gil Spencer. Who sent you to your boxing friend." A long, theatrical sigh. "Trevor, I've got digital surveillance everywhere. You should have figured. That I would hear you buzzing. I'm way ahead of you. Have been from the beginning."

"Vance Zaduck," I replied. "It's you."

A laugh at the other end.

"Vance, please tell me, where is Heather?"

"You know, normally Starbucks coffee—which of course contains a high-octane dose of caffeine—ought to wake people up. Strangely, though, your daughter, Heather—oh, such a pretty and charming girl—anyway, when she had that cup of coffee with me a while ago, she just sort of slipped away . . . actually, semiparalyzed by now, it looks like."

"Tell me where she is!"

My driver was glancing at me in the rearview mirror. I could hear him praying quietly.

Vance was yelling back. "You're in no position to make demands. You don't realize it, do you? How you're so very screwed. No matter how you look at it. Which way you turn. But maybe, just maybe, you can still cut your losses."

I blew back at him. "Where—?"

But he screamed, "You want your daughter? You can have her. After I'm through with her. She won't be much to look at. Oh yes, she'll be very, very dead. Now, if you want her alive, then you better do exactly what I tell you."

"Okay, okay. What do I do?"

"Get to the Washington Monument. Make your way through the crowd at the bottom. There's an incident going on, so, well, you just better make it inside, and without telling the cops that you and I have been talking. Otherwise, she's dead."

"Then what?"

"Call me the second you're inside the monument. Oh, and

you've only got fifteen minutes. If you're late, I'll send her down to ground level. Very fast."

The call went dead.

I yelled to the driver to hurry up to the Washington Monument. "This is life or death."

"Traffic very bad," he said. "Constitution Avenue jammed. Do my best . . ."

"Pass everything in front of you," I pleaded. "I have to be at the foot of the Washington Monument in fifteen minutes or she's going to die."

"That means we get there in ten minutes," he said. "A few minutes for you to run from the street to the monument."

He swooped into the center lane marked with an arrow for turning left, gunned it through the yellow light, and swung back into the travel lane in front of a Mercedes that blasted its horn. Another light had turned yellow, and up ahead we saw dead-stop traffic on Constitution. The cabbie hammered his horn and cut in front of traffic to turn onto Seventh Street.

The cabbie was narrating his route. "This way to Independence Avenue and then north on Fifteenth, that will get you closest to monument."

"Yes, go, go, go!"

A few minutes later he was racing past the reflections of the Tidal Basin and then turning onto Fifteenth. He slammed the taxi to a halt.

When I grabbed for my wallet, the driver yelled, "No pay, no pay, just run!"

I was at a full sprint, coattails flying as I ran over the grounds toward the famous white obelisk towering 555 feet over me. By then I could already see that a ring of Metro and park police had cordoned off the bottom. In the distance I could hear sirens approaching.

When I reached the police line, I spotted an officer who looked like a sergeant. I yelled, "My daughter is in danger here at the monument!"

"What's her name?"

I told him my name and Heather's, showed my driver's license, and gave a rapid physical description of her.

The sergeant stepped aside and spoke to someone on his radio. I checked my watch. It had been thirteen minutes and a few seconds since my talk with Zaduck. "Hurry," I pleaded.

The sergeant stepped back to me. "Someone is up there with her," he said. "A federal official. Trying to coax her back. We don't know how this happened. But we don't want to scare her into doing something stupid."

"She'll want me up there," I cried. "I can keep her safe."

Another call on the sergeant's radio. Another look at my watch. I now had less than a minute to get inside the monument.

I wasn't waiting any longer. I broke through the ring of police and started sprinting to the ground-level doorway. At first the sergeant called for me to stop. Then put the radio to his ear again. I picked up the pace, now only about thirty feet from the doorway to the monument stairwell. Two other cops were now chasing after me.

But the sergeant yelled for them to let me go, waving me toward the monument entrance with both hands.

Once inside, I called my cell phone number. It rang seven times. I held my breath. "Dear God, rescue us," I prayed.

Eight rings.

Then Zaduck picked up.

"It's called Rohypnol," he said. "Technically called flunitrazepam. Ten times more powerful than Valium. Not allowed by the FDA yet. But readily available in Mexico. Could be worse." He chortled. "Just be glad it wasn't Calabar bean extract."

"Picked that up on your trip to Matamoros?" I said. "Was that before or after you partnered with voodoo priests and demons?"

"Let me tell you something," he screamed. "I'm a general in my outfit. You're just a buck private in yours, you little puke bucket."

"I want Heather."

"Come and get her," he said. "Oh, and sorry, you'll have to climb the stairs."

"Where are you now?" I demanded.

"Aren't you listening?" he said. "At the top deck. So get climbing. There are 897 steps. Average time for runners, before they closed the stairway to the general public, used to be, oh, I think about twenty minutes. I'm a fair man. So I'll give you twenty-five."

I started sprinting up the stairs, huffing and puffing. I cursed the day back in New York that I had stopped my workouts.

Push, push, push, I was telling myself now. I stripped my suit coat off and dumped it in the stairwell and kept charging upward.

A third of the way up, already winded, I met two EMTs and

four cops stationed in the stairwell. They checked my ID as I checked my watch. I told them every minute counted. One of them called on his radio. Then he nodded to me. "Good luck, sir," he said. "That federal attorney up there is trying to keep her calm until you get there. Sorry about the stairs. Elevator is usually closed to the public ever since the East Coast earthquake."

"Where is she?"

"The top level. The observation deck. Somebody smashed the triple-thick window glass, which we thought was impossible. The US attorney happened to be up there, thank goodness, and said she was ready to jump. He caught her by a rope. I guess one of the safety lines left behind when they repaired the top after the quake."

That last bit was an ice pick right into my heart. Zaduck was already framing it as attempted suicide. A perverse trick. Whatever was happening up there, I knew that if I didn't make it in time, she would die a terrifying death. Zaduck had to be under complete demonic control. Heather's death was unthinkable but a win for the other side. Roars of victory from hell.

I took to the stairs again, glancing at the watch, feeling the sweat soaking through my shirt and pouring down my face. Exhaustion was taking over. I tried to take two steps at a time but tripped and smashed my face on the concrete steps before picking myself up and starting again.

I passed two more EMTs in the stairway. Then two more cops after that, who didn't stop me but cheered me on instead.

I had tried to keep track of the steps. Was I at 800 or 810? I was losing track. But I didn't care. At that moment, nothing mattered except rescuing Heather. I couldn't bear the thought of her hurtling down from the top of the monument.

But as I stumbled up the stairs, I had another thought. And it horrified me. Not about the demons who had taken hold of Vance Zaduck or about the evil that he and his twisted cohorts were practicing across the globe as they captured young girls—grist for their grotesque Internet mill, Chicken Fox Videos.

No. It was about me.

Was I the cause of this? All because I had insisted on pursuing the Jason Forester case? Pride? Arrogance? Indictment after indictment flooded my brain. I could practically hear the coarse whisper of my accuser, tormenting me.

Finally I yelled to that chief of horror, "Get behind me." And then, in bursts of breathless cries, I called out to Christ, my Redeemer. For help. For strength. To rescue my daughter.

I was nearing the observation deck. Just seconds away. Just a few more feet. And then I would meet this demon face-to-face.

67

I was about to rush onto the interior observation deck. Before that, I had only one thing left to do. I punched three numbers into my disposable cell phone and dropped it in my shirt pocket.

On that top deck, Vance Zaduck was alone, leaning against the wall, waiting for me. In Zaduck's hand was the end of a rope. He was holding it delicately between his thumb and index finger. As if it were nothing. As if it were a mere string. The rope was pulled taut and threaded through the open window, just large enough for a person to squeeze through. There was something outside on the other end of the rope, out of my sight. I had only seconds to size things up.

Broken glass scattered on the floor. The metal window frame

twisted by an inhuman power, yet only half-wrenched from its place in the square marble opening. I could feel the wind gusting though the open window. The Potomac River was in the distance, shimmering in the fading daylight. Heather was nowhere to be seen.

As I faced him, I announced myself loudly. "Here I am, Zaduck. Top of the Washington Monument. Just like you asked. Now it's your turn. Where's my daughter?"

When the answer came, it was what I had dreaded. And even though it was no surprise, I had vainly hoped against it.

"She's at the end of her rope," Vance said and tittered like an adolescent at his own sick humor.

He added, "Don't worry. It's tied firmly around her ankle. But just to show you I'm not *that* diabolical, after the drugs I added to her coffee, she's been napping peacefully."

Then a sound. A voice. A few seconds later, the voice again. Then louder. It was Heather screaming outside.

"I believe your little darling has awakened," Zaduck said.

"You'll never get away with this," I yelled.

"Oh? Well, simplest scenario—I let go and your daughter takes a thrill ride to ground level. And about my getting away with things . . . When the police come up here, I think I can sell this situation very convincingly."

He took a step toward me, his supernatural power so great that he was still delicately pinching the rope between his fingers even with Heather dangling at the other end. "So tell me the truth. You want to see what is inside, don't you? You're curious. The kind of demon that can drive a powerful man like me to create an extraordinary enterprise. Meeting the deepest needs of men around the world who want the pleasure of something very, very special. Admit it, Trevor. You want to see the face of the thing that is unspeakable to you. Perhaps because you fear that you will see a power greater than your puny God."

"This is about you and me, Zaduck, not Heather. Bring her in. Then you can toss me out that window if that's what you want."

"You'd like that, wouldn't you? A failure in life, yet a hero in death. No, I don't think I'll give you the pleasure. Besides, I already gave you a chance to get out of town. Tried to tell you on that Metro ride. Made a special effort. But no, you had to stay, didn't you."

It was horrifically clear.

He said, "You didn't really think I was going to a birthday party for my niece, did you? I don't even have a niece or a sister." He laughed. "Uh-oh," he said in a mocking voice, "Trevor Black didn't do his homework."

"So this is a game after all, isn't it?"

"At last. Now you're getting it. Yes, yes. A game. Here's the final score: I win. You lose."

I shouted, "The kidnapping of girls. Perverted abuse. And when they become inconvenient to control as slaves, dumping them in a bayou somewhere or in a shallow grave. That's no game. God help you, Vance, you're demonic. Depraved."

"*Depraved.* That old legal term. Good for you. Thinking like a lawyer. But you ought to try my new skill set. Thinking like a demon. Nothing like it. And please . . . do me a favor: don't bring God into this."

"Too late. He's already here. And because he's God, he wins.

The forces inside you, they're doomed." I began to plead with him. "But believe me, there's still hope for you. Redemption is right here. All you have to do—"

Zaduck bellowed back with a sound that was unlike anything human. His voice was changing. Rumbling. A volcano ready to erupt. Like the groaning of things breaking and shifting deep in the earth.

"Your talk is nothing! It's nauseating. Nietzsche was right. Power and the will to use it is everything. Like when I walked into Jason Forester's office with perfect timing. Then showed him my power. My true self. That's all it took. The weakling's heart burst wide-open. Fulfilling our prophecy in the FedEx letter. That makes me just like God, doesn't it? That's why I can control anyone. Men like Larry Rudabow. Get them to butcher those gullible idiots, Paul Pullmen and Henry Bosant. Especially Pullmen. Such beautiful bones. I prefer the delicate bones of the hand, by the way. Which is why I have been able to run a global Internet phenomenon that even the DOJ can't figure out. It all comes down to smart power. Constanzo came close. But he was clumsy. And stupid. I, on the other hand . . . I am the perfection of that power."

Something was happening to Zaduck physically. As Zaduck began to morph, he was no longer just a man. A furnace had opened up from within, and though he had the outline of a man, his form was filled with a glimmering, smoldering fire, like the color of a lava flow vomiting from a volcano. As if he were a man who had been set on fire from the inside.

The fire monster roared, "Now you will see my power."

"You have no real power."

"No?" he screamed back. "Then take the test. I dare you."

I braced myself. "Test?"

"Just declare it. So simple. Declare Christ to be a coward for not taking the challenge our master gave him in the desert. When he refused to throw himself from the pinnacle of the Temple. Didn't you ever wonder what he was afraid of? Maybe that those angels might not save him. So, Trevor, it's your turn. Call him a fool for preaching love. Use your brain, man. Love? We live in a universe full of exploding supernovas and burning stars, where power and energy and survival is all that there is. A planet in a constant state of war. Disasters. Starvation. Where parents kill their children. And husbands and wives slay each other. Just admit the folly and futility of your Jesus, and everything will be fine."

I shook my head. I knew, God help me, that I couldn't deny the Savior who had saved me. My legs weakened. I pleaded for him not to do it, while I inched toward him.

But the fire monster in front of me burst into a hideous cackle. "No matter. I'll still finish it."

"What?" I yelled back.

"The test of your phony faith. Giving your daughter, Heather, the chance that your Christ refused to take."

"Chance?"

"To survive the fall, of course. It's only five hundred feet to the ground."

I pleaded in the name of Christ for him to show mercy. To spare my daughter. But the creature roared at me, "You worm. Now you'll watch my power over life and death."

He opened his hand and let go. I saw the rope and its knotted end vanish from his fingers and fly through the open window. I heard a distant scream from Heather as Zaduck stepped in front of the window and blocked my view.

I rushed wildly toward the window, but my enemy blasted me backward to the floor with a gesture of his hand. I leaped to my feet, horrified.

The monster shouted, "Don't worry. Your turn is next, going through that window after her. I'll tell the police you over-powered me and I couldn't stop you from your own suicide. People already know you're crazy. After all, you see demons."

Crushed with grief, I rushed to the window again, and again with one movement of his hand, he tossed me back. The fire creature howled, "And because Vance Zaduck is so cyber-smart, I've even created a 'suicide note' in an e-mail sent to you from Heather, right here on your own cell phone." He held up my smartphone and moved slightly to the side, which gave me a view of the window that had been smashed open.

That was when I saw it. A blinding light in the window like a hundred suns. I shielded my eyes. Then a shape in the light. Holding the end of the rope and reaching down, wrapping it securely around the twisted metal of the window frame. The rope was holding fast.

An instant later, the figure of light was no longer there. I started breathing again.

But the creature inside of Vance didn't see it, any of it. The fire monster was looking straight at me, waiting to see my despair. Thinking that my God had abandoned me and wait-ing for me to collapse in agony.

I shouted my response in a voice crushed with emotion: "When I am weak, that is when his power is perfected in me."

The monster roared. I shouted it again.

He roared louder, stepping toward me. "This is just the beginning of my vengeance."

"No, it isn't," I cried. *"It is finished."*

The fire monster recoiled at the words.

And then the sound of feet. A lot of them.

Police, with service pistols aimed, rushing onto the observation deck.

No more fire monster standing before me, but instead Vance Zaduck, looking cool and collected.

Zaduck said, "Thank goodness you're here. I didn't know how long I could hold on to the rope for that poor girl. But her crazy father here tried to . . ."

Vance reached toward the end of the rope that was caught in the bent window frame, a final attempt to make it look plausible, but he never got there. Three officers wrestled him to the ground first.

Two men from the rescue squad gingerly hoisted Heather up by the rope that was still knotted around her ankle, up to the window, through the opening, and into the room. She was shaking and crying hysterically and couldn't catch her breath. As soon as her feet touched the floor, Heather rushed into my arms.

Vance cried out to the police that they had it all wrong.

"No," I said as I clutched Heather, who was weeping loudly, shaking, and holding me tight. "They have it perfectly right. And so does that 911 operator." I pulled out the cell from my pocket and spoke into it. "This is Trevor Black. Thank you for hanging on. Are you still there?"

"Yes, sir," she responded. "Is your daughter safe?"

After assuring her that Heather was in my arms, I asked, "Did you catch the conversation?"

"Loud and clear," the 911 operator said. "Every word. I relayed to Metro police. They're with you now? And the suspect's in custody?" I told her yes to both.

As Vance was led away, he announced with an eerie calm that he would be cleared and that "Trevor Black will be the one destroyed by this, you'll see."

All that I knew, all I cared about, was that Heather had been protected.

EPILOGUE

Heather and I walked along the gravel road that ran past the lighthouse on the left. Up ahead was the little harbor where the boats at anchor bobbed gently against the waves. The news reports had warned of a tropical storm and suggested it might turn into a hurricane.

"Did you ever experience one?"

"A hurricane?" I asked, to which she nodded. "Two of them since I moved to the island," I said.

"Did you go inland or sit it out?"

"I stayed on the island."

Heather took a deep breath. She seemed strong and healthy, despite the horrors of the ordeal that she had weathered in Washington.

She'd met with a psychologist and a team of counselors over the next week while we lingered in Washington. She agreed to continue talking to someone about her harrowing experience. They were concerned about PTSD. But Heather was insistent. "Take me back to your island," she'd told me. "Please."

I glanced at Heather during our walk past the lighthouse. She caught my smile and asked me what I was thinking.

"Just that, in a very short period of time, the two of us have had some interesting experiences together."

She gave a little laugh. I asked why. Heather shot back, "Demons, car chases, and hanging by a rope from the Washington Monument. Is that what they mean by 'quality time'?"

I was amazed that she could muster any humor about it. But then, I was her dad, so I still couldn't.

We avoided talking about the details of what happened up there at the top of the Washington Monument. I wanted to let her open the discussion, not me. But even with her casual joking, I knew there was a well of dark emotions beneath the surface. I could see that despite the courage, there was pain and fear in her eyes. I would give her time before we would talk about it.

As for me, I was still haunted by the terror of what nearly happened at the monument. It came out in my dreams. Ever since the incident, those events were being replayed in my sleep, every detail. It was expected, of course. Traumatic memories, embedded in the mind, are powerful things. But I knew something much more powerful still. That perfect power was my hope. The substance of my certainty.

Gil Spencer called regularly to keep me up-to-date. Vance Zaduck was facing a grand jury and possible indictment on twenty-four counts, including conspiracy to commit murder, kidnapping, child pornography, and criminal racketeering. He had hired the most prestigious criminal defense firm in Washington to defend him. The case would be a legal blood-bath, and I knew that both Heather and I would be called as witnesses at trial. Yet because it might cause strategic problems equally for both the prosecution and the defense, the real evil underbelly of the case—the demonic underworld and the voo-doo cult that had become Zaduck's portal of entry into that realm—was unlikely ever to be aired in a courtroom.

The best news, though, came from Dick Valentine. Four hours after Zaduck's arrest, the FBI searched his condo in Bethesda, Maryland, and extracted the data from his computer.

It not only revealed the secret locations where victims were being held overseas; it also detailed the routes of ships and pri-vate planes that would have moved young female sex slaves to their international destinations.

Would have but didn't. On the Mississippi River, a police blockade, aided by the Coast Guard, caught two ships full of girls.

In Mexico, Guatemala, Denmark, Bulgaria, and Russia, agents raided barns, warehouses, and cellar dungeons, freeing hundreds of girls. One of them, a young middle schooler named Peggy Tanner, was released and returned to her New Orleans family, who had been waiting in torment until that day. It was now time for the posters about her disappearance to finally be taken down from the alleys of that city.

Attorney Morgan Canterelle called me a few days after the news broke.

There was an apologetic tone to his voice as he admitted he had "a confession of sorts" he needed to make. Knowing Morgan Canterelle, I was all ears.

He told me that in addition to being retained by Belle Sabatier to investigate the poisoning of her mother, Minerva, and representing the family of Peggy Tanner, the abducted girl, he was also private legal counsel for someone else.

"Louisa Deidre Gaudet," he announced. "She hired me to try to get to the bottom of her sister's murder. I was bound by her wishes not to tell y'all unless and until things were resolved satisfactorily. Given her sensitive government position, of course. Sorry about that."

"I understand confidentiality," I replied.

"But now that y'all have blown this wide-open, we're hoping the authorities can tie up all the loose ends. Round up everyone who's part of this devilish scheme. And track down Minerva's house cook, who was responsible for her death. A good place to start might be with Lawrence Rudabow."

According to Canterelle, the New Orleans housing inspector had been captured in Laredo, Texas, trying to slip into Mexico through the Juárez-Lincoln port of entry. That led to a search of Rudabow's home and the discovery of a pair of familiar sunglasses, a little bebop hat, and a construction map of the Six Flags site with markings for entry points.

Canterelle ended the conversation by saying, "By the way, I was there when Peggy Tanner and her parents were reunited. And I cried like a big ol' baby. Yes sir, miracles still happen, Trevor. They surely do."

Attorney General George Shazzar held a press conference,

announcing the arrests in connection with the criminal enterprise known as Chicken Fox Videos. When questioned about the fact that Vance Zaduck, US attorney for the District of Columbia, was suspected of being the mastermind behind the horrid crimes, he gave the expected response: it would be "improper to comment before the investigation is completed." What he really meant, of course, was before the grand jury released its anticipated indictments.

But the attorney general did add, "As for our pursuing offenses involving child exploitation, endangerment, and other human trafficking, particularly those fueled by dangerous cults, we are looking forward to a robust new task force to prosecute those crimes. Particularly now that an internal impediment has been removed." That was as close to mentioning Vance Zaduck as he came, at least at that early stage in the case.

By the time Heather and I had reached the harbor on our walk, the sky had turned black and the wind was picking up. She looked up and studied the signs of the changing weather. I told Heather that if she wanted, we could close up my cottage and head to the mainland.

"No," she said. "I can't tell you why exactly, but I want to stay here. Both of us. Right here together."

Then she asked a coy question. About a visit from Belle Sabatier.

A few days before, Belle had called me, and we had a short conversation. The first thing she said was that she was moving out of the Sabatier mansion in New Orleans.

"I'm reopening my art studio," Belle explained. "White magic, black magic—either way, I don't want to live here in the house with all the voodoo memories." She added, "I've been thinking about something you said."

"Oh?"

"About opening doors. Giving the devil an unintended opportunity. Heather reminded me of what you said about that at Bayou Bon Coeur. It made an impression. On her and on me."

I wondered—is every father as stunned as I was just then, realizing his daughter actually remembered his advice?

Belle said she wanted to visit me on my island. "I've been invited to display my work at an art show in the Outer Banks. Close to you. It's a small show. Nothing grandiose. But it's a start. I'd love to visit you and Heather."

I told Belle that she was always welcome, but I had no idea how long my daughter would be staying with me. And as we walked, I shared all that with Heather.

As I said it, reality set in. I didn't want Heather to leave, but at some point I would have to let her go. She had her master's thesis to finish and then wherever that would lead her in her future life. Most certainly somewhere apart from me. Which was as it ought to be. Though it was painful to imagine.

Heather and I stopped at a spot on the road where we still had a view of the whitewashed brick lighthouse. Though the power of the wind was mussing her hair, Heather didn't seem to mind. Instead she closed her eyes and leaned her head back, letting the rising storm lift her hair in the air like sea grass dancing in the wind.

"Storms seem so powerful on the island," she said. "Makes you feel small."

A thought came to mind—about power. And about God.

That when you connect with his power, and when you find him, and he rescues you, there is no smallness in it. Just the opposite. You are enlarged and empowered. Because even though unworthy, you know that you are loved and loved infinitely. Which is where the real power lies.

I reached over, laid my hand on Heather's shoulder as we walked, and told my daughter that I loved her.

She paused. "Love ya too," she replied a few seconds later.

We walked in silence for a while.

Then Heather blurted out, "I did it because I wanted to know where I came from. And to figure out who I am."

I asked what she was talking about.

"My neck tattoo," she said. "The umbrella tree. Roots. Branches. Belonging. You know, family. That's the reason I chose a tattoo with a picture of a tree. Silly in retrospect, I guess. Because now I know where I belong."

Together, we both looked at the white tapered lighthouse. High above its two small windows, there was a glass-enclosed beacon at the top, designed to flash a strong beam out to the tumultuous ocean. Light into darkness. Over the ages, guiding to safety all who were in peril on the sea.

Heather took a few more seconds to study it. After that, she spoke in a voice so casual that the full power of it might have been missed.

"Hey, Dad, let's go home."

A NOTE FROM THE AUTHOR

While this is a work of fiction, there is also a storehouse of data both astonishing and disturbing that undergirds two aspects of this tale. First, current figures indicate that, worldwide, some forty-six million people are enslaved in some form of human trafficking. Those exploited victims are often female, and many of them are young. Second, technology has regrettably provided a kind of petri dish where this trafficking enterprise is grown and harvested. The "dark web"—that dirty underbelly of the Internet where these criminal activities flourish—is reported to enjoy some 2.5 million visitors every day.

As for the element of this story dealing with the dangers of a certain cultic practice, I believe there is evidence to support a genuine concern. Where do these various forms of evil come from? The reader is perfectly free to read this novel as entertainment and to dismiss the question. On the other hand, the reader may consider the thesis in this novel, that there exist two invisible yet life-impacting kingdoms, one of darkness and one of light. If that is true, then our choosing one rather than the other will necessarily have far-reaching, even staggering consequences.

DISCUSSION QUESTIONS

1. At the beginning of the novel, Trevor and Heather are still nearly strangers to each other. What did you think of their efforts to connect as father and daughter? Heather has lived into adulthood without knowing her father's identity; how would you react to new information like this?

2. At the ABA convention, Trevor knows he's in unfriendly territory, yet he doesn't shy away from tackling unpopular topics head-on. How do you approach situations like this, when people aren't receptive to the truth? How do you determine when to be silent, when to be tactful, and when to speak out with boldness?

3. The Bible tells us the devil "prowls around like a roaring lion, looking for someone to devour" (1 Peter 5:8). Where did you see this play out in the novel? Which characters were in danger of the enemy's clutches?

4. Heather and Belle each have an interest in voodoo. Why does this worry Trevor? Do you agree that other religions can be gateways for demonic activity? Is this true of every other religion, or only some?

5. We can't smell or otherwise physically sense demons, so how can we discern spiritual activity in the world around us? Do you find this easier in large or in small situations? How can you sharpen your sense of discernment?

6. In the subway scene, Trevor was rescued by angels. The Bible clearly talks about angels and their actions in the world. How are angels at work today? In what ways has your view been shaped by cultural depictions of angels rather than by biblical ones?

7. "The human heart is the most deceitful of all things, and desperately wicked" (Jeremiah 17:9). Where does the world's evil come from? How much of it is due to Satan and his forces, and how much can be blamed on humanity's own proclivity for evil?

8. Though he'd never been part of any kind of exorcism, Trevor trusted God and stepped forward in faith to deliver a man from demonic possession. What other kinds of deliverance do people need? How can we be part of that redemption process?

9. "We are not fighting against flesh-and-blood enemies, but against evil rulers and authorities of the unseen world, against mighty powers in this dark world, and against evil

spirits in the heavenly places" (Ephesians 6:12). How does this information shape our approach to evil in the world? How does it change our approach to people who do evil?

10. Is there anything in your life that you need to be delivered from? Can you think of someone you trust who might help you in that spiritual battle?

ACKNOWLEDGMENTS

I realize that the seeds of this story were planted in my mind slowly, and over many years, and in a variety of ways, and I have many to thank because of it. I am sure that the lawyers in the Wisconsin law firm known at the time as Hippenmeyer, Reilly & Arenz, who hired me fresh out of law school and thrust me into a wide-ranging trial practice, had no idea how those initial legal experiences would later give me the inspiration for a great deal of courtroom fiction, some of which makes an appearance in this book.

My friend, mentor, and previous fiction coauthor Tim LaHaye, who passed away before the publication of my first book in this series, *The Occupied*, generously nourished my fiction career. Tim and I shared a common vision that novels can provide an opportunity to reach people and to touch minds and hearts, and I owe him a great debt of gratitude.

During my too-short association with Enough is Enough, an Internet safety group, and its founder, Donna Rice Hughes, I sharpened my understanding of the potential harm that digital interactivity can pose to unsuspecting young people. But more than that, I was encouraged by our meetings with tech giants when they demonstrated digital programs that parents can use to protect their children when they are online, reminding me that risky situations can have happy endings after all.

The legal organization for which I act as special counsel, the American Center for Law and Justice, provided me with a real-life example of the dangers of Internet exploitation of young women when they asked me to help them to forge legal arguments that would be used in a recent state supreme court case. A state law prohibiting the sexual enticement of young people over the Internet was being challenged by an online predator, and our ultimate victory arguing in favor of that restriction not only protected the teenager in that case, but likely rescued future victims as well. That stuck with me, and I am sure that in some way it motivated me to pursue a few of the plot lines that show up in this story.

As always, my editor at Tyndale, Caleb Sjogren, provided insightful and necessary suggestions about the manuscript, while also patiently enduring my sometimes-intractable positions about what should remain and why it should not be stricken. In the end, his hand in this process has been invaluable, and I and this book are the better for it. The staff members at Tyndale have provided me with boundless encouragement and practical help; in particular Jan Stob, and on the marketing and promotion side, Maggie Rowe and Cheryl Kerwin. Karen Campbell of Karen Campbell Media was quick to grasp the real essence of this story, and she has artfully and passionately communicated it far and wide. My literary agency, AGI Vigliano, and specifically Thomas Flannery Jr. and David Vigliano, have continued to provide excellent representation. As a result, they have freed me up to focus on my writing rather than on numerous transactional issues, a blessing beyond description.

Last but certainly not least, my wife, Janet, has always been, and always will be, the best friend, the sharpest listening ear, and the most pragmatic voice that a writer/husband could ever hope for. She is the lifeblood, in one way or another, of every story that has been, or ever will be, tapped on my keyboard.

ABOUT THE AUTHOR

CRAIG PARSHALL is a fiction writer who has authored or coauthored twelve suspense novels. His fiction work has appeared on the *New York Times* Best Seller List and on the CBA bestseller list.

Craig is also a current events columnist and has coauthored several nonfiction books with his wife, Janet, a national syndicated radio talk show host on Moody Radio. As a constitutional attorney, Craig serves as special counsel to the American Center for Law and Justice on matters before the US Supreme Court, on Capitol Hill, and before state supreme courts.

Craig is also a commentator on issues involving culture, faith, freedom, law, media, and technology, and he frequently debates the most controversial and engaging issues of the day with atheist groups, separation-of-church-and-state leaders, and cultural pundits. He also speaks nationally on topics such as Washington policy and politics, religious liberty, Internet freedom of speech, and worldview, as well as debating artistic and creative issues with movie directors in Hollywood.

On constitutional matters, Craig has testified frequently before committees of the US Senate and House of Representatives, as well as before the Federal Communications Commission on broadcasting freedoms and the future of media. As a veteran trial and appellate attorney, Parshall has represented clients in civil liberty and church/state cases before the US Supreme Court, the majority of US Courts of Appeal across the United States, and numerous federal trial courts and state supreme courts.

Craig was the founding director of the John Milton Project for Free Speech, a pioneering venture advocating for freedom of speech and religious liberty on the Internet that he launched in his previous capacity as senior vice president, general counsel, and senior adviser for law and policy for National Religious Broadcasters.

Craig's appearances before national media as a fiction author, cultural commentator, and constitutional attorney have included television and radio interviews on FOX News, CBS, CNN, NBC's *Today* Show, *Inside Edition*, PBS, NPR, CBN News, and Court TV, among numerous others. He has been interviewed or featured in major newspapers and magazines including the *New York Times*, *National Law Journal*, *Chicago Tribune*, *LA Times*, *Boston Herald*, *Boston Globe*, *Milwaukee Journal Sentinel*, *Atlanta Journal-Constitution*, *Charlotte Observer*, *Des Moines Register*, *Newsweek*, and *US News and World Report*.

Catch Craig on his website (CraigParshallAuthor.com), on Facebook (Craig Parshall Author), on Twitter (@CraigParshall), or on LinkedIn (Craig Parshall—Principal at Parshall Policy).